P9-AFM-391

PRAISE FOR LÁSZLÓ KRASZNAHORKAI

"Throughout Krasznahorkai's work, what strikes the reader above all are the extraordinary sentences, sentences of incredible length that go to incredible lengths, their tone switching from solemn to madcap to quizzical to desolate as they go their wayward way; epic sentences that, like a lint roll, pick up all sorts of odd and unexpected things as they accumulate inexorably into paragraphs that are as monumental as they are scabrous and musical." **Man International Booker Prize judges' citation**

"Krasznahorkai's subject is a total disenchantment with the world, and yet the manner in which he presents this disenchantment is hypnotically enchanting. He is one of the great inventors of new forms in contemporary literature." ***New York Review of Books***

"László Krasznahorkhai offers us stories that are relentlessly generative and defiantly irresolvable. They are haunting, pleasantly weird and, ultimately, bigger than the worlds they inhabit." ***International Herald Tribune***

"Krasznahorkai is clearly fascinated by apocalypse, by broken revelation, indecipherable messages. To be always 'on the threshold of some decisive perception' is as natural to a Krasznahorkai character as thinking about God is to a Dostoyevsky character; the Krasznahorkai world is a Dostoyevskian one from which God has been removed." ***New Yorker***

"The rolling continuity of Krasznahorkai's prose slides between viewpoints, tracks back and forth in repetition and re-emphasis, steps aside to remember a different time, resembling the flux of memory, which at any moment may be jolted into the present. After many pages of being suspended in the unending, the approach to a full stop can bring a sense of dread, which Krasznahorkai most often justifies in his final phrase or two: the prose lifts us up: then we drop." ***Times Literary Supplement***

ALSO BY LÁSZLÓ KRASZNAHORKAI

Animalinside

The Melancholy of Resistance

Satantango

War & War

SEIOBO THERE BELOW

LÁSZLÓ KRASZNAHORKAI

Translated from the Hungarian by Ottilie Mulzet

Tuskar Rock Press

A complete catalogue record for this book can
be obtained from the British Library on request

First published as *Seibo járt odalent* in 2008

The translator acknowledges the kind support of the Hungarian Translators' House in Balatonfured, Hungary, where this translation was partially completed.

Publisher's Note: The epigraph, which recasts a Thelonious Monk line once quoted by Thomas Pynchon, is a creation of the author.

First published in this translation in the USA in 2013 by New Directions Books

First published in the UK in 2015 by Tuskar Rock Press,
an imprint of Profile Books Ltd
3 Holford Yard
Bevin Way
London
WC1X 9HD

ISBN 978 1 78125 510 0
eISBN 978 1 78283 188 4

Designed by Erik Rieselbach

Printed by Clays, Bungay, Suffolk

1 3 5 7 9 10 8 6 4 2

Either it's night, or we don't need light.
—Thelonious Monk — Thomas Pynchon

CONTENTS

SEIOBO THERE BELOW

1
KAMO-HUNTER

Everything around it moves, as if just this one time and one time only, as if the message of Heraclitus has arrived here through some deep current, from the distance of an entire universe, in spite of all the senseless obstacles, because the water moves, it flows, it arrives, and cascades; now and then the silken breeze sways, the mountains quiver in the scourging heat, but this heat itself also moves, trembles, and vibrates in the land, as do the tall scattered grass-islands, the grass, blade by blade, in the riverbed; each individual shallow wave, as it falls, tumbles over the low weirs, and then, every inconceivable fleeting element of this subsiding wave, and all the individual glitterings of light flashing on the surface of this fleeting element, this surface suddenly emerging and just as quickly collapsing, with its drops of light dying down, scintillating, and then reeling in all directions, inexpressible in words; clouds are gathering; the restless, jarring blue sky high above; the sun is concentrated with horrific strength, yet still indescribable, extending onto the entire momentary creation, maddeningly brilliant, blindingly radiant; the fish and the frogs and the beetles and the tiny reptiles are in the river; the cars and the buses, from the northbound number 3 to the number 32 up to the number 38, inexorably creep along on the steaming asphalt roads built parallel on both embankments, then the rapidly propelled bicycles below the breakwaters, the men and women strolling next to the river along paths that were built or inscribed into the dust, and the blocking stones, too, set down artificially and asymmetrically underneath the mass of gliding water: everything is at play or alive, so that things happen, move on, dash along, proceed forward, sink down, rise up, disappear, emerge again, run and flow and rush somewhere, only it, the Ooshirosagi, does not move at all, this enormous snow-white bird, open to attack by all, not concealing its defenselessness; this hunter, it leans forward, its neck folded in an S-form, and it now extends its head and long hard beak out from this S-form, and strains the whole, but at the same time it is strained downward, its wings pressed tightly against its body, its thin legs searching for a firm point beneath the water's surface; it fixes its gaze on the flowing surface of the water, the surface, yes, while it sees, crystal-clear, what lies beneath this surface, down below in the refractions of light, however rapidly it may arrive, if it does arrive, if it ends up there, if a fish, a frog, a beetle, a tiny reptile arrives with the water that gurgles as the flow is broken and foams up again, with one single precise and quick movement, the bird shall strike with its beak, and lift something up, it's not even possible to see what it is, everything happens with such lightning speed, it's not possible to see, only to know that it is a fish—an amago, an ayu, a huna, a kamotsuka, a mugitsuku or an unagi or something else—and that is why it stood there, almost in the middle of the Kamo River, in the shallow water; and there it stands, in one time, immeasurable in its passing, and yet beyond all doubt extant, one time proceeding neither forward nor backward, but just swirling and moving nowhere, like an inconceivably complex net, cast out into time; and this motionlessness, despite all its strength, must be born and sustained, and it would only be fitting to grasp this simultaneously, but it is precisely that, this simultaneous grasping, that cannot be realized, so it remains unsaid, and even the entirety of the words that want to describe it do not appear, not even the separate words; yet still the bird must lean upon one single moment all at once, and in doing so, must obstruct all movement: all alone, within its own self, in the frenzy of events, in the exact center of an absolute, swarming, teeming world, it must remain there in this cast-out moment, so that this moment as it were closes down upon it, and then the moment is closed, so that the bird may bring its snow-white body to a dead halt in the exact center of this furious movement, so that it may impress its own motionlessness against the dreadful forces breaking over it from all directions, because what comes only much later is that once again it will take part in this furious motion, in the total frenzy of everything, and it too will move, in a lightning-quick strike, together with everything else; for now, however, it remains within this enclosing moment, at the beginning of the hunt.

It comes from a world where eternal hunger is the ruler, so to state that it hunts means that it takes part in the general hunt, for all around it every living being falls upon its prescribed prey in the eternal hunt: falls upon it, strikes down upon it, approaches and seizes it, grabs its neck, breaks its spine or snaps it in the middle, then grazing on it, sniffing at it, licking it clean, puncturing it, sucking at it, despoiling it, nosing through it, biting it, swallowing it whole, and so on; hence the bird too stands in the inexhaustibility of the hunt, compelled to the goal of hunting, because in this way and this way only can it get at nourishment in this eternal starvation, in the obligatory hunt, extending accordingly to all: the hunt here is exclusively, or rather in this special case, enriched with another meaning as well—as the bird takes up its place, that is, as it plants its legs in the water, and so to speak stiffens itself: a meaning that this word usually does not provide, and so quoting the famous three sentences of Al-Zahad ibn Shahib, now with increased complexity: "A bird flies home across the sky. It appears to be tired, it had a difficult day. It returns from the hunt, it was hunted"; well, we need to alter this somehow, shifting the emphasis a little; that although it had a direct goal, it did not have a distant one, it existed in a space in which any sort of distant goal, any distant cause, was essentially impossible, yet making all the denser the weave of immediate goals and causes from which it was cast, and from which one day it shall necessarily perish.

Its one single natural enemy, however, the human being—the creature exiled into the daily enchantment of Evil and Sloth over there on the embankment—is not watching it, as on the paths inscribed into the dust on either side of the riverbed right now, he walks, jogs, cycles homeward or away from it, or respectively, just sitting on a bench spending his lunch hour there with his nigiri—that is, rice-triangles wrapped in seaweed, purchased at the nearby 7-Eleven—not now does he watch it, not today; maybe tomorrow or some other time, if there is any reason; but even if there were someone to look, the bird wouldn't even take much notice, it has got used to the humans on the embankment, just as they have got used to the large bird standing around in the middle of the shallow river; today, however, this is not occurring on either side of the river, neither one is taking any notice of the other, although someone could observe that there it is, in the middle of the Kamo, the water largely reaching up to its knees, hence the truly quite shallow weir, interspersed with small grassy enclaves, hence truly peculiar, if not the most bizarre river upon the globe, and the bird just stands, without a single movement, its body strained forward, waiting staggeringly long minutes for the day's quarry, now already ten minutes, then a half-hour passes as well; in this waiting and attentiveness and motionlessness, time is cruelly long, and still it does not move, standing exactly the same, in exactly the same pose, not a single feather trembles, it stands, leaning forward, its beak bent at an acute angle over the mirror of the gurgling water; no one is looking, no one sees it, and if it's not seen today then it is not seen for all eternity, the inexpressible beauty with which it stands shall remain concealed, the unique enchantment of its regal stillness shall remain unperceived: here with it, in the middle of the Kamo, in this motionlessness, in this snow-white tautness, something is lost before it even has a chance to appear, and there shall be no one to bear witness to the recognition that it is the one that gives meaning to everything around it, gives meaning to the spinning churning world of movement, to the dry parching heat, the vibrations, every whirling sound, scent, and picture, because it is a completely unique feature of this land, the unyielding artist of this landscape, who in its aesthetic of unparalleled motionlessness, as the fulfillment of unswerving artistic observation, rises once and for all above that to which it gives meaning, rises above it, above the frantic cavalcade of all the surrounding things, and introduces a kind of aimlessness—beautiful as well—above the local meaning permeating everything, as well as above that of its own actual activity, because what is the point of being beautiful, especially when it is just a white bird standing and waiting for something to appear below the surface of the water that, with its ruthlessly accurate beak and will, it then spears.

All of this occurs in Kyōto, and Kyōto is the City of Infinite Demeanor, the Tribunal of those Condemned to Correct Behavior, the Paradise of the Maintenance of Correct Attitude, the Penal Colony of Omission. The maze of this city emerges from the labyrinth of Demeanor, Behavior, Attitude, from the infinite complexity of stipulations of the affinity to things. There is no palace and no garden, there are no streets and inner spaces, there is no sky above the city, no nature, no momiji turning scarlet in the autumn in the distant mountains that surround and embrace the city, or any pearlwort in the courtyards of the monastery, there is no network of the remaining Nishijin silk-weaving workshops, there is no Geisha quarter with Fukuzuru-san concealed next to the Kitano-Tenmangū shrine; there is no Katsura Rikyū with its pure architectural discipline, no Nijō-jō with the dazzle of the paintings of the Kano family, the uncertain memory of the bleak setting of Rashōmon; no sweet intersection of the Shijō-Kawaramachi in the city center in the frenzied summer of 2005, and there is no charming arch of the Shijobashi—the bridge which directs one to the eternally elegant and enigmatic Gion—and there are not those two enchanting dimples on the little face of one of the dancing geishas of Kitano-odori: there is only the Colossal Agglomeration of Stipulations, the etiquette that functions above all things and extends to all things; this order that cannot, however, be completely grasped by a human being, this Prison of Complexity—at once unalterable and mercurial—between things and people, people and people, and furthermore, between things and things, for it is only like this, through this, that existence may be granted to all the palaces and gardens, the streets aligned in a grid pattern and the sky and nature, and the Nishijin-quarter and Fukuzuru-san and the Katsura Rikyū and the place where Rashōmon was and those two enchanting dimples in the little face of the Kitano-odori geisha, as this geisha, born into charm, turns her fan away from her face for a mere fraction of an instant, so that everyone can see—but really just for a single instant—those two immortally beautiful dimples, that unaffected, bewitching, captivating and corrupting smile before the public comprised of the base gazes of the filthy rich patrons.

Kyōto is the City of Endless Allusions, where nothing is identical to itself, and never could have been, every individual part points backward to the great collective, to some unpreservable Glory, from where its own self of today originates, a Glory that subsists in the hazy past, or which the mere fact of the past created, so that it is not even possible to grasp it in one of its elements, or even to glimpse it in something which is here, because he who tries to see into the city loses even the very first element of it: who, as a visitor would, alighting at the monumental Kyōto Station from the Shinkansen bullet train, arriving from the old Edo, if, getting out, he finds the right exit and strolls into the underground passages resembling an amusement park in their complexity, strolls into the head of the Karasumi-dori, and glimpses, let's say, on the left side of the road leading directly to the north, the long, yellow exterior walls, commanding respect, of the Higashi-Honganji Buddhist temple, already visible from the station; in that very moment, he has already left the space of possibility, the possibility that he could see the Higashi-Honganji of today, as the Higashi-Honganji of today does not exist; as the eye looks upon it, the Higashi-Honganji of today is immediately submerged by what would be most inaccurately designated as the past of the Higashi-Honganji, for the Higashi-Honganji never had a past, or a yesterday or a day before yesterday, there are only thousands and thousands of Allusions to the obscure pasts of the Higashi-Honganji, so that the most impossible situation is created, that there is, so to speak, no Higashi-Honganji of today, just as there never was a Higashi-Honganji at one time, only an Allusion, commanding respect, there is one, there *was* one, and this Allusion floats across the entire city, as one enters into it, as one tramps across this prodigious empire of wonders, from the Tō-ji temple to the Enryaku-ji, from the Katsura Rikyū to the Tōfuku-ji, and finally reaching the given section of the Kamo—largely at the same elevation as the Kamigamo shrine—at the point where the river gurgles, to where it, the Ooshirasagi, stands: the only one for whom in a particular fashion there is just as much present as there is past, in that it has neither: for in reality it never existed in time moving forward or backward—it is granted the artist's powers of observation, so that it may represent that which adjusts the axes of the place and the things in this ghostly city, so that it may represent the ungraspable, the inconceivable—as it is unreal—in other words: unbearable beauty.

A bird fishing in the water: to an indifferent bystander, if he were to notice, perhaps that is all he would see—he would, however, not just have to notice but would have to know in the widening comprehension of the first glance, at least to know and to see just how much this motionless bird, fishing there in between the grassy islets of the shallow water, how much this bird was accursedly superfluous; indeed he would have to be conscious, immediately conscious, of how much this enormous snow-white dignified creature is defenseless—because it was superfluous and defenseless, yes, and as so often, the one satisfactorily accounted for the other, namely, its superfluity made it defenseless and its defenselessness made it superfluous: a defenseless and superfluous sublimity; this, then, is the Ooshirosagi in the shallow waters of the Kamogawa, but of course the indifferent bystander never turns up; over there on the embankment people are walking, bicycles are rolling by, buses are running, but the Ooshirosagi just stands there imperturbably, its gaze cast beneath the surface of the foaming water, and the enduring value of its own incessant observation never changes, as the act of observation of this defenseless and superfluous artist leaves no doubt that its observation is truly unceasing, all one and the same if a fish, a tiny reptile, a beetle, or a crab comes along, which it will strike down with an unerring, merciless blow in that one single possible moment, just as it is certain that it came here from somewhere upon the dawn sky with the heavy, slow, and noble flapping of its wings, and that it shall return back there if twilight begins to fall, with the same flapping; it is certain as well that there is a nest somewhere back there, namely that there is something behind it, just as there could theoretically be something before it: a story, an event, hence a sequence of occurrences in its life; just that, well, the unceasingness of its observation, its watchfulness, its motionless pose betray that all of this is not even worth mentioning, namely that in its, the Ooshirosagi's, case, matters such as these have no weight, are nothing—they're foam, froth, spray, and spume—because for it, there is only its own unceasing observation, only this has weight; its story, which is unique; it is completely solitary, which also means that the motionless watching of this artist is the only thing that made and makes it the Ooshirosagi, without this, it could not even take part in existence, the unreal peak of which it is; that is why it was sent here, and why one day it will be called back.

There is not even the slightest trembling to indicate that at one point it will move from its state of utter motionlessness into that lightning-quick spearing, and that is why up until now this utter stillness decisively creates the impression that here, at the place that it occupies on the Kamogawa, there is not a snow-white great heron, it is nothingness standing there; and yet this nothingness is so intense, this watching, this observation, this unceasingness; this perfect nothingness, with its full potential, is clearly identical with anything that can happen, I can do anything, it suggests as it stands there, at any time and for any reason, but even though what it does will be anything, anywhere, and for any reason, for it, however, this will not mean upheaval but just a sharp instantaneous tilting, so that from this enormous space—the space of possibilities—there will be something; the world tilts, because something will happen out of the absolute character of its motionlessness, from this motionlessness strained to the utmost, it follows that at one point this infinite concentration will burst, and if the direct cause will be a fish—an amago, a kamotsuka, or an unagi—the goal is to swallow it down in one piece, to maintain its own life by spearing it, the entire scene is already far beyond itself; here, before our eyes, whether on the northbound number 3 bus or a battered bike, or strolling down below on the path inscribed into the dust of the banks of the Kamo; we are nonetheless all of us blind: we proceed alongside it having grown used to it, and if we were asked the question how is it possible for it to live, we would say we were beyond all that; there is only the hope now that from time to time there might be someone among us who might glance over there for no reason, completely by chance, and there his gaze would be fixed and for a time he wouldn't even look away; he would somehow get mixed up in something he did not particularly want to get mixed up in, namely with this gaze—the intensity of his own gaze writhes, of course, in eternal undulations—he looks at it; it is simply not possible to hold a human gaze in such a state of unceasing tension, which however would be very necessary right now—namely, it is virtually impossible to maintain the same peak of intensity, and it follows that at a certain slack point in the trough of the wave of observation, the so-called lowest, perhaps even the absolutely lowest section of the wave of attentiveness—the spear strikes down, so that unfortunately the pair of eyes glancing over there by accident sees nothing, just a motionless bird leaning forward, doing nothing: such a person, with his brain in the trough of observation, would have been the only one among us—and perhaps he will never see anything else ever again and will remain that way for his entire life, and what could have given his life meaning is passed over, and because of that his life will be sad, impoverished, worn, dreary with bitterness: a life without hope, risk, or greatness, without the sense of any higher order—though all he would have had to do would have been to glance over while on the northbound number 3 bus, or on the battered bicycle, or while strolling on the path inscribed into the dust of the banks of the Kamo, to take a glance and see what was over there in the water, to see what the big white bird was doing there, motionlessly, as extending its neck, its head, its beak forward, it fixedly gazes at the foam-tossed surface of the water.

There is no other river like it in the world, if someone sees it for the first time he simply can't believe his eyes, he just can't believe it, and standing on one of the bridges—let us say, the Gojo-ohashi—he asks his companion, if there is one, what exactly is this here below us, in this wide riverbed, where at first water, but only in the narrowest of veins, trickles here and there between the completely absurd-looking islets; because this is the question, whether someone can believe what they are seeing or not; the Kamogawa is a relatively wide river in which there is so little water that in the riverbed the little islets, hundreds of them, are formed from silt, islets now overgrown with grass, the entire Kamogawa is full of such haphazard silt-islets overgrown with grass, knee- or chest-high, and it is between these that the little bit of water meanders, as if on the verge of completely drying up; what has happened here, a person asks his companion, if there is one; maybe some catastrophe or what, why has the river dried up so much?—he, however, must be content with the reply that oh, the Kamo was a very wild river, and beautiful, and certainly downstream by the Shijo-ohashi it still is, and sometimes here too, when the rainy season sets in, even now it can be filled up with water, until 1935 it flooded on a regular basis, for centuries they couldn't control it, even in the Heike Monogatari it is described how they couldn't control it, then Toyotami Hideyori ordered the regulation of the river, and a certain Suminokura Soan and his father Ryōi began to do so; indeed Ryōi completed the Takase canal and then its channel was straightened, and then by 1894 the Biwa canal was completed, but of course there were still floods, and the last time, precisely in 1935, so great was the flooding that nearly all of the bridges were destroyed, and there were many deaths, and unspeakable damage; well at that point, it was decided that they would finally put an end to its destructive strength, they decided they would build this and they would build that, and not just along the embankments but down there in the riverbed as well, a kind of system of irregular dams made of blocking stones, which would then break up the flow of the water that was excessively turbulent as it fell in torrents from the northwestern mountains; and so they broke it, says the local companion, if there is one, as is clearly visible, they were able to break its strength, there is no more flooding, no more death, no more damage, only these tricklings; these blocking stones, this system of dams work very effectively and, well, the birds—from the middle of the Gojo-ohashi—the local companion points upward and downward, many kilometers into the distance, and toward the riverbed; these countless birds, they come from the Biwa lake; but even he doesn't know exactly from where, and there is everything here—Yurikamome, Kawasemi, Magamo, Onagagamo and Hidorigamo, Mejiro and Kinkurohajiro—really all different sorts and this kind and that, and little dragonflies dart about here and there, it is just the snow-white great heron that the local companion, if there is one, does not mention; he doesn't mention it because he doesn't see it, as he points over there, because of its continual motionlessness, everyone has got so used to it, it is always down there, they don't even notice anymore, yet it is there as if it weren't even there, it stands motionlessly, not even a single feather quivering, it leans forward, raking with its gaze the foamy froth of the water trickling down, the snow-white unceasingness of the Kamo, the axis of the city, the artist who is no more, who is invisible, who is needed by no one.

It would be better for you to turn around and go into the thick grasses, there where one of those strange grassy islets in the riverbed will completely cover you, it would be better if you do this for once and for all, because if you come back tomorrow, or after tomorrow, there will be no one at all to understand, no one to look, not even a single one among all your natural enemies that will be able to see who you really are; it would be better for you to go away this very evening when twilight begins to fall, it would be better for you to retreat with the others, if night begins to descend, and you should not come back if tomorrow, or after tomorrow, dawn breaks, because for you it will be much better for there to be no tomorrow and no day after tomorrow; so hide away now in the grass, sink down, fall onto your side, let your eyes slowly close, and die, for there is no point in the sublimity that you bear, die at midnight in the grass, sink down and fall, and let it be like that—breathe your last.

2
THE EXILED QUEEN

Quiz Biblici online, maintained by the website La Nuova Via, offered its readers in the autumn of 2006 the following crossword puzzle, which in number 54 across compelled its readers to a decisive conclusion:

CRUCIVERBA 21

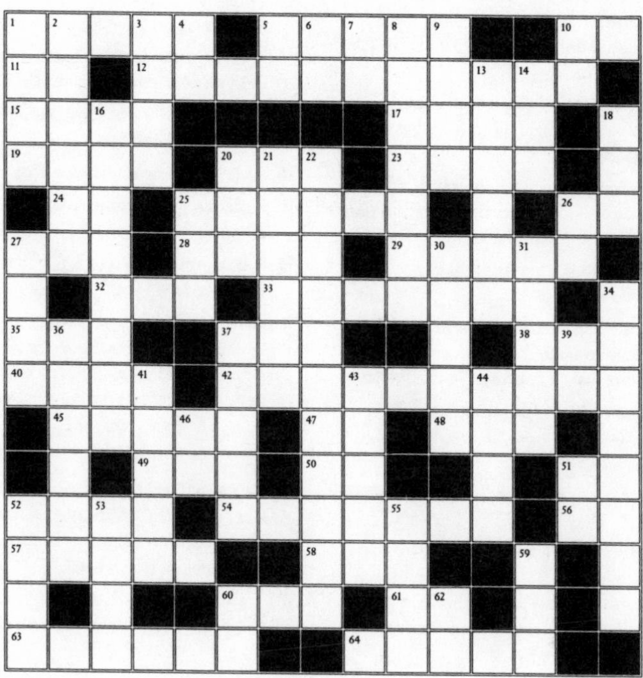

Orizzontali:

1 E sulla ... e sulla coscia porta scritto questo nome: RE DEI RE, SIGNOR DEI SIGNORI

5 Il marito di Ada e Zilla

10 Il Signore ... trarre i pii dalla tentazione

11 ... questa stagione io verrò, e Sara avrà un figliuolo

12 La legge è fatta non per il giusto, ma per gl'iniqui e i ribelli, per gli empî e i peccatori, per gli scellerati e gl'..., per i percuotitori di padre e madre

15 Poiché egli fu crocifisso per la sua debolezza; ma ... per la potenza di Dio

17 Re d'Israele

19 Perciò pure per mezzo di lui si pronunzia l'... alla gloria di Dio, in grazia del nostro ministerio

20 Una testa d'asino vi si vendeva ottanta sicli d'argento, e il quarto d'un ... di sterco di colombi, cinque sicli d'argento

23 Perché mille anni, agli occhi tuoi, sono come il giorno d'... quand'è passato

24 Quando sono stato in grandi pensieri dentro di ..., le tue consolazioni han rallegrato l'anima mia

25 Figliuolo d'Eleazar, figliuolo d'Aaronne

26 ... amerai dunque l'Eterno, il tuo Dio, con tutto il cuore, con tutta l'anima tua e con tutte le tue forze

27 Allora l'ira di Elihu, figliuolo di Barakeel il Buzita della tribù di ..., s'accese

28 Questi sono i figliuoli di Dishan: Uts e ...

29 Perciò Iddio li ha abbandonati a passioni infami: poiché le loro femmine hanno mutato l'uso naturale in quello che è contro natura; e similmente anche i maschi, lasciando l'uso naturale della donna, si sono infiammati nella loro libidine gli uni per gli altri, commettendo uomini con uomini cose ..., e ricevendo in loro stessi la condegna mercede del propio taviamento

32 Elkana ed Anna immolarono il giovenco, e menarono il fanciullo ad ...

33 Io do alla tua progenie questo paese, dal fiume d'Egitto al gran fiume, il fiume Eufrate; i Kenei, i ..., i Kadmonei

35 ... dal primo giorno toglierete ogni lievito dale vostre case

37 Davide rimase nel deserto in luoghi forti; e se ne stette nella contrada montuosa del deserto di ...

38 Or Abner, figliuolo di ..., capo dell'esercito di Saul

40 Figliuoli di Tola: ..., refaia, Jeriel, Jahmai, Jbsam e Samuele

42 Fa' presto ... accordo col tuo avversario mentre sei ancora per via con lui

45 Questi tornò a Jzreel per farsi curare delle ferite che avea ricevute dai Sirî a ...

47 ... n'è di quelli che strappano dalla mammella l'orfano

48 ... la si ottiene in cambio d'oro

49 Non han più ritegno, m'umiliano, rompono ogni freno in ... presenza

50 Il mio amico m'è un grappolo di cipro delle vigne d'...-ghedi

51 La città rumorosa sarà resa deserta, la collina e la torre saran per sempre ridotte in caverne, in luogo di spasso per gli onàgri e di pascolo ...' greggi

52 Il suo capo è oro finissimo, le sue chiome sono crespe, ... come il corvo

54 La regina Vashti ha ... non solo verso il re, ma anche verso tutti i principi e tutti i popoli che sono in tutte le province del re Assuero

56 ... dunque, figliuoli, ascoltatemi, e non vi dipartite dale parole della mia bocca

57 Il cuore allegro rende … il volto
58 Mahlah, Thirtsah, Hoglah, Milcah e Noah, figliuole di Tselofehad, si maritarono coi figliuoli dei loro …
60 Uno dei valorosi guerrieri al servizio del re Davide
61 Oggi tu stai per passare i confini di Moab, … Ar
63 La moglie di Achab, re d'Israele
64 Fu giudice d'Israele per 23 anni, era della tribù d'Issacar

Verticali:

1 Ma quella che si dà ai piaceri, benché …, è morta
2 Sansone disse loro: 'Io vi proporrò un …
3 Perché Iddio … gli occhi aperti sulle vie de' mortali, e vede tutti i lor passi
4 Figliuolo di Giuda, figliuolo di Giacobbe
5 … porte della morte ti son esse state scoperte?
6 … solo udir parlare di me, m'hanno ubbidito
7 … rendono male per bene; derelitta è l'anima mia
8 Gli uomini saranno …, amanti del danaro, vanagloriosi
9 O monte di Dio, o monte di Basan, o monte dalle molte …, o monte di Basan
10 … rallegrino i cieli e gioisca la terra
13 Io ho veduto gli sleali e ne ho provato …
14 … attento al mio grido, perché son ridotto in molto misero stato
16 Or i capi sacerdoti e gli scribi stavan là, acusandolo con …
18 Figliuoli di Caleb figliulo di Gefunne: …, Ela e Naam, i figliuoli d'Ela e Kenaz
20 Rimpiangete, costernati, le schiacciate, d'uva di …-Hareseth!
21 Prima vi abitavano gli Emim: popolo grande, numeroso, alto di statura come gli …
22 E non dimenticate di esercitar la …
25 E l'Eterno gli disse: »… tu bene a irritarti così?«
26 E in quell'istante, accostatosi a Gesù, gli disse: … saluto, Maestro!
27 Per la tribù di Beniamino: Palti, figliuolo di …
30 Efraim ebbe per figliuola Sceera, che edificò Beth-horon, la inferiore e la superiore, ed …-Sceera
31 Uno dei capi di Edom
34 … notte e giorno, e non sarai sicuro della tua esistenza
36 Davide sposò anche Ahinoam di …
37 Essa gli partorì questi figliuoli: Jeush, Scemaria e …
39 Dio in lingua ebraica
41 Dopo di loro Tsadok, figliuolo d'…, lavorò dirimpetto alla sua casa
43 I dormiglioni n'andran vestiti di …
44 Quand'hai fatto un … a Dio, non indugiare ad adempierlo
46 Amica mia io t'assomiglio alla mia cavalla che s'attacca … carri di Faraone
51 Non sapete voi che un …' di lievito fa lievitare tutta la pasta
52 Li hanno gli uccelli dei cieli
53 E i suoi piedi eran simili a terso …, arroventato in una fornace
55 E questi sono i figliuoli di Tsibeon: … e Ana
59 Or Amram prese per moglie Iokebed, sua …
60 … vostro agnello sia senza difetto, maschio, dell'anno
62 Ecco, io ti … di quelli della sinagoga di Satana

At about the same time as this, a firm registered at the address of Mitchelton 4053, Qld, Australia made an update to its internet page, vashtiskin.com, so as to correspond with the new spirit of the times, and as one can sense, this act is not a trifling one, for as they write, Vashti Purely Natural Skin Care, distantly related to the website www.3roos.com/forums/showthread.php?t=194376, has a unique range that supports health and well-being by using nature's gifts to work in synergy to rejuvenate the body and uplift the soul. *Their products, which include skin cleansers, body lotions, hair lotions, and baby products,* are handmade from the finest plant-based ingredients that mimic the naturally occurring constituents in the skin, reduce free radical damage, and encourage hydration, blood supply, and cellular regrowth. *In addition, they inform us that Vashti* uses only quality ingredients, *and also wish to tell us that their products are 100% vegan-friendly, that they* respect humans by avoiding the use of synthetic ingredients and artificial colors and fragrances. *Finally, they add that they* respect animals by not supporting testing on them.

Radical Damage

She was never much loved in the Persian court; she was exalted and envied, praised and condemned; she enchanted everyone and they said of her that she wasn't, accordingly, so beautiful, but she was beautiful, very beautiful, surpassing every measure known up until then, and consequently more dazzling than anyone else: but love was withheld from her: it never occurred to anyone to approach her in a loving way; neither those who could be in her very presence nor those who had only heard of her, and everyone in Susa knew—no less than everyone across the whole of the Achaemenid Empire—that she lived in the Emperor's palace under the burden of a perpetual deprivation of love, and that was even so before she became the spouse of the Great King, because at the very moment of her birth her destiny had been sealed, for it was claimed mistakenly that she was the descendent of Bel-sarra-usur, sunk into religious frenzy, and Nabu-kudurri-ushur, the bountiful robber-chieftain king; and from the beginning they treated her, regardless of her age, as someone whom a great future awaited, although they could not have suspected just how great a future it would be, until the end of time itself, because when the sovereign of the gigantic Empire of the Persians made her his first wife, selecting her and pronouncing the marriage, it so happened, when the queenly crown was placed upon her magnificent head, a Babylonian head—so, the Great King couldn't find anyone suitable among the ladies of Persia, Parysatis let drop in fury; no, the Great King succinctly replied, and indeed it really was so, because no one else existed for him apart from Queen Vashti; he had never seen such beauty as he had perceived in her from that very first glance, neither before nor anywhere else ever since, and yet since the time of Cyrus the Great, the Empire had grown quite large, for surely it was the greatest in all of the world within the grasp of reason, and where to be precise there was no lack of beauties: Medes, Scythians, Parthians, Lydians, Syrians, and Jews, impossible to list just how many peoples and how many kinds of beauty, but not one of them even came close to the godlike beauty radiating from the Babylonian queen; the Great King is in love, they whispered in the Persian court, which continually shifted its quarters between Pasargade, Persepolis, Ecbatana, and Susa, according to the season; if he is in the queen's presence, they said of the sovereign in Pasargade, it's as if he's lost his mind; if he as much as gazes at the queen, they whispered in Persepolis, he can't look away from her; if he is in the queen's proximity, the foreign emissaries repeated at home when they had returned from Susa, he doesn't pay attention, and it is impossible to discuss anything with him; and all of this corresponded to reality; at times, if the Great King was attending a resplendent supper in the zenana, he nearly forgot to eat, for he only gazed at the Queen, and could not bear to free himself from the sight of her magnificent, thick, golden-hued hair, as it fell in plaits below the elegant nape of her neck onto her back—he too marveled at her, lauded her, extolled her, and he felt ill at ease when the court rumors that he was in love reached his ear, for he didn't know what it was that bound him—whether tightly or slackly—to that feeling through whose power he felt he had to marvel at her, laud her, and extol her, the Great King was helpless, yet he was happy and proud, and could have been capable of murdering with his bare hands anyone at all who might dare to utter her name—not only his mother, Parysatis, which would have been natural, not only the women residing in the secluded world of the palace zenana, which was in itself tradition, but even the subjugated princes and kings—if they dared to speak of his marvelous Queen, saying that she was *excessively* proud in the court, that she *excessively* sought the people's favor, he would, in all certainty, have killed that person, for in addition what they said was not so far from the truth; for Vashti proved in reality to be reclusive during the zenana-feasts ordered for the king, and Vashti was only made happy by being able to take part in a procession in Persepolis or Ecbatana, or Pasargade or, during the winter months, before the people of Susa, winning, in this way, immeasurable popularity; ever more popular, noted the sovereign's mother, who was her greatest enemy in the circle of the royal councilors, with murderously glittering eyes; ever more popular, the Persian retinue murmured uneasily, turning gloomy at the mere thought of the male successor to arrive in no time at all no doubt, who thanks to his mother would be half Babylonian; ever more popular, as was reported to the Great King, who hearing the news was in such high spirits as if seeing the people rejoice at his own treasure, believing that this popularity would shine through to him as well; this, however, was not the case, this popularity applied to the Queen alone; an unbridled enthusiasm which, apart from the fact that the procession of the Queen of the Persian Empire was not a custom and therefore not possible, arose from the feeling of this populace that Queen Vashti was using every opportunity to take part in a procession in her gilded carriage before the celebrating crowds because she loved them, the people; the Great Queen, as she was called, by decree and by their sensibilities, however, wanted only to see how they loved *her*; although this was not true, for if they rejoiced at the sight of her, if they shouted from joy being able to catch a glimpse of her, the people were in fact enthralled only because they *could see* her, they *could glimpse* her, which in reality fell far short of the Great Queen's covetous wishes; but she didn't notice anything, the people rejoiced and shouted, and yet the court trembled; first and foremost the mother of the Great King, Parysatis, who sensed in all of this the premonition of greater, more treacherous changes, and who would have gladly smothered one hundred peasants of the Babylonian Empire in ashes, just out of deterrence, if not the Great Queen herself—at least for now, she said to her most trusted confidantes; it was impossible, she made accusations in the presence of the Great King, how this vagrant Babylonian had the gall to flout the conventions of the Empire at every possible opportunity, whether under the pretext of making a sacrifice to Mithra or showing gratitude to Anahita, to go out among the crowds, to leave the quarters of the zenana, to have herself feted by the rabble; so let them fete her, the Great King remarked with shining eyes, she is the only one in the entire Empire, he said, gesturing toward the zenana, who deserves to be feted, at which Parysatis snorted loudly and stormed off, and the Great King merely smiled to himself, and had no concern for his mother, his only concern was for the Great Queen, and in his decrees he upheld the cult of Mithra, and of Anahita, while he himself, in accordance with tradition, subjugated himself to the veneration and worship of the Most Supreme, Ahura Mazda; let her go, he pronounced to his entourage, and sacrifice as she wishes to Mithra and Anahita, it will hurt neither the Empire nor the people, and it didn't hurt him in particular if he himself didn't take part in these queenly processions, it was enough for him to imagine to himself how, amidst her most dazzling ornaments, in her most dazzling attire, she flung, on the way to the shrine of Mithra, her unparalleled beauty out to the people; this was pleasing to the Great King, this magnificence and this dissipation, as, so to speak, she squandered the inimitable splendor of her own person onto those unworthy of it, this in particular enraptured the Great King, this insolent caprice, for he had not the slightest inkling of why Vashti felt an insatiable desire to be loved; and among the jubilation and screaming of the crowds in Susa and Persepolis, she could imagine that here, on either side of the sacred path, were people filled with love for their queen—a jubilation and shouting which she heard now, too, in the torturing silence, when the theater of her ruin had commenced, and in accordance with the judgment and custom, she was compelled to leave the palace apartments alone, deprived of her jewels, with no one to accompany her, through the queen's courtyard and toward the Northern Gate, to all others closed.

Sandro had said that while he was away, they should accept even the smallest commission; the workshop had been in operation for only a year and a half altogether, in other words was still unknown, and moreover, the distinguished neighbor himself, Signor Giorgio Antonio Vespucci, had sent the venerable caftaned Jews to them while others had not, so that alluding to the absence of the master painter of the workshop, Alessandro Battigello, who was presently working at the request of Signor Tommaso Soderini for the Sei della Mercanzia—in other words the Chamber of Merchants—Filippo di Filippi Lippi explained that he would consequently negotiate with them, and he requested with great respect that they take a seat; they, however, only looked around at each other perplexed, not knowing what to do, they could hardly discuss this matter with such a whelp of a boy, clearly only an apprentice here, but he, understanding the game that was being played out in their glances, informed them that no matter how young he might seem, he was neither apprentice nor servant in this painting atelier, nor any sort of sluggard, but instead Filippino Lippi, the most fully authorized *fel-low-mas-ter* of Signor Alessandro di Mariano Filipepi, better known as Sandro Battigello, and—as they might have guessed from his name, he was none other than the only son of the renowned Fra Filippo Lippi, so they could compose themselves and at last take a seat, and hold forth in all tranquility as to the matter that had brought them here, he would be of assistance to them inasmuch as he possibly could, and they only stared at the adroit youth; then the eldest among them surveyed him for a bit and then smiled, nodded to the others, and so it happened that the commission for the preparation of the two forzieri was handled by Filippino himself, by himself and in full; it was the very first commission of its kind for the workshop; there is to be a wedding ceremony, the old Jew explained at length, fingering his white beard, nuptials—and here followed a name that Filippino, even when asking to hear it again, could not grasp—in a certain family, and on this occasion they were, at the recommendation of the younger sister of Signor Vespucci, turning to the workshop of Signor Alessandro di Mariano to ask if he would undertake this commission, which was to be completed by the last day of the year; ah, two forzieri, nodded Filippino very seriously, but suddenly he fell silent and his lips were pursed, like one who is pondering whether his workshop could take on yet one more commission alongside so many others, yes, replied the old man, and from this point on he looked at the figure of the fourteen- or fifteen-year-old boy more decisively; with the usual measurements, he said, but not the usual technique; he lifted up his long index finger, for they—that is to say the family—meaning the family of the bride, he continued, forming his words slowly, desired this pair of forzieri not to be carved, as was often the case, but it had to be painted, and that was why they had come to Signor Sandro di Mariano: they wished the young master to paint the story of Esther, from the Hebrew Bible, onto the two forzieri; the surfaces of the longer and shorter sides of the chest would be employed but not the lid, and the back part should also be left untouched, as it would be resting against the wall in the bedroom of the newly wedded pair, so that, in brief, altogether there were two long rectangular surfaces and two roughly square-shaped ones, the old man explained, and that means that Signor Sandro di Mariano, taking everything into account, has two larger and four smaller surfaces at his disposal, but of course—the old man looked around the somewhat disorderly workshop, not bothering to conceal his doubts—all the work has to be undertaken by the master, so that he will have to arrange for the carpentry and the goldsmithing as well; that is no problem at all, Filippino interrupted him, as for a goldsmith one could not find anyone better matched to the task than the master's older brother Antonio, and as for the carpentry, for many years now they had worked in collaboration with Giuliano da Sangallo, the celebrated master carpenter, at which the old man raised his bushy eyebrows, yes, replied Filippino just as decisively as he possibly could, they'd been familiar with his work for quite a long time, and were greatly satisfied with it, but at this the entire family—principally the younger members, who were seated in the back, near the entranceway, listening in to the conversation from there—began to smile; so would the gentleman please state first what size of forziera he had in mind, asked Filippino as he leaned toward the old man with a serious gaze, for he did not like this general mirth; well, the old man gestured with both his hands, about this big; fine, said Filippino, nodding at the measurement; he snatched up a longish slat of wood, drawing a notch in it, and took it over to the old man, is this what you were thinking for the length, he asked; as he measured with his hands the length he had just demonstrated to the boy, the old man was clearly astounded, as it clearly corresponded to the length notched into the slat; then, as it were, beginning to speak seriously and directing the boy back in front of himself with his distinguished eyebrows, he gestured backward to one of the younger members of the family, and there appeared in an instant in his hand a piece of fabric with a drawing on it, clearly showing the desired forziera, indicating the precise measurements—well let us see, and now the old man gazed deeply into Filippino's eyes, repeat to me exactly what we want, as afterward you will have to repeat it to your . . . fellow painter, if he comes back; then he leaned back a little in his chair, which however had no back, as it was only a simple wooden stool, as was used in such workshops; Filippino smiled for a brief moment but then immediately and ceremoniously began to speak, saying that the distinguished guests had, on the eleventh of August, in the year of Our Lord 1470, in the workshop of Sandro Battigello, ordered the construction of two forzieri in the proportions indicated on the section of homespun and, as I see it, he continued, raising the piece of fabric closer to his eyes, it shall be from the very finest poplar wood, thus all of the carpentry as well as the goldsmithing work shall be combined with this particular commission, according to which the *workshop* of the master under discussion shall paint the story of the entire Book of Esther onto the two front-panels and the sides of the forzieri; the date of completion, however, shall be designated as the last day of the year, so let that be as well the date for receipt of the stipulated remuneration of fifteen golden florins per piece, in such a way—here the old Jew, taking up the conversation, gazed at the boy with ever-growing satisfaction, but as if not having heard the recommendation concerning the price; he recommended that on the one main panel there should be the depiction of Esther pleading for mercy before the king, and on the other the portrayal of the gratitude of the Jewish people; the side panels, however, should portray the main protagonists—Ahasuerus, Haman, Mordechai, naturally with Esther in the foreground; of course, replied Filippino coolly, with a severe frown, of course Sandro Battigello will be the one to conceive first, in what manner, how it will be possible to convey one entire book of the Holy Writ onto a total of six panels, in such a way that the essence is transmitted, he shall be the one to decide; at which point the old man—who was more or less expecting such a response—smiled, gazed back at the others, bowed to Filippino, and answered him, saying yes, my dear boy, I envisaged it just as you said, and with that he rose from his seat and looking at the boy with a warm glance, motioned to the others, stepped out onto the Via Nuova, then, shaking his head, serenely murmured to himself, what next, you little urchin, fifteen gold florins, and per piece!—then he clasped his hands behind his back and with his extensive clan behind him, who had already broken out into loud conversation, merrily analyzing just what kind of a workshop this was, he withdrew from the scorching sun, so that the entire company under his guidance continued slowly to vanish into the shaded side of the Chiesa di Ognissanti.

Although founded by Cyrus the Great, and expanded by Darius, the Persian Empire became truly great only through Artaxerxes Mnemon II, this—in the view of his contemporaries and later the historians—feeble, susceptible, enervated, and at first, this delicate and generous man, who was originally called *Ṛtaxšaçā* in his own language, and then later called Artsaces by the Greeks, and who for a long time could not get over having had to bury the eunuch Tiridates, the boy-love of his youth, before—as perhaps Herodotus has noted—he had a chance to emerge from childhood; his grief was so great that he ordered the assumption and the practicing of the deepest mourning across the entire Empire, at which his mother, in the hopes of bringing it to an end, threw all her might into the creation of a marital union auspicious for the Empire, through which she also wished to obstruct him, Artsaces, from gaining the throne, for in her heart—if in the case of Parysatis we can even speak of such a thing as a heart—she intended the throne for her second-born, but in vain, not even one of her plans came to fruition, for she had to behold as her favorite, the passionate Cyrus the Younger, created to rule, died at Cunaxa, and it was precisely the despised first-born, and then again the Babylonian slut designated for the marriage not only didn't encumber Artaxerxes II's ascension to the throne, but actually directly expedited it, for that accursed foreign serpent, as Parysatis called her among her closest devotees, had become so popular practically since her very first public appearance, when, in procession behind her husband, the Emperor, she was able to take part in a large festival dedicated to Ahura Mazda, that the people wanted to see her on the queen's throne immediately, and there they saw her, because the Emperor wanted to see her there too, and the magi of the Medes placed the crown on her head, and she became the Great Queen of the powerful Empire, and she became as well the one for whom the Emperor, in one swift blow, could forget his bereavement over Tiridates, for it was enough to look at Vashti and he was bewitched; Parysatis tried everything humanly possible against her, availing herself of the wives secluded in the zenana, particularly the jealous Ionian Asparia, pushed into the gray background of the zenana because of Vashti; she used all the machinations of zenana-intrigue, she used the priests of the faith of Marduk and the priests opposed to the faith of Marduk, as well as the so-called "male societies" formed to resist the autocracy of Ahura Mazda, as well as the antipathies of the Zoroastrian priests who repudiated these "male societies," she tried everything but without result, her first-born, and not high-born, was blinded by the Babylonian beauty, who sat upon the throne and wore the crown on her sweetly curling flaxen hair as if she had always been seated upon that throne, and as if that crown had always been meant for her; simply put, nothing could touch her, nothing in the entire God-given world, Vashti's position grew ever more solid, in parallel with the Empire, which again only strengthened the position of the Great Queen as it grew and became ever more powerful, never had there been an Empire of this extent in all the world within the reason's grasp, in addition the residents of the Empire relished the great peace in the wake of the great wars, which they ascribed to the personal talents of the Emperor, taking it as equal proof that the most supreme Deity of the Heavens, Ahura Mazda, was happy to see the Great King upon the throne; in short, Vashti seemed unassailable; the Queen Mother fretted in her apartments, maddened by the impotence of her fury, only able to trust now that something would happen to bring about the end—as it usually did—to this nauseating peace in the Empire and this deplorable romance in the royal palace, she watched the Great King, growing ever stouter, and she was besieged by splitting headaches, she watched the radiant Babylonian slut and she was nauseated, but for the time being there was nothing she could do, just keep watching, Parysatis said to herself in between the headaches and the nausea, one day this too will come to an end, because Ahura Mazda in the heavens wished it so, and thus it came about, and her waiting and her torment were not in vain, for the end did come, so easily, so self-evidently that she herself, Parysatis, was the most surprised of all, when she heard after the conclusion of the official celebration of the monarch's ascension to the throne that the Great King was held by even his closest devotees to be incapable of the most trifling of decisions, and the word had began to spread as well in the subjugated provinces that the Emperor was weak; Artaxerxes would permit anything at all, but not this, so that after the rejoicing, lasting 180 days, a festival of seven days was ordered for the old and newly conquered princes, the old and newly conquered kings, to be held on the opposite bank of the river, in the Apadana, built as it were to face the palace of Darius in Susa in order to demonstrate the dignity of his right to the throne and his strength—but from this point on everything became very confused, and even Parysatis could only follow the events with difficulty, as for a while she had believed that the Great King was incapable of true wrath; the first reports of this had already arrived, the only problem being that custom did not allow her to approach the Apadana herself, to witness with her own two eyes at this so-called celebration, descended into drunken roistering, this anger, in any case the second report spoke of violent rage, the eunuchs practically flying between the zenana and the Apadana, the Emperor is foaming at the mouth, they whispered into her ear, he is jabbering and yammering and howling and bawling, and all of the guests are in shock; the celebration has fallen apart and come to an end; they reported, in the palaces of Susa, of the unexpected events; and Parysatis was happy once again, for the mere fact that the Emperor's repulsive yet seemingly unassailable sense that there could be no problems at all between him and Vashti, for whatever foolishly squalid reasons, thrilled her, so that both her headaches and her nausea immediately disappeared; she felt wonderful, her eyes glittered, her brow unfurrowed, her back straightened, once again assuming that immovable face, so dreaded by all those around her, while Vashti herself was writhing between proud dignity and wounded humiliation, sitting in the audience hall of the Queen's apartments convinced of the justness of her own response, and waited for him, the one of whom and from whom such appalling reports arrived, she waited for the Great King but he did not come, only more and more reports, and Vashti fell deeper and deeper into shock, and grew despondent, and she could know already what was to follow, for there was nothing else that could follow, she knew how the council—the convening of which she had been, in keeping with tradition, immediately informed—would decide, just as they were, drunken and starving for a fatal scandal, that she would have to proceed from the queen's apartments across the desolate palace to the forbidden gate, she would have to follow the centuries-old mandate and take the first steps of exile, so that in the end she would be no more than one smothered in ashes, like a dog that had disobeyed.

They asserted everything, and then they asserted the opposite as well, it simply was unbelievable that in the case of a practically "new" masterpiece—the ensemble of panel-paintings depicting the story of Esther was altogether five hundred years old—so little was known, still, they didn't know anything; this is not a question of the "wider public"—even though this term encompasses fewer and fewer people, this lack of knowledge going along side by side with erudition—but rather of the endless hordes of experts, who have sacrificed numerous works of scholarship to demonstrating that, of course, Sandro Botticelli painted the series of panels depicting Esther's story, as well as others demonstrating that Sandro Botticelli did not paint them; then to prove that perhaps he only painted the essential parts, and then not even that; maybe he just created the undersketch for Lippi, to show him what he had to paint, and then that the panel entitled "La Derelitta"—one of the most mysterious artworks of the quattrocento—was of course the fourth piece, one of the side-panels, earlier believed to be lost, of the cassoni, as the forzieri—that is to say, the two large chests that were bestowed as a dowry by the bride's family, to hold the bridal trousseau as well as preserve other valuable objects—were called; then later on someone else came along, who eliminating all doubts—hmm—hypothesized that the renowned "La Derelitta" was the work of Botticelli but it did not form, and never had formed, a part of the cassoni, of which it is not known who commissioned them, or when the order was issued by that person who commissioned them, and which were later scattered in as many directions as there were separate pieces: there is a witness to the fact that in the gallery of the Palazzo Torrigiani in the nineteenth century the six panels were still placed together, but then the individual sections turned up along the most obscure of routes, in six different museums, from Chantilly to the Horne Foundation; then came the twentieth century when—now in possession of technological possibilities previously unknown—it was possible to hope that the researchers who study these forzieri or cassoni would come up with something, well they came up with the fact that Filippino Lippi, born out of the forbidden passion of the former monk Fra Filippo Lippi and the former nun Lucrezia Buti, could have something to do with it, namely that the young child who had inherited in a truly astonishing fashion all of his father's genius, was an apprentice—perhaps at the age of fourteen, shortly after his father's death in 1470 or 1471—in the workshop of Botticelli, himself previously an assistant in *his* father's workshop, so that—the contemporary experts opined—it is highly likely that the adolescent Lippi worked on the series of panels depicting the story of Esther; later on, however, we found out from Edgar Wind and André Chastel that, well, not exactly; they painted the panels together, but it was impossible to say who had painted what, and presumably Botticelli did play some role in their creation, and we can read in the very latest promisingly monumental monograph published in 2004 by a certain Patrizia Zambrano who, doubtless ranking among the greatest masters of saying absolutely nothing, herself reached the conclusion that both Botticelli and Lippi could have painted the panels, perhaps the two of them working together, or in such a way that Botticelli somehow worked on the pictures, perhaps in the planning or the undersketches, and then Lippi did the painting; or conversely that Lippi worked completely alone—the elasticity, if it can be expressed like that, with which Ms. Zambrano covers all the possibilities, is unbelievable—and it can even be worthy of high praise that she was able to knead together, into one single study, all the hypotheses that have arisen in the difficult question of attribution since the time of the quattrocento until now; to put it briefly, we know nothing, as was always the case; it's just as if in the matter there would now be a kind of consensus that "La Derelitta," at least, was painted by Botticelli alone, which is quite obvious—inasmuch as one looks at the painting itself—and it is impossible to comprehend the presumed difficulty of separating it from Lippi's oeuvre, or how one can establish that it in no way formed a part of the Esther panels, in other words, we can remain in the barren steppe of the last descriptive scholarly contribution, that is to say the work of Alfred Scharf, published in 1935, which awkwardly and laboriously ponders over the date of creation for the panels, but—thankfully—nothing more, as the author is compelled to demonstrate simply what can be seen in the individual paintings, and how all this is connected to other similar forzieri created by Lippi, and more generally, how these are connected to Lippi's life work, and that's it already, that's enough, 1935, Alfred Scharf, and we're done, because in the end what is the point of bothering with the deliberations of the scholars, if the bucket in which they are mixing their brew is completely empty; and so is it not sufficient, not deserving enough of awe, that in the terrifying and unknown machinations of chance and accident, these panels have actually been passed down to us?—for after all these speculations, at least it is not possible to doubt in their existence, to contradict the fact that they exist.

For so-called historical research has cast doubt on the existence of Vashti, the existence of Esther, the story of Vashti and the story of Esther; it was so from the very beginning and even today there is a kind of suspicion around the whole thing, around Esther and particularly around Vashti, and Ahasuerus and Mordechai and Haman and the feast of the Emperor, a suspicion that everything that occurred there did not occur, because as the historians write, everything that stands in the Book of Esther is so indemonstrable, so unlocalizable, so unidentifiable and confabulatory, that it simply cannot stand; so that it would be better if we thought of it as a fable—we should think of Esther, Vashti, Ahasuerus, Mordechai, and Haman as the characters of a fable, or perhaps a little more exaltedly, of a myth, since—as is claimed, and people who understand these matters largely agree with these claims—the entire Book of Esther, and so too Vashti, who assumes merely a minor role in it, simply has *no foundation in reality*, so that well, if this *no* is not even the essence of Purim, its origins are at the very least obscure, and it can be presumed that the connection of the Book of Esther with the Hebrew text, as with the Greek canon, only occurred later, for the matter begins with the fact that historical scholarship is unable convincingly to identify the main protagonist—inasmuch as he can even be regarded as such—Ahasuerus, as for a long time the conviction reigned that this same Ahasuerus was actually Xerxes I and the entire fable reaches back to the Babylonian captivity, and this viewpoint still, even today, raises its head at times, but all in vain, for there are ever more—naturally, among those for whom the unclear origins of Purim are troubling, that is to say, what are we celebrating during Purim anyway—who remain silent in the face of the unparalleled expertise of the arguments set forth in Jacob Hoschander's 1923 study: that, for example, the identification of Ahasuerus with Xerxes and, thus, the dating of the story of Esther to the time of the Babylonian captivity is a mistake, because Ahasuerus is none other than Artaxerxes II himself, brought forth as a leading figure during the period of decline of the Achaemenid dynasty—Artaxerxes Mnemon II, the ruler mentioned before his coronation as king under his Greek name of Artsaces—the inevitable murderer of his younger sibling, the victor in the battle at Cunaxa, the inciter of the plot in Xenophon's masterpiece, the *Anabasis*, the faithful first-born of his mother, immortalized as the evil intriguer Parysatis, who had a ravishingly beautiful wife Statiera, whom Hoschander, and not just with any kind of reasoning, identifies as Vashti; so coolly, so indisputably convincing does his argumentation proceed, that it is hardly denied—neither by Christian biblical researchers nor by more neutral historians; not even by rabbinical tradition, and although there is of course some divergence between these two groups on this point, the concordance is more conspicuous, even if the formulations of the rabbinical scholars are more severe, that is to say even if they deviate in a more austere trajectory from Hoschander's analysis, which accepts the conflict between the old and the new faiths as sufficient explanation for the background to the Book of Esther, namely, for example, that Vashti, inasmuch as the story is true, did not really fulfill the king's command—the gist of which was that she must appear among the drunkenly clamoring princes and kings, before the Great King, who desired, with his wife's beauty, to confirm the insurpassability of his own Empire; namely, his command was such that she must leave her own gathering, held for the illustrious ladies of the Persian court in the audience-hall of the queen's apartments in the zenana, which in keeping with tradition occurred simultaneously with the week-long celebration of the Emperor, prescribed in such cases by Persian and even older tradition, and during which she must not be absent, and at which she sat until it was over, her person completely veiled—well, if all of that is really true and it occurred like that, but then again—according, that is, to the rabbinical commentators—it was not like that, the cause was not the pride of the Great Queen, but an illness that Vashti had been hiding from the Emperor for weeks now, so that to no avail, the Hebrew and the Christian bibles relate, it was whispered and whispered again into her ear that she had to leave the women's feast, and had to appear immediately before the Emperor, to no avail did the eunuchs keep repeating it nervously, alarmed by what they saw in the Empress's eyes, for what they saw in those incomparable eyes was that, as for the Emperor's truly unusual request—in opposition to every kind of courtly decorum—that mandated she would have to show herself wearing nothing more than a crown, that is to say disrobed, displaying her beauty before the male assembly descended into a drunken rabble, that she was not going to fulfill it, to no avail did they urge her and whisper the reasons into her ear, just as tradition, too, strives to no avail to engrave this picture into memory, for in actuality, as these interpreters claim, with a sudden harshness and devoid of mercy, Vashti was leprous, and the illness, albeit still in the early stages, had disfigured her face and her entire body, and it was for this reason that she did not dare to show herself before her king, so that she would not lose his love and his admiration, and it was precisely this knowledge that had reached Parysatis' ear earlier, who immediately sensed that in such a shaping of events the time of reckoning had come; she therefore sent a message to the Emperor at a suitable time, which was hardly unheard of or out of keeping with custom; she sent a message, however, saying that if he were to summon his ravishing queen now, she would certainly deny him his request, for she was too proud to appear in such a company, at which point Artaxerxes, prostrate from the several days' worth of drunken carousing, and forever grappling with the uncertain nature of his worth as sovereign, immediately gave the order to the eunuchs, of the sort that—with all the logical irrationality that followed from the situation—she must come, she must come immediately in her full beauty, namely that she must not wear anything but the crown on her head—Parysatis, it is said, was in jubilation; Vashti realized that this was the end; however Artaxerxes, in his bitterness, permitted every council and agreed with everything, because all he could think of was that if Vashti, as she had been doing for weeks, disgraced him and denied him again, then the Empire would also deny its last Great Emperor, and although in his dim, slow, drunkenly flickering brain he knew what judgment he was pronouncing on her whom he loved most in all the world within reason's grasp, he also felt that

Vashti's fate—and here the Hebrew commentators of the text lower their voice—was a mirror of the fate of the Empire, and that if Vashti were lost, the entire colossal Persian Empire itself was lost, lost forever.

He already knew how to draw a Madonna even before he knew what a Madonna was, but it wasn't only in this that he displayed an extraordinary talent, but in nearly everything else too, for he was able to read and write, master the skills of carpentry, use the tools of the workshop, grind and mix the pigments to perfection, gild frames in such a way that no one ever had to teach him, so that in Prato his father always followed his progress with laudatory attention, keeping an eye on his every movement, and he only caressed the boy when little Filippino had the inclination to sit on his lap, and this period somehow passed very quickly, the child had hardly reached his sixth year when his father began to notice that he didn't like to be touched, that he had no need to be embraced, indeed—to put it more directly—he detested it, although he was treated with particular love in his father's dwelling as well as in the workshop; the family, the numerous and often-changing ranks of assistants and pupils, even the distinguished patrons, if they came to negotiate with the famous master, never failed to praise him, saying what a beautiful child, just as they never failed to gape in astonishment (although they did not truly believe that this wee mite had made the drawing so proudly displayed by the master); hence he grew up in the warmest possible of settings, but still it did not, for a long time, quell the unease felt by his parents, for it was distressing enough, from the time of his birth, to consider what an accursed life would be the share of one brought sinfully into the world, to consider the circumstances in which one of the parents had been a Carmelite monk, the chaplain in the Santa Margherita monastery, and the mother, to their even greater shame, was a nun in the same monastery at the time of conception, so truly they were sinners indeed, the manifest sinners in a scandal discussed all across Firenze for months, albeit relatively ordinary sinners, but sinners all the same, who would have remained so for a long time to come, perhaps even up until the very gates of Hell, if the extraordinary genius of Filippo Lippi, renowned all across Italy, had not, under the pressure of the Medicis, brought about a papal absolution from Pius II, who resolved the affair by "canceling them out," that is, exempting them from their monastic vows—but he could only save them, he did not help the child any further, so that the stamp would remain forever upon little Filippo, whom his father, in vain, inundated with love, every sign of passionate love; never could he free himself from the anxiety of what would become of the child when he grew up, and this anxiety persisted for years and years, until the point when the child began to show that there was no need to be anxious on his behalf, because he would be able to stand on his own two feet and his talent would compensate for his impure birth, for he demonstrated such unparalleled intellectual sensitivity, and so adept at learning was he that he simply dumbfounded everyone around him; it was possible to see that this boy would be a great man, just like his father; he was, however, never instructed—neither by his father nor by anyone else; instead he only observed, continually, regardless of who was doing what in the workshop, or at home, or on the street, the child watched silently, and he asked questions, and when he saw his father beginning to draw, he began to draw too, he took a wooden board and a bit of charcoal and he copied every movement precisely, observing how his father made a large sweeping arc with the charcoal, and the arc on his drawing curved astonishingly in the same way, but it was like that with everything, the child observed everything thoroughly, he was able to sit silently for up to an hour beside the blacksmith of Prato and watch how perhaps three pairs of horses were shod, he was able to spend long hours on the banks of the stream, observing the ripples in the water, and the light on the rippling surface, in short when he had achieved his sixth year, his parents were no longer anxious for him; his father was certain that the fruit of his deeply passionate love, sinful and yet preordained, had been taken into the protection of the Lord, he brought his son with him wherever he could, even to Spoleto, where he was at work on the Cathedral; on the building site the child, alongside the chief scribe, performed the duties of a kind of assistant, for he was capable of that too, confirming his aptitude everywhere and in everything, and in addition swept everyone off their feet with his gentleness and sensitivity, although as a result his parents were subjected to a different kind of worry, that is to say that the child's health was not in good order; he was always catching a cold, he wouldn't dress warmly enough; his throat was already swollen and he would be bedridden for days, so the problem was then the state of his health; his parents never managed to tell him enough that he had to take great care, even in 1469, when his father lay on his deathbed, and charged the boy with the completion of the fresco of the Holy Virgin that he had begun in the Cathedral; no, not even then, and even there, did he fail to remind his son to dress very warmly while he was working, as in the Cathedral it was always too chill, and under no circumstances should he drink cold water while at work; and of course what could Filippino do but promise to adhere to his father's words, but then he didn't keep it and it was practically all the same anyway, because if he happened to think of his health and dressed properly on a very cold winter day, simply to air out the workshop briefly was enough to make him bedridden again; there was no solution, he could never be circumspect enough, for he was laid open to illness, as it was expressed to him, even Battigello—his older friend who served as an apprentice alongside him in his father's workshop, who later opened up his own workshop in Firenze where Filippino followed him—even he said so, Battigello—that name clung to him with such injustice, because as a matter of fact it was a jeer directed at his stout older brother Giovanni, who haggled with the customers in the pawnshop—in a word, even he, this Battigello who was soon to become one of the greatest painters of Firenze and of all of Italy, even he pointed out to Filippino that if he didn't look after himself, then when a serious epidemic struck, that would be the end, it would take him and he could look back then; it was just that Filippino was powerless, this was the cross he bore, and perhaps this was the price for his sensitivity from the very beginning, on a spiritual level, as his father said, because in reality this was what separated him the most from his cohorts: while they were playing outside, Filippino sat inside, happily reading, and he read everything that Battigello pressed into his hands, and as for what Battigello pressed into his hands, it was everything, and very often such works as really should not be pressed into the hand of a eleven- or twelve-year-old youth—Ficino and Pico della Mirandola and Agnoto Poliziano, for example—and maybe Filippino didn't understand, how would he even understand the sentences, but the spirit of the thoughts behind them reached him, and this spirit made him pensive, even then he began to spend hours brooding below the workshop window, huddled into a corner, if there happened to be no book in his hand, and when he turned fourteen, even Battigello himself was forced to recognize his ability to penetrate everything intuitively, so that roughly during the time when Battigello became to be called Botticelli, and the young master began to be mentioned and praised all across Firenze, one day he informed Filippino that he no longer regarded him as an apprentice, he had in fact never done so; Filippino should instead regard himself as a fellow painter in the workshop, as he had already been, strictly speaking, for a long time now, maybe even from the very day when, stepping into Battigello's workshop, he had begun to work with him; because for grinding the pigments, burning the wood for charcoal, boiling up the sizing and so on, a real assistant or two was always turning up; Battigello always gave Filippino such tasks as: well, do you see that Madonna, paint the Infant in her arms with two angels, all right?—fine, Filippino would answer, and an Infant and two angels would appear upon the painting, such that no one would have ever been able to say that Battigello had not done them himself; this Filippino had an unbelievable ability to penetrate everything intuitively; he only had to observe, for example, the movements of Battigello's hand, his thoughts, his colors and his drawings, his themes and his figures and his backgrounds—all beyond his father's painterly world—and from that point on he was able to paint any kind of a Battigello at any time; so that he, Battigello—when he received the commission from the new master of the Merchants' Guild to paint an allegory of one of the seven virtues, and this commission took up all of his time—he entrusted Filippino to prepare, from start to finish, all of the other projects of lesser import in the workshop, and so it happened that the commission of the panels, depicting the story of Esther, of the two forzieri was given to Filippino, who after discussing the manner of elaboration of the theme with Battigello, completed them to the greatest satisfaction of the patron, and even on time, indeed completed them the day before the date agreed upon, which was truly not a characteristic of Battigello or the greater number of masters in Firenze at all, and perhaps not even of Filippino, but, well, this was a bridal gift and there could be no question of delay, and the commission itself, the workshop's first genuinely serious commission in this respect, stimulated Filippino in an extraordinary fashion, so that he worked on it night and day, and the two larger panels were ready within two months, and he had already painted the second side-panel when Master Sangallo had finished constructing the two chests and Antonio had prepared the goldsmithing; Battigello was satisfied and praised the work of Filippino, but tactfully avoided expressing the thought that it all looked as if he himself, Battigello, had painted it; Filippino, however, was not fooled by this, because when the beginning of the last month of the year came around, and only one panel remained to be painted and placed into the chest, he decided that he would work not in the spirit of Battigello, but according to the dictates of his own imagination; namely, he completed the commission, creating the companion picture of the side panel "Esther arrives at the palace of Susa" so as not to upset the balance of the entire work, but he did paint the chief figure in the picture, Queen Vashti, as he saw fit, and he saw fit to paint her in such a way that this exile would reflect forth every humiliation, every indignity, every human collapse, and that moreover in this humiliation, in this indignity, in this collapse, Queen Vashti would not lose any of her extraordinary beauty, for as Filippino sensed, it was only with the deepest beauty that this humiliation, indignity, collapse could be expressed—this was different to what Battigello had seen up until now, so very different, and on the day before the last day of the year, the patron came with his extensive and merry family, as well as a tumbrel hired for the two heavy chests, and on this occasion—for the reckoning of the bill had to take place as well—Battigello had to be present, and so he arrived a few hours early, and while waiting, he examined the chests once again, at length, for the last time, including the last side-panel, and Filippino could tell how he was struck just as wordless as when he had examined them for the first time, and then he looks at him, Filippino, with a sad, endlessly mournful gaze, and it is as if his words were not addressed any longer to his companion, as he looks away from him, and then he says in his own velvety, gentle voice: if only one day I could find such beauty as that in someone, Filippino, if only one day I could find it too.

They entitled it "La regina Vashti lascia il palazzo reale," that is to say "Queen Vashti Leaves the Royal Palace," but originally it had no title at all, if we are not to regard as a title that designation that Filippino had given to it just before while in discussion, when it was time to present the forzieri, finishing with the presentation of the carpentry and the truly splendid goldsmithing to the family, who were visibly greatly pleased; he explained, proceeding from one picture to the next, one scene to the next, what picture and what scene was depicted on the side panels; perhaps it was the title the head of the family himself later gave it, when in a moment of solemnity at the bridal ceremony itself he explained to the young couple—Sarah and Guido—that upon the sides of the dowry chest that they had just received as a gift there was depicted none other than the story of Esther according to Hebrew tradition, which—at least in the view of the family patriarch—illustrates marital fidelity, as well as the deeper significance of Purim, and preserves it for memory—but of course these accidental designations could never qualify as titles, there wasn't even any point to bestowing a title, for in the times that followed, wherever the two forzieri happened to turn up, they were regarded everywhere as what they were, two very beautifully painted dowry chests, and later when only money and jewels were kept in them, they were seen merely as two old safe-boxes which, as one owner—the wife of a textile merchant from Ferrara—put it, were "decorated with pleasantly painted scenes"—a title only became necessary when the chests fell apart, the beautiful copper linings were stripped away, and in their value was determined separately, as well as that of the paintings, of course, the price of which unexpectedly shot up to the heavens by the length of time that had passed, and due to the not very impartial craze for the quattrocento; in a word, when the pictures began their existence as individual pictures, that is to say, after Torrigiana, then in that moment of course each one needed to have a title; one was needed in Chantilly for the Musée Condé, and one was needed in Vaduz for the Lichtenstein collection, and one was needed in Paris as well, and mainly one was needed in Firenze for the Horne Foundation, particularly here because it was with that title that they hoped to express that the determination of the picture as an object was now a closed matter, and that from now on the panel depicting Vashti would have to bear the title of "Queen Vashti Leaves the Royal Palace" and that was it; it went under this title as part of the huge Botticelli exhibit in Paris, in the Grand Palais, which for many was and remained an unforgettable experience, and although according to the scholar at the Horne Foundation it was given a rather unworthy setting, still, whoever had eyes to see—squashed up against a side door—saw within the work the greatness that was *around* Botticelli, in other words that of Filippino Lippi; still completely unrecognized, the genius, the restless, vibrant brushstrokes, the tautened vibration, the explosive force, the proto-Baroque of Lippi the younger, and with that the figure of Vashti, broken in suffering, stepped with finality into that mysterious Empire, which was even more mysterious than the one from which the main figure in the picture had come; into an Empire, where this figure, tortured from suffering and broken in soul, stepping out through the royal palace's—no, it was more like a fortress now—Northern Gate, finds herself on a terrace that leads nowhere, and there she comes to a halt, the landscape before this fortress is nearly called into question by her beauty and her pain, her radiant being and her forsakenness, what should be done with this enchantment cast into human form, with this sovereign nobility, in the desolation of its own bleakness—but this is only called into question, there is no need for reply, and all of Susa is quiet, for everyone knows what will happen now before the palace, because what follows is not exile, that was merely the induction of the judgment according to the tradition of Marduk, but behind Vashti, the hulking executioner brought from Egypt shall appear, he will seize her, and drag her back into a designated palace courtyard, and there he will smother her under the ashes of legend, he will crush that milk-white delicate neck with his bull-strong right hand, until that milk-white delicate neck is broken and the legs writhing below cease their dance of death, and the body at last collapses, for once and for all, prostrate upon the ground.

3

THE PRESERVATION OF A BUDDHA

For the greater glory of Our Lord, Jesus Christ

Inazawa knows everything, but Inazawa is manifestly an industrial city, where the presence of a monastery hardly ever visited by tourists is of no importance whatever, and this morning it is closed, that is to say the gates are not being opened, so that the monks, in a supposedly secret ritual, may bid farewell to one of their Buddhas; a statue that—in the opinion of the committee in charge of the cultural heritage of the prefecture—bears particular value, yet its condition has, in the course of the centuries, greatly deteriorated, and the restoration—as the abbot and the leadership of the five main rinzai temples have decided—can be delayed no longer; Inazawa simply isn't interested, not even in the slightest, in what is occurring in this Zen monastery somewhat secluded from the city; it is only the most extravagant spectacles that arouse any interest: for example the yearly Hadaka Matsuri, in which men, almost completely naked except for their fundoshi—that is to say a small loincloth—carouse drunkenly on the streets along the path of the Naked Man; following a tradition now completely empty, every February the residents have to reach out and touch them, to preserve the city from Evil; yes, that is needed here, this Shintō circus, this entertainment, because that is the single event that is not only inundated with tourists, but also followed even by the NHK in Tokyo, broadcasting at these times a crowded scene for several long minutes; no, the imagination of the residents of Inazawa is not moved by an insignificant rinzai temple, and especially not this one, this Zengen-ji—if they have any imagination at all, for even their brains are now used to the industrial grayness; life here, and anything that could be imagined about it, is monotonous—the Zengen-ji, really, is just as gray and lifeless as everything else here, people shrug at the textile factories or the assembly lines, and it will remain like that, this general lack of interest, even in the very last week, no curiosity whatsoever arises; yet there inside, in the monastery, the excitement is palpable, at last something is going to happen, the monks—understandably excluded from the Hadaka Matsuri—are thinking to themselves, at last an end to these monotonous days, to the weeks and the months if not years, a sudden and extraordinary change is coming—for this can after all be called sudden and extraordinary, taking the view from the inside, if the Amida statue of the Zengen-ji, which according to the expert opinion and the temple clerisy, is of far greater worth than that claimed in the documents issued by the prefecture committee, after long procrastination, the decisive reason for which is the torturously difficult procurement of the enormous restoration costs, as well as the delivery arrangements, which proved to be similarly complicated, and to a lesser extent that they are *not happy* to move the most sacred of sacredness from its place; in short, this treasure, exceeding its estimated and presumed worth many times over, would simply be picked up and moved, well, this really counts as an extraordinary event, although understandably even the wisest among them did not reach this decision willingly, indeed, certain individuals, seeking a suitable date between the summer and the winter ango, explicitly delayed the transportation, for truly such an occurrence as this was so rare—they shook their heads—here in the monasteries of Aichi prefecture, no one could recall any such event, and in truth even the abbot—himself of wide-ranging experience—and the most respected monks did not know for a while what the ritual requirements actually would be; whatever was needed to be done they would of course do; one thing was certain, it took months for the leading authorities to acquaint themselves with the ritual stipulations prescribed for such circumstances, and it must be acknowledged that they were prepared for a difficult task, demanding great caution, but not for one so exhausting, complicated, and intricate; one that in addition required practice; that is to say that all of the monastery residents had to be trained so that everything would follow according to plan, the authorities had to expand upon the tiniest details in their explanations; even if in terms of the lesser-ranking monks, they had to explain who should do what, and when; it wasn't even worthwhile to deal with the question of the essence of the ceremony as well as its variegated details, it was good enough, the abbot indicated to the leader of the temple administration, if they correctly chanted the sūtras and recited the mantras, if the musicians knew exactly when to bang away and when to stay quiet, and in general it would be enough if everyone clearly understood the structure of the ritual awaiting them, and if the components of it could be carried out faultlessly, that would really be enough; well, that is—the abbot rubbed his shorn pate, as the designated day approached—well, that is a lot too, for he could surely see that here lay precisely the hard part: there could be no errors, by no one, from the rōshi to the deshi, nothing that was not allowed, their coming and going, standing and kneeling, to begin and end the sacred chant when necessary—that was the hardest part, the abbot said, vexedly rubbing his itchy skull once more; he had already seen much and he knew that it wouldn't work, it would not be perfect, someone always makes a mistake, standing up too late, or kneeling down too late; even he was unclear at times, either beginning a little too slowly than was necessary, or too quickly, or being uncertain for a moment: where to now, the left?—or maybe even ... to the right? oh no, groaned the abbot on the evening before the appointed day, when the special moving van ordered here for delivery by the Bijutsu-in—that is the National Treasure Institute for the Restoration of Wooden Statues—had already arrived from Kyōto, and the driver, after the measurements of the statue had been taken and the large kiri-wood transit crate had been made, was happily snoring away in one of the guestrooms, oh no, what now, how are we going to fulfill our obligations properly, the abbot rubbed his shaven scalp worriedly, but then he quelled the anxiety within himself; if he could not, on that day, completely suppress his excitement, in any case when he arose the next day, that is today, at four in the morning to the sound of the great bell, the ogane, and quickly washed, he felt neither anxiety nor any kind of excitement, only the obligation to carry out the tasks that awaited him, just the order of things to be done: the first, then the second, so that simply no time remained to reflect on such matters as how, being the jushoku—that is, the abbot of the temple—or simply a Zen monk, how could he even have been anxious or excited in the past weeks and days, because now that the whole thing was beginning, he couldn't pay attention to anything else but taking the very next step, then the next after that and so on, and so it is and so it would be proper, in this way, for the day to begin by simultaneously giving the order to close—that is not to open—the gates; to check the day's events, affixed to the kiku-board, making sure that everything was written out correctly, to see if the work was going on in the kitchen and at the spot designated for packing up the statue next to the van; to see if the monks had begun their procession with the jikijitsu at the front into the zendō; to see if the musicians had been asked for the last time if they knew the exact sequence of events; all of these orders had to be given at once, and at the same time they had to be supervised: first the closing, that is the non-opening of the gates—in this matter he wished to see it with his own eyes—that is first to go to the Sanmon, the main gate, then to seek out the others in turn, even nudging them with his hand, were they really closed, only this would convince him, only in this way would he believe that yes, the monastery was closed, and still it was hardly half past four, or maybe a quarter to five in the morning, and the monastery was hermetically sealed, no way to get in, no way to get out, the abbot notes to himself, everyone remaining on the temple grounds knows this, all who could, as well as those who had to remain inside, are aware, but it is felt by those, too, who attempt to follow the so-called secret events from without, because there are, for that reason, a few standing around out there on the street by one of the gates, trying to listen, to figure out, somehow, what is going on inside, smaller groupings of lay believers, recruited by happenstance simply from local elderly insomniacs, standing at the monastery gates that are positioned according to the four directions; or there are those who aren't too sluggish to get dressed and come here at the crack of dawn, so gnawed by curiosity—surely nothing like this had ever happened before, they mutter in front of the gates, instead of opening the gates they've shut them, or rather the gates are closed—and there they stand, and they would not be willing to move from there for any sum of money, they try to capture some sense from the half-audible voices of what is going on in there right now, well, and even if something like that emerges, they can't get too far with such sounds, even if they hear from a distance the silent shuffling coming from inside, as the monks, after the chanting of the sūtras filters out, walk in procession, to the rhythm of the mokugyo and the handbells, from the zendō to somewhere, indeed, as they largely agree at each gate, they are most likely walking toward the Buddha Hall, the hondō, and even if they hear that, even if they can agree that yes, it's the Buddha Hall, they can only be going toward the Great Hall where the Amida Buddha is located, they know nothing of the ceremony itself, and that is really how it is, for here the listeners, at all of the gates, are mistaken when it comes to this, for the entire monastic collective, after the recitation of the sūtras in the zendō, are really not proceeding toward the Great Hall of the Buddha, but in the opposite direction, away from it, the farthest possible distance from the Hall of the Buddha, in actuality, to their own quarters, to seclude themselves and to wait: since during the so-called secret ceremony, beginning with the truly secret rituals of its commencement, no one else may be present, only the jushoku and two older rōshi, as well as the jikijitsu and three jōkei in all—these being three assistant monks chosen for the occasion who handle the instruments of the Buddha Hall—only them, seven in total, so that not only the curious crowd outside, but even they, the resident members of the order, listen in vain to the sounds of the keisu, the rin, or the mokugyo filtering out from time to time, in vain does a seemingly familiar phrase from one of the sūtras strike their ears, they haven't the slightest notion of the secret part of the ceremony nor will they ever, and they could never even form any notion of it, for only the following sections of the Hakken Kuyo ritual, coming after this truly secretive beginning, concern them, only then can they take part, and for all that they must do so with great devotion and a great sense of duty, when they gather again, emerging from their quarters, and proceeding together in the same direction, toward the hondō, because then their shuffling truly means that they are proceeding to the sound of the densho, the great drum, proceeding to the hondō, into the Great Hall where the Buddha sits—and as they, the monks, the residents of Zengen-ji, take their places before the Buddha's infinitely radiating gaze, something irrevocable has happened.

Something has happened to it, immediately they sense this, as they sit down in their respective places in the Great Hall facing the lotus throne, but of course it doesn't pass through their minds that this infinitely diffusing gaze *is no longer here*, they don't think about that at all, not even because they don't dare to look at it; their heads are bowed, everyone concentrates solely on not treading on the feet of the monk in front of him, or not bumping into someone else when that monk suddenly comes to a stop in front, or on concluding a movement—albeit in general if moderate confusion—exactly when it must be concluded, the heads always bowed down, every movement as silent as possible; the monastery is used to this already, and already knows especially how to change places without a sound, to rise and to kneel, to step forward and step backward, to stand in a disciplined manner, to sit in a disciplined manner and walk in a disciplined manner when necessary, while their discipline, as always, extends not only to this, but to their not posing questions to themselves, because even if they think about the fact that something has happened, they do not, in any way, ask what, not even in their innermost thoughts; at the very most, the new arrivals, the little novice deshis, ask themselves, for example, if the deepest meaning of the Hakken Kuyo ritual, that is the temporary removal, departure, diversion of the Light radiating from the Buddha's eyes, has already occurred within the framework of the secret ceremony—as they had been previously instructed, that this, the ceremony enabling the Sacred Statue to be moved at all, would occur as they waited in their quarters; so what then is the ceremony that follows upon it, or more childishly, what is the point of the whole hocus-pocus *afterward*, to be completed by all of them, the entire Zengen-ji gathered here in the hondō, the temple-apprentices still ask themselves this, but then somehow in the general silence and devotion the question dies out even within them too, for along with the others, it is surely enough for their little souls, they are permeated with the consciousness of how uplifting it is even just to take part in the ceremony, for them to be able to assume their role in the Hakken Kuyo, and this is enough—the ones outside cannot, in the end, experience this, the profane curiosity-seekers up at dawn outside the gates, they only hear the sounds filtering out; one of them loudly and with great pride announcing to the others that this was now the Incense-Lighting Hymn or the Amida-kyō, now the Invocation, now the Triple Vow, now the greeting of the Zengen-ji Bodhisattva, now the Prayer of the Sangharama, come on, that's enough already, the others hiss him down, we can see that you really know what's going on in there, they jeer at him, but we've heard enough already, so that the speaker retreats into wounded silence; just the sounds of the great drum and the rin, then the keisu, which is the gong and the mokugyo filter out beyond the gates; and morning has not yet come, they still stand around in the darkness, they stand around and try to listen, patiently, however, like people who are waiting for something, but just don't know what it is they are waiting for; some of them, chiefly those who live nearby, drift away for a while, to drink a cup of hot tea because in mid-March it is still chilly at dawn, it could be warmer, but this year, somehow, it's taking longer than usual for spring to arrive, only the huge pale pink-tinted flowers of the magnolia have bloomed so far to indicate that winter has definitely come to an end— a sip or two of hot tea, then they come back, those who just now disappeared from the group standing around in front of the gate; they shall not, however, be any the wiser, for from outside only the sounds of sūtras, fading away, filter out through the gates, then not even that, there shall be a great silence inside, a long motionless silence, during which the ones outside wait for a newer sound or movement, but in vain, for absolutely nothing can be heard, as everyone inside the hondō is now turning toward the Amida Buddha, then kneeling once, getting up, kneeling a second time and getting up again, and kneeling a third time and at last getting up, concluding thus the ceremony taking place within, the Hakken Kuyo has achieved its goal, the statue may be moved from the lotus throne, even if it is not moved immediately, for the monks first need to leave the space of the hall, and it is only then, only when the last one reaches the courtyard and all of them, at the signaling of meal-time, direct their steps to the jikidō, when only the abbot, the two rōshi and the jikijitsu remain inside and four strong young jōkei, selected in advance, then the jushoku motions to the youths who, approaching the statue and after bowing three times, lift up Amida with great caution from the lotus throne, taking tiny steps under the enormous weight, they take the statue out from the hondō to the designated spot next to the moving van, and from that point on, everything plays out quickly, the kiri-crate, already tied up, appears, the bottom of it is covered with silicone gel, acid-free paper, and fabric, the body of the statue in turn is tightly wrapped in thick moisture-absorbing cambric, the entire wrapping is carefully fastened, and then the Buddha is lowered into the crate; they begin to fill the empty space between the body of the statue and the walls of the crate with even more deliberation than before, so that—while the monastery is finishing breakfast in the jikidō—the Zengen-ji Amida Buddha is already inside the storage compartment of the moving van, expertly tethered, immobile, and nothing remains but to give the signal to the driver to start now for Kyōto, and then to return to the hondō for a bit, and temporarily cover the vacant space where the Buddha was with an orange-red embroidered silk cloth, that is all; and the abbot can at least say to himself that the Hakken Kuyo has been completed, the Hakken Kuyo proceeded as it should have, and that now one just has to wait, to wait like this for eleven or twelve months for the Buddha to return in renewed form, for the rest is up to the driver, who at this moment is cautiously pulling out through the circle of fortunate curiosity-seekers by the western gate of the Zengen-ji, and turning into the street leading out of the city, so as to quickly reach the highway toward Ichinomiya, and from there to merge onto the Meishin Expressway, because he truly feels confident there, on this highway in the colossal traffic heading toward Kyōto, he feels as if it were not himself driving the van, but as if it were being driven by some kind of higher force, together with the billowing tide of innumerable cars on the Meishin Expressway, he feels confident indeed, here in this crazily dense traffic heading in one direction; he knows his precious consignment to be utterly safe, though there is hardly any cause for concern anyway, it's not the first time that he's transporting something like this, this is his job, he's no beginner, he's made trips with items said to be of extraordinary national value in the enclosed platform perhaps hundreds of times before, yet still despite that, this time, as always, he feels a little excitement as he passes the distance markers, or rather a kind of pleasurable tension, which will only come to an end—as he already knows from experience—when the consignment will be taken from him in Kyōto; up till then, well, there was just still the Sekigahara exit, then Maibara and Hikone, the entire route of 170 kilometers until Otsu, because in Otsu he feels like he's home already, from that point on everything is familiar, to drive into the city, taking a short cut, and after Fujinomori, through the Fukakusa district right up to the Takeda intersection, because there he has to turn right, at exactly a 90-degree angle, onto the Takeda Kaido, from which it usually takes a mere half-hour—for at this hour the traffic is moving—to reach the large gate beside the National Museum by the Sanjūsangen-dō, and wave to the gatekeeper, who is already leaping up and opening the gate; he can come to a stop already in front of the Bijutsu-in delivery entrance, because from there on it's no longer any of his business, he has the papers signed, hands it over, and the rest is for the workers of the Bijutsu-in, with that his work here is done, he can pick up the next consignment, the workers are taking down the crate, then put it into the elevator and take it up to the mezzanine where later on, the unpacking of the crate will take place, but not today, there is no time for that today, the Bijutsu-in has so much work that the Inazawa material, as it is called from this day on, remains unopened for days; there it sits in the enormous space of the Bijutsu-in with its open galleries running along each floor, put aside in a corner, and for the time being only the statue itself knows that it is one meter, thirty-seven centimeters, and two millimeters tall, made of hinoki cyprus, known as jōseki-zukuri—that is, assembled from many parts, structured with a hollow interior, held together by small iron nails and reinforced by pieces of lacquer-soaked fabric—the statue presumably dates from the beginning of the Kamakura era, and one could enumerate where the diadems are individually placed into the head, where they can also be accordingly individually removed from the head, as well as both the ears and the chest, all of that; and the harmonious body sits in the lotus position, covered by folds of fabric, carved with miraculous sensitivity, although of course the most precious thing of all in the statue are the eyes, and this is also what makes it so celebrated in the opinion of experts—the half-lowered eyelids or, put another way, the only half-opened eyes, miraculous, astounding; they give the statue and every Amida statue, as its essence, the infinite suggestion of one immortal gaze, the influence of which one cannot avoid; it is a question all in all, of that one single gaze; so that the sculptor, sometime around the year 1367, wished to depict, to capture with his own unfathomable genius of artistic technique that *one single gaze*, and this depiction and this capturing, even in the most restrained sense of the word, was successful—there it sits in the corner, and it is the dreaded master of the restorers of the Bijutsu-in—the forever ill-tempered, forever irritable and dissatisfied and grumbling and gloomy and dry and humorless, Fujimori Seiichi—who will decide, which means no peeking out of curiosity; the statue will remain wrapped up in the cambric until he gives an explicit instruction; no one can mess with it, that is no one can look at it; later if the time will come, Master Fujimori wrinkles his thick eyebrows, just keep yourselves busy with the work that is in front of you now, there are deadlines to be met here, he paces up and down among the various component parts of Fugan-ji, Manjushri, and Shakyamuni statues piled up on the floor and on the tables, as well as among the restorers, their faces masks of discipline, they appear to be slightly amused—but there are urgent deadlines all the same; he stares fixedly at the craftsmen from beneath his thick eyebrows, and the deadlines must be met and your work completed, and there should not be any messing around with that Zengen-ji statue, no matter how famous, how tempting, it stays in the corner, he repeats again, so that after this no one in this spacious lofty hall of the workshop has any desire to break the prohibition, in any event the time really will come, the restorers note among themselves quietly, as it does come in actuality, for in less than two weeks, as they are all finishing their own portion of work, one day, after breakfast, the master of the workshop, his expression even more gloomy than usual, nervously fixing the side part in his thinning hair, says, well, let's take off the cambric now, and everyone knows that he's thinking of the Zengen-ji Amida Buddha, let's take it down, Master Fujimori repeats and that means—that *let's take it down*—that they should take it down, his subordinates should take off the cambric, because Fujimori Seiichi always speaks in the first-person plural, but thinks in the imperative mood; so they take it off, carefully, almost thread by thread, warp by woof, lest a scrap of pigmentation or fragment of wood clinging to the surface, if there is any such thing, should fall off, here every individual piece counts, here nothing can be lost, not even a tiny speck of dust, for—as the workshop-master never tires of repeating during the dreaded and dreadfully boring weekly meeting sessions—even that speck of dust may date from the Heian period, and a speck of dust from the Heian period is worth more—the master at this point, during the meeting sessions, raises his voice—than you yourselves, that is to say the restorers in this workshop taken all together, and so, well, of course they know that he observes them in this spirit too, so the level of caution is particularly high, a caution that is sustained even in his absence, for all of the restorers in this workshop are blessed with a special quality of conscience, all are from the nation's most important workshops for restoration of ancient statuary, craftsmen with specific talents and specific training, who know full well, without any prompting, the significance of a speck of Heian dust.

The administration must exceptionally and immediately—so that they hardly have time to look and see what is beneath the layers of cambric—create a description of the statue's general state for the so-called Blue Dossier, they must create a description of practically everything they perceive about it, concerning the possibly most minute details, circumstances, and even impressions; following, however, the sequence specified by the Office of Cultural Properties so that even at the very first, they must provide an account of the material from which the work is created and its structure, the measurements within a hair's breadth of accuracy, whether the traces of previous restoration work can be discerned, what specific damage has occurred, so as to formulate a plan for its later rectification, and finally what all of this will approximately cost; but then they have to give an account of the delivery process as well, which they simply take from the shared notations of the driver and the abbot of the Zengen-ji, while making note at the same time in what year, on what day, at what hour and at what minute they took possession of the statue, with what protective measures, from whom, and with what designated goal, then follows the notation of the year, month, day, hour, and minute of the unpacking of the crate, Master Fujimori is in his element, he knows this very well, this obligatory administrative sequence, so that his words come sputtering out—questions here, statements there—it all goes into the Blue Dossier, the work-book treated and venerated almost as much as if it were a sacred sūtra, for it is this, precisely this Blue Dossier, which—if, in agreement with a pre-designated schedule, a so-called supervisory inspection is carried out—the highly respected and even more powerful Office of Cultural Properties may examine as the single real evidence of the work that is taking place here, for certainly the Tokyo authorities do not, or at least hardly ever, have any encounter with the work itself; it is only through an acquaintance with the contents of the Blue Dossier that they can form an expert opinion as to what is going on here, if things are proceeding as they should, exclusively from the Blue Dossier, the significance of which is, accordingly, huge; and Master Fujimori knows this better than anyone else, it all depends on this, what is in the Blue Dossier, on what the special committee—they are methodical and of the highest authority—reads from the Blue Dossier; no wonder, then, if the description of the circumstances of the interventions taking place here are nearly laughable in their painstaking minuteness; Master Fujimori dictates, or asks questions; or he asks questions while making statements, or makes statements while asking questions, while the others—crouched and circled around him and the statue, now placed on the floor—very quickly nod, one after the other, in agreement, and mumble and approve, and always in chorus, as they are now, saying yes, absolutely, of course, the most serious traces of exterior damage are visible at first glance on the right side of the chest, on the throat, the arms, the back of the skull, in the figure's lap, and on the statue's base, that is true, they all say yes and firmly nod, the restorers in chorus; this must be noted down and this too is noted down in the Blue Dossier; and hours pass, however unbelievable it may seem, literally hours, until they have finished recording this administrative reception in the Blue Dossier, for the diagnosis must determine not only the symptoms but the presumed causes, it is almost noon already when the statue is carefully lifted up and placed onto the hydraulic table, and the restorers set about photographing the statue from every conceivable angle; this too will be part of the obligatory documentation: how the work of art appeared—in its entirety—when it was taken in for restoration; then the procedure is completed, the photographing, for safety's sake a second camera is used as well, and then with the greatest caution they lift the statue down from the hydraulic table, and take it directly into the fumigation chamber, where the Amida Buddha receives his first so-called general defumigation, devised especially for such cases, for always or nearly always this is actually the first order of business, if a wooden statue is brought into the Bijutsu-in, if even merely for the protection of the hordes of national treasures already undergoing restoration here, because no one can recall even a single case in which damage by vermin was not a factor—at times decisive—in a statue's material disintegration; insects and bacteria are always a factor, centuries have gone by here, most often the objects in need of rescue brought here date from the Edo or alternately the early Kamakura dynasty; since this is a rescue, it has to be gassed, and with that, after the Inspection, the Registration of the Current State, and the Photographic Documentation of the entire statue, the Operation proper begins, so that just as is mandated by the letter and the spirit of law no. 318—the Act for the Protection of Cultural Goods introduced on December 24, 1951, and amended or supplemented every year or two up to the present day—give it strong methyl bromide, comes the command from Master Fujimori, when the statue is placed in the fumigation chamber, as it was clear even after the first examination that here, as in so many cases, they are faced with the so-called dry-rot insects of the Lyctidae, Bostrichidae, Anobiidae, and Cerambycidae families, and before anything it needs a good shower of gas, as the fumigation in the chamber is called, first the whole at once; then follows the procedure, in fact the most delicate part, in which they disassemble the Amida Buddha from the Zengen-ji into its minutest components on the hydraulic table, separating the tiniest possible parts from the rest, so that, disassembled pell-mell, the damage to the details thus exposed can be examined and determined, and at the same time specifying—collectively, always with the entire group of restorers, but of course under the supervision of the workshop's master—the methods, materials, sequence, and timing of the repairs of the damage, always following the letter and the spirit of the law of December 24, 1951, that is to say, never losing sight of the fact that their task here in the Bijutstu-in is not the restoration of carefully guarded national treasures, but their material conservation, not RESTORATION but CONSERVATION; Master Fujimori takes this section of the law from 1951 so seriously that when he pronounces it, he essentially screams; his subordinates are convinced the reason why is that he *fears* this word; it is not our task to repair mistakes, Master Fujimori states, his voice, at such times, already rising, but rather to secure the current extant state, this is our task, and here he repeats it, he repeats it a few times, placing so much stress on every syllable that the syllables nearly falter in the stresses, just like the restorers themselves, and there lying strewn about all in pieces on the hydraulic table is Amida Buddha, as above their heads the just-shouted MATERIAL CONSERVATION fades away; they lean over the hydraulic table and everyone picks up one single piece, or in the more delicate cases, leans down very close to examine and decide what kind of damage has occurred here, and what should be done about it; that is to say, the wondrous gaze of the Amida Buddha lies in pieces on the hydraulic table, this is a very delicate point, and always is a very delicate point in the life of a restorer, an Amida Buddha so nicely laid out, just like this one from the Zengen-ji is now, nicely arranged on the large surface, so that it can all be nicely differentiated, nicely discernable in the photo documentation to come, and so where is that renowned gaze?—that is the sensitive question; to which of course Fujimori-san has an answer, namely that it is nowhere else, and nowhere else during the entire course of the restoration, but within the souls of the restorers; fine, comes their reply, because even if they can sense that, and they actually do sense there is something in their souls when they glimpse it for the first time, and the unquestionable respect felt in their souls does not cease during the entire course of the work up to its completion, but . . . when the *whole* lies here in tiny pieces, it can hardly be said that the *whole* of it is there, that is to say the *whole*, gathered here in pieces isn't there, only the pieces are there, and the *whole* isn't anywhere, so that as always, there is a certain unease in the matter, as they complete the disassembly and the carefully separated parts are documented, that is, photographed from above by a camera mounted on tracks and therefore easily adjustable, on the upper floor, as well of course by employing the lifting mechanism of the hydraulic table, they take, that is, a full overview shot from above, clearly showing each individual piece, because in the Blue Dossier every individual component part has to be marked with the appropriate symbol and designated so that at the end—after reassembly—they will be able to demonstrate, with fresh photographic documentation as well as drawings of the internal structure, where the pieces have been, and what condition they are in; there is, accordingly, disquiet, some discomposure, in the soul, the place, in other words, where, according to Fujimori Seiichi, Amida Buddha would be; everything goes smoothly, restorers are not chatty people, they are used to silence, and even if a talkative sort happens to turn up among them, he too becomes used to no conversation after a year or two; the work, the entire process of taking apart the statue occurs in nearly total silence, and the same goes for the automated photographing of the statue from above; and then, the various disassembled components are carried again in small groupings into the gas chamber, and these groupings of components are given a second gas-shower, the intensity and quantity of which is measured specifically for them, respectively, until the various specialists begin to carry away the individual pieces to their own work tables, and until the specialized restoration of the individual components thus begins—up until this point, there is a touch of disquiet in their souls, if they happen to glance at each other, a mild discomposure; somehow, though, when Master Fujimori designates the specific tasks, it is obscured, and everyone can at last withdraw with their own piece of the statue to the worktable, because from that point on the only interest lies in the task at hand: to establish the extent of the fissures, the cracks, the internal structural damage caused by the borings of the vermin, the amount of paint that has peeled off, to decide—of course after having reached agreement with the Director of the workshop—what is the best course of action for the restor . . . for the preservation of the statue, would it be more efficient to introduce the mugi-urushi or the various synthetic resins and emulsions by injection, or work them into the fissures of this or that smaller or larger cavity with a small thin-bladed knife; or should we now strip off the Edo-period veneer from the surface and retain the original Kamakura one; should we use funori or another kind of animal-based adhesive for gluing or keep the Edo-period glue and stabilize that; in a word, it has begun, and everything goes smoothly, and Master Fujimori—to the extent that his soul, tensed in continual readiness, permits at all—notes with a certain satisfaction that work has commenced, and that it is proceeding in its own order and way, life goes on in the Bijutsu-in, and of course more and more statues are brought, meaning that the attention of the workshop must be divided among various activities, but this does not in the least concern Master Fujimori, every statue that is brought here receives its own warranted attention, and the work proceeds in parallel, summer passes and then autumn, a mild winter coming in December, only January and February are unusually chill, the chill lasts a long time, they note at the end of one day or another as they step out from the Bijutsu-in building into the courtyard, once again winter has lasted too long, it wasn't like this in the old times, they mutter to each other as a few set off, going part of the way together, toward bus number 206 or 208; in the old days not only were the magnolias already blooming in mid-February but the plum-trees as well, not to mention that at this time of year—in the old days—a jacket was sufficient and not a coat like today, somehow everything is going to the dogs, the restorers mutter to each other in the cold wind as they head toward the bus stop; if at such times some of them head out together after a typical day, no one is thinking that at the same time they are carrying, as they get into the bus and go home, according to the original consensus, the soul of the Amida Buddha in their own souls, which they then take home, give it something to eat for dinner, sit down with it in front of the TV, then lie down to rest with it and finally the next day bring it back to the Bijutsu-in, continuing their meticulous work on the section that has been entrusted to them; for example, the restorer with the magnifying glass strapped to his head, whose task it is to preserve and protect the carved hand making the gesture of "Mida no jōin," thinks exactly that, and that is how he explains it to his seven-year-old son at home, of course the boy starts to make cheeky remarks and ask silly questions which are impossible to answer, so that the restorer grows annoyed, shoos the child away, and continues to work away industriously in the Bijutsu-in, so that the quality of the carved hand making the gesture of "Mida no jōin," will be clearly discernible, because there is exactly where the problem lies: the borders of the fingertips touching each other, and the contours of the back of the hand, are completely blurred, so that you can hardly tell what mudra the hand is posed in; this is especially important in a statue of the Amida Buddha, Master Fujimori mentions on such occasions—three or four times a day—standing behind the back of the restorer, which is of course incredibly irritating, because he has to keep looking away from the magnifying glass in order to look back at the Workshop Director, and not only that, but keep nodding in agreement with the strap on his forehead, which can fall off at any moment, because for a while now he hasn't been able to properly pull the strap tight enough; but still his situation is a happy one; it's that young restorer, a certain Koinomi Shunzo, that Master Fujimori torments most of all, the one who has been entrusted with the restoration of the statue's eyes, as one of the undoubtedly most talented—well, this Koinomi's nerves can hardly hold up, in December, it is already plain to see that he cannot withstand the constant badgering, the continual supervision, the eternal reminders and anxiety-provoking remarks, and even more so, that Master Fujimori is somehow capable of moving around, of being in the workshop, in such a way that no matter where he is, he gives the impression that it is he, Koinomi, who is the perpetual focus of his attention: if he is by the gas chamber because he has something to do there at that moment, it's as if he's watching from there; if he is by the courtyard window, then from there; indeed, this Koinomi has the sense that if Fujimori-san goes out of the workshop to do something on the second or third floor, or if he goes over to the administrative manager of the Bijutsu-in, he still somehow leaves himself behind; Koinomi can hardly focus on his work, he continually blinks at the thick sliding door of the workshop, at the handle, waiting for it to turn in the next moment and the workshop head to return, that is to say that he cannot relax even if Fujimori leaves him to his work by going out for a bit, but only if Fujimori does not go out at all, because at least then he cannot delude himself by saying he isn't here, at last he can breathe a sigh of relief, for the possibility that he can return at any moment is far worse than when he is here, strolling among them with his hands behind his back, so that it is this Koinomi who suffers the most, although he is completing his task—a born eye-specialist is what they call him—with extraordinary skill, and that is just what is so necessary, as everyone knows full well the significance of what will happen to the eyes of the Amida Buddha here in the workshop, because on the day of arrival, the renowned gaze, if examined up close, seemed just a little faded; the entire workshop expects a great deal from Koinomi, exactly what, would be difficult for them to formulate in words, but it is a lot, that's what they even tell him as a form of encouragement, if he heads home with them on the way to the 206 or 208 bus stop, but in any case, not within earshot of the director of the workshop, that is to say they would never dare to risk allowing Master Fujimori to overhear such encouragement, because then it would somehow seem as if the workers of the atelier were openly defying him, whereas such defiance, especially openly, cannot be expressed; we're not living in America, one colleague raises his voice at one point, definitely not, they all nod in agreement, not a word is spoken and everything remains as before, that is to say that on the one hand Koinomi's colleagues all work on the basis of an anticipatory, encouraging trust, on the other hand among the eternally dissatisfied, critical, wounding, confidence-destroying, and degrading comments from the Workshop Director; just one thing is certain: one day, toward the end of February, when Koinomi states to the workshop that he's finished and Fujimori immediately appears there behind him, ready to snarl, with a shake of his head, what impudence to say that one has finished, given such a task, it is he, Master Fujimori, who will decide if it is finished; the only problem is that when Master Fujimori stands behind the back of the young restorer and leans forward above his shoulder to examine the head and the two eyes, the words choke in his throat; the eyes, that is, really are finished, there can be no doubt to an expert, as Fujimori is himself, that his subordinate spoke correctly, the restoration of the two eyes is complete; it is, however, difficult to say exactly how this can be known, yet in any event, it is sufficient merely to look at the head of the Buddha affixed to Koinomi's worktable, the diadems are still not screwed back into place, as someone else at another table is stabilizing their surface; it is enough to cast one glance to know perfectly that Koinomi is speaking the truth—the gaze is exactly what it should be, as it might have been originally in that year, sometime around 1367, when an unknown artist sought out by the Zengen-ji or recommended to them carved it; someone standing near the back formulates this thought in a muted voice when, at Koinomi's announcement, everyone gathers around Koinomi and the workshop director: the gaze has "returned" and everyone is visibly in agreement; indeed, captivated, they stare at this gaze, this look that ascends from below the two half-closed eyes, the gaze of this looking, for these are experts, outstanding experts if not some of the most outstanding anywhere, they don't need, for example to screw the diadems back onto the head, have no need to complete the painting of the face, i.e. the fixation of the former hues, to see that the gaze is finished, and with that too, they sense that the most decisive part of the restoration has been completed, and that is not so much of an exaggeration, because somehow after this, everything in the workshop speeds up, if it is the Zengen-ji Amida we are speaking of, all the parts end up back in place more quickly than before, the fastening and adhesive substances, largely prepared from urushi, are spread more rapidly onto the surfaces than before, and Master Fujimori states quite soon that the workshop is now ready to put all the disassembled components back together, so now the workers are already hurrying to the hydraulic table, already the red and saffron nails which will replace the rusted originals have been gathered up, and in the meantime they nearly forget to photograph the seperate, now restored components for the Blue Dossier—but only, of course, if Master Fujimori weren't there, who of course is there for this occasion as well, keeping a keen eye on things and reminding the restorers of the necessary sequence of their work, repeating over and over in rebuking tones that to disregard law no. 318, the Act for the Protection of Cultural Goods, effective as of December 24, 1951, is not customary, as he terms it, in this institution—and so, in a word, the pieces are photographed one by one; then there comes at last the great day when the restored components are re-assembled, in the afternoon; the promised date of delivery is now drawing near when it is placed on the hydraulic table in its original radiance, and once again whole, the statue of Amida Buddha from the Zengen-ji, and its own gaze of unutterable strength, broadly scourging, sweeps across the entire staff of the Bijutsu-in, as if they had been struck by a windstorm, and even Fujimori Seiichi feels it, for the first time now he bends his head before the statue, lowering his eyes, for a time unable to withstand that tranquility—immense, ponderous, terrifying, and enigmatic—the likes of which here, even he, a workshop director at the Bijutsu-in, who has seen so much, has never yet encountered.

Winter has come to an end in the monastery, the cold is for the most part behind them: the uplifting memory of the ango meditation lasting three and a half months, but also that of their eternal daily torments, the biting cold, the heavy snowfalls, the numbing frosts, the icy winds; their hearts are filled with joy, they can now stand in between the choka at dawn and the peal of the evening bells, immersed in the beauty of the enormous magnolia tree behind the hondō, they can see how life begins to take shape on the early-blossoming trees, as the first buds appear on the plum-tree's branches, how the morning is ever more bounteous, if they open their windows upon rising, with the humming of birds—in short, the Zengen-ji is replete with a sense of relief and happy excitement, and the children, the jishas, run around during the rare pauses more freely, although they feel in their souls, after the trials of the winter, a somewhat more serious hue, and the food in the jikadō tastes better, and the afternoon work in the monastery's vegetable gardens is more appealing, and everything, but everything is filled with ever more hope that it shall be, it shall come, that spring is nearly here, when the abbot makes the announcement that word has come from Kyōto, the work has been completed, and hence they request the monastery to decide which day, before the beginning of the springtime ango, should be designated as the precise date of delivery, the beginning of March, they write back, there is not much time for reflection, a group of the most eminent monks immediately sit down together and even contest the authority of the abbot over what day would be the best, essentially everything has been prepared, everything has been studied and memorized, they know nearly every element—by heart, interjects the abbot, by heart!—of the great ceremony, the kaigen shiki, that awaits them, says the shikaryo; we'll see about that, says the abbot, shaking his head; but later on, even he has to recognize that they have done all they could, the invitations to the two guest abbots and many other illustrious guests were sent off long ago, now only the specific date has to be announced to the citizens of Inazawa, from whence—with regard to the spectacular nature of the ceremony—a larger mass of visitors (and perhaps of donations as well!) can be expected; the determination of the exact conditions for delivery is child's play, for it is exactly the same, the abbot notes, only in reverse order; it's only that—for a moment he falls silent—it's only that, he continues, shaking his freshly shaven pate again, there is a problem with preparing the kaigen shiki beforehand, in his view the monks are prepared only in their heads, that is to say as for the actual practice in how to proceed in this ceremony without error—well, he shakes his head again, they are doing pretty badly with the concluding section of the kaigen shiki, that is the ceremonial preparation for the return of the Buddha, because—the abbot rubs his bald head forward and backward—they don't know the sequence of the kaigen shiki well enough when practicing it; it's one thing to have something in your head and entirely another thing for it to work out in reality, he will have to see, because it's difficult, he shakes his head, of course he knows full well this ceremony is difficult and complicated, indeed much, much more difficult than the Hakken Kuyo a year ago, difficult, he repeats, and that doesn't mean that it can be treated in such an undisciplined manner, because in his view there is simply not enough rigor in the Zengen-ji, and that can be seen when, during their practice of the kaigen shiki, the monks all *make mistakes,* on every occasion they *make mistakes,* either they don't know the sequence or one of the musicians comes in at the wrong place, not to speak of themselves, to begin with *themselves* first and foremost, since even they, yes, precisely they, the foremost monks of the monastery, with he himself the foremost of the foremost of the continually uncertain: either there is a problem with the memorization of the texts—used less and less or even not at all—of the sacred sūtras and dhāranīs, or accordingly, during this or that point in the ceremony, even knowing where their place is, and even more, grumbles the abbot, for everyone to know where they should stand and where they should go often causes problems, it can't be like this; he raises his voice with a bit of irritation, he requests, starting tomorrow, greater discipline from everyone, and they will have to explain this to the rest as well, but first and foremost they themselves should fully understand that the kaigen shiki is a *public* ceremony, and there could be many attendees, the abbot of Nanzen-ji monastery will be here, and the abbot of Tōfuku-ji monastery, and quite a few lay people, they have to be ready for that, and they have to prepare for it—this is true, the shikaryo interrupts, but so much has already happened, let us not forget, the shikaryo says, slightly offended, how much has been done already, particularly under his, the shikaryo's guidance, because please kindly consider, esteemed abbot, all of the countless invitations, writing them out, putting them in the envelopes, sealing them, addressing them, mailing them, then all the planning: who will receive the guests, where will they be accommodated, which monks will be receiving visitors; then the memorization, here the jikijitsu decorously takes up the thread of the discussion, teaching them sūtras they've never even heard before, beating the dhāranīs into their heads, drilling them on who has to go where and when, how many times have I myself tried with them as well, sighs the jikijitsu, how many times—fine, says the abbot with a conciliatory expression, but then scratches his freshly shaven head again; all of this is fine, but everyone clearly agrees that things are not proceeding without error; time is pressing, so he has no desire for any more fruitless chatter on this question, let us begin from tomorrow, everyone with his own task, with redoubled zeal; and that is how they leave it, with redoubled zeal, all of the monks taking part in the discussions accept this, it's just that from the next day onward the abbot somehow does not sense that redoubled zeal, or it does not somehow appear at all that the zeal of anyone entrusted with drilling the monks in a given task has been redoubled, the abbot walks through the monastery rooms, he hears the monks reciting the sūtras, he watches attentively when a jikijitsu or a rōshi holds a rehearsal in the hondō, and he sees what he sees, he just rubs and ever more nervously rubs his skull, which, as the hair begins to grow in again, is ever more itchy, because he hears, he sees, he senses that not only is it not flawless, not only is it not yet correct, let alone perfect, but it will never ever be so, given the material in the Zengen-ji that they are able to summon forth; it will never be any better than this; he paces back and forth from the western gate to the eastern gate, from the northern gate to the Sanmon, and then one day he is suddenly filled with tranquility, for he senses that he has accepted, somehow, in the course of things he has reconciled to this: that they are what they are and not any better, he has given in: that put together like this, from the rōshi to the battan, the shikaryo to the kakuryoosha, from the jushoku to the ensuryo, they are altogether capable of this much, and this perception for once does not fill him with sadness, or more nervousness and dissatisfaction, but rather with tranquility, it's the intention, he says to himself in the evening before retiring, if the intention is correct, then there is nothing else to wish for, so that the next day, summoning the monastic leadership for a discussion, the exact date and time of the delivery, and also that of the kaigen shiki, is determined, the letter has already been dispatched to Kyōto, and the responses are already coming back from the invited expressing how wonderful it is, the date—mid-March—is perfect, they will be here, everything is proceeding impeccably, and the time has already come for the monks to proceed to the samu, that is they begin to clean and tidy in a manner that has never been seen before, far out-stripping the usual tidying up, they set to work on cleaning the buildings from within, they set to cleaning the monastery from without, a broom and a floor mop make their appearance in every corner, outside, in the courtyard and the back courtyard and the rear-most courtyard, not a single square meter remains where a rake and a broom have not made their presence felt, the fever is general, it has infected everyone by now, the great day is coming, they take out and survey yet again their attire to ensure that between the koromos and the obis, the kesas and the kimonos, everything is in order, that they are clean enough, ironed, undamaged, that they are suitable for the great ceremony of the kaigen shiki; and everyone finds, that somehow . . . everything is ready, it's strange, but along with the shared and gratifying excitement, there will also be, growing ever stronger amidst the entire monastic community, an inner certitude that during the forthcoming ceremony everything will be fine, everything will proceed with decorum, as the great day approaches, ever fewer disquieted countenances are seen, a deshi, a battan, or a jisha running about here and there, and on every face there is joyful anticipation, so that when the news arrives, late in the morning one day, almost around the same time as the day's first meal in the monastery, that a special delivery van with their Buddha has set off, the monks signal with joyful eyes that they have understood, it has begun, although according to general agreement the kaigen shiki is actually not supposed to begin here in the hondō as they file in, but when the special delivery van from far-off Kyōto turns out of the gates of the Bijutsu-in, traversing the still sleeping city, reaching the Takeda Kaido, cutting southward up to the Takeda intersection, and there turning ninety-degrees to the left onto the Meishin Expressway, making the one hundred and seventy kilometers from Ōtsu past Hikone and Maibara to Sekigahara without stopping, as is happening right now, and after a half-hour the competent driver turns off at the designated exit from the Meishin Expressway and even if he is moving now a little more slowly than on the freeway, he still, despite all the twists and turns and tiny little villages, reaches Ikinomiya in good time, and without hesitation finds the road to Inazawa, and in the Zengen-ji, as if they sensed exactly where he is, the western gate, just when he appears at the end of the street leading up to it, is opened by chance, and no one bothers himself about the fact that even before the driver's arrival they kept opening up the gates again and again, peeking outside to see if he was here already, we opened the gates just by chance exactly at the moment when he appeared at the end of the street, the deshis waiting at the western gate later recount, so we just left it open, really, as they then relate further, it just so happened that the shikaryo gave us the order right then to open up all of the gates, and we opened them, as actually did occur, because in reality, according to the original plan devised by the abbot and the others during the final planning sessions, they are the ones who were meant to open the monastery gates, not at the usual hour, but rather at the time of the arrival of the van, that is of the Amida Buddha, they opened the western, the eastern, and the northern gates, and even the Sanmon, and it is actually with this, the opening of the Sanmon, that the monks of the Zengen-ji inform the residents of Inazawa that they are joyfully welcome upon this illustrious day as, within the context of a rare ceremony, their most sacred of sacredness, now restored, shall be returned to its rightful place, and to the same extent that the citizens of Inazawa, one year earlier, had been unmoved by the news of the secret farewell ceremony, now with the Festival of the Return of the Buddha, moved by the possibility of seeing today a colorful, unique, and rare event, they go to the Zengen-ji, the word spreads everywhere, this time it really is worthwhile, and so the city sets off from the textile mills and the rows of machine works, already at around seven in the morning several hundred have gathered in the temple courtyard across from the Hall of Buddha; there are at least three hundred of them, one of the young monks, his eyes glittering, but fearful of exaggeration, whispers with cautious appraisal into the ear of the jushoku; three hundred, repeats the abbot dumbfounded; yes, at the very least, repeats the boy a little uncertainly, not knowing if this is a little or a lot, and huddling up, he does not move from the abbot's side, as if to say that perhaps he is wrong, but how could he tell for sure how many there are, that is, he couldn't take any responsibility for his words; three hundred, the abbot murmurs to himself once again, ill-temperedly, and signals to the boy that there is no problem, it is not the boy's words that he doubts, and it is not because of them that he is in a bad mood, but rather, how are we going to be able to move around in here, he says aloud, so the boy hears it, and the boy's anxiety subsides—so many won't be able to fit into the hondō; he spreads his arms apart to the boy, who, of course, grows concerned as well, for the abbot himself is speaking of such fateful questions with him, but at the same time sad ones too, for the news that he has brought has made the abbot sad, well, no matter, he waves his hand, he smiles at the deshi, and sends him somewhere on a task and already he has come out of his quarters to look for the two illustrious guests, the two abbots from Kyōto, with whom he will lead the ceremony of the kaigen shiki—as all the same it is most auspicious, the answer to his query having arrived from Kyōto months earlier, it is the most auspicious to conduct the ceremony is in the presence of three abbots—and the abbots have slept well, they say, and you can see from their plump cheerful faces as they enter—he steps toward them, greeting them with three deep bows—that they slept well indeed, sweetly, like the sleep of children, they repeat; following the prescribed ritual, they receive the greeting of the host, then together they proceed out of the building, the crowd opening before them, in front walks the abbot of Nanzen-ji with two monks accompanying him, and in his wake the abbot of Tōfuku-ji with two accompanying monks as well, and at the end walks the host-abbot among his own jishas, they proceed thus across the middle of the wide courtyard, where by now there may be even a thousand, and they step, in the same order, into the hondō, where on the right side, in the prescribed order, are the elder monks, on the left side the younger unsuis, the deshis, the battans, and so on, all facing each other, and to the back, next to the main entrance are the jikijitsu and the musicians, so that they can be observed by the lay public, the merely curious and the tourists, then in the silence the high clangorous peal of the shokei resounds, and the congregation with the three abbots facing the altar of the Buddha in front kneels down, then another musician beats the hokku, the large drum, at which point the abbots stand up; all of this is performed three times in a row: the ringing sound of the shokei, the kneeling, the thumping of the hokku; getting up, shokei, kneeling down, the great drum; getting up—and then the same thing for the last time, and then the jikijitsu is already striking the large drum, the mokugyo sounds forth as well, and the gathering place their hands in the gesture of gasho-in—as does the abbot, who now turning to the left takes two and a half steps, then turning to the right steps over to the incense stand, then kneels and gets up, so as to bow to the altar where the Buddha is to be placed, then he kneels down, gets up, again steps before the incense stand, takes with his right hand a stick of incense from his assistant, holding it horizontally with both hands between his thumbs and index fingers, and raises it up to his eyebrows, then he kneels down with it and gets up; with his left hand he plants it into a vase filled with ashes, and then he does the same with another stick of incense on the right-hand side of the vase, and then with a third stick of incense; it seems that the essence of the matter is that he always takes it with his *right* hand, then raises it with both at once to hold it *horizontally*, and with his *left* hand he places it into the ashes, while his gaze passes all around the incense-stand, then he bows to the altar, places his hands together, takes two and a half steps to the right, then once again moves to the right, and with that he returns to his place, then turning to the left he makes two and a half steps again, and stands before the main prayer bench, which has been placed between the three abbots and the altar, but by then the recitation of the first great sūtra has long since begun to resound to the rhythm of the mokugyo—the Sacred Water-Prayer, addressed to the Mahasattva Bodhisattva, followed by the brief three-line invocation to Avalokiteśvara, so that the ceremony then goes beyond the boundaries of prayerful activity, that is, while the entire gathering in resounding chorus, under the direction of the voice of the jikijitsu, chants in special unison: all that is unclean and foul and decayed and impure is now being made pure here; the abbot slowly bows toward the altar, then raises a tiny water bowl prepared in advance, in which one single tiny tree-branch is blossoming, he raises the little branch with the middle and index fingers of his left hand, then with the middle and index fingers of his right hand he bends it into a ring, so that the bottom of the stem passes through it, tying the ring into itself, exactly at the point when the sūtra, in the voice of the jikijitsu, as it rises out of the chorus, indicates that this entire hall and the whole of this place are being purified by this moment of the ritual and the prayers, the voice of the jikijitsu soars above the chorus of monks, which at times seems to resound with higher ascendancies in some distant, ever so distant rapport—then, along with the clang of the gong dying out, the enchantment of this purification dies away, and from that point on, for quite a while and without the jikijitsu, only the congregation has the word, the word which is understood by no one now, or perhaps was never understood by anyone, as the gathering now recites in broken Sanskrit:

NA MO HO LA TA NO TO LA YEH YEH
NA MO A LI YEH P'O LU CHIE TI SHUO
PO LA YEH P'U T'I SA TO P'O YEH MO
HO SA TO P'O YEH MO HO CHIA LU NI . . .

and the mokugyo beats in the same rhythm as the words, and at times the large gong sounds, the gathering visibly recites with confidence that of which no one understands one single word, but they know that the kinhin is to follow, that is from this point on, they move from their places and in single file, one nicely after the other, they circumambulate the great hall, with the jikijitsu in front, after him the mokugyo-beaters, and only then the monks, according to rank, age, authority, and prescribed order, they go in circles, they pronounce the sacred dhāranīs, resounding in a tongue incomprehensible to them; last to come are the women and at the very end are the three abbots with their accompanying monks, they just circle and circle around and around along the walls of the hall, away before the altar; and so that the procession can finally come to an end, the host-abbot stops his colleagues when they reach the spot in front of the altar, in an arc, then taking up their original places—and the congregation too returns to its original place—the jikijitsu stands again by the front entrance, from where he directs the ceremony, he raises his voice and in this raised voice recites the last words of the dhāranī, according to which:

LA TA NO TO LA YEH YEH NA MO A
LI YEH P'O LU CHI TI SHUO P'O LA YEH
SO P'O HO AN HSI TIEH TU MAN TO LA
PO T'O YEH SO P'O HO

so that here, his voice, descending at the very last line, slows down and expands like a river flowing into the ocean, and he begins already the recitation of the Hannya Shingyō—the Heart Sūtra—then the Mahāprajñāpāramitā, then the praise of Avalokiteśvara, then the Song of Parināmanā, and at last the Triple Vow, after which the entire gathering bows three times before the altar, each time to the clashing of the great gong, in the knowledge that the altar-place has been purified, so that the first chapter of this particular coming together and return has been concluded, and now the next may commence, in which, as an invocation, the four strong, young monks who one year ago took the Buddha out now bring in, underneath a golden brocade, and with small cautious steps, the Amida Buddha of the Zengen-ji, raise it to the altar, someone pulls away the silk cloth that had been covering the Buddha's seat, and they place Him there, Him whom they have awaited for so long, and for whose gaze so many hundreds of pairs of eyes, in the crowded hondō, are now contending.

The leader of the ceremony, the jikijitsu, strikes the gong three times; according to precept the large drum then sounds too, and in the space of the hondō above the gathering a greater ceremoniousness than before can be felt, leading the less well-informed among them to think, well, at least now they're finally going to take the brocade off and we can finally get to see the Buddha; but no, they are wrong, the time for that has not yet come, now it is time for the three abbots to pray together; after what is known as the purification of the lotus throne, the emphasis of the ritual in this crucial second part shifts onto the abbots, and there are more offerings made with the incense, then the recitation of the sacred names, and after the three abbots kneel down together, the congregation, under the leadership of the jikijitsu, begins to sing the Amida-kyō, in which the sūtra, with miraculous power and at length, venerates the Amida Buddha and the inconceivable greatness, timelessness, harmony, and fragrances of the Pure Land; then there comes the time to acknowledge defilements, where one must kneel down at the end of every sentence, even the three abbots kneel, and recite with them, and all those taking part in the ceremony kneel down at the end of each sentence as well, we have produced hellish karmas, they all murmur—the mokugyo sharply cracks underneath the thin stick—through desire, through hatred, and through impatience we bring them forth and sustain them in time, the source of what we all are is our mere bodies, our mere words, and our mere minds, and we *deplore this greatly now*; this is what they murmur, they sing this in a louder, unifying harmony, then everyone rises and now, somehow, the emphasis shifts to where it should be; the three abbots, that is, again take up the direction of the ceremony, so that from this point on they are the ones who grant permission to speak, and they grant it right away: three times in order, the wish is chanted that glory may come to the monastery, to the Three Jewels of Mahāyāna, and now the eldest and most respected monk, having earlier been prepared, is called forward to go to the incense stand to complete the ritual of incense-purification; then when the jikijitsu causes the gong to sound, and during its long reverberation the document called the Announcement of Explication is placed in the monk's hands, the smoke snakes upward, entwines around the old man and the document as well, and he begins, his head trembling, in a tremulous voice, to read aloud that here and now appears the Body of the Buddha, here illuminates the karma that brings happiness to all living beings, and the magnificent Form, in its own boundlessness, is unmoving, and this place is now the hall of the Exaltation of the Light, that we, within the Eastern Realm, are on the island known as Japan, where this monastery belonging to the Rinzai lineage is located, the old monk reads in his tremulous voice that now here they have sung a few sacred sentences with the gathering, with which the Dharma is protected, and pure faith remains preserved; he then lowers the document, for the next few sentences no paper is needed, and he announces that the monastery has collected every donation it possibly could in order to protect the sacred statue of the Amida Buddha from the harm of centuries, and now the day has come when, this protection ensured, they have received Him back, and He shall be placed back there, from whence He was earlier taken, so He has arrived, murmurs the old monk, behold the auspicious, happy, great day, and they have gathered in this hall, which is the space of contemplation, that is to say of the soul, and they have come here together, because for them both this space and this soul are of the utmost necessity, and he leans once again over the text, and reads out that the return of the Amida was the heart's desire of the faithful, and the hope of those who await from it the renewal of their faith, to receive, in the barren, ruinous heat, the cool relief of the tree of Dharma, may the garden wreathed in gold again be tended for the prayers to come, for they are now making a vow, he says, looking up from the document, and they make this vow with great joy, and they make this vow precisely today, in the year 2050 on the fourteenth day of the third month in between the morning hours of nine and ten o'clock, they make a vow, and they have set the lotus throne back in its place once again, and once again they survey the entire magnificent Form, truly complete, and they trust that once again they shall see the Precious Light and they supplicate and, bowing their heads, they utter the profound wish that this treasure-laden throne shall be resplendent until the end of time, when the body itself shall vanish, and that the light between the Buddha's eyebrows may once again issue forth, and that one ray of this light may spread across the entire Realm of Dharma; I, says the old monk showing his hands folded in prayer, and bowing his head, I bow my head, and I fold my hands in prayer, and everything good shall like a tree take root, the utterance of the feelings arising in our hearts, the feelings drawn in by the happiness and wisdom emanating from the altar, we supplicate in gratitude and thanks, he continues, movingly, wishing tranquility and peace for the Son of the Sun and the people, we wish for the Dharma once again to be majestic among us, and we wish for the wise and beautiful path to come to the Zengen-ji monastery of Inazawa; today, he says, we have recited sūtras, and the melody, the song of this gathering, is like the brocade upon Him here in the center of the Altarplace; later on, it shall fall away and beneath it the eye shall see what it has been awaiting, and then the old man begins to say, as he lowers the document for the final time, that through the Explication just uttered he supplicates the Three Jewels to create the certainty that this Buddha statue is now perfect and without flaw, for the sacred statue of the Amida Buddha has been rectified and placed back on its base, and all of this has taken place within the framework of the ceremony conducted by jikijitsu Zhushan on the fourteenth day of the third month of the year 2050 according to the Buddhist calendar, in the presence and with the cooperation of the abbots Nanzenji-san and Tōfukuji-san; from the mouth of the monk Shooshin, he says, and he withdraws; and already the assistants have set three small tables in place of the prayer benches in front of the abbots, a piece of yellow silk is placed on each table, and finally in the center of each table a flower-stalk is placed, and already the sacred deities are being invoked in the sūtra recited by the gathering, and the abbots take up the three flower-stalks, they raise them and hold them aloft, as first the Nanzen-ji abbot joins the congregation and sings that the abbot of Nanzen-ji beholds this flower, and he holds it aloft, and supplicates with all of his heart, he calls the Lord of the World, the Master Shakyāmuni Buddha, he supplicates the Lord of Faith of the Eastern Realm, Dainichi Nyorai, who is the Tathāgata of crystal light, he supplicates and calls the Lord of Faith of the Western Realm, Amida Buddha, and the Buddha of the World to Come, Maitreya, Miroku Bosatsu, and every Buddha who can penetrate the Realm of Dharma through the air, he says, and he bows his head, adding softly that he only wishes never to break his own vows, that now, with a humble and full heart, he wishes that He for whom it is fitting should take His place upon the lotus throne, but the entire last part of his words referring to his vows is sung by the gathering as well—each person pronouncing his or her own name—and then something happens which has not happened yet, that is to say silence, and in this silence the three abbots place the three flower-stalks back onto the little tables, the sound of the hand-held gong reverberates, the congregation kneels and prostrates before the Buddha, then the shokei sings out again, everyone rises, and in the sustained silence the jikijitsu asks the participants of the ritual to call forth the Amida Buddha within their own selves, to look at the contours discernable underneath the brocade on the lotus throne, and to let millions of Amidas appear in their imaginations, this is what they must invoke, this is what they must think about, the jikijitsu's words sound out in the silence, and with this it is the turn of the host-abbot, who lifts the single flower once again into the air and says: may the Amida fill the entire world, and look upon all the living beings, so that he and everyone present here may avoid suffering arising from Origination, and, finally, may the throne on the altar truly become a throne, but at this point the entire gathering, led by the jikijitsu, is singing, so as to invoke, with their individual and their shared strength, the Mañjuśrī Buddha, in all aspects perfected, the Samanthabhadra, the Bodhisattva Avalokiteśvara of great compassion, in all deeds accomplished, the Ksitigarbha Bodhisattva, who realizes every desire, the Bodhisattvas of the ten world-directions, the Mahāsattva Bodhisattva, and their only wish—here the sūtra comes to a close, the unity of the singing enriched by a lower fifth—is never to break their vows, and that the Buddha, compassionate to all sentient beings, may appear and take His place upon the lotus throne, which stands before them covered in brocade, and when, at the last word, the shokei again is struck, everyone kneels, then they arise, for it all to be repeated first by the shikaryo, then the jikijitsu, and finally by the entire gathering, for everything to be repeated, but at the same time, somehow, everything begins to rise in the midst of this repeating, there is something now in the Hall which is difficult to put into words, but everyone present can sense it, a sweet weight in the soul, a sublime devotion in the air, *as if someone were here,* and it is most evident on the faces of the non-believers, the merely curious, the tourists, in a word the faces of those who are indifferent, it can be seen that they are genuinely surprised, because it can be felt that something is happening, or has happened, or is going to happen, the expectation is nearly tangible, although everyone knows exactly what it is that is happening, or is going to happen, no one has any doubt at all that perhaps there will be another, and then still another, and then still yet another sūtra, another supplication, another prayer, another vow, and they will yank the covering off the statue, and everyone will finally see the Amida, but that is precisely the curious thing: everyone knows what will follow, and of course when it will follow, still everyone stands dumbfounded, and looks, looks until it ensues that the host-abbot arises, holding aloft a stick of incense, kneels, rises, the gong is heard, and the abbot recites: Revered One of the Returning World, of whom there is none higher, today, according to the teachings, I venerate your throne, I only wish that you might kindly receive it, that every Buddha and Bodhisattva now present here in this room may see and feel that there are no more obstacles, this place has been blessed through the tranquility of an unnameable peace; the abbot speaks and speaks without error and everyone hears precisely what is being said, but from here on the general attentiveness becomes somehow so diffused in expectation that the individual components of the ceremony fall apart, the gathering at one point pays attention to the abbot's words, as he is just now stating that Amida's body is golden, His eyes illuminating the four seas, the light streaming forth from them circling Mount Sumeru five times, and at another point the jikijitsu strikes the gong; here, a few people on the left-hand side of the hall bow down, then a few voices are raised again, and then those standing on the right-hand side bow down; then the eloquent voice of the Nanzen-ji abbot can be heard, as he speaks of his wish to be reborn in the Pure Land of the Western Realm, for nine different kinds of lotus flowers to be his mother and his father, that as these flowers open may he glimpse the Buddha, and that he may awaken to the great truth of non-birth, words that nearly dissolve into the ones spoken by the Tōfuku-ji abbot to the right of the host-abbot, saying, namely, may every single Buddha appear in the world, because of one single great thing, and may the entire consciousness of the thus enlightened Buddha, he supplicates, be present here, and may all Buddhas and Bodhisattvas have mercy upon all living beings, may their causes be perceived and may they be led to the Dharma, may they receive enlightenment as to the non-self-evidence of knowledge, for *knowledge lies within the baneful obscuration of the cause of suffering,* and that is why we are here, who, upon this day, in the year 2050 on the eleventh day of the third month, have come here to consecrate the statue of the Amida Buddha, for him to make us understand, says the abbot of Tōfuku-ji, that this statue before us is knowledge given form, but it is not knowledge itself; at that point, however, a kind of disorder begins to arise in the hondō, some kind of confusion in the devotion, or more precisely it is the confusion of the devotion itself, as the strength begins to seep out of the words, they blur into each other, no longer is each word built upon the next, but the words begin to mean the same thing one after the other, this confusion is significant, as is obvious, significant, as it, so to speak, indicates the path upon which the gathering has been lead by the words, to that point where only the consummation of the final moment is necessary, and then truly everything is taking place in this spirit; it could not be stated that the gathering is really concentrating on the most essential elements of the ceremony; they do not notice, for example—or it may be that in the crowd of people they cannot see—that the abbots, before their words just uttered, have each taken up a mirror from the tables placed before them, wiping it with a fine cloth, and then all three have turned the mirrors toward the Buddha; the gathering—at least most of them—are gaping here and there, most of them can only hear what the host-abbot is saying, for right at this moment he is saying that we who consecrate the Buddha are in no way identical with the consecration, we only now do, in the name of the Buddha, what is required, it is not we who can approach Him, but rather that He penetrates us completely with His wisdom, He, the Buddha, who is present here, the imperceptible and supreme Form in its own infinite radiance, that if we speak, the abbot's veiled, weary voice is heard, if we recite sūtras, through these utterances the light of the Buddha illuminates billions and billions of worlds; that much is heard, then their attention is led by the gong and the great drum, so that they no longer can make out the words of the abbot of the monastery as he says that the wisdom of the Buddha, at the same time, finds a means within us, having taken physical form, returns back to each one of us—that already goes unheard, only the clanging of the gong, and the deep thumping of the drum, but by now it is so hard to pay attention to anything at all, the gathering has by now been here for hours, legs, backs, heads ache; and the scene is swimming before their eyes, nonetheless, at such times, who can say what is essential and what isn't—one thing is certain: whether there is tiredness here or there, no one wants to miss out on the essence, so that the great majority of them shift their heads back and forth, now trying to listen attentively, now trying to see what is going on, the boundary, in a word, between the important and the less important begins to blur; this has not been, up until now, a cause for concern, but from this point on the monks themselves are not even certain that they are taking in the most essential elements of what is happening in the hondō; all, however, monks and visitors alike, are certain that the ceremony is moving forward, *intensely*, in strained expectation, where then, in this strained expectation, in this *intensity*, the abbot of Tōfuku-ji slowly, very slowly, circumambulates with the mirror held aloft, yet in such a way that the light from the mirror illuminates, with a flickering, trembling beam, around the entire hall, and then he places the mirror back onto the table, then taking up from it a paintbrush (with his right hand) and a tiny jar (with his left hand), he dips the brush into the jar, in which there is paint of a vermilion hue, then he raises the brush full of paint toward the presumed direction of the eyes of the Buddha statue, searching with the tip of the brush the height of the eyes, and then two young monks, who had been positioned on either side of the altar quite a while ago, step toward the statue, cautiously remove the brocade covering, step to one side with it, and the crowd holds its breath and just stares to see what has become of the Amida Buddha in far-off Kyōto, the abbot locates the proper height, and the brush is at the same height as the Buddha's eyes, with utmost exactitude, it is held there for a bit, motionless, the silence is complete, then he shouts out in the silence to OPEN, at which point of course the gathering can no longer restrain itself and, breaching the ritual's ceremonial rigor, then cry out, the gong sounds, the drum sounds, the shokei and all of the instruments on either side of the main entrance sound out, but by that point the jikijitsu has begun to recite the sūtra of the Opening of the Light, the gathering, mesmerized, joins in and they recite, sing, and murmur the words of the sūtra, but they cannot bear to look away from Amida, for most of the believers remember very well how the statue looked across the decades, a dark shadow on the altar, with almost no contour, almost no light, yet now it is truly resplendent, resplendent in the wondrous face the wondrous eyes, but this pair of eyes, if even touching lightly upon them, does not see them but looks onto a further place, onto a distance that no one here is able to conceive, everyone senses that, and the tension is extinguished in one blow, on every face great joy can be seen, no matter the tiredness, no matter the exhaustion, now it is as if their gaze were reflecting something of that radiance that comes from the altar, they recite, happy and relieved, after the jikijitsu that they now are making a vow to the Buddha, wishing for every being to find the path, that this unsurpassable wish may be fulfilled, and they make a vow to the Dharma, they recite, and they wish that all living beings may penetrate into the wisdom of the sūtras like the ocean, and they make a vow to the Sangha, they announce last of all together, and ask that every being in the gathering may be protected, and all misfortunes averted, and that they may reach that redoubtably distant, beautiful pure land onto which the returned Amida Buddha now gazes.

He waves for a long time as the elegant, sparkling black cars wind out of the western gates, then for yet a long time, as the two abbots from Kyōto disappear into the traffic in the street leading away from the monastery, he waves, and he feels unspeakable relief that at last, at the end, after they discussed every possibility, they too have departed, and that generally everything had gone well yesterday, and the kaigen shiki came to an end with no greater problems, and he slowly strolls back to his quarters; however—for he is somehow very tired and feels even much older than his years—he decides that he will not take part in the daily morning meditation in the zendō, but will, exceptionally, take a nap, so that as he saunters in the chill wind on the narrow paths of smoothly raked white stones between the gardens, he thinks: Exalted Buddha, how fallible they were, how unworthy, how many mistakes, how many errors, how many times they faltered in the texts, how often the great drum beat at the wrong time, and above all how many wrong steps before the altar, how many uncertain and perplexed moments, from which they could not free themselves, and all the same, they did it, they were capable of that much, they had not fallen short of their abilities, he strolls in the chilly, early spring wind, to remain apart a little while, still hearing the voices led by the jikijitsu, reciting the sūtra in the zendō, he looks all around at the beautiful order and the tranquil pavilions of the monastery, and then suddenly an idea springs to mind, or well it really isn't an idea, but rather just that … he slows down, comes to a standstill, then turns around, heading back toward the zendō, he walks in front of it, again hearing the monks' sūtras, and the rhythmic thumps of the mokugyo, and suddenly he finds himself in front of the hondō, and then comes to his senses, as if he were about to ask himself what he was doing here, and why he wasn't he going to take a rest already—then he forgets what he even wanted to inquire about within himself, and slips out of his sandals and straightens his robes, as if he were about to go into the main entrance; but he doesn't head up the steps that would take him there, instead—he himself doesn't even know how—he stands on one of the lower steps, he looks around, no one is in sight, everyone is in the zendō, so he sits down on one of the steps and he remains there, the early spring sun shines on him, at times he shivers in a stronger breeze of the chill air, but he doesn't move from there, he just sits on the step, leaning forward a bit with his elbows pressed onto his knees, looking ahead, and now at last he is able to pose the question to himself: what in the world was he doing here, he is able to ask himself, he just can't find the answer, or rather he cannot understand: even if what he hears there within his soul does exist, it all adds up to just this much: nothing, he is doing nothing at all in the entire world, he just sat down here because he felt like it, to sit here and know that, there inside the hondō, Amida Buddha is now enthroned upon the altar, and he sees what no one else but himself can see, only and exclusively he, he sits there on the steps, his stomach growls, he scratches his bald head, he stares into space, onto the steps below, the steps of dried-out old hinoki cypress, and in one of the cracks he now notices a tiny ant, well, and from that point on he only watches that ant as it goes about on its funny little legs, climbing, hurrying and then slowing down in this crack, as it starts forward, then stops, then turns around and lifting up its little ball of a head, hurries off again, but once more it comes to a dead halt, climbing out from the crack, but only to crawl right back into it, and starts off again, then after a while coming to a halt again, it stops, turns around, and just as sprightly as it can, goes again backward in the crack, and all the while the early spring sun shines on it, at times a draft of the wind strikes it, you can see the ant struggling not to be carried off by the wind, little ant, says the abbot, shaking his head, little ant in the deep crack of the step, forever.

5

CHRISTO MORTO

He was generally not the type who walks with banging steps, he was not the resounding, military, lock-stepping Hussar type; yet because he liked the leather soles of his shoes and the heels of the leather soles to last a long time, the soles and the heels were fitted with proper old-fashioned shoe taps, which, however, echoed to such a degree, with every single step he took, in the narrow back street that it was becoming increasing obvious with each meter that these shoes, these black leather oxfords, did not belong here, not in Venice, and particularly not now, not in this silent neighborhood, during this total siesta; he did not, however, want to return and change them; and he might have tried to walk more softly on the old paving stones, only that he couldn't, so that he felt continuously, passing before each house, that inside, the occupants inside were flinging curses upon him: why couldn't he just go away and die somewhere, and what was he doing outside anyway, and especially a character with such damned well-shod black oxfords; he stepped with his left foot, he stepped with his right foot, and that was enough, he already took it as a given that the tranquility of the siesta had come to an end within these buildings with their closed façades, cloaked in muteness, because here outside—thanks to him—the silence had been broken; there was not a God-given soul in the little alleyways, not even a tourist, which was rare indeed, so that there were only the Venetians, there inside, with their failed attempts at a siesta, and him, here outside, with his solidly-made oxfords, so it seemed that only the two of them existed in the exact center of the sestiere of San Polo, in this sweet and narrow labyrinth this afternoon—he could practically hear the curses breaking out from behind the closed wooden shutters: off to stinking putrid hell with you, with those wretched black oxfords—but in this he was mistaken, for it was not only the two of them in the sweet and narrow labyrinth of the sestiere of San Polo: there was someone else as well, who at some point just appeared behind him, lagging considerably behind though in any event trailing after him with more or less the same speed: a thin gangly figure in a light-pink shirt, but of such a light pink that it stood out immediately as this very light pink flashed now and then at a turning point behind him; he didn't know when he had been joined by him, he had no idea when he had begun to be followed, if indeed he was being followed, but somehow he sensed right away that yes, when he had set off from the San Giovanni Evangelista, where he had stayed for one night at the address of San Polo 2366, in the Calle del Pistor or the Campiella del Forner o del Marangon, he definitely was not behind him, indeed not even—he tried to recall—when he cut across the Campo S. Stin in the strong sunlight toward the Ponte dell'Archivio, or still yet, he suddenly reflected, it was possible that this figure had already been waiting for him when he stepped out through the courtyard, open to the heavens, of the San Giovanni Evangelista, and came out of the entrance of the house with its elegant, useless entrance arch designed by Pietro Lombardi, to make his way toward the Frari; it was possible, it flashed through his mind, even very possible, and he felt that at the mere conjecture that someone wanted to attack him, his stomach convulsed into a knot, and he began to feel cold, as he always did when he was afraid; he stopped at the end of the square that opened up before the Ponte dell'Archivio, like someone trying to find the right way, someone who is ruminating—as is often the case with foreigners in Venice—if it would really be a good thing to cross this bridge now or instead to turn away; and he did ruminate, but really just so that his shoes would stop making that huge clattering and he could gaze back—and he did gaze back—and the chilly sensation in his body was transformed from the chill of an uncertain anxiety to that of a decidedly sharp fear, and he had turned away already, in his echoing black oxfords, toward the Ponte, wishing to cross it hastily, but what does he want?—his step quickened in fright—to rob me? beat me? strike me down? stab me?—ah, somehow no, he shook his head, somehow the whole thing was not *like that*, the character behind him did not particularly give the impression of being a robber or a murderer, instead it seemed as if he, the visitor to Venice, was the one leading him, pulling him, drawing him onward with the clattering of his painfully echoing oxfords, or as if this otherwise rather laughable figure couldn't resist the clattering of his shoes, a figure who was moreover bent like the letter S, with collapsing legs, a rump thrusting backward, a crooked back, and a head that sloped forward, yes, he said to himself, passing along by the Ponte dell'Archivio, no he doesn't want to rob me or murder me, this character in the pink shirt was simply not a robber or a murderer, but of course he could have a gun on him, who knows; he fretted on and on, walking with unflagging speed, in no way displaying how much he was afraid, he went further along the Fondamenta dei Frari toward the square, all the while understanding what was happening less and less; in the first place, why he was so afraid; this figure coming after him clearly wanted something but that was still no cause to be so afraid; he was, however, very afraid, he admitted that, and this acknowledgement was made even more tormenting by the fact that he was freezing, at the same time sensing that the situation was ridiculous, because what if it emerged that it was all just a misunderstanding, that this figure wasn't even there because of him, but just by happenstance, such happenstance often occurs, and finally there was no one on the streets, but no one, not a single soul; it could be natural that he too was headed for the same place, and with the same gait, for he had noticed in the meantime that the beanpole had not come closer, but was always on his trail; he did not lag behind, but neither did he draw near, there was always just one street-corner between them as they proceeded onward, or none at all, he noted, his heart in his throat, because right now in fact it was as if that distance separating them were somehow a little less, a little shorter—he attempted to estimate just by how much—until now, that is, there had always been one corner between them, regardless of the distance from one corner to the next, but now, here, on the Fondamenta there was unequivocally no corner at all between them, that is to say that Pink-shirt was, beyond a doubt, approaching, which caused his stomach to clench into an even tighter knot; he's chasing me, he said to himself, and at that word he shuddered, he grew chill, or he was freezing from fear, he couldn't decide which; yet he was also frightened now by the very fact that he had to fret over such things; what was going on anyway, he had no idea, there was something in the whole story, something unreal, something unlikely, some misunderstanding, some *mistake* that he, who had practically just arrived in Venice, and who had just stepped out of the pension's entrance, was being pursued by someone, the whole thing was just not right, no and no, he kept repeating to himself, then he stopped in front of the entrance to the Frari with an unexpected idea, like someone who is looking to see when it will be open again, he stopped, to bring everything to a head, and to see what the other was doing, indeed, not even waiting for what step he might take, proceeding beside the entrance to the Frari; then, he went to the other end of the church and there—the enormous building was buttressed with a supporting ledge, which, as it were, stood out from the smooth façade about one meter above the ground so that you could sit down on it—he too sat down, because the sun was shining there, he collected himself and sat down as one who is interrupting his journey for the sake of taking in a bit of sunshine; but misfortune had already found its recipient, as on the far side of the Campo dei Frari a little café, the Toppo, was open in spite of the siesta, even though there was not a single customer; the sunlight did not reach over there—in any event *he* could stop there, indeed, so that when he sat down in the sunlight by the wall of the Frari—the other sat down in a chair in the shade under a sun-umbrella, as if having decided to take a drink in the city, in this brief tranquil interval, and it was precisely here, on the ever more tranquil Campo dei Frari this afternoon that, in a word, nothing, but nothing came to light; until now, the thought that the beanpole had followed him accidentally had seemed a possibility, and perhaps he was looking for nothing more than a place open for business where he could just sit down, where he could rest those tired legs of his, collapsing with each and every step—it could have seemed a possibility if he, here and now, sitting on the ledge of the wall of the Frari, had been capable of believing in it, but he did not believe it; on the contrary he took it as a given that as he sat down, the other, too, sat down right away, as if their movements were synchronized; he had betrayed himself—I am being followed, he concluded decisively, and although he wasn't aware of it, he nodded at him; the sunlight began to work his chilled hands, from which the conclusion could be reached that fear (one clearly fully justified!) had made them so, but besides all this it still was a little chilly outside, you could feel it in the air, it was only April after all, and in mid-April it could certainly happen that from one hour to the next, in these places in the city not exposed to sunlight, it would suddenly turn cool, everything changes quickly here, including the weather, he sat on the protrusion from the wall, he warmed himself in the pleasant sunshine, all the while, naturally, not for a moment taking his eyes off his pursuer, who sitting on the other side of the square was just now placing his order with the café proprietor, when for no particular reason at all something came into his head, a newspaper article, as it happened, which had nothing to do with anything—most likely his brain was fatigued in the midst of these fearful states and had wandered off—sitting on a small but splendid eighteenth-century marble table in the proprietress's sitting room of the pension where the mail of the occupants of the house was kept, there was a newspaper he had seen, in which he read a little about what Benedict XVI had recently said, but it was not necessarily the article itself that drew his attention, but the headline, and it was this that had remained in his memory, and because of this, his attention now slipped, wandering off, back here to that moment—even if his gaze remained fixed on the other over there, as he sipped his coffee, for it seemed that no sooner was the order given than it was fulfilled; almost in the exact moment of the order a cup of coffee appeared on the little table beneath the sun-umbrella—slipped back to the headline, which read something like this:

HELL REALLY EXISTS

and below which it was repeated that, according to Benedict, who had recently spoken at a convocation in a northern district of Rome, it was an error to think, as more and more people did, that hell was just a kind of metaphor, an emblem, an abstraction; because, reported Benedict, it has a physical reality—this, the article on the front page of the Corriere della Sera, was what came into his mind, what an impossible situation, he thought, sitting two hundred meters away from me is someone who has followed me, someone who is watching me, and here I am, beside the Frari, with this idiotic thing in my brain, I've lost my mind; he tried to pull himself together, but he couldn't because it then came into his mind that while John Paul II was of the opinion, as the Corriere stated, that heaven and purgatory were not really extant, Benedict went so far, continued the reporter, as to state with full emphasis at this convocation in the north of Rome that it was possible that heaven and purgatory did not really exist, but that hell did, moreover in the concrete physical sense, where the word, that is to say physical, had been set in italics, there in the daily mail of the occupants of the house on the little marble table; but what could this possibly mean, he thought, but only this much: well, let's just stop here, what is this, so there's no heaven, no purgatory, that's fine, to hell with the whole thing, that's fine—but he did not continue the thought, as suddenly a feeling arose that he was flirting imprudently with danger, a danger that possibly didn't have any basis, but if this were not the case, then he was, with complete utter carelessness, flirting with it; he jumped up suddenly and set off for the narrow alleyway that ran alongside the apse of the Frari, but just as suddenly regretted doing so, turning back to the Campo dei Frari, and quickly crossed the square on the near side—in opposition to his plan, that is to say, actually, contrary to his intended direction, he turned into a back alley just as narrow and dark and damp and chill, in order to draw attention away from where he was really going, but he nearly ruined it, it shot through him; he nearly revealed against his own will where he was going with those resounding steps of the black oxfords, he nearly betrayed to his pursuer his destination; he himself hardly understood how he could have been so rash, but it's fine now, he thought, calming down a bit, there is no way anyone could now tell where he was headed, which, as senseless as that might have seemed, still could be the case; that is, not to reveal where he was headed, inasmuch as there was no question whatsoever of pursuit, inasmuch as it was, however, a question of pursuit; it will all soon come to light, he kept looking backward in the alleyway; and so, as to allow that chance to occur, he stopped, trying to discern if he heard steps in the quiet that suddenly sprang forth from the silencing of his own hard-soled shoes, but he didn't hear anything, only a small breeze struck him, coming in both directions from the damp walls; in any case, because he had to know if that character was on his trail again, he slowly began to move backward in the alleyway, cautiously, on tiptoe lest the shoe taps betray him yet again, and hiding his body behind the wall, he leaned out, looking out onto the square, but there was no one sitting on the other side at the little table beneath the sun-umbrella, on the contrary, he was nowhere on the square, he had disappeared, had been absorbed, evaporated, he stated to himself, and stayed there for a few moments longer, until he could cut across the small intersections without his heart jumping into his mouth—as he reflected, for a while, Pink-Shirt could pop up in front of him at any moment, surprising him at any one of these little intersections—but as one intersection came right after the next, and nothing of the sort occurred, he slowly began to calm down; he stopped, he listened, then after he turned and went back toward the Campo dei Frari, he found the square in exactly the same state as before, that is to say completely deserted, he now had the courage to turn definitively into his own alleyway, so that taking it he could reach the Scuola Grande di San Rocco, which was his goal, he went to the end of the Salizzada S. Rocco, which now did not seem as narrow as it had a moment ago, when no one at all was walking there, perhaps because now, as he turned into the alleyway, he caught sight of a few pedestrians who were already approaching from the opposite direction, from the San Rocco to the Frari, that is to say in the opposite direction to himself; in any event these few encounters, as each stray pedestrian passed by, felt as if someone were shaking him by the shoulders, saying wake up already, it's all over, it was just a bad dream, don't worry about it, that was his mood as he reached the Campo dei S. Rocco where nearly the whole of the little square was filled with sunlight, and there to the left stood the marvelous Scuola Grande di S. Rocco, for whose plan we can thank a certain master builder of the name of Bartolomeo Bon, although for the entire building itself—in other words the entirety of the San Rocco in all of its full glory—our thanks are due to Sante Lombardo and Antonio Scarpagnino, so that after 1549, Giangiacomo dei Grigi had nothing to do but finish it, that is to create the gestures still missing from the structure, so that it could stand in all of its beauty resplendent before the visitors, just as it stood today before him, who even at first went toward the iron gate of the plot of land facing the building and stood there, and turned around to gaze at this creation which in the opinion of all Venice-goers responds to the most exalted and perfect architectonic conception—simply to give himself over not only to the wonder, as he had already stumbled upon this, amazed, when he had been here for the first time, but to his memories as well, because it was, as a matter of speaking, about this too; it was for the sake of this that he had come to Venice, for the sake of this one single building, because once, when he had come here for the first time, he had been so overpowered there inside that in fact he had shuddered; he stood in the sunlight and looked at the elegant façade of the San Rocco, but his gaze strayed again and again to the entrance, where he himself would step inside, as he had stepped inside once before, but not now, he composed himself; now, for the time being, he had to catch his breath, free himself from the horrifying dream of just a few minutes before, to expel from his head this entire nightmarish pursuit, because really, looking at it from here, he thought—amid the smaller crowds of people that already, at the end of the siesta, were inundating here and there between the entrance and exit points of the tiny square—it seemed completely impossible that someone would start pursuing him as soon as he stepped out of the doorway of the pensione, some guy in a pink shirt, a ridiculous gangly sort with his strange S-shaped body, his collapsing knees, his head dangling forward, how could he even have imagined it, and even more so that this figure had targeted him, it was really totally absurd, he decided, because why the hell would anyone be looking for him in Venice, where he knew virtually no one, what reason could there possibly have been for anyone to trail him among the tens of thousands of tourists, especially him, who in the whole God-given world had no ties at all to Italy, let alone Venice, and moreover, he was not one of those who kept coming back here again and again, in pursuit of so-called illusory pleasures, giving himself over to the blank drift of superficial and frankly idiotic raptures—he was not in any way like one of them!?—actually he did not truly admire Venice: as far as he was concerned, Venice reminded him too much of a woman, for him, there was in Venice a kind of immoderate feminine delusion and fraudulence, no, this city was not his cup of tea, though of course he could not deny that it was truly beautiful, that there was in Venice an unparalleled beauty, this strange city—from the Ca'Doro to the San Giovanni e Paolo, from the San Marco to the Accademia, the Hotel Giorgione to La Fenice, and so on—but admiration was denied to him and he did not love Venice, he was instead afraid of it, the way he would be of a murderously cunning individual who ensnares his victims, dazing them, and finally sucking all the strength from them, taking everything away from them that they ever had, then tossing them away on the banks of a canal somewhere, like a rag; yes, this was how he now saw this laughable situation; he didn't even come here very often, in the course of his long life this was the second time he had been here, and now, he thought, smiling at his own fears, what a crazy, terrifying, perhaps excessive, if he could put it that way, fantastical start, he was fortunate, he added to himself, completely relaxing now in the midst of the crowd, that he didn't have to go to the Ca'Foscari or the Palazzo Ducale, nowhere at all, he didn't have to budge from here, and a vaporetto wasn't much so that he didn't have to pay a lot; if he wanted, apart from the S. Rocco, he didn't have to see anything of Venice—just the one single thing he had traveled here to see; the visitation of which was more important to him than his entire mediocre, senseless, barren, and superfluous life.

He began with Titian, because first of all Cavalcasalle had done so, then Fischel and Berenson decisively, then Suida with doubts, and finally in 1955, a certain Coletti reached the definite conclusion that the creator of the painting was none other than Titian, yet this attribution, if the word itself applies, can be accepted only with the same difficulty as that which followed afterward; above all, if we look at it from today, the principles employed were just as baseless as what was stated afterward; in any case Signor Pignatti came along and announced—twice to be exact, in 1955 and 1978—that all of this Titian-attribution was a mistake, for the analysis of the painted surfaces as well as the dolcezza in the use of color made it clear that it was the circle of Giorgione that could be thanked for the canvas, a view as surprising as much as it was incomprehensible, for he, that is Giorgione, was at that time not considered a religious painter, no pictures of his on sacral themes have survived; the only one we know originating from him on any such motif, the "Castelfranco Madonna," is a work commissioned to this mysterious genius by Amateo Constanzo for the burial of his son Matteo; in a word, utter confusion dominated the question of who painted the picture, a confusion that was finally crowned by the commencement in 1988 of a mutually reinforcing war of hypotheses, which was begun by Mauro Lucco, who stated: well, my honored ladies and gentlemen, please forgive me, but the painting almost certainly originated from the brush of Giovanni Bellini; let us place it side by side with the work entitled "The Drunkenness of Noah," which can be seen in Besançon; and after this there was no stopping, Michel Laclotte came along, pointed his short index finger at the "Cristo morto nel sepolcro" and said "Bellini," and then Anchise Tempestini stepped in, and finally Miss Goffen, and they said "Bellini," just as did the postcards of scandalously poor quality displayed on the tables behind the ticket counter, unambiguously indicating with no discussion, with not even one tiny question mark at the end, the great Bellini, despite the fact that by then scholars had at their disposal the expert opinion of the distinguished Hans Belting, who considered the authorship of the given painting by Titian as self-evident, and moreover in such a fashion that he was the only one who did not make any argument but simply referred to "the painting by

Titian" and that was it; so that the uncertainty could have been absolute had not the Confraternita—containing more than a few Bellini-proponents—closed the matter for once and for all, declaring Giovanni Bellini as the author of the picture, so that after this point no one raised the question again, the matter seemed to be closed and it very well could have remained so, in this atmosphere of mutually exclusive attributions, had not the art historian of the Confraternita, Dr. Agnese Chiari, been troubled by something about this valued treasure of S. Rocco, and not brought it to the attention of Dr. Fatima Terzo, who shortly before the turn of the millennium had paid a visit here from the Vicenza branch of Banca Intesa, that is from the Palazzo Leoni Montanori, she had said that there's something else here, among all the sensational Tintorettos: a little picture, the whole thing no larger than 56 by 81 cm., clearly belonging to the imago pietatis tradition as posited by Belting and hence referring back to the Byzantine heritage; it was in such poor condition that it deserved a little attention; Dr. Chiari glanced meaningfully at Dr. Terzo, who was responsible for all cultural matters at the bank, while she arranged for her to see in more tranquil surroundings, in the little camarilla on the second floor to the right, what was at play here; it could, she repeated with an innocent face, do with a little repair, because it's very beautiful, isn't it, asked Agnesee Chiari, and let the protective brocade fall before her guest in the narrow space of the camarilla, beautiful, replied Dr. Terzo in astonishment upon seeing the picture, so that afterward, with no further discussion, the picture turned up in the hands of the master Egidio Arlango, and the always risky undertaking of restoration work began, the chief goal of which, for Agnese Chiari and the Scuola Grande Arciconfraternita di San Rocco, was to bring to a halt the evident disintegration of the picture, its physical stabilization, declared Dr. Chiari to the council members at the voting colloquium of the Confraternita, because truly, in the upper and lower sections of the work, where the canvas had been stretched onto its frame, and was thus at its tautest, serious damage was visible, even to the naked eye, so now, when Mr. Arlango examined it more carefully with his magnifying glass, to note in the inventory where exactly the most serious problems lay, and of what character they were, it became obvious that if no intervention were made, the work would begin to crack apart within a few years at these given spots, the paint would chip off, and hence the damage caused by the long delay would be irreparable; but in the restoration workshop of Mr. Arlango they found other problems as well, here a patch where the strength of the color had waned, there a crown of thorns that had lost its outline, then the faded Greek initial letters on both sides of the head, and the generally dark, seemingly homogeneous background itself, which already cried out with its countless fissures for the hand of Mr. Arlango; so that of course for all of them—the Banca Intesa, Mr. Arlango, and Dr. Agnese Chiari—the undeniable overriding intention was to repair the artwork and halt its further decay; thus, for all of them, but particularly the ambitious art historian, a much more deeply hidden goal was at work: to know, that is to decide through the means of restoration, who was in fact the true painter, and particularly so that they could say it was without doubt Tiziano, or without doubt Bellini, or without a doubt Giorgione, and the San Rocco collection would be enriched by a major artwork of clear attribution, so that Dr. Chiari came to look at the restorer's workshop nearly every single day, to ask: Giorgione? Tiziano? Giovanni Bellini?—Mr. Arlango, though, did not reply for a long time; in addition, Mr. Arlango, with his squashed-together face, was a person of fairly disagreeable aspect, perhaps because of his physical deformity or perhaps because of something else, he was decidedly humorless, unfriendly, and taciturn, an individual who disliked strangers coming into his workshop; he didn't even pause to answer if someone asked a question but only spoke when it was truly necessary, and in this case it was certainly not necessary one bit, because nothing had been determined, and how could anything have been determined anyway; when they had photographed the painting from all angles, with the greatest possible caution, and had begun to remove the canvas from the frame—even figuring out how to perform this task took a week to decide—then the examination of the frame itself followed, and Dr. Chiari realized that she had to deal with Mr. Arlango in an altogether different manner, that it would be better to let him work undisturbed, to reduce the number of her visits; indeed, she asked for his advice as to when it would be good to come back, to which of course the broadest smile possible appeared on Mr. Arlango's sour face as he happily announced, Come back in a year's time, then abruptly turning away from Dr. Chiari, he addressed himself to another painting, as he began to dig away with a tiny scraping knife at the joists of the frame, his back turned toward her, and the broad smile of a moment ago became a prolonged smile of satisfaction displaying his yellow teeth; this smile lasted for quite a while, this inimitable gaiety practically affixed to his sour face, so that the yellow teeth stinking of nicotine only disappeared beneath the chapped lips in Mr. Arlango's squashed-together countenance when he heard, over the sounds of the knife scraping against the frame, someone leaving the studio and closing the door quietly behind herself.

Mr. Arlango could have said that, contrary to all expectations, the picture was not at all in as bad a condition as would have been expected at first sight, and he could have said that this was due to the picture's already having been restored five or six decades previously; for if, within the internal parlance of Mr. Arlango, this earlier restoration could be termed philistine and irresponsible, it was nonetheless helpful, very helpful, that the original canvas had been backed up against and then stretched onto another canvas, and the reinforced picture had been placed again upon a frame; they, however, had made use of three unacceptable procedures, as it happened; for one, Signor Arlango muttered to himself, they did not take into account how the paint was cracking and peeling away from the canvas; two—he counted to himself on his fingers—they retouched, indeed repainted the right eyebrow of Christ our Lord, the hair of Christ our Lord, and the shoulder of Christ our Lord; and three, grabbing his thumb, index and middle fingers and squeezing them together in rage, they had simply smeared the surface of the painting with some cheap junk, some kind of lacquer-like substance, which in the course of time had oxidized and yellowed, and with that, the fate of the picture was sealed, because that for the most part ruined it, more precisely—and with the increasing inner force of his words he punched into the air—they *falsified* the original effect of the painting, chopping up and finally destroying the picture itself, because this had caused the entire artwork to change, which is unforgivable on the part of a restorer, whose business it is precisely to give back to the work the spirit of its original creation, but these ones, Mr. Arlango motioned with his hand resignedly, they could not have been restorers, a restorer would never do such a thing, methods such as these are used only by amateurs, by dilettante art-bunglers, and pronouncing these words—dilettante art-bunglers—Mr. Arlango calmed down; because when in the course of his work he came into contact with dilettantes, he pronounced his judgment, named them for what they were, and that was that, he was finished, no longer bothering with the matter, only with how to render them harmless, if it was still possible; at such times as now, he fell into deep concentration, looking at the picture for hours on end, thinking through what was to be done, what work must be completed, in what order it should proceed, what materials to use, what examinations to be performed—then he set to work, and at such times it really was not desirable to disturb him, for that matter it was not desirable to disturb him in general, as Dr. Agnese

Chiari had already experienced in her own case; so she couldn't have known what was going on in the workshop, nothing about the examinations, about what materials were being used, what working methods, and in what order they were being performed—so when the day arrived, that is to say when the examinations had begun and the picture was under the illumination of a special X-ray machine, the result was so surprising that even Signor Arlango hardly dared risk not informing the client, because he knew what was at stake, and it was hardly incidental—to establish, in other words, who was the artist—although looking at the picture closely, it had already been clear to him, from the nature of the draftsmanship as well as the varying quality of the details, that the work was the result of the effort of not one, but two artists; but he himself was quite surprised as—in the course of X-raying the picture, perceiving the difference in the pigments as well as the layers of imprimatura and gesso lying on top of each other, trying to determine their quality, condition, and kind—he glimpsed the name, the signature painted in the usual manner of the cinquecento onto the wooden board itself, it was placed deliberately—or in any event, before the painting of the work had begun—into the pictorial space: then he no longer hesitated, he notified the Confraternita to send someone, for he had something important to show them on the picture, so that after Dr. Agnese Chiari from the San Rocco had arrived once again, Mr. Arlango merely placed the picture behind the X-ray device, chased his guest out of the workshop, pressed the remote control in his hand, withdrew the slide, and developed it, and only then did he call the guest waiting in the corridor back in, sat her down in a chair, but said nothing to her, altogether he said not one word, only snatched up the X-ray image now hanging from a string tautened across the workshop window and handed it to her, withdrawing wordlessly to his work table, and he made as if he were scraping away at something again; but all the while he was observing the client, who looked at the picture for a while in silence, then got up from her chair, coming closer to see better in the light, but there was no doubt: in the upper left-hand corner of the X-ray image was written legibly the name VICTOR and on the other side BELLINAS, and Dr. Chiari just looked, and she didn't want to believe what she was seeing, because it just couldn't be, and she just looked, looked at the name, her gaze now fixed on Victor, now on Bellinas, it wasn't possible that this almost nameless nobody could have ... it was unimaginable, nobody was going to believe her, but still the board of San Rocco, all waited with bated breath for her ceremonious announcement: my dear colleagues, it has been determined, to the exclusion of all doubt, that the creator of this work is Tiziano, or my dear colleagues, now there is no doubt whatsoever that the picture was painted by Giorgione, or possibly, I have the pleasure to inform you that, due to the result of our investigations, the creator of this exceptional work shall no longer be the subject of uncertainty, for it has been demonstrated that the author is Giovanni Bellini and no one else—except that it was someone else, Agnese Chiari now thought to herself, and consternated, thought it best to sit back down in the chair, because the name was finally so clearly legible, Victor Bellinas, who was none other than Bellini's—the great Bellini, Giovanni's—most indefatigable assistant, about whom—Dr. Chiari tried to call forth from her memory—we know almost nothing, so insignificant was he; of course, there are perhaps one or two pictures that can be attributed to him, "Crocifisso adorato da un devoto" in the Carrara Museum in Bergamo, and maybe a few others; a fresher memory of a painting, perhaps of two young men, loomed forth from Dr. Chiari's memory, but in reality he was not known as a painter, only a painter's assistant, to whom Bellini left part of his estate, that is after the loss of his wife and the decease of his son, and he did not marry again, he had no heirs, for his bad relationship with his brother Gentile, as well as his even worse relationship with his father Jacopo, was common knowledge at the time, so for him it would have seemed most fitting to adopt this faithful, industrious, trustworthy assistant, this Vittore di Matteo, as he was originally called, to adopt him simply as his grandson and bequeath to him the most valuable of what would remain after he was gone, that is to say the workshop, counted as the most illustrious in Venice in 1516, when Bellini died; this was bequeathed as an inheritance to the disciple of Venice's most famous painter as the chief asset along with, Agnese Chiari thought to herself—it now seemed, one or two unfinished pictures; she now rose from her seat and, as the master restorer continued to scrape away exhibiting the greatest possible indifference to the matter, she went over to the picture again, looked at it more thoroughly, and perhaps not so accidentally reached the sudden conclusion as the workshop's master had reached at the very beginning, for she now saw at once that the head, well, it was somehow different from the whole, ravishing in and of itself, while everything else seemed to have been painted in a completely divergent, greatly inferior fashion: it was a flash, but Agnese Chiari understood instantly that the head was Bellini's, and the rest had been completed after the death of his great mentor by Vittore di Matteo, called Belliniano in his honor, according to his own talent, which was not exactly scandalous but just in no way comparable to the genius of the creator of the head; there stood the envoy of San Rocco and she did not know what to do; should she try to talk with this dreadful Mr. Arlango and ask his opinion—what for?—she cast aside the idea, it would be enough to persuade the council of the Confraternita of San Rocco to swallow this surprising result, and accept that life is surely a little more complicated than those present here, the current generation, would like to admit; that is to say the picture is completely immaculate, Agnese Chiari explained to the council, enthusiastically raising again and again the enlargement taken from the X-ray image, it is immaculate in every possible meaning of the word, she said, in once sense because master Arlango, after necessary chemical testing, mixed a certain solvent with which the "protective lacquer" originating from the unknown yet dilettantish hand was removed, and now it shines forth in its own immaculate, its own original character; but it is immaculate in the sense too that we now know, beyond a shadow of a doubt, who painted it, at which point the members of the council exchanged significant glances and looked at the art historian with great expectation, and if they were not made unequivocally happy by what they heard, it was because, now was it Bellini—or not Bellini?—they asked each other; do you understand? the question went back and forth, I for one don't, came the answer from here and there, and as Dr. Chiari could see just how difficult it was for the council members to take in the truth, she repeated again and again that the head, and her voice resounded triumphantly in the room—was Bellini's; the picture, however, she continued, originates from various hands; it can be hypothesized that this certain Belliniano found this marvelous head among the canvases that had been begun by his master in the workshop bequeathed to him, and cleverly, so that he could be there and yet not be there—he could hardly bear to write the name of his own person, having finally emerged from his master's shadow, and yet he could not bear not to write it—he accordingly wrote his own name, dividing it between the left and the right sides of the head, and then painted over it, in other words concealing the entire thing; for surely he knew well that he could sell it as a Bellini painting for a huge sum anywhere and anytime, whereas an unfinished Bellini, actually a hardly started Bellini—not to mention, if he were to betray that apart from the head he had painted the entire picture—wouldn't get him anything, only a few coins, so he painted what was missing as best he could; the three Greek letters on either side of the head, the naked torso, the shoulder, the two hands as they intertwine in the front of the picture, and he created for all of this a dark background, so that the face, whose enthralling power he would never have been able to conjure up himself, would burst forth as it were from the darkness, with its boundless docility, something like that occurred, it is certain—Dr. Chiari reported to the members of the council—and so the endless dilly-dallying could finally come to an end, at which the council members, slightly confused, began to nod their heads, and consented to everything that the art historian recommended, namely that the painting should not be put back into its old corner in the Albergo, but that it should be put on a stand in a prominent spot in the great hall, and an article should be written about it, because they could be completely certain—Agnese Chiari reassured her colleagues—that the art historians, if they had not done so before, would now take notice of this picture, so let it be displayed with all the respect due to a great creator, it should be lit with a spotlight and then they would see that the name of S. Rocco would become even more illustrious, for it was not any old finding that they had been able to discover with this Vittore, mark my words, repeated Dr. Chiari, everyone will be talking about this; in which, however, the scholar was greatly mistaken, because in total a notice of a few lines was published in a professional journal for restorers, penned by an unknown art historian, Giovanna Nepi Sciré, and the whole thing remained confined to the pages of Restituzioni 2000, which, because of the far too specialized nature of the journal's orientation, could not reach the personages most affected, so that they knew nothing of this discovery, not Tempestini, not Goffer, not Belting; and the wider public, finally, knew nothing at all, so that now, standing in the square before the San Rocco in the sunlight that filtered through the iron gate, as he made ready to enter the building at last and seek out the work for the second time in its usual spot; inside, on the ground floor, the vendor behind the ticket desk awaited the tourists, continually arranging the exact same postcard with the exact same signature taken from the famous painting, exactly as eleven years ago, when he had come here for the first time, had entered and come into sudden contact with the Dead Christ, up there on the second floor, the little room opening up on the left from the wide landing, in the corner of the Albergo, not even lit by a single light.

The group with which he had arrived did not, as a matter of fact, wish to return to the heart of the city; due to the general fatigue, the direction proposed seemed like the journey back, but nobody wanted to turn back, no one was thinking that this Venetian excursion had to come to an end, and they would return to the station; they wanted to rest, that was the truth, but not to have it come to an end, to relax, and eat and drink, because they were truly exhausted from having walked all day; when he proposed that, before sitting down in a restaurant somewhere, they should absolutely, at the very least, see the San Rocco while it was still open, at first a uniform and drawn-out "no" was the response, the children in particular began to whimper and then to scream at full volume at even the mere mention of a museum visit, but then he said that it was possible to sit down in the San Rocco, and that according to the guidebook there was, on the Campo San Rocco, or nearby, a fountain, moreover on the way, there was also a very special ice-cream parlor, well with this he was victorious, the company began to incline toward the idea, good, they said, San Rocco, fine, but this is the last stop before the restaurant and if there was neither a fountain nor ice-cream parlor, they would wring his neck, mark their words—they were merry and intoxicated with what is termed the dazzling beauty of Venice, and there was an ice-cream vendor on the Campo S. Margarita, where they suddenly emerged, slightly diverging from the direct route, but then, finding a shadowy spot, when they withdrew toward the wall of one building to lick their ice cream, they noticed that there were at least two attractive-seeming restaurants open for business on the square; first they tried to talk him out of the whole idea of San

Rocco, saying that Tintoretto—it was because of him that they had come—was just an overweening "something," as one lady of the group put it, so they should just drop the whole thing; then, however, when they saw that he really was dead set on it, and wanted to go there no matter what, they advised him that this Campo S. Margarita was alluring enough for everyone to sit down in one of the two restaurants, and if he was so set upon it, well he could go, on the map San Rocco wasn't so far from here, and really it wasn't, although once again he got lost at the Rio Foscari, but then someone helped him, pointing him in the right direction, so that barely ten minutes later he was already standing in front of San Rocco; as it was too hot on the square he went straight into the building, thinking he would have a quick look, that he wouldn't miss Tintoretto after all, then hurry back, for his feet were really burning by now, and he too was certainly quite hungry and thirsty, so just Tintoretto, he decided, he would regret it later on if, citing his fatigue, he had to admit having seen nothing of it, so he went inside, buying an entrance ticket that was more expensive than usual but forgetting to take the museum's guide along with the ticket, so that at first he thought this is the whole thing, the ground floor, that it was the entire Scuola Grande di San Rocco, and he began to look for the Tintorettos and even found eight of them, but not a single one had any effect on him at all, that is to say that these Tintorettos were not the real thing, here in this one large room, that was cold, not very beautiful, and a little forbidding, with a grumbling ticket-puncher at the entrance and behind her, on a few tables, the offerings of cheap reproductions by the illustrious names of the place, and an equally grumpy employee, so can this really be right, he reflected, it's inconceivable that there are no real Tintorettos here, and he was about to start back to the ticket desk to inquire where the real Tintorettos were, when to his left he spied a broad staircase, and as there was no sign on it stating that tourists were not allowed, he began to walk up it, a little timorously; his first steps were hesitant, but then, when no one called after him, he grew ever more decisive, and so wound his way up to the landing, like someone who knew from the start exactly where he was going, and there at the landing he realized he was a fool, a yokel from eastern Europe, an irredeemably insensate figure, for at the landing the two fresco panels by Pietro Negri and Antonio Zanchi revealed that he was in the right place now, that this was where he should have come right away, and then, on this upper floor—of course it was the same with everyone who comes here for the first time, it was also his first time up here—it then occurred to him that he had forgotten to catch his breath, because it was so unexpected, and for him this heavy magnificence awaiting the visitor fell so unexpectedly upon him: the ceiling painted in gold, the richly molded stucco, and in the midst of all this the real Tintoretto, his overpowering paintings striking him with such force, and the geometrical patterns in the marble floor beneath his feet left him so taken aback by their physical beauty that he didn't know how not to step on them; so that his movements were only directed by that, and there remained still a kind of uncertainty as if he were continually dizzy, and he was dizzy, at first he stepped onto the marble floor with a bad feeling, as if he were not worthy to take these steps, and at first he didn't even dare to look at the ceiling for a long time, for he felt he was really losing his balance, good lord, he sighed, as he slowly began to slide here and there, he had no idea where to begin or with what, because what should he do with these real but gigantic Tintorettos, what should he do with this blinding light affixed to the windows, for in this light, things were being laid open to him that he simply did not deserve, he thought, troubled, then he started off again, went over to the facing wall, and quickly sat down upon a chair, an uncomfortable modern one that could be folded shut and re-opened, an entire row of which was assembled all along both of the lengthwise walls, and just then he could have collected himself a bit, when from the back of the hall the guard headed very decisively toward him, and pointed at something behind the chairs: where underneath the windows, every meter or so, there was some kind of paper on the wall, stuck onto the marvelous carved decorations, the guard pointed at these and muttered something in Italian, of which he understood not one word, until finally one of the papers was pressed into his hand, where it was also written in English, DO NOT SIT DOWN!; nodding, he sprang up and not asking where else, or why the chairs had even been put there in the first place, he slowly began to walk by the windows, but the sunlight kept blinding him, so that he could hardly even see the huge Tintorettos; finally he made his way around and once again began the slow sliding, here gaping at the ceiling, here at the Tintorettos, and so it went, and he could not even conceive that, in this palatial hall, such bounty as had been created, marvelous but still too weighty for him, could even be possible, because it was too much, he was too weighted down by this rich beauty and excess, so that it was with relief that he discovered an open door at the end of the hall, which opened onto a little side-room; he quickly scurried in, for he believed that there would be less splendor here, and chiefly that he wouldn't be so much under the gaze of the guard, who—as he was the only visitor capable of trying something, as he had dared to sit down—perpetually attempted to stand in his path, practically chasing him, not leaving him in peace for a moment; of course the guard acted as if he weren't watching him, but he kept returning to the door of the little side-room to see what he was up to, but what could he have done, he asked himself, but slowly inch along the walls before the colossal paintings, and just as he was about to leave the room, with the intention of quitting the museum as soon as possible—as the museum-guard was too much for him, as was indeed the entire palace—and he now really did need to rest, he needed a rest from all this unparalleled yet complex pomp and monumentality and he was about to go back into the large hall from the smaller side-room, when he noticed that there stood a picture-stand in the corner—buried away as if it weren't any object of great consideration—and the picture-stand held a little painting; his gaze happened upon it and he stepped back with a serious demeanor, to reassure the guard who was staring at him again, he stood in front of it like a proper museum-goer, or at least how he imagined a proper museum-goer should stand, he stood in front of the little painting, which depicted a half-naked Christ, whose head was so gently inclined to one side, and on his face was such an endless and otherworldly peace, he could not determine whether the figure was lying or standing, in any event, somewhere in front of the stomach the two hands intertwined, and the slightly awkwardly-painted blood could be clearly seen as it dripped from the wounded hands, but on the face there was not the slightest trace of suffering, it was a very unusual likeness; Christ's hair, shining gold, fell in curling locks onto his slender shoulders, and again and again that terrible docility and resignation because—and he had discovered this first—in contrast to all the tranquility and peace, a profound desolation inexpressible in words was upon that face, and the whole image shone forth from a darkness, like gold against the deepest night, he looked, he looked at this strange Christ, and he could not bear to look away, he was no longer bothered by the guard, who just now was not only looking in but actually standing in the doorway with the most obvious expression of suspicion, to watch him to see if he was about to attempt another scandalous move as he had just done in the other room with the chairs, but although this happened, he didn't see him anymore, he didn't even realize that the guard was watching him, just then he saw nothing, for he was looking at Christ's eyes, to figure out just what made this Christ so distinctive and demanded his full attention, he looked into those eyes which were so mesmerizing, because that is what happened: the picture, this imago pietatis-like figure of Christ had mesmerized him, he searched for some point of support but there was no helpful explanation, not under the picture nor on the stand which had been set up, nor on the wall before which he stood, nothing regarding the painter or the subject, they had simply put up this Christ-torso by the wall in the corner, as if the exhibition planners of San Rocco wanted to say—well, we have this picture as well, it's not too interesting but as long as it's around we'll just put it over here, so have a look at it if you're interested, and he was interested, he really couldn't look away from it, and then he suddenly realized why: both of Christ's eyes were shut, ah yes, he sighed, like someone who had found the clue, but he had not found it at all, and that was even more unsettling, because he had to look some more, now however he looked at just the two closed eyelids, and he had to endure the knowledge that he wasn't finding out the clue to the strangeness, he looked again at the whole—the fragile shoulders, the head inclined to one side, the mouth, the fine wisps of beard, the scrawny arms, and the two hands placed so oddly together—when suddenly he became aware that the eyelid of Christ seemed, as it were, to have moved a bit, as if these two eyelids had fluttered; he had not lost his sanity, so he said to himself no that's impossible, he looked away then looked again, and the two eyes flickered yet again, this is sheer impossibility, he thought, frightened, and he was on the point of abruptly leaving the room, for it was clear that his fatigue was playing games with him, or that he had simply stared at the picture for too long and was hallucinating, so he went out of the little room and passing the guard, set off decisively for the staircase, but there, before he actually placed his foot onto the stairs, he thought again and turned, just as decisively as he had gone out, he came back in, even looking at the guard, and this helped him too, for the expression on the guard's face was easy to judge as he turned abruptly back, and who was looking at him even more suspiciously than before, if that was possible; it was clear that as far as the guard was concerned he was an insolent nutcase, whose every move had to be watched carefully; and actually there was something to that, he was not entirely certain that he hadn't gone mad, because what was up with this whole Christ in there, he asked himself, he did not go into the little room but, defying the guard, plunked himself down in the chair nearest to the little room; the guard, however, did not wish, or rather did not see the point in making him get up; here, however, he did perceive from the corner of his eye the notice printed on the pieces of paper telling people not to sit down; let's consider this one more time, he thought with a quaking stomach, is this possible?—it is not possible, inside there is a picture, a body of Christ, with the head bent to one side, a gentle *abandoned* Christ; someone painted him, someone turned him into an ideal, and someone is looking at him, in this case myself, he said, and he wasn't quite sure if he were speaking aloud or not, in any event the guard was coming quite close to him, so that when he decided that he would go in to confirm everything, he practically brushed up against his clothes, the two of them didn't fit into the doorway, and he stood again before the torso of Christ, he constrained himself not to look at it for a bit, but then of course he looked at it, because this is why he had come in, and the two eyelids of Christ flickered again, but now he could not look away at all, but rather his gaze was fixed, and he looked gaping at these closed eyes, he knew without a doubt that the eyes of this Christ were trembling, and that they would tremble again, because this Christ WANTED TO OPEN HIS EYES ... but then, as he realized this, he was already in the great hall on his way toward the staircase, already running down the stairs, turning onto the landing and he was already on the lower floor, out from beside the postcard vendor and the ticket-seller, out into the open air, into the throngs of people who, suspecting nothing, were undulating here and there in the friendly sunshine of the Campo San Rocco.

He had been here for the last time eleven years ago, but apart from his hair having turned completely gray, it was as if nothing at all had changed, and this was shocking to him, because normally at the very least a cobblestone is overturned, a gutter-spout breaks off, or where there was a pizzeria there is now a café, or there is a new fountain, or something like that; here, however—he looked again all around the square—there was not, in the entire God-given world, one single difference; yes, it was true that the Scuola Grande had been restored, but it had only become a little cleaner, a little more uniform; it had not changed, it was neither fresher nor livelier nor brighter, and not even, as in "modern times," as so often happens in other cities, when a building is restored, because in that case it really is restored and an effort is made to return it to an image of its original state, which is a complete impossibility; for every material is different, the air is different, the humidity is different, the pollution is different, and those who endure all of this, who look at it, who walk around it are all different as well; here, however, no such error had been committed; everything in a word had remained as it was, he determined, drawing closer to the sunlit part of the square, he now faced the magnificent windows of the main façade; he sat down by the iron gate, the sun warming his limbs pleasantly, and nothing remained from his being chased around by the pink shirt than a failed mistaken story, which perhaps had never even happened, although once again the article on the front page of the Corriere della Sera came into his mind and with that—completely irrelevantly and senselessly—his memory somehow cast up the word Gehenna, translated as the word of Jesus in the Hungarian Bible as signifying Hell, yet in actuality signifying Ge-Hinnom, near Jerusalem, where waste was burnt, so that as he observed the integrated beauty of the building, and as he allowed the sun to warm his aged body, all of this became so utterly inappropriate to where he actually was—a thought-fragment without meaning, zigzagging and fleeting, brought about by mere coincidence, just like Pink-Shirt himself, as well as his pursuit and this whole trip here—and all of this had so little, so little to do with the scene of normality proffered by the crowds walking around on the square, it had so little, so little to do with him, or why he was in Venice now, or with what finally awaited him there inside the building, so that consciously and finally he wiped it all out from his brain, if he could still not yet summon up the courage to head inside *immediately*, for there inside, on the second floor, was the one significant thing in his entire meaningless existence: and his entire meaningless existence, as it were, bore down upon that painting of small scale; he had thought of it so often in the past eleven years, had so often conjured it up, so often taking into his hands that little frame containing the reproduction sold in the form of a postcard and allowing him to preserve a likeness of the painting even if of horrendous quality, and so often had he tried to discover how what had happened could have happened up there in the corner of the Albergo—so now, as he stood twenty or twenty-five steps from the entrance, he could resolve to go in only with difficulty; the sun, however, was beginning to set, the shadows grew ever longer on the square, the strip of sunlight was narrowing more and more, so that he had to consider that the museum had opening hours as well, of which the last two were necessary to him, for this was his plan: to come in fact, just before closing time, when there would perhaps be the fewest people inside, there would be two hours, then back to S. Polo 2366, a dinner with the friendly owner of the pension, then the next morning away from Venice, back to the Aeroporto S. Marco for the plane, for this was the question: what had happened then, and how it could have happened, and does that kind of thing happen generally, as well as the larger question of what if it happens again, if there will be a repetition of this ... something, since he could not pronounce the word miracle, even to himself, or perhaps he didn't feel like pronouncing it; he cleared his throat for a while as if anyone in the crowd could have heard his thoughts, but well no, so he left off clearing his throat, he got up, went into the entrance, bought a ticket—seven euros? he asked in surprise, remembering the entrance fee differently—and like a blind man who knows the way with dead certainty—

he was already hurrying forward in his black oxfords, which clattered on the marble floors, ringing out so clearly that the postcard seller and the woman at the ticket desk, who had already seen all kinds here, gazed after him with ever-rising indignation—in vain, the gray head commanding respect—until he reached the other side of the room, the entrance to the staircase in the middle, and then up the stairs to the right—onto the landing, and he was already standing in the upper hall of the Scalone, with its breathtaking magnificence, but he didn't even look up at the ceiling or at the walls, or down at the marble floor, he just immediately turned to the left and went into the Albergo, he instantly turned left and was standing there in the corner, where the picture-stand should have been, but nothing stood in this corner, the Albergo had been completely rearranged, there were some sort of Renaissance chairs in it, and this room, which had originally served as the working area of the person who managed the daily affairs of the Scuola, was filled with them, only the ceilings were left untouched, only the walls were left untouched, everywhere the same pictures were hanging, of course again Tintoretto, once a member of the order; but the special painting-stands from the Albergo, upon which two works had been displayed, one of them the work he now sought, were nowhere to be seen; but there's nothing now, all's been swept clean, what has happened here, he looked around uncomprehendingly, what have they done here, he began to pace nervously from one side of the Albergo to the other, but the picture wasn't anywhere, and then suddenly the same convulsion was squeezing his stomach together and he was struck by the same cold draft as when he was being chased near the Frari, the same convulsion and the same chill, he straggled here and there, I have to find someone whom I can get to understand what I want, he thought, and began to head toward someone who looked like a guard, who sat in one of the chairs in the back row of the great hall, visibly deeply immersed in whatever he was reading, of course all the while taking in everything that was going on in the great hall, this cannot be imitated, it is not possible to guess how they do it, impossible to figure out; he could feel, however, that the attendant noticed him immediately as he reeled from the thought that the picture was no longer here, as he appeared at the door of the Albergo in the oxfords that banged and clanged strangely against the marble floor, and headed toward him, the guard saw the figure with the snow-white hair clearly but he did not move, he didn't even look up from the book, on the contrary before he even got there he turned over the leaf and ruffled the pages a little, slightly raising his head like someone who has reached the beginning of a new page, so when he heard the question, in a makeshift patchwork of Italian-Spanish-French-English, asking where the little picture was, and was shown its approximate size and where it had been, inside in the left-hand corner of the Albergo on an easel-stand, in other words he was shown rather than spoken to, the guard spread open his hands, and shook his head, indicating unequivocally that he did not understand what the visitor wanted, and he was already lowering himself to sit down and read again, but at this the visitor was visibly in despair, and began to explain even more vehemently, now mixing his own language in with Italian, and he just pointed and gesticulated, at which point the guard once again and for the last time shook his head and signaled with his hands that he didn't understand, the visitor should realize that he didn't understand—and with that he finally sat down in his chair, crossed one leg over the other, he clearly hated tourists and especially their questions; he opened his book, then, with an irritated expression, began to try to find where he had left off before he was interrupted, and the visitor, in his helplessness, left him there and set off, forward, blindly, the Tintorettos on the colossal walls just hanging, hanging next to him, when suddenly, like someone whose foot has grown a root into the ground, he stopped short, pressed his head forward, and straining his eyes in the front part of the room, bathed in a rather dim light, he gaped in the direction of the gigantic scene of San Rocco placed in exactly the center of the wall, more precisely he gaped straight ahead, to the left of the Altarpiece, because that is where it was, that is where they had put it, from there it gazed at him, from a distance—the great hall had been rearranged, so that the scene of San Rocco was separated from the rest of the hall by a somewhat bulky knee-high marble balustrade, and the picture-stand—as if it were an ordinary easel—had been placed within this area, just enough toward the back so that no visitor would be able to touch it physically, and thus no harm could come to it, yet close enough, and brilliantly lit in the dimness, so that whoever wished could feel himself directly in its presence; and this is what he wished; he left definitively behind him the museum guard leafing through his book and slowly, ever more slowly, sliding his feet forward ever so cautiously, so that the nerve-wracking heel guards would barely brush against the floor, he went forward, he went until the black oxford with the reinforced soles came up against the three broad steps leading directly upward to the marble balustrade, so that one could, if one chose to do so, get as close as possible to the picture; he still wanted to get as close as possible to the picture, but as he stood there, it disturbed him so much to see Christ once again shining from the darkness, so much did it affect him that he couldn't even bear to look properly, so that he didn't even see anything properly, and in particular not the picture as a whole, for he saw only details, his gaze jumped from one detail to another, as if his intention to take in the entire picture with his troubled gaze was deliberately made impossible by his very own self, with this jumping around from detail to detail; suddenly, then, he looked around, and felt himself to be ridiculous, like a hysteric, he thought, and stepped back onto the floor, obliged as he did so to look ahead toward the steps, so that he could bear to descend them, so when he faced it again, he had to look upward again, and by that point he had calmed down somewhat, there were hardly any people around, just the museum guard, sitting in the back with his book, the conditions were very nearly ideal, he could have said, all was silent, for now the Tintorettos and the opulent woodcarvings on the wall had swallowed up even the last echo from his shoes, there was silence and complete peacefulness, just an elderly couple with cameras dangling from their necks, but they were far away, near the entrance of the Albergo; he looked at the picture, he looked at Christ, and that which so laughably had not succeeded at first was now self-evident, that is he looked Christ in the face, finally he looked at the two closed eyes, and suddenly he felt very warm, with not even one knot in his stomach or chill in his body, nothing but this warmth that inundated him; he took one step back and then he felt he was tired: he had to sit down, he mumbled perhaps in an undertone, and he looked back at the guard, but he did not look like someone who was about to leap up and come running over here if he took a seat, so not even bothering with the strips of paper placed behind the chairs just as they had been eleven years ago, he lowered himself into the seat closest to the picture of Christ, to look at it from there; he waited for perhaps a minute and then realized with relief that the guard had not even pricked up his ears, he just kept on reading, and so he seated himself more comfortably and began to look with all of his strength to see what remained of the Christ of eleven years ago, he looked with all of his strength and he now dared to risk resting his gaze solely onto Christ's eyes, he sat motionless, turned a little to the left so as to take in the canvas, and his gaze sunk deeper into the eyes of Christ and he waited, he waited to see if the eyelashes would quiver, and if what had happened once in this building would happen yet again, he looked at the painting, sitting rigidly; a light had been set up and the entire thing was perhaps overly illuminated; this light, however, made every detail perfectly visible, even from here, from the chair: the endless solitude of the naked torso, the shoulders and arms painted rather awkwardly—an awkwardness that showed only more plainly their fragility; and he saw perfectly that the two eyes were not flickering, but slowly opening—he was so frightened that he quickly looked at the right eye as well to see if what had occurred with the left eye was true, but then he lost his clarity of vision, the two eyes once again returned to a state of being closed, what is going on here, am I hallucinating or is this some optical illusion, what is this, he bent forward and lowered his elbows to his knees, and buried his face in his hands, then he looked around again to see if anyone was watching him, but nothing, the elderly couple was still here, how much time had passed anyway?—then others came in as well, a middle-aged man, alone, then two young girls who immediately began to play with one of the mirrors placed by the table for the museum visitors, allowing them, if they held it the right way, to take a closer look at any part of the ceiling ornamentation that might interest them; altogether that was who was there and no one bothered with him, with the figure hunched forward, just looking at the image of Christ, just looking and not even moving, BUT HE IS OPENING HIS EYES, he registered within himself; then again he tried to muster the courage to fix his gaze onto the two eyes of Christ, BUT HOW DARK are these eyes, it was spine-chilling as although NOW THEY REALLY WERE ALMOST COMPLETELY OPEN, you could hardly see the pupils, and nothing of the white of the eyes, it was completely clouded, a dark obscurity lay in these eyes, and it seemed unbearable that this dark obscurity was emanating such an endless sadness, and not the sadness of one who suffers but of one who has suffered—but not even that; he got up, and then leaned back in the chair, it is not a question here of suffering but only of sorrow, a sorrow impossible to grasp in its entirety, and entirely incomprehensible to him, an immeasurable sorrow, he looked into Christ's eyes and he saw nothing else there, just this pure sorrow, as if it were a sorrow without cause, he froze at the thought of it, SORROW, JUST LIKE THAT, FOR EVERYTHING, for creation, for existence, for beings, for time, for suffering and for passion, for birth and destruction—and suddenly a noise of some kind struck his ears, his head cleared for an instant, and after a while he realized that it was sifting in from outside to here, oh, these strollers on the square, it's coming from there, he thought, then he was struck with terror at the thought of Christ and his sorrow, and outside, the crowds, mostly young boys and girls teeming merrily, he recalled the people he had seen outside; this incomprehensible sorrow, it burst into him, was somehow *lost* in the corso of young boys and girls outside; everything, however, is still there and everything now is like that, and everything now is still there, and everything is like that—BUT FOR WHAT, something within him asked, and he felt this question as if he had been struck by lightning, not the flash of the lightning of recognition, however, but a flash of the lightning of shame—for he was ashamed that it had occurred like this, that here was Christ in the fullest and most horrible sense of the word—an orphan—and here is Christ REALLY AND TRULY, but no one needed him—*time had passed him by,* passed him by, and now He was saying farewell, for He was leaving this earth, he shuddered as he heard these sentences in his head, and oh my God what now, what horrible thoughts—I must get up, he decided, I've finally seen what I came here to see, now I can go, so that he saw himself as he got up, and went down the steps, stepping out among the youths of the Campo San Rocco, and he mixed into the eddy of early evening; he didn't move, he just sat there in the chair and saw himself heading down the stairs, he saw himself leaving the building and boarding a vaporetto, forfeiting his dinner and leaving his bags at S. Polo 2366, having himself taken from San Tomà directly to the Stazione, and from there to the Aeroporto San Marco, to escape from Venice, back to where he came from, yes, he saw how he really set off down the famous steps—only he didn't know that for him there would never be any exit from this building, not ever.

8

UP ON THE ACROPOLIS

The taxi drivers pestered him continuously in the horrendous crowd, no, no, leave me alone, he said at first, then he didn't answer and, rebuffing them, tried to avoid them, in the meantime signifying with his glance no, no, only it was impossible either to avoid them or to get them to stop pushing up against him, they practically encircled you and droned this into your ear: Syntagma, and Acropolis, and Monastrikai, and Pireus, Agora, Plaka, and of course, hotel, hotel, and hotel, verri cheep and verri cheep, they shrieked and smiled, and that smile was the most horrendous of all, and they came from the back, then you changed directions with your suitcase, but then—zap!—you were already ploughing into them in front, because within a single split second they either shot out behind you or in front of you, the entire situation in the Aerodromia Eleftherios Venizelos was as if it were not a question of your arrival but a mistake, which the arriving person realized only when it was already too late, since he has arrived already, and has stepped into the horrendous crowd of the colossal waiting room, from everywhere groups or individuals were struggling to move in some direction or other, all in completely different directions, children screamed for their parents, and the parents screamed for the children not to go too far ahead or not remain too far behind, elderly couples with their lost gazes shuffled along always moving ahead, the leaders of school groups yelled at frightened pupils to stick together, and Japanese tour guides with their little flags and megaphones yelled at the frightened Japanese tourists to stay together, and sweat poured off of everyone, as the heat in the hangar was insufferable, it was summer, an infernal pandemonium, a madhouse unannounced in advance, as you attempted, with your suitcase, to fight toward the direction where the exit was expected to be, but even there outside it didn't really come to an end: on the one hand because only then did you feel the meaning of heat in Athens in the summertime; on the other hand, as the taxi drivers, at least three or four of them, were still following right behind him and they just spoke and spoke and smiled and smiled and reached after his suitcase, by the time he was able to break free of this insanity he was a corpse; he sat down in a waiting taxi and said to the gum-chewing, bored-looking driver, who was reading a tabloid newspaper, *in the near of Syntagma, Odos-Ermou-Odos Voulis, parakalo,* at which point the driver looked at him as if to say who is this old geezer, then nodded, leaned back in the driver's seat; he didn't look where the taxi was going, although he had with him a rough sketch of the streets from one of his Greek acquaintances, so that he would not be ripped off in the taxi—or at least not too much, as one of his acquaintances from Athens explained in an e-mail, because they will anyway to a certain extent, let them, it's the custom here, otherwise it will make them ill, but it wasn't because of the e-mail; his strength was gone, and his nerves just couldn't take it anymore; he was so worn out by the landing and then what came after it, as his suitcase had not been where it was supposed to be: completely by chance, as he was looking with a frightened expression for the Lost Luggage counter, his gaze happened upon a familiar object, circling around in solitude on a distant conveyor belt promising baggage from a Kiev flight four hours earlier, then he went on to the customs officials who, searching for hashish, took apart his unfortunate suitcase, and finally there was the unrestrained labyrinth of the waiting area, so that really it was enough, no one from his circle of acquaintances was waiting for him in the arrivals lounge, in vain did he loiter for a while in that frantic crowd, so that well, after one hour he set off, that is he would have set off but then the taxi drivers flung themselves at him, so that in a word now, sitting in the back seat of a taxi chosen by himself and utterly exhausted, he gaped out the window at the city that was almost completely devoid of people due to the early hour, and for a while he wasn't even really looking where they were going, or watching the meter, he could only conclude when he saw that not even one of the street names written on the piece of paper coincided with those outside—and he began to suspect, for that matter, justifiably—that the taxi was not taking him by the most direct route, so that when the reading on the meter had already surpassed the sum in euros mentioned to him by his acquaintances as the absolute maximum he should pay, he tried somehow in English to make himself understood to the taxi driver, but at first it was as if the driver didn't even hear him, he just turned to the right, then turned to the left, until at a red light he deigned to glance backward benevolently and jab at the street name on the piece of paper being extended to him, indicating where they were at that moment, and this was certainly not only very far from Syntagma but from the city center as well, so that he tried to assert himself and gestured that the whole thing wasn't good at all, and he was overcome with anger, and he pointed at his watch and pointed at the name of Syntagma on his paper, but to no avail, the taxi driver phlegmatically chewed his chewing gum and nothing, nothing at all disturbed him and he clearly was the type that nothing ever would disturb, he just kept on heading in the direction he thought was right, and he reassured his passenger that everything was fine, don't worry, be happy, he said toward the back seat from time to time, reassuringly, so that the passenger's stomach had completely clenched into a stiff knot, when suddenly the driver braked at the edge of a busy intersection, opened the door and said—pointing around, with a sudden faint smile at the corners of his mouth—so here is Syntagma, or didn't you want to come here?—he then held out to the driver the amount that had been decided by his acquaintances, but at this, as if suddenly awakening from slumber, the driver bellowed at him so unexpectedly, and began to shake him by the shoulders; hardly had a minute passed and already a small group of Greeks was standing around them; at last, with their assistance, a compromise was reached, and they agreed upon a price which was twice the true going rate, but he was fed up already, I spit upon Athens, he said in Hungarian to the Greeks loitering around him, but they just slapped him on the shoulders, everything was fine, perfect, come and have a drink, no way am I going to have a drink, he broke away from the circle, because of course he could not discern that these people surrounding him did not intend to fleece him, but out of sympathy for his hopeless skirmish with the taxi driver they genuinely wanted to invite him for a drink so that he could calm down, taxi drivers are just like that, you can't argue with them, even if you bargain with them they always find a way to rip you off, especially so early in the morning, come on then, they said in Greek, and they pointed at the tables, set out beside the street, of a nearby restaurant, from where they had arisen just a few moments ago, but he was so terrified of them that he quickly grabbed his suitcase and set off on foot into the chaos of the intersection, just like that, diagonally into the traffic, which was a mistake, for not only did it increase the general chaos, although that didn't cause any commotion, but it did put him in considerable danger, and he was not even conscious of the fact that once he had reached the other side he had directly and needlessly risked his life among the honking cars perhaps three times; to the other side then, with a suitcase, which although not heavy, thank God, nonetheless hindered him in further unconstrained movement, and particularly in planning these movements; nothing, that is to say, came into his mind as to what to do now, he should call his acquaintances to find out where they were already, so they could come and help him, but the taxi driver had cheated him to such an extent that his diminished reserves were not enough even for one phone call, so he just stood there for a while, and the group from a moment ago had already sat down again, and as from here they did not at all look like robbers, after a time he decided to go back to them and ask for directions, he even stepped off of the sidewalk, but a car really almost swept him away this time, so that he thought it wiser to look for some kind of official crossing, of course here too he had to be on his guard for he could not tell if the green light across the way was actually referring to him, then when after a while it emerged that indeed it was, he also had to grasp that the green light here was just a kind of theoretical yes to the crossing of the street, in practical terms it could be understood as green, yes, but only as long as this plan was not opposed by another, more powerful force, and opposed it was, whether by a truck rushing alongside him, or a bus that generated a whirlwind flinging him backward, whether by this or whether by that, but then, happily, other would-be pedestrians appeared on the scene as well, so that together at one point they initiated a common passage during a green light, well, that was successful, and there he stood on the terrace of the restaurant among the group of young people who were sipping away—nonchalantly and with a kind of serene indifference—at their drinks; they greeted him in a friendly manner and on every face the thought was plainly written that they had told him already that before cooking up any plans it would have been much better to have a drink with them; they asked him if he wanted a beer, or a kafes, or perhaps a raki, oh no, he protested, just an ellinikos kafes, okay, ellinikos kafes, they passed on the order to the waiter, and the conversation began, the Greeks really were young but not too young, not too far past the age of thirty, and they knew English pretty well, only their accent was peculiar, and he too could hardly deny where he came from because of his accent, so they understood each other well, so much so that suddenly he felt at once a kind of natural trust toward them, and he told his story briefly, who he was and why he had come here, that he had had rather enough of the world, or of himself, or both, so that he thought he would come to Athens, where he had never been before but which he had always longed to visit, so that it was a kind of farewell for him, but that he himself didn't understand too clearly just what he was bidding farewell to here; the company listened, nodding their heads, and honored him with a long silence, then slowly a kind of discussion began, and his new friends wanted, in the first place, to dissuade him at all costs from ... from everything, as it turned out, but mainly from the idea that he should call his acquaintances, because if they weren't waiting for him at the airport, and they weren't around here at the time agreed upon, for safety's sake, at nine o'clock, at the intersection of Ermou and Voulis, and it was already past nine, wasn't it, so there was really no rush, they said; however, they advised, he should remain with them, since fate had already brought him this way, believe us, even like this things will be fine; why, he asked, what were their plans, ah, our plans, they looked at each other and on their faces a kind of amusement was plainly visible, well, as for their plans, there weren't any, that is to say that, well, their plan was to sit here and drink yet another beer, and with a kind of sincere grimace they indicated that they did not belong among those who make plans, to sit here was everything, they had been doing that since yesterday evening, and as long as their money lasted, this would be their plan, to drink another beer slowly and look around, said one oaf who introduced himself as Adonis; they were intelligent and sympathetic, yet still, as he took a sip of the ellinikos kafes, he was suddenly struck by the sense that if he let everything stay like this, he would never see anything of Athens, namely that when he had been speaking of why he was here, to know what Athens was like, he was greeted by an unmistakably loud silence, as if they wanted to say that to know anything at all, especially about Athens, well, that was totally useless;

Yorgos, sitting beside him, who, however, called himself George, seemed to be entertained by the idea: still Athens, this Yorgos said, and he grew somber; you know, my friend, what Athens is like, it is a huge pile of stinking shit, that's what it is, and he drank from his glass, and there was too much bitterness in the whole thing to ask why he had said that; fish cast out onto the shore, he thought later on, good-natured and pleasant idlers, he determined; still he had to acknowledge that in their midst he was feeling better and better, and something in him grew alarmed as well, that all the same it was dangerous, very dangerous to sit here on his very first morning and listen to them as they talked about the song "Guns of Brixton" and whether the Arcade Fire or the Clash version was better, then to be silent with them for a long while, and to look around for a long while, to look at the dense traffic coming from the direction of Syntagma and the Odos Voulis, to watch as the cars senselessly, but so senselessly, rushed here and there in the already dreadful heat and the dreadful stench, it was all too pleasant being here with them, and alluringly despondent, like a kind of sweet weight that pulls one down—if he didn't move right away, he said to himself in fright, then he would remain here and everything would turn out completely differently than what he wished from the depths of his heart, so that suddenly he stood up and announced that he wanted to see at least the Acropolis, since childhood it had been one of his greatest desires to see the Acropolis one day, and now that he was getting old—ah, so *at least* this Acropolis, Adonis winked at him; the Acropolis, Yorgos looked at him as well, sourly, well you know after all, they said to him, after all you're here for the first time, why not, although I think it's really idiotic, said Yorgos, I think so too, said Adonis, but well, fine, go if you want to go so much, but wait, what about—a girl from the group, whose name was Ela, now advised him—this thing, and she pointed to his suitcase, you don't have to take that the whole way, you can put it somewhere, if you don't find us here, just wait, but where, and she looked around—at Maniopulos's, Yorgos recommended; okay it's nearby, and so it was, Maniopulos was a merchant or something like that, in a completely dilapidated little shop in the dilapidated street behind the restaurant, maybe it sold computer parts, it was not easy to determine, but it sold something like that, in any event the youth in the shop immediately said yes, and put the suitcase behind a kind of curtain, and gestured to him that everything was fine, he could come back for the suitcase anytime, when he was done, and with that they were already outside on the terrace, they were explaining the route to him, advising him that although it was hot, he should go on foot, because there wouldn't be so many tourists, and then, he could see something of the Plaka, the old city, just keep on going that way, Yorgos pointed in one direction, and he started off toward the crossing, just keep going that way, although it would have been better, they immediately noted among themselves, if he had waited a few hours, that is to say until evening, as the sun up there will be scorching, dreadfully so, but he was already on the other side, and he began to make his way into the narrow alleyways of the Plaka, he was still waving to them, they waved back amiably, and even though he had felt so good in their midst—or exactly because he had felt so good in their midst—he now breathed a sigh of relief, at last now he was on the way, on the way to the Acropolis, because *at least the Acropolis,* he said to himself, and he thought of those very first murky pictures which he had preserved in his memory since childhood, and he felt joy that they had not been able to seduce him, although there was some murkiness *in everything,* even in this seduction, as even that was also murky if he thought about it, how those ancient pictures of the Acropolis never really had any contours, how they never even had any clarity, especially in regard to the proportions, that is he could never picture to himself how large the Acropolis actually was and how big its buildings were—how big, for instance, was the Propylaea, and how big was the Parthenon—one could not, that is, on the basis of descriptions or drawings or photographs, be sure of the dimensions, if one tried to judge the size of this temenos, as the Athenians called the district of their sacred buildings; it was impossible, and this was somehow a great problem, that one could not be sure of the proportions, it made the construction of the entire Acropolis in one's mind nearly impossible; somehow everything depended upon the proportions, he always felt this, and he thought so now as well, as he went along the street; he bought a sandwich for an exorbitant sum, he drank a can of more or less chilled cola for an even more shameless price, but it didn't matter, as the only thing that mattered was that he was getting ever closer to the Acropolis in the scorching heat, and that he was going to see the Temple of Nike, and he was going to see the Erechtheion, and of course, crowning it all, the unsurpassable Parthenon—and most of all he would be up on the summit of the Acropolis, for he had always wished for this, he wished for it now as well, as a farewell, he wanted to see it very much, as the Greeks had seen it, let's say, 2439 years ago.

He went along the Voulis into the district of Plaka, and in reality only a few hundred tourists were wandering toward him, beside him, or leaving him behind, so he could have even described himself as lucky; then he progressed for a while along Flessa, at one point he got lost, and he was confused, and he had no idea if it was right to continue along the Odos Erechtheus; in any event he continued along that street and after the narrow alleyways of Stratonos and Thrasyllou he suddenly came upon a wide street with busy traffic called Dionysiou Areopagitou, from where he could already see the temenos high above, true, it had suddenly been visible at one point or another previously, when in the narrow alleyways now and then a gap opened up for a fleeting moment, but now on this Dionysiou Areopagitou he saw it for the first time in its entirety, and that also meant for the first time in his life—and from this point on, for a good while, nothing concerned him, he judged that he was close to his goal, that he was at the foot of the Acropolis; even to think that thought was beautiful, the sun was scorching dreadfully, the traffic was horrendous, it could have been around ten or eleven o'clock, he didn't know exactly, his watch had stopped on the plane coming here as he had forgotten to have the battery changed, and now this already ... what, he thought to himself, it's not enough just to be here?!—and he trudged along in the scorching heat, but there were suspiciously few tourists headed this way, indeed, he was seeing ever fewer and fewer tourists, no matter, he was not dissuaded, for here at his right was the Acropolis, at one point he would arrive at the way up, and if he had to go around the entire thing, he would go around it, and that was that, who cares, he reassured himself happily, but he went along this street for really quite a long time, the air had a dreadful stench which he had to suck in, and the noise from the traffic was practically unbearable; and he had just decided to ask directions from the very next passerby, when suddenly he came upon a serpentine path, reinforced with limestone, zigzagging upward, and he saw up there, at the summit of the long upward-rising path, a kind of booth; he climbed up the path with difficulty and the booth was a ticket counter, but the sign on it did not say tamio; but upon it was written AKROPOLIS, which he saw as laughable, for it was as if they had written on the path leading up here, dromos, which was a path, as everyone knew, and here is the Acropolis, so what was the point, probably for the entrance fee, he thought, and that surely was the reason, for an entrance fee was collected, a particularly high entrance fee at that, at first it was twelve euros, then when he protested, gesticulating, it was six euros, at last he had his ticket, he could go in, and he set off, glancing upward to see that here was the Acropolis, but he couldn't bear the light, he had to look down; but it wasn't even such a simple matter as that, for he looked down to rest his eyes in some patch of darker shade down below along the path, and he couldn't do it, as the path simply *did not have any darker shades*, the paving below his feet blinded him just as much as that from which he had quickly averted his gaze; the paving below was of white marble, that is to say, the same material from which the steps were made, and no blade of grass or weed whatsoever sprouted up, upward he went and he only knew that he was beside the Propylaea, in the new entranceway to the Acropolis, which had been built by Mnesicles, and he groped his way upward knowing that there on the left rose the so-called Pinacotheca of the Propylaea, and on the right was the garrison building, then high above it the Temple of Athena Nike, with its four wondrous columns; but he only knew this, he couldn't see anything, he just went upward, squinting, for so he had resolved: fine, so here I am blinded, well then, after the steps I'll find a spot underneath a tree or I'll take cover in a building and have a rest, and then I'll come back here, and I will examine the Propylaea more thoroughly, and so he stumbled on, but the path leading through the Propylaea not only did not improve things, but actually made them worse, for instead of soil, limestone covered everything; the entire temenos was built on a colossal snow-white limestone cliff, and so the path into it ran along a blinding limestone surface among cunning little pieces of limestone; the Acropolis, he stated to himself, his eyes dazzled, was therefore completely, in its entirety, set out on a mass of pure limestone on this bare mountain; this Acropolis, he thought, stupefied, but for a while he still did not dare to completely think about what it meant that the mountain was *completely* bare, that there was nothing, but nothing apart from the limestone cliff, and the famous temples on the limestone cliff, built from varying materials, but partially from Pentelikon white marble, he did not dare to think about it, because he could not really believe it, so that he just went on, he tried to keep his eyelids lowered so that he wouldn't fall flat on his face, but so as to also not let in the dreadful scorching fire of the sun, because the sunlight truly proved to be merciless, although it didn't bother him that his skull, his back, his arms, his legs, everything was burning, he somehow withstood this, but what completely astounded him, the grave import of which he was not at all aware, was the effect of the sunlight on the limestone, he was not prepared for this intense, ghastly brilliance, nor could he have been, and why, what kind of guidebook, what kind of art-historical treatise relates such information as watch out, the sunlight on the Acropolis is so strong that in particular, travelers with weak eyes should definitely take advance precautions, so that he, who consequently belonged to this group of travelers with weak eyes, had not taken any sort of advance precautions at all, with the result that now he could not take any preventive measures, how could he do so—he had nothing with him, just a suitcase, that's it, it flashed through him suddenly, and arriving in front of the shrine of Artemis Brauronia, he decided that the suitcase here in his hand would save him, what luck that he had brought it with him—from which it already was clear just how much he did not, due to the fatigue, heat, and blindness, have his wits about him, as it only occurred to him that the suitcase was certainly not in his hand, but had remained down below in the city with the boy, Maniopulos, when he withdrew to the wall of the shrine to open it and take out a piece of clothing; the sun at this moment was right above his head; no kind of soothing corner, niche, roof, or recess could be seen anywhere, not right here, not further on, the light crashed down on him without obstruction, arrow-straight, vertically, so that there was no shade at all in the entire Acropolis, although he didn't even know that at this point, and therefore he took out, as he had nothing else, a used paper napkin from his jeans pocket, folded it in several places and put it before his eyes, but to his misfortune even the white of the napkin was irritating, so that he pressed the palms of his hands onto his eyes and went forward like that, trusting that, well, sooner or later he would get somewhere, to some resting place, or anyplace where he could retreat and rest his eyes; and he went forward, he went further up on the Acropolis, that place that he had longed, since his childhood, to see the most, and where, as it soon became clear, there was now only him and a German couple in the distance, by the Parthenon, unlike himself, he thought, they of course had come totally prepared, both of them had tropical helmet-like sun visors, they wore wide, dark sunglasses, they had backpacks from which, just as he happened to glance over at them, they pulled out liter bottles of mineral water, as a result of which he felt a torturous thirst, but he could do nothing to quench it, for here—in contrast to his every hope—there was no refreshment stand, as usually was the case in tourist spots, or someone selling drinks or anything like that, *there was simply nothing on the Acropolis, only the Acropolis,* but by now he was suffering very much, he came to the place where Athena's statue had stood and the path continued toward the Erechtheion, but like a blind man, he felt the path before him with his foot, as it was utterly impossible to look up by now, just as it was even to glance upward, tears rolled down from both of his eyes, they weren't hurting yet then, they only really began to hurt when his tears had dried up; he had cried out, so to speak, everything, as he reached the caryatids of the Erechtheion, where he of course could not go in—particularly from here, from the southern side—or even touch the maidens of Karyai with his glance, as the balustrade was high, and thus the caryatids were unreachable, he looked around despairingly, pain stung his eyes, here and there on the rocky surface enormous pieces of cut stone lay, most likely the Dörpfeld Temple, or the remains of the altarpiece of Athena, who knew where they came from, he was in any event able to take in this much in a moment, and then he dared to open his eyes again, and it was as if some god high above took mercy on him for a short time, for he was led to the southwestern façade of the Erechtheion, behind the caryatids, and there he glimpsed a tree, a tree, my God; the blinded worshipper of the Acropolis hurried over there; just that when he got there, he threw his back against the trunk, and attempted to open his eyes; nothing had changed, for he could not bear to open his eyes even here; the tree was a small fig-tree, an almost completely dessicated tiny dwarf of a tree, its stalk-thin trunk with its branches above were so thin, holding up a flimsy crown like it was butterfly wings, through which the light could pass with no obstruction, and when he gazed at the ground at his feet—in disbelief, he didn't even see the shadow of these tiny branches—he then understood that what he had come here for would remain forever unseen by him: not only, he thought bitterly, not only would he never know the scale of the dimensions of the Acropolis, but he was never even going to see the Acropolis, even though he was here at the Acropolis—the gods had not designated the little tree as a place of relief for him, but rather the northern façade of the Erechtheion, there, that is, to the extent that the sun had shifted up there in the heavens, so that the foreground lay in shadow, he ran over there, crazed; the German couple were there already, they were cheerful, the husband was just changing the film in his camera, the lady was eating a huge gyro, they were fat, their complexions almost bursting with health, the gods truly favored them, he noted to himself, growing sadder—sadder and ungrateful, for finally he had reached a spot where he could rest his eyes, tortured by the pain, and generally speaking, when he did open his eyes, it was true, apart from the lower column-stumps of the old Parthenon, he could see nothing at all of the so-called Acropolis that he had longed to see his entire life, because his back was turned to it; well, this is absurd after all, he thought, after he had pulled himself together, and he did not wish in any way to reconcile himself, the Germans set off toward the Parthenon to take pictures, he, however, stayed, for he knew what would happen if he stepped out of the relief-granting prostatis of the Erechtheion, maybe he should try to sleep, he thought, to wait while the sun completed its momentous journey high above, and down here the proportion of sun and shadow would be altered, yet immediately he knew it was a bad idea, for he would not be able to hold out without any water, it was this, precisely this, that he had not foreseen, he should have brought water here—he leaned back against the wall, and he thought of Callicrates and of Ictinos, who had built it, then of Pheidias, who with his enormous gilded ivory statue of Athena had given it meaning, and leaning back against the wall, he pictured himself stepping closer to the Parthenon, indeed, directly, standing there by the wondrous columns of the Parthenon, by the exquisite Doric and Ionic orders of the columns, and he thought about the spaces of the pronaos, the naos and the opistodomos, and he thought about how when all this was built, the temple was still the place of faith, it was the backdrop and the goal of the Panathenaea, and he exerted his throbbing brain to take it all in, to see it all at once, and thus to be able to preserve for himself, as a way of bidding farewell, the most beautiful architectural creation of the western world—and still then, he thought that actually he should weep, because he was here, and yet not here at all, he should weep, because he had attained what he had dreamed of, and yet had not attained it at all.

It was horrible to pick his way down from the Acropolis, horrible to admit that this whole Athens trip had, due to such a ridiculous, commonplace, ordinary detail, turned out to be an ignominious failure; he stumbled downward, shielding his eyes with both hands, and he would have been very happy to kick apart the ticket booth, but of course he didn't kick anything apart, he only wandered, meandered slowly downward on the path in the merciless heat, he reached the traffic of Dionysiou Areopagitou below, and decided that he would head in the other direction around the Acropolis, which he didn't even feel like looking up at anymore, although now he was recovered enough that his eyes down here could bear the light; he could of course have gone back in the same direction that he had arrived from, but he had no desire to, just as he had no desire for anything else from this point on, he was not interested in the National Museum, he was not interested in the Temple of Zeus, he was not interested in the Theater of Dionysus, and he was not interested in the Agora, because he was no longer interested in Athens, and because of that he was not even interested in those points along the way from which he could have had a view from down here of the Acropolis; I spit on the Acropolis, he rashly said to himself aloud, he said it, but it was only the sadness speaking in him, he knew that himself as well, it was sadness for all that was imperceptible here, for he now interpreted it like this, as at first he sought and found a profound symbolic significance in what had happened to him, and rightly so perhaps, so he could somehow endure it, so he could in some way comprehend the events of the past hours, that is his own farewell, the meaning of which was only now slowly beginning to take shape within him, and he only looked at the sidewalk beneath his feet, and everything hurt, chiefly his eyes were still hurting, but his feet were hurting a great deal as well, he had blisters on his heels from his shoes, at every step he had to try to place his weight on his right, and then his left foot, so that they would slide forward a little in the shoes, so his heels wouldn't touch them, and his head was still hurting terribly, as he was hungry, and his stomach was also hurting terribly, he hadn't had a sip of anything for hours, he proceeded in this direction on the narrow sidewalk of the Dionysiou Areopagitou, which seemed longer, indeed unbearably long, and he didn't and didn't look up, because *up there*—as he now began to call the Acropolis so that he wouldn't have to utter the name itself—nothing more remained which, in the course of another attempt, whether tomorrow or tonight, he might see, he knew that it would be futile to return, he would never ever see the reality of the Acropolis, because he came here on the wrong day, because he was born in the wrong time, because he had been born, it was all wrong from the very beginning, he should have known, should have sensed, that today was not the day to begin anything, nor was tomorrow, there were no days before him now, as there had never even been any, just as there was not and never would be a day—as opposed to this one—in which he could have ascended successfully on that upward path of cunningly packed limestone, why had he even embarked upon this—the corners of his mouth were turned down—why was it so urgent, and he berated himself, and hung his head, and, utterly weary, he went on with his bleeding heels in the loathsome shoes along the foot of the Acropolis, and it took a very, very long time until circling it, he went back into a street where he was once before, early that morning, he had turned into it coming here, Stratonos was the name of the little street, then he continued into the Erechtheos, and from there it immediately took him out onto the Apollonos and across to Voulis at the Ermou intersection—and he already saw his companions from that morning on the other side, he hardly wanted to believe what he was seeing, but almost all of them were there, only the one girl, Ela, was missing, he could make out that much from here, from the other side, they noticed him as well, and they were waving at him already, clearly he had the effect on them, when they recognized him, like that of some kind of refreshment in a scorching heat, and it was unspeakably gratifying for him, after so much torture, after so much unnecessary torture up there, to return among them, for as he glimpsed them and his heart began to throb, finally it had somehow been resolved, what it was that made the entire company so attractive, it was, well, precisely the fact that they weren't doing anything and didn't want anything, and that they were good, he thought now, rather moved, in his exhausted state, as he looked at them, and waved across to them, so that, well, it seemed so obvious that the only sensible thing to do was to sit down with them, here in Athens, where this company had accepted him from the very first moment: to sit in their midst, to order an ellinikos kafes, and to become lost here, in Athens, what's the point of wanting anything, so that now, after this dreadful and dreadfully laughable day, nothing seemed quite as ridiculous as when he thought back on how much he had wanted something here this morning, how ridiculous was this entire wanting, when he would have been so much happier staying among them, and drinking yet another ellinikos kafes, and watching the traffic, as the cars, the buses, and the trucks rushed by frenziedly here and there; he felt dead tired, so there was no question of what he was going to do from this point on, he was going to sit down among them, and do nothing, just like them, and eat something and drink something, then there could be another ice-cold ellinikos kafes, and then that sweet, slack, eternal melancholy, and he was going to take off his shoes and he was going to stretch out his legs, and after narrating what had happened to him up there—not sparing self-ironic observations—he himself would take part in the general mirth as to how could someone be such an idiot as to come to Athens in the summer, and then, on the very first day climb up to the Acropolis in the strongest sunshine, be amazed that he saw nothing of the Acropolis, someone like that deserves it, Yorgos was going to say amidst all the laughter, someone like that really demands the title of imbecile, Adonis would add, without a trace of offense, someone like him who on a scorching day goes up to the Acropolis and doesn't even bring sunglasses—they would laugh at that for a while, he thought, here at the intersection: this adventurer of the Acropolis, and perhaps it would be at this point, namely, that he would say why he had set off without sunglasses, it was because the Acropolis in sunglasses has nothing to do with the Acropolis; they waved to him again to stop dilly-dallying, to come over already, he, however, from a feeling of joy that actually here he was a little bit at home, at home among his new friends, set off without a thought into the dense traffic toward the terrace on the other side, and was immediately, in the blink of an eye, struck down, and crushed to death on the inner lane by a fast-moving truck.

13

HE RISES AT DAWN

He rises at dawn, more or less at the same time as the birds; he is a bad sleeper, only falling asleep is easy for him—in the evenings this happens quite often, although afterward there are frequent startled awakenings, where he's drenched in sweat, worn out from a dream, and it goes on like this till dawn, when finally the skies begin to turn gray in the neighborhood of Kita, located above the Koetsuji Temple in Shakadani, after each difficult night he gets up in the large house in which he lives alone, and it's as if he is not only living alone in the house, but in the entire vicinity, as this is one of the most expensive residential areas in Kyōto, the expensive neighborhoods are nonetheless always the quietest, the most depopulated, in a word the most inhuman as well, there is no sign at all that people live in the buildings next door, even more solitary than his; at times, now and then, a car passes by very cautiously and quietly, someone is going somewhere, someone is returning home, but it is as if they too were alone, if there even was anyone at all like him; he has lived for long, indeterminable years alone in the enormous, impeccably outfitted and tidy house; very frequently three or four days can pass without him talking to anyone, or wanting to talk to anyone, and even then it is usually by telephone; he has no domestic animals, he does not use any devices to play music, he only has a battered TV, and an even more battered computer, and a little garden in the tiny courtyard behind the house, he lives, in a word, in total silence, it seems fairly likely that he wants to live in total silence, and the reason why is an enigma, just as his entire life is an enigma, which means that he is entirely concealed between the early evening slumber and the awakening at dawn, something is barricaded off, inasmuch as the inclination, the unconditional demand for complete silence, for solitude, for cleanliness and order definitely creates the impression that there is a story behind it, but then what this story could possibly be is a secret which he conscientiously watches over, if at times he takes on a few students for a short period, or if now and then on some evening or another an occasional friend spends some time with him—nothing from the story can ever be glimpsed, everything is well concealed: the early slumber, the bad nights, the awakenings at dawn, then a quick breakfast, often taken standing up in the Western-style kitchen facing out onto the garden, and he goes up already to the first floor, where he has set up his studio in a little room facing south, as the light there is the strongest, at times even excessively strong and excessively sharp, so that during the long summers, which last from May to September, he must frequently draw the curtain across the window, and he sits down in the middle of the studio in a work-box carpentered by himself and the work-box faces the windows, he sits, then, from early morning to early evening in this box, where—you could say—everything is within arm's reach; he puts on his glasses, draws his legs together and lowers himself down; then he takes a piece of hinoki cyprus into his lap, he looks at it, turning it around, he prepared it already yesterday, that is to say he cut it to measure, to the desired rectangular size, indeed, he has, using the cardboard stencil, already drawn the chief contours onto it, and it is these now that he is looking at, as well as the two little photographs of the model, placed in the work-box in front of him near his legs, in the photographs a hannya mask can be seen, a mask, with its demonically terrifying features, known as the shiro-hannya mask, used in the Aoi no Ue Noh drama, this is the ideal to be sought, he must, in his own way, be up to that task, the creation of which he plunges into automatically, which for the most part tends to last one and a half or two months, maybe a little shorter for a hannya mask—it always depends on how much work he gets done in a day, and has successfully this work turns out—a month and a half, so, roughly, that much time, here on the tatami placed in his work-box from early morning to early evening, and as for speaking, he doesn't speak, not even to himself; if he makes any sounds at all, it's only that he is lifting the piece of wood and quietly blowing off the wood shavings chiseled off the mask, and sometimes when he changes his physical position in the work-box and sighs while doing so, and once again he bends toward the block of wood, for at first it all begins with the Okari wood-merchant located in the one-time Imperial Palace, below Gosho to the south, in the person of Okari-san, who is of about the same stature as he, therefore very short, a good fifteen years older, and fairly gloomy, Okari-san, from whom he has been buying wood for years—he just bought this newer piece—he trusts him, the price is always good, the annual rings are thin and dense, the lines are without defects, namely the hinoki from which the chosen block of wood originates grew slowly; in addition, the wood is delivered from Bishu, in the prefecture of Gifu, from a forest that has the highest reputation, from a forest renowned for the quality of its material—the whole thing is a simple rectangular-shaped block of wood, that is how it all begins, with the circular cutting with the saw on the basis of the stencil to the desired proportions; he does not think, because he doesn't have to, his hand moves by its own accord, he does not have to control its direction, the saw and the chisels know by themselves what they have to do, so it is no wonder that this first, this very first phase of the work is the fastest, the most free from the later, frequently tormenting anxiety; the saw, the large chisel, the mallet, then the vacuuming up of the wood shavings, just like that, he sits in his work-box, using a small vacuum cleaner adapted to his own needs, so that nothing will remain outside of the work-box, no dirt whatsoever on the sensitive tatami, that is what the work-box, where he is sitting, is for, from where, reaching out, he vacuums, and in which the level of wood shavings is growing ever higher; it is so that in the midst of working he can somehow keep up a little cleanliness, he removes the larger pieces with the saw, then with the large chisel and mallet, but this occurs only in the first few days; later, beginning the third of fourth day, he naturally uses ever smaller chisels, varying in degrees of sharpness, and he no longer strikes the chisel with the hammer, but holds it in his hands, and in this way, holding the block of wood tightly in his left hand, he chisels into the soft material, using tiny, accurate, certain and quick movements with his right hand, but always in such a way that he simultaneously holds up the exact stencil needed—taken from countless others—up to the surface being worked upon; he prepares an enormous quantity of stencils in advance from the so-called original, which is usually lent to him under a tight deadline, that is, for a maximum of two or three days, by the owner—then he takes down, let's say, the measurements, as he cuts out an enormous quantity of cardboard sheets based upon this original, so that there are specifications accurate within a hair's width, for the forehead, the eyebrows, the eyes, the nose, the cheeks, the chin, and every other single detail of the face, horizontally and vertically, diagonally, and in relation to all the other parts as well, in a word, from every possible dimension, every important angle of vision, these are the stencils, only the stencils, so that in the first two weeks only the outlines of the stencils—taken and drawn from the original, then cut out from cardboard—assist the chisel in his hand, so that their significance is, accordingly, huge, and that is why if someone were able to look at him from afar, which of course would be impossible, as there is no way this could ever happen, then that someone would see something like a person such as Ito Ryōsuke of the Kanze school, the Noh master mask-maker, who just now is chiseling something, and is already trying out the necessary stencil to see if things are proceeding in the right direction—was this last bit of stenciling correct, how much is still missing for this and precisely this proportion—proportion to the whole!—to be completed, to see consequently how much there is still to be carved away, so that the expression will then faultlessly emerge in the Noh mask, made from the block of hinoki-cypress, the original expression as seen upon a hannya mask on the theater stages of the Kanze-school in Kyōto or Osaka is what he has in mind; he saws, he chisels, he cleans up, then he just chisels and blows away the shavings of the soft hinoki, and if he is making it for the Kanze ultimately—as for a commission, there usually are none—the matter begins with him seeing a Noh play, and he sees in the Noh—for instance, as in this case—he sees Aoi no Ue, and in that he sees a hannya mask on the main character known as the shite, then he pictures a different mask from the one he saw, and from that, the feeling that he has seen a Noh mask arises, but he doesn't want one like that, but another one of that sort has just come into his mind, well, then, he wants to carve one himself, but for this naturally he needs a mask that is as close as possible to what he wants, and naturally he needs a hannya mask from his master, the famous Hori Yasuemon, hence he needs one to prepare the stencils from and the other to use as a model; he has hardly begun, here it is already the third or fourth day when the piece of word he is working on is now drawing toward the imagined end result, he can essentially tell less and less what is going to happen on a given day, in terms of the coarsened view of things, his life is filled with successive imperceptible changes, all the while with every tiny, exact, certain, and quick carving, he gets closer and closer to the mask he has sensed, it's just that until that point, so very many days and so very many hours, so many early mornings and noontimes and evenings are yet needed, roughly a month and half's worth of them, perhaps two entire months; he may be uncertain, and with the details burnished together with more difficulty; or—as does occur now and then—he may make a mistake, and have to to correct it, it is a loss of time, although he works quickly, as mostly he works by natural light, he chisels, he lifts it up, he blows away the shavings, he tests the stencil, and he chisels again, the silence is great, inside the house it is complete, and from outside only very rarely do sounds filter in, so that it is he in the first place who breaks the silence, and most often, amidst his rapid movements, by putting down now and then the chisel on the floor of the box, or little further away, but still next to him, he puts it outside of the work-box, on the tatami mat; he puts it down, or rather in the vehemence of movement he tosses it down, he lets drop a chisel in order to exchange it for another, or holding it away from himself he looks at the mask from a distance, and at such times it happens that the chisel he has tossed down makes a loud clattering sound as it hits against the others, but usually there is just the sound of breathing, a dull thump, as he sometimes changes his bodily position in the box, and he sighs, there are no other sounds, essentially he works in total silence, from early morning to early evening, that is to say more precisely, first from early morning until noon, as he then takes a short break for so-called lunch-time—this cannot exceed one half-hour, although in contrast to breakfast he sits down at lunchtime, either inside, in the kitchen, or if the weather is good, by the little table set up in the shady garden; he eats for the most part, only vegetables, meat almost never, perhaps fish, but for the most part vegetables and more vegetables, he starts with some kurama vegetables, cut into thin strips and marinated in sour brine, then a miso soup follows, then with his favourite gemma rice, three or four fried avocado halves, fried mushrooms, fried tofu, cooked bamboo, or he makes an udon or a soba, with perhaps yube, that is, tofu-skin, soybean sprouts, or clustered edamame beans, finally there may be a little natto—fermented soy bean—then a little sour plum, namely the umeboshi, which he particularly likes; all the while just mineral water and mineral water, and all of this of course within the space of only one half-hour, because he has to work, he has to go back to the studio, because in the meantime, while he has been eating, he didn't even really break away from that phase of work or that problem to be solved, from which he only somewhat distanced himself during lunchtime, so that already he is up there, on the second floor, he lowers himself down into the work-box, he picks up and holds the mask he's preparing at a distance, and he looks, slowly turning it around in his hands, he looks, at last, with a somber face; he begins again, he takes the chisel, he blows away the shavings, he raises the mask, looking at it, then he takes it and chisels into it again, he holds the stencil up to it, and he chisels and he blows, and he looks, then he chisels into it again, he holds the stencil up to it, and he chisels, and he blows, and he looks, and in the meantime, he doesn't, as it were, think about anything, particularly not about whether he is now preparing a wonderful hannya mask, or just a satisfactory one, within him there is no desire for the exquisite; if there ever even was, his master taught him in his youth—or rather fulfilling the prophecy of his master, his own experience taught him that if there is within him the desire to create an exquisite mask, then he will unavoidably and unconditionally create the ugliest mask possible, this is always, and is unconditionally always so, hence for a long time now that desire has not been within him, to put it precisely, there is nothing at all within him, the thoughts don't whirl around, his head is empty as is if he had been stunned by something; only his hand knows, the chisel knows why this must happen; his head has become empty, but in a sharp way, however, it is sharp when his hands hold up the mask under preparation, and he looks at it to see if things are proceeding in the right direction, only then is his head clear, but only while he is still looking at the mask under preparation; then he lets it fall back into his lap, and his hand, holding the chisel, sets to the task again, then again his head is not clear, but rather completely and immediately empty; various thoughts extinguishing each other do not twist and turn, whirl and swirl, do not wriggle here and there, only the complete emptiness in his head, there is the complete emptiness in the house, and there isn't even anything in particular to think about, for there is emptiness in the house, and there is emptiness in the neighborhood, and if someone were to inquire of him, as the students, taken on for short periods, in every single instance are wont to do, asking for example, how from this piece of hinoki there will emerge a mask—it is free, in his view, from all mystical intervention; that is, after a series of not particularly special sculptural operations, the mask will in his judgment be completed—a Noh mask that will terrify people; in other words what makes something like this spellbinding, what makes it not spellbinding—what are the fine or not-so-fine differentiations that decide this question, particularly, by the comprehending eye, unequivocally and immediately—whether the work here has been successful and the mask is splendid, or just an awkward, a painfully unskillful ignominious disaster, and thus not even worthy of mention; finally, what does the Noh want, what is the Aoi no Ue, by chance, all about, and so on, such questions, in his studio inside his work-box, visibly trouble him, not only because the mere fact of someone asking him any question at all troubles him, but in his completely empty head, there is really nothing with which, even if he were to rely on it, he could, for that matter, reply, he does not to occupy himself with such questions as what is the Noh, and what makes a mask "spellbinding," he merely occupies himself with doing the very best he can within the limits of his abilities, and with the aid of prayers recited secretly in shrines; he only knows movements, methods of work—chiseling, carving, polishing—that is to say the method, the entire practical order of operations, but not the so-called "big questions," he has absolutely no business with those, no one ever taught him what to do with that, so that this empty head always was and always remains his only response, a head that contains nothing in response to questions that contain nothing, but how can this be stated, there's no way, especially to the students coming from the West, so that at such times the situation is such that an empty head stands facing the seemingly weighty, unexpected, and—due to their unexpected nature—even too crudely grasping questions, and not only does he not have any answers, but it is also very hard for him to cope with having to break the silence to say something, so that he begins to stammer, in the strict sense of the word he stammers when he speaks, as if he were searching for the English word in the language of his visitors, he would, however find it faultlessly and quickly if he were in the habit of using language, any language; he stammers out something, but it is, as he himself knows full well, not even audible, and he himself sees that it can't go on like this, the students mutely, a little dumbfounded, prod him on to say something already, something essential, but well, what can he do, nothing essential to reply to the posed question comes to mind, his head is buzzing, he tries to step out of the vortex in which he lives, he tries to understand the glances of the visitors who have questions and who would listen, and it seems that he is hoping that finally he won't have to say anything at all, but then it appears that well, this hope is in vain, for the gazes—curious and insistent, urging him to say something already, for god's sake—are fixated upon him; then he pulls himself together, and he says something in reference to the given question, very cautiously and circumspectly, with elegant restraint, and refraining from using big words, he says something, something about the mask, that here is such and such a mask, and in a certain play, it more or less means this and this, but when it comes to what does the Noh want, or what is the essence of the Noh, and so forth—the dreadfully tactless questions—he doesn't know what to do, he genuinely doesn't understand, he can't even understand how someone can even ask such a question, the kinds of questions children ask, if at all, not grown-up people, there is no place for such questions here, in the simple studio of a simple maker of Noh masks, as he calls himself; for that, Ito Ryōsuke says, stammering, we would have to ask the great masters, not him, he just does what he can within the limits of his abilities, but he doesn't want to hurt their feelings when he sees, on the faces of these Western students admitted to his studio for a brief time, obvious disappointment, he doesn't want—and not because of them, but rather because of himself—to see this disappointment, it is unpleasant, he still has to say something, so he pulls together with great difficulty a few sentences to answer one of the complicated questions, he musters up something from his memory of what he heard from some great master, and he presents it, haltingly, in his own particular way of speaking, and then the relief in him is far greater when he sees that those around him are satisfied with the response, as this satisfaction can be seen on their faces, so much for that, he leans back again over his work, then looks up occasionally to see if the signs of satisfaction really can be seen on their faces, then he can hardly wait for the visit to come to an end, or for the time that they decided upon to come to a close, but the entire visit has unsettled him so, that when they have finally gone, and he has decided that he will never again, as much as possible, admit anymore Western curiosity-seekers, he is for a long while incapable of returning to his work, he does not sit back down in the work-box, just paces up and down, straightening an object now and then in the studio, then he begins to put things in order, he vacuums up, he arranges the tools around himself as if that were meaningful when he has no need for that now, the proper time for straightening up is at the end of the day; he rises, and he puts everything in order, packing up and cleaning, he is so discomfited after such a meeting that everything in his head churns back and forth, the questions swirl around there in larger and smaller broken fragments: what is the Noh, and what is the meaning of the hannya mask, and how can there be "something sacred" from a simple hinoki tree, but what kinds of questions are these—Ito Ryōsuke shakes his head despairingly—how can this be; and he sighs; when everything has been put back he sits down in his place, takes the piece of hinoki being worked on, holds it at a distance with his left hand and as much as possible, leans back in the work-box, so as yet to see it from the greatest possible distance, he looks at it then lets it fall again into his lap, takes the appropriate chisel in his hand, and he chisels, and he lifts it up, and he blows the wood shavings away, and that night he finishes a little earlier; he packs up again, he puts things in order, he cleans up, so that the next morning the studio will await him as it should every morning; then he goes out of the house, he takes his specially designed bicycle, and sets off before dinner to cycle out of himself all the assembled disturbances of the visit, for that, the bicycle, is his one recreation, and his is a completely particular model, not simply a mountain bike, but a specially designed bike that can do anything, or almost anything, its gears, its ease, its fittings, everything about it is satisfactory—at one point a long time ago, he decided to get one and to begin cycling in the mountains—he turns out from the house, and he is already racing down the steep slope of Shakadani, then within ten minutes he is out by the northern mountains, and now the hardest part begins, the drive to the top, and he gets properly sweaty, he just keeps pressing the pedals going uphill, the perspiration streams down from him by the time he reaches the point he has decided upon that day, but then comes the downward run, and the wondrous, the inexpressible tranquility of the forest, its refreshing beauty, its inconceivable monumentality, its silence and purity, and the fragrance of the air, and the muscles at rest and the speed, as he only has to glide along going down, glide, gliding back into the city, at such times he would be happy not even to use the brakes; this descent is so good, for it takes him back once again to the emptiness that is within him, and which was disturbed; but it has been restored by the time he gets back and puts the bike in its place against the wall of the house, the peace within him is complete, there is no trace whatsoever in his head of confusion or nervousness; he sits outside in the garden or sets the table inside in the kitchen, and he has dinner, so that early tomorrow morning he can sit again with the hannya mask in his hand, holding it at a distance, leaning backward, and looking at it, then taking it into his lap, with his left hand and with his right, he begins to chisel, now with only completely minute movements, just as delicately as he possibly can, for now even a single cut that is too deep or too long can ruin it; so in part he makes ever smaller cuts, in part he still tries out the stencil frequently—at short intervals—to see how much, how much yet he needs to remove in order to finally reach that phase when it is not merely just the stencil, just the stencil, that is when the use of stencils is not enough; this is the point from which he is no longer able to decide if he should remain in the work-box and look at it in his outstretched hand, when it is already not enough for him to turn the mask around as frequently as is possible, slowly, first to one side, then to the other, once looking at the front, and once in semi-profile—the time has arrived, he determines at such moments—as it occurs now—for him to come out of the work-box, and to look at the mask in the special system of mirrors that he has set up; it is hard to decide when a day like that comes, but it does come; when he is leaving off work on an early evening, he feels that it is close; maybe tomorrow, he thinks, then the next day, early in the morning, taking the mask again into his hands, it is clear that it is not maybe, but now, this is the morning, now he must look at it, or to put it more precisely, the time has come to look at it in the mirrors, which are set up in such a fashion that he sits with the mask in his hand, and he faces the open door of the workshop that looks out onto a narrow hallway, as does the small tilting mirror already set up on the tatami behind him but highly visible from his work-box; and then facing him at the end of the narrow hallway, thus a good ten meters away, is a large mirror covering the wall; then there is roughly in the middle of the hallway, temporarily installed, a little tilting mirror, or rather a mirror that can be adjusted to the desired angle; there is also a little mirror on the hallway's ceiling, exactly above the little mirror placed in the middle: this is the system, and he, facing the large mirror, accordingly displays with his right hand the mask to the large mirror, picking it up with greater caution than before and lifting it above his right shoulder; he sees first of all in the large mirror what he is displaying, what he has been doing during these long days, and of course he also sees his own face too and above his right shoulder, the mask at this point in the work-process—but he doesn't look there, of course, but only and exclusively at the mask—slowly, along an invisible central axis—he turns to the right, then suddenly he pulls the mask back, so that, held at a moderate angle, it shows the left profile, as a Shite might do very frequently later on upon the Noh stage, and generally he is not very pleased with these first inspections in the system of mirrors, something is not really right in the face, that is, on his face, his features grow even more somber, if that is possible; he almost speaks, saying something, but then not even that, only the somber face remains, and he sits back down in the work-box, and continues carving at a different tempo, this is therefore always an essential development, this first and then second and third reflection in the mirrors, for a fundamental error always emerges only, but only, in this way, which does not mean that the problem will be solved, just that he suddenly sees that he is going in a wrong direction: something there beneath the eyes, as is the case now, has been deepened too much, or not deepened enough, this must be fixed; he takes up a different kind of chisel than the one he was working with before, but then he stops to think, and he exchanges this chisel for a third one, he bends a little bit forward, and in this different, somewhat more feverish tempo, again he begins to work, at times displaying—so as to check his work—the mask in the little tilting mirror facing him on the tatami, above which, as well, as in the double mirror on the hallway's ceiling, he displays the part to be fixed, he shows it there above his shoulder, but in a curious fashion, as if he weren't even looking, as if he weren't even really examining it again, he holds it up and glances into the little mirror, and he lets the mask fall back already into his lap, as if knowing automatically where the problem is, he does not need the little mirror for that, as if he were saying that he doesn't need any helping devices, he automatically knows that something is not good in the creases under the eyes this time, they are not deep enough, or they are, precisely, too deep, he is perceptibly nervous, only he knows why, that here, in this workshop, one movement can destroy everything, and until he fixes it, it will not be clear if it can be fixed at all; now, however, yes, this time it can be fixed, it is clear as the minutes pass how he takes in air in a more tranquil rhythm, and now really he just casts a glance from time to time, as he holds it up to the little mirror, then he switches to a completely fine chisel, then to sandpaper, and finally he smoothes the detail being worked upon only with his hands, then once again he stands up and sits down facing the large mirror, holding the mask up above his right shoulder, again he turns it slowly a little to the right, then a little to the left, it really is clear that this time he was able to correct the mistake, and how far away the end still is, how many more times shall he make an obvious mistake, the whole thing is as if he were coming down from Nakagawa-cho on the serpentine path, but without braking even once until the end, coming down from the border of Nakagawa-cho, let's say from the bridge over the brook, all the way to Gorufu jō mae—there, where a famous Noh actor lives, if he passes by the Gorufu jō mae, which occurs often as this is one of his favorite bike routes into Nakagawa—he often thinks of this Noh-Shite, that he lives here—just that, never anything else—in a word, that route is from Nakagawa to Gorufu jō mae, well, and who could believe it, that it would be possible to come down from there, from the bridge over the creek to the city—

completely freely, without braking—impossible, he would say, the path is so steep, there are so many turns, and the bicycle would accelerate so much, that in seconds the whole thing would be a labyrinth of speed, and a hairsbreadth wrong movement with the handlebars, for just a split second, and that would be it, the thought itself is unimaginable, this would be the general consensus, and even he wouldn't take it on, even with the special mountain bike; this example, however, frequently comes to mind and not by accident, for even this workshop with its own speed, is at the very least, such a labyrinth, at the very least such a life-threatening, perilous labyrinth, where in every single movement of every single phase of the work there exists the possibility of error, beginning with the question of whether he picked out the correct tree at Okari-san's, whether he ascertained correctly the line-structure of the hinoki—for one must know with utter certainty where the individual lines are placed in the tree, because everything, but everything has to be determined on the basis of these lines, as this decides the location of the central axis, and through that, every single line to be drawn from the stencils—but then comes the drawing of the contours, the decision as to where the tip of the nose will be, then the eyebrows, the forehead, the nostrils of the nose, the depth of the chin, and the ear, he cannot err in any single moment with a single stroke of the chisel, and then where is the end to this—here he isn't even close to the midpoint, when he must deepen the individual contours of the mask, when he can begin carving the surface of the eye socket, the nose, the cheeks, the ears and the mouth, and where is the end to all of this, he isn't even at the midpoint, because the days just come one after the other, and he has to carve out the completely concave back half of the mask, then bore through the place where the eyeballs will be, he must attend to the formation of the mouth and the teeth, and only then can he say that he has arrived more or less at the midpoint of the work, and then comes the point when he takes a small nylon bag filled with lacquer and soaks the mask, as well as the horns, which have been carved in the meantime; then he has to wait a good long while, then take the whole thing out of the lacquer, and then place it in boiling water, then dry it, fit the horns into the right points on the forehead and fasten them into place, and only then comes the gilding of the eyes, then the overlay of the teeth with copper, the entire process now requires a different kind of sensitivity and aptitude from a person who suddenly must be a goldsmith and coppersmith, he must have at his disposal these sensitivities and these aptitudes, just as when the inner surface of the mask is being scraped clean, then painted, first with lacquer, then after drying, with the famed and dangerous urushi, then the whole thing is placed in a special drying appliance, then it is removed from the drying appliance, for then what follows is the actual painting: that is, the spraying of the mask's surface with a white pigment of his own mixture, and then there is the restoration of the gilding of the eyes and the copper overlay of the teeth through the process known as reburnishing, then the application of red paint onto the lips; and in general the operation of the painting of the mask is complex and many-sided—he must paint the hannya mask as well, and he must paint the hair, indeed the individual strands of hair must be painted individually—he must be able to form, on the surface of the mask that is painted white, the blemishes of the skin, its gentle pock marks, and only here, at this point can he say that he is able to begin the last phase of the work, that is, he has to sew from silk, and again, just by himself, the protective pouch for the mask: first to cut out the inner casing from thin white silk, then to prepare the proper lining from torn felt, giving the pouch the soft, thick lining; and finally he has to be able to select, and to select correctly, from the gorgeous woven silks of varying patterns, the one that is truly suitable, the one that will be fitting for this mask and this mask only, then to cut that out as well, and sew the whole thing together, and all of this without a single mistake, but this is impossible: I frequently make mistakes, he has acknowledged to his students—who are admitted again and again into his studio for only brief periods, only from time to time—frequently, he says to them, smiling and nodding; he does not in general show his worry, yet it is perceptible that, at such times, he is angry, in vain does he smile, because one cannot make any mistakes at all, he explains, and despite that, he always and frequently makes mistakes, not to mention the one instance that really threatens him with complete nervous collapse, when the entire completed mask is a mistake, if he may explain it like that, namely that when he has been looking at a mask for two or three days with pleasure, when he feels that he can inspect it with satisfaction, because this mask—clearly thanks to chance—has been successfully completed, then suddenly he just senses a chill around his heart, and he is looking at it with a cold and impartial feeling, he immediately sees that it is bad, that he has ruined it, and do you know why, he then raises his eyebrows, and he himself immediately supplies the answer, at this point he never stammers, he looks around at the students, who are there only occasionally: because no one can make a good mask by chance, to make a good mask by chance is impossible, chance has absolutely no role whatsoever in this, all the while you can't know of course what does have a role; maybe, he lowers his voice, practice and experience have a role, and only these two things, nothing else, because the mask is just a piece of wood, a painted and carved piece of wood, on the surface of which we glimpse a face, and he can even say this now, and he feels this now too, when the day arrives, pronouncing his latest work, known thus by its exact name, shiro-hannya, the demon-head created for the Noh play entitled Aoi no Ue; he sets to sewing the silk pouch and then he sews it, and he looks for a while at the terrifying creature, at the monster with its huge gaping mouth, its bulging eyes, and the horns on its forehead; he looks at it, he examines his latest masterwork, then he carefully puts it into its final place, into the silk pouch, and he doesn't even suspect yet—the thought never even occurs to him—that in the space of hardly more than a month and a half, what his hands have brought into the world is a demon, and that it will do harm.

21

A MURDERER IS BORN

He set off from the deepest of hatreds and arrived, from deep below, and from far away, from so far below and so far away—that then, at the beginning of the beginning, he had not the slightest idea where he was heading; indeed, he didn't even suspect that there was a route toward anything at all, he had come to hate the country where he lived, come to hate the city where he resided, come to hate the people among whom he stepped onto the metro every morning at dawn, and with whom he traveled home in the evening, it is futile, he said to himself, I have no one here, nothing ties me to this place, let the whole thing go to hell and rot away; since for a good long while he could not decide, he just went with the morning metro and came back with the evening one, back home, and when the day arrived, one morning at dawn, that he no longer stepped onto that metro with the others, he just stood for a while on the platform, there was nothing in his head, he just stood, and he was pushed around, here and there; he picked up one of the free advertising newspapers, then had a beer standing at the counter, and he looked at the want ads and picked out a country along with a job offer, because he knew nothing about it, Spain, that's a good distance away, so let it be Spain, and from that point on things sped up, and a cheap airline was already dragging him along, he was traveling by plane for the first time in his life, yet he felt nothing other than fear and hatred, for he was afraid of them: he hated the self-confident stewardesses, the self-confident travelers, and even the self-confident clouds that whirled around below him, and he hated the sun and the sparkling light as well—and then he was nearly plummeting down, plummeting down straight into that city, and hardly had he set foot here then he had already been swindled, for of course there was no job behind the job offer, and the money he had saved up was almost immediately gone—it had gone toward the traveling, accommodation for the first few days, and food, so that he could start here, there was no going back, no going back at all—he could start to look for work in this foreign land, which of course he didn't find, everywhere the "Romanian vagrants" and those of their ilk were chased away, he just wandered around in this beautiful city, and no one would give him any kind of work, and a week passed, and then another and then another, and then another Saturday came along again, so he set off, alone as always, for the city, but this time without hope of work, the weekends were particularly the worst, but he just sauntered, from hate, into it, into anywhere, from one Barcelona street to the next, in the thick Saturday-night multitude of people inebriated by wealth and the pleasures of life; he only had fifty euros, hunger gnawed uselessly in his stomach, he didn't dare to go in anywhere, because, of course, of his clothes, in these clothes—he looked at himself—it was completely understandable if they wouldn't let him in anywhere here, and then it happened, he was at that moment walking down the Passeig de Gràcia, that the crowd of people at the intersection swelled to such a density, and all of them in such elegant clothing swelled together and he was forced to stop, he withdrew next to a wall and looked at them from there, because he just didn't want to be swept along from there, to move on from there, so he stayed by the wall, and because his back was pressed against it, he began to look at the building behind him and he was completely stupefied, for he had already seen many similar perversities in this city, but never anything like this; yet he had come this way before, he must have seen this one as well, but he had passed it in vain, he hadn't noticed it until now, which was already strange enough, he thought, because this building at the corner of the Passeig de Gràcia and the Carrer de Provença was so colossal, so unwieldy, it weighed down so heavily on the intersection that actually it would be hard not to notice, he slouched further along the wall, then spotted a tourist plaque introducing this spot, which stated that this was the Casa Míla and below, in parentheses, that it was La Pedrera—it was indicating this place precisely—so that this had to mean that the name of the building was Casa Míla, that is, it must be some kind of famous building, well of course, he thought, here in Barcelona, in this district, they could put that on a lot of buildings, not even because it was famous but because it was built by a lunatic, then he took a closer look at the façade, at least as much as he could in the throng of people, and although it was much, but really much uglier than the others, he disliked it for exactly the same reason as he did its companions, as in general he did not like anything that was not *orderly*, and this was very much not so, this looked like a gigantic stomach, like a huge gut that had somehow, due to its weight, plopped out onto the sidewalk and sprawled there, it sickened him, indeed: now that he looked more closely at the colossal weighty façade, it somehow began to enervate him, to oppress him, he found it in every sense of the word repugnant, and he could not understand why someone had been deliberately allowed to build something like this, in this loathsomely beautiful and rich city; it could have been half-past five and it was still completely light, only he called it evening, as for him half-past five was still evening, he couldn't help it, the multitudes desirous of entertainment or shopping just undulated on and on, turned, whirled at the corner, and wouldn't let him go any further so he could get away from here unimpeded, on the contrary when he noticed that the entire thing seemed to be growing, even swelling, and not only here in the intersection but in both directions along the Passeig de Gràcia, he then decided that he would leave the neighborhood, go into the Carrer de

Provença, and try to find some much, much cheaper neighborhood, one suitable for him, which on the one hand would be along the way to his new free accommodations, and where also he could finally eat something; and he went along the wall for a bit—to be completely accurate, the distance of a few steps—to an open entranceway, clearly the entrance of that La Pedrera itself, or whatever they called it; he looked in, but saw inside there not a single living soul, only a kind of ornamental staircase decorated with morbid ivy-tendrils that somehow curled, morbidly, upward in the slightly darkened entrance hall, they curled between five dreadfully hideous columns and some kind of painted marble-like wall; there must be some kind of event taking place inside, a wedding or something like that, he thought, but he didn't move from the entrance, he just waited, waited for a guard to appear, or a valet, or someone like that, he was positive that this would happen, because he nearly wanted them to throw him out, but no one appeared so that, led on by a quick and foolish idea, he made a step toward the inside, and loitered there for a minute, looking around in the entrance hall that was obviously carved and painted in the most insane way possible, he loitered and … no one came, there was such silence as if this Saturday evening rabble, heaving and straining, were not clamoring right outside the entrance a few meters from here—silence, this was really strange, the door was open, he set off along the five columns up the ornamented staircase, he knew how insolent he was being, for surely if anyone had no business being there it was he; just out of curiosity, a voice said within, I'll go a bit further up out of curiosity, and so he reached the first floor, where he again found a wide-open door, but the strangest thing was that there was no one even here, he was certain that he wouldn't be able to go any farther, but no, inside, past the wide-open door a longish corridor opened up, in the corridor, there was only an empty table and an empty chair standing orphaned on the side there, he stepped into the corridor, and he noticed that to the left of the table there was a similarly opened, narrower door, then he saw eight steps leading upward, and still beyond that, looking from down here, another space opened up, or a room—he stood on his tiptoes, the better to see, very cautiously, what was up inside there, but up inside, in that raised room, only a dim obscurity appeared to him, from which further dimly obscure rooms opened up, and in the rooms there was not, as far as he could judge from here by the entrance in front of the eight steps, a single living soul; on the walls in these rooms were some kind of old-fashioned religious pictures, old-fashioned and beautiful and not right for this place, they all shone with gold, oh no, he thought, now he really had to leave, and he turned around uncertainly, like someone wishing to return to the main corridor and from here down the stairs and out into the street, he would run and, uninhibitedly, he would breathe the air deeply in at last, for here he was completely holding his breath; but even then he didn't leave, he just took a few steps toward the opened door next to the table, he looked at the eight upward steps that led into the first room and looked again into that first room; suddenly these gilded pictures had begun to attract him; he didn't want to steal them, no such thought arose in him—more precisely it did arise but he immediately chased it away—he wanted to see how they shone, really just to look a little bit more, at least until they threw him out, since he didn't have anything to do anyway, when suddenly, from behind his back, there came from outside, from the ornamented staircase, with such faint steps that he didn't even hear them, a middle-aged, well-dressed couple, arm in arm, they separated behind him, walked around him, and then returned to each other's side, and in the meantime the person they had walked around trembled barely perceptibly with his entire body, the woman slipped her arm through the man's again and they headed up the eight steps and stepped into the room, disappearing from view there, which decided the question of whether he should go in or not, as he immediately started after them, whatever happens will happen, at the very most they would throw him out, whatever, even then he would see a little more of what had shone in his eyes so much from below, so that he too, his legs still slightly trembling, went up the eight steps, and stepping across the threshold, he ventured in after the middle-aged couple—it was dark, moreover there were only lights above the individual pictures; he didn't stop right away but went in further to create the impression that he was already inside, indeed, maybe even more inside than those who had come up from behind him, so that it was not the first picture, not the second, and he didn't even know how many pictures it was, and suddenly Jesus Christ was looking at him, sitting on a kind of throne in the middle of a triptych, in one hand he held a book, namely the Scripture, which was open, and in the other he was ominously signaling something to him who was looking, signaling outward from the picture, and really, everything around him shone—they made it with gold leaf, he determined, as earlier he had been in restorers' workshops, even if now he was only on building sites; with gold leaf—he leaned closer, but almost immediately stepped quickly back—the gold leaf almost adheres to the base by itself, clearly this had been prepared with it—he looked at Christ, but strongly avoided looking into his eyes even once, for this Christ, although he knew it was only a painting, stared at him so sternly that the gaze could hardly be borne—it was, moreover, beautiful—that was the only word for it, beautiful—and a bit as if the painter had painted it in a time when people didn't yet know how to paint properly, or at least it seemed so to him, for there was something elementary in the formation of the head and in the entire picture, in the background there was no landscape at all or any buildings as he was used to seeing in church paintings, there were only angels with bent heads, and saints with bent heads, and everywhere the illumination of this gold, and in a surprising way this showed Christ from completely close-up, so close that after a while he had to step back, because it's too close, he thought, and he also blamed it on the painter; he suspected that these primitive pictures had been exhibited here on purpose, as well as in the subsequent rooms, in every space he could glimpse from here, as he also immediately perceived that there were some people in the farther rooms, and then he thought right away that it would be better to sidle backward; yet a long moment followed, and they didn't come to usher him out, moreover, one of the people dispersed in the farther rooms came here, into the room where he was, and took no notice of him, then he thought, he's just a visitor, *just like me*, and he began to feel more self-confident, and he looked at the Christ some more, but he didn't see anything, he was not observing the picture but what the person next to him was doing; but he wasn't doing anything, only going from one picture to the next, he's really not a guard, he thought, finally relaxing, and he looked again at the Christ, above Him there was something like a very faint cross-hatching, but impossible to decipher, and so he tried to read what was written below the picture which might as well have been in Catalan, as he didn't understand a word, then he took one step farther to the next picture; the background of that one was also completely gold, and it could have been made a very long time ago, because the wood on which it had been painted was already thoroughly chewed up by woodworms and the paints were peeling off to a considerable degree, but what he saw was very *beautiful* again, the Virgin Mother sat there in a picture within the picture, the Infant on her arm; the Infant particularly pleased him, as he pressed his little face as close as he could to the Virgin Mary's, who however was not looking at the Infant but somehow in front of herself, outside of the picture, at him, who was looking at it, and her gaze was very sad, as if she knew what would happen later to her little son, such that he stopped looking at her and stared at the gold background until it dazzled him, and the third picture and the fourth picture and the fifth picture were all very similar, they were all painted onto wood, they all had gold backgrounds, in all of them the Virgin or Christ, or some Saint, were childishly painted, for there was some kind of Saint in each picture, frequently there were several, but the essential thing, he determined, was that these Marys and Jesuses and Saints, painted in vivid colors with gold backgrounds, were—well, as if children had created them, at least that's what came to his mind—of course then he tossed it away as nonsense, for what could be expected of him anyway, he didn't understand, he had, it was true, once worked for a few months in an art restorer's workshop, but still!—anything here, well no, what he saw was certainly not childish, rather just only . . . probably very old, he concurred with himself, so old that people didn't know the rules of painting, or that painting could have had a different set of rules; he went from one to the other, here leaning his head to the left and there leaning it to the right, and if the strained readiness to jump out of there at the first ominous sign had not ceased in him, he now lingered in front of each picture in a more orderly way, because not including the Christ here at the end of the room, whose stern gaze he had encountered at the very beginning, the rest of the Saints, the Infants, and the Kings looked at him with complete tenderness, so that he really did calm down a little, and still no one came to put him in his place or to ask for an entrance ticket, if it was an exhibit, it remained so, indeed, he didn't go back into the first room he had blindly hurried across when he first came in, he continued on into the next one, where it was just as dark and where only little lamps also illuminated each one of the pictures from above, here too were the Saints with the Virgin Mary or with Christ, here too was no end of gold and illumination, which practically radiated out from them, as if they didn't need a single lamp above them, because the light came from within them; he walked up and down with complete self-confidence now, given his circumstances, he went from one room to the next, he looked at the Saints and the Kings and the other Beatified Ones, and instead of feeling gratitude to the heavens for being able to be here undisturbed, he was overcome—exactly in that place where the eternal hatred was—by a kind of sadness, and he felt alone—ever since he had arrived here, he hadn't felt anything like that; he stared at the illumination, he stared at the gold leaf, and something began to hurt violently within him, and he didn't know what it was: if it was really being alone that hurt so much, the pain coming upon him suddenly; or that he had wandered into this happenstance so dispossessed, while everyone outside was wandering around so happily; or if it was that immeasurable distance that hurt so much, making him realize how unbearably far away were these Saints, these Kings, these Beatified Ones, Marys and Christs—and that illumination.

The influence of Byzantium and Constantinople was immeasurable, but of course that statement needs to be amended, for without Byzantium and Constantinople not even the Slavs themselves would have assumed Christianity across such a vast area, so, of course, it is natural that, on the subject of icon-painting, everything goes back to Byzantine origins, everything points in that direction, to the Byzantine Greek Orthodoxy; from there the first miracle-working images emerged, and from these the first miracle-working icon painters emerged; the Russians went to study with them in Byzantium, to the unprecedentedly wealthy and powerful city of Constantinople, preparing for immortality—it was from here that the stern outlines on the motionless face of the mighty Pantokrator that were painted onto the arches and cupolas originated, from here it was transmitted, before anywhere else, to Kiev, then to Novgorod, Pskov, Vladimir and Suzdal, to Radonezh, Pereslavl, Rostov and Yaroslavl, then to Kostroma, and finally to Moscow, to Moscow—all these countless chastising glances, these countless somber Virgin Mothers in mourning, those fierce rhythms, those immobile judgmental colors, and that extraordinary tautness and finality and steadfastness and unshakeable spirit and eternal life, but the Russians created something utterly different, something that was replete with gentle affection, reassurance, peace, sympathy, and reverence; that of course reached consummation only in the fifteenth century, because there—at least in the historical sense, from Kievan Rus' to the Grand Duchy of Moscow, a long road had to be traversed, which moreover should not be envisaged as one unbroken line but as a kind of sketch, the main direction of which is indisputable but which stops from time to time at a certain point, like islands flashing in all directions, radiating outward like stars, leaving a trace on the map of the first five centuries of ancient Russian art, which at last culminates in the icon-painting of Moscow, and creates that tradition which renders it unmistakable, binding together Vladimir's Mother of God and the Virgin of Volokolamsk, and so with that the ancient Russian art of icon painting could come into being—that which did not require time to be born, but immersion, which did not come about in one single process—time, therefore, was not the central element, but rather it was the glimpse, the sudden comprehension, the lightning-quick recognition, the sight of which was incomprehensible, unrecognizable, unseeable—this was the thinking of every saint—from the two sons of the Grand Duke of Kievan Rus', Boris and Gleb, to the igumen of Pecherskaya Lavra, Feodosiy, to the abbot Saint Sergey of the immortal Monastery of the Trinity of Radonezh; truly everyone, the named and the nameless, who took part in this immersion—even those among them already able to feel the wonders of Creation—were aided in this magical atmosphere created by the icon painter, almost always working in complete obscurity; drawing closer, in his own tortuous way to the incomprehensible and the unrecognizable, and the invisible; for the icons explained to them clearly that the world was at an end, and that this world had an end; and that if they kissed the icon and looked *into* it, then they would be assured that something exists more miraculous than the miraculous itself, that there is mercy and there is forgiveness and there is hope, and there is strength in faith, and then there were the shrines of Desyatinnaya and Sofiya, created on the model of the Byzantine cruciform chapel, there was the Uspensky Cathedral of Kiev, and the Spas chapel of Neredica and the Paraskeva Pyatnitsa temple of Chernigov, there was the Pecherskaya Lavra and the Temple of the Gate, and the church of Berestovo and the monastery of Vidubitsky, but these were still the first wave of the glorious shrines, monasteries, and churches built in the joy of the new faith, as this was followed by the renowned Moscow Period with the Uspensky, the Andronikov, and the Troitskaya-Sergieva Lavra, so that the newer shrines and monasteries and churches were built one after the other to the north, as far north as Vologda and Ferapontov, and everywhere icons were created in the hundreds and thousands, the iconostases were raised, and the walls and the columns and the ceilings covered in frescoes, and the people were immersed in faith, and they stepped into the narthex and from there into the naos, and holding three fingers together, in a wide arc they made the sign of the cross, once in the middle of the forehead, once below the navel, then once to the right, finally to the left, then they bowed, and after a brief supplication they went forward to the analogion, the icon-stand, making the sign of the cross twice in front of it, and they kissed the edge of the icon, then again they made the sign of the cross once and they kneeled, and they bought a bundle of sacred candles and they lit the candles in the candelabra placed at certain points in the church, and here, after reciting the mandatory prayers and all the while crossing themselves again, they purified their hearts, at last they took their places in the shrines, the monasteries, and the churches, the women on the left side, the men on the right side, namely, the women in the narthex and the men in the naos, and they heard the voice of the priest leading the ceremony, that in the name of the Father, the Son, and the Holy Ghost, Amin, have mercy upon me, a sinner, our Lord Jesus Christ, The Son of God, for the sake of the prayers of Thy most pure Mother, the Saintly Ones, our Godly Fathers, of every Saint, have mercy on us, and Glory to Thee, Our Lord, Glory to Thee, O Heavenly King, Bringer of Comfort, Soul of Truth, Who art everywhere present and fillest all things, Treasury of all the Good, and Giver of Life, come abide within us, and cleanse us of all sins, and redeem, O Benevolence, our souls, and they heard the reverberations of the choir, the polyphony growing ever richer, constructed on the basis of the diatonic, chromatic, and enharmonic scales, they gave themselves over to the ikos, sounded in the scale of eight voices and its forty modulations, and they said the Amin if the time came in the liturgy of St. John Chrysostom, and made the sign of the cross, as if scattering crosses, flinging one cross after another for hours, while this great Liturgy was taking place, until the priest kissed the cross and after the distribution of the prosfora, called upon them to leave; and they believed in God, because they saw the icons, because these icons demonstrated to them, and proved definitively to their impressionable souls that what stood before them on the icon-stand or what they could see hanging on the wall before them, the icon, was truly that *place* where they might glimpse into another world, a world above all else, so that their lives passed in one single prayer, or if that was not entirely the case, as in the midst of writhing struggle between the lesser and greater sins, committed over and over, it was difficult to maintain the intensity of the concentration demanded by constant prayer; yet there still remained wonder, the sincere rapturous wonder of those for whom this state of continuous prayer was not a superhuman task but was itself the only single imaginable form of this worldly life—truly one long uninterrupted prayer—for this was the case of those who chose the sacred path, of every cropped-headed votary of the subjects of Orthodox devotion, who following one of the twofold traditions of Byzantium, chose to pass their lives in that which the Lord had meted out for them: either a strict kinovion or a more free-spirited idiorhythmic type of monastery; nonetheless they lived in both places in this state of continual prayer, if not explicitly confined within this prayer, as were the most constant heroes of the faith, the Hesychasts; well, perhaps these monks couldn't even have done otherwise, as for them anything else would have been unimaginable; therefore they lived as an inner mute prayer, immersed in perfect reticence, in a silence where no worldly sound was ever heard, not even the faint murmur of the prayers of the other monks, not even the murmur that could be heard from the whole of the Russian lands, which in accordance with the so-called spirit of history was slowly moving in a turbulent swirl toward union, for in the meantime the Russians had become enamored with Christ and the Virgin Mother, and with sincere murmuring fear in their hearts paid tribute to Our Lord the Creator, who looked down upon them as the Pantokrator from the heights of the church cupolas, they were enchanted by the dazzling beauty of the churches, by the endless riches that rained down upon them on Sundays and during every mandatory prayer on the church holidays; under the weight of their sins, they took part with the most profound trust—with the promise of redemption—in the long ceremonies, which in and of themselves were prayers; all the seven Byzantine synods of the Orthodox faith wanted this and ordered it as such, where everything, including the smallest details of life, was regulated, and thus everything could accordingly serve the everlasting sustenance of the Church in the enormous territory of Russia, emerging as a great power, everything could serve the everlasting sustenance of the buildings of its faith—polished, intricate, and infinitely refined—so that every object and every hymn and every supplication and every movement would conjure up amazement and preserve the sense in the believer, with his wretched existence, that here he was close to Paradise, close to Our Lord, close to Christ and the Holy Mother of God, close to the Unseeable, to that which was more Miraculous than the Miraculous, so that he would be filled with the heart-wrenching reverberations of the choir's chant and the Word; his soul would be, after sorrow, penetrated with infinite joy, so that he would believe, truly believe, that his wretched life was nothing; for everything was above, was there in the beyond, was there if he looked, before kissing the icon's edge, in the incomprehensible spectacle opening within the gates of the icon, it was there ... there ... somewhere.

He decided to leave, that was all he needed, to give himself over to this weakness, to the glutinous substance of a sadness that had precipitously descended upon him, all he needed now was to give in, especially in this place that was not for him, merely because the pictures on the wall here looked at him with such illumination; it was out of the question, get out now, the whole thing was totally absurd, he could not allow himself this, he had nothing at all, neither proper accommodation nor money nor work; not only did he have to be strong inside but he had to feel that way, facing whomever he would encounter on Monday while searching again for work; wandering around in here was pure lunacy, I'm out of here, to hell with it, and he was already going, that is to say backward, because one could not be certain, as he was not, that there was, at the opposite end of the series of rooms arranged like a labyrinth, an exit; he recognized this already, he did not have to ruminate: well, which way now, this way, he said to himself, and he went, backward, to where he had come from; he didn't look at the pictures now, he was very angry at himself and felt it had been idiotic to sneak in here; he retreated from one room to the next, and he had already reached the first room, and was already below on the eight steps, and he was about to walk through the door that opened wide onto the corridor so he could then run down the crazy staircase and outside, out of this crazy building, once again into the crowd and then into the Carrer de Provença, and from there quickly toward a district suitable for him, so he could eat in some cheap buffet to hold out until tomorrow when, in the first room through which he had blindly hurried through when he first came in, yes, now he remembered clearly, that here in this first room he hadn't really looked at anything at all, he hadn't even seen anything, as if he'd had to shut his eyes; for the life of him, he didn't remember anything of what was here, he had, in a word, headed inside unseeing, yet now, on his way out, he cast a glance at a picture of much larger dimensions than the others, altogether one glance, and he had already turned his head away, and he had already raised his leg to step across the threshold, yet he stopped, somehow he faltered in his movement, he could not complete it and because of this he nearly stumbled clumsily in front of the eight steps—almost, for at the last moment he was able to pull his leg back, and he was even able to keep his balance, he only clutched at the door frame and looked back once again, and, well, there would not have actually been any particular reason for him to be so troubled, for in this first room there was only one picture to be seen; true, it had been positioned differently, and it was also true that apart from this picture, nothing else had been placed there—an easel, a kind of painter's easel had been set up in this first room, and on this, obliquely, that is at a slight backward tilt, and much bigger than the others—a painting nearly life sized had been placed, and, because the easel was high above the floor level, it so to speak welcomed the visitor, and if already from the beginning it would have been hard for him to explain why he had slipped into here, and what the hell he was looking for here, then now he knew even less why he had come to a dead halt before this picture, so that he nearly fell on his nose from the sudden stop, that is, in any event, how it occurred: he braked, he came to a dead halt, he leaned against the door frame, he regained his balance, and he turned in the direction of the large picture, and in the picture he saw three mighty, delicate, supplicant men, as these three men sat around a table; that was what he saw first, but he quickly discovered that these three men, each of them, had wings, it was not, moreover, easy to discover this as the painting was in fairly bad condition, it was immediately visible that many parts that had once been painted in were missing, but the three figures who, due to their wings, were obviously angels, had remained relatively intact, only a scar extended all the way down the middle of the picture, as if the wood on which it had been painted had split, and as if after this fissure had occurred, something else had been spilled there, resulting in a thick streak where some of the color was lost; but then he determined that there was, to the right, a similar though thinner streak where the same thing might have occurred; aha, he realized suddenly, these fissures occur in the two places where so long ago the boards were fitted to each other, there is a problem with the join, he thought worriedly, the material is warping and had already warped a bit, in other words it had cupped, as people who work with wood are wont to say, and in that first minute he didn't even know why the hell he was interested, and what had made him anxious and why he wasn't moving on already, what the hell was he doing standing around here and why was it so important to him, to him of all people, that there were two scars on this picture and what they were from, when he awoke to the realization that these angels ... it was as if they had stopped him, it seemed like pure lunacy but there had to be something in it, he perceived that he was now staring only at the background, perhaps even more terrifyingly shining and golden than the previous ones, and that he wasn't taking his eyes off of it, his eyes were dazzled from the illumination, just so he didn't have to look at the angels—but already, he was well aware that he *did not dare* to look at the angels—so, this really takes the cake, have I gone crazy as well?! and he looked at the angels and almost immediately at the sight he collapsed, for he knew right away, as he looked at them, that these angels were real.

It would have been simpler if he had just immediately run down the steps, and then really had gotten out of here, only that from his point of view, looking at it from here inside, things weren't like that: on the contrary, it seemed to him simplest not to flee through that door that the angels were guarding, but to go backward, backward once again, across the rooms, and there to look for a real exit, and he even did so, although of course he hadn't thought it through; he was too frightened for that, it was his reflexes, not his brain, that were making the decisions, his simple sensory reflexes, so that he fled, and truly he ran, across the first room, then he ran across the second, then in the third one he slowed down—they weren't actually coming after him—nonetheless in the fourth room he already tried to conceal his running, so then he ran further in a hidden running; if anyone standing in the rear rooms was looking at him, then they wouldn't have encountered anything particularly conspicuous, it's true he looked like someone who was dragging his feet a little strangely across the floor, but simply hurrying through the rooms, clearly he had some business to attend to, something undone somewhere, any one of the visitors to the exhibit might have thought this if they had cast a glance at him, only, they didn't cast any glance, no one could have cared less where he was going, and since all were examining the icons such as, perhaps, the familiar couple from the beginning, who were softly whispering before each picture, but really, he engaged the attention of no one here until he reached the last room, where he saw a door that was not opened wide, it had to be opened if someone wanted to go through it, but it seemed obvious that it led outside, so he didn't reflect too much over where to go, already he had stepped up there, and already he had opened the door, but stepping through it, he saw sitting, facing him, next to a little table, a large-framed, bearded old man, who immediately looked up when he appeared, hurrying through the door; he was already suspicious as to why someone was leaving the last room so hurriedly; oh no, that's all I need, he thought, suddenly slowing his pace, but to no avail, it was too late, the old man got up from his chair and looked him in the face, at which he quickly looked away, and stood by a wall just as monstrous as the one on the first floor, he leaned back as much as he could against the pockmarked wall and puckered his mouth, looking at the floor before him, like someone who had just come out of the room to rest, or like someone who was just thinking about what he had just seen; he observed that having done so, the old man sat down again, or, more precisely, he slowly lowered himself down to his chair, but he was looking, not removing his gaze from him, because, well, of course he was suspicious, he thought, I would be suspicious too in his place, so that he stayed there; something was jutting horribly into his back, some kind of bauble jutting out from the wall, clearly some kind of wretched ornament, how much longer am I going to have to stand around here, he reflected irritatedly, when the old man somehow motioned to the rooms with his head and spoke to him, saying "Is Vasilka there?" which of course he did not understand, on the one hand because he didn't speak Catalan—he had only learned a few basic expressions in Spanish, and on the other because the old man was not speaking Catalan and not even Spanish, but in all likelihood Russian, or in any event some kind of Slavic language, so he stood there doubly distanced from this presumed Russian language, and as always, when someone said something to him in this country, he nodded cautiously, so cautiously that it could be understood to mean anything, in any event he said not a single word, and just continued to stand there by the wall; the old man, as if put at his ease by the nod, sat back in his chair; he however looked at the old man now for the first time more closely, and he saw that this person, who had clearly been placed here in some sort of supervisory position, was not simply just old, he was downright ancient, his beard was thick and snow-white, and reached down to his chest, he was continually twisting the end of it, but his eyes, which were of a kind of blue like the cloaks of the angels inside, were fixed unblinkingly upon him, he said nothing for a while, then he began to hem and haw, and like someone who took it completely for granted that the other one understood what he was beginning to say in his own language in this foreign city, spoke again in what, as before, was most likely Russian, saying that he could not stand it anymore, all this slacking off, he'd chewed it over a hundred times already why these pictures were here, and what their purpose was, that the two of them were the Gallery itself, but as for that one, he gestured in vexation, it was a waste of time even to talk about it, he was just a slacker, oh, that Vasilka, the old man sighed, shaking his head at length, to which he responded again with a nod of the head, and with that he finally convinced the old man that he understood what he was saying, moreover that he agreed with him, and that Vasilka really should have been sitting there, obviously in front of something by the entrance where the angels were; yes, he must mean the entrance; the old man, sensing his concurrence, nodded in gratitude, since, he explained, the treasures inside there were of inestimable value, because there were things here, selected items, not only from the Moscow collections but material from Kiev and Novgorod and Pskov and Yaroslavl and from more recent times too, these just could not be left unsupervised, with no protection, there was no way this could be entrusted to the Catalans, they would have their heads off if they found even a single spot on any of them, he had kept explaining this to Vasilka, continuously, but you could explain all you wanted, Vasilka slipped away like a lizard and of course he knew—the old man pointed to himself—that if he went through the rooms, then there wouldn't be anyone here, so what could he do; every morning he said, look, Vasilka, the devil will seize you if you slip away so much, you'll never get back home—because they were sent here from home—and so on, he just kept on saying that they were the two room-guards for the Gallery, and that he had pleaded in vain for them not to stick him with Vasilka for this traveling exhibition, anyone but that Vasilka, but the main boss didn't listen to him, because no one had listened to him for a long time now; he had grown old, in his left ear—and he showed him the spot—he was completely deaf, and he didn't even see that well, but don't tell that to anyone, no one had to know that, because they then would kick him out of the Gallery, he would die immediately if that happened, for the gentleman could well believe him, and again he pointed at himself with both hands, he had worked as a guard in the Gallery for more than forty years now, everything, he had lived through everything already that was just possible to live through: this one left, that one came, this one left again, that one was appointed again, it was a pure madhouse, that is why he had always stuck to being a guard, no one was envious of that, yet he was, he noted—a confidential expression on his face—a born Vzdornov, yes, he gave a brief laugh, from *that* branch, from the famous and renowned family of Vzdornov, not even as far removed from the most famous of all, batyushka Gerold Ivanovich, who for that matter was now living in Ferapontov, completely withdrawn from the world, so that every single day he could look at the world-famous frescoes of Dionisiy, which—they say—also had made him go a bit mad but that doesn't really matter because, getting back to himself, they—Gerold Ivanovich here, Gerold Ivanovich there—they could talk all they wanted, he would never leave his position as a museum guard for any amount of money, this had always suited him and in the most perfect way imaginable, because here at least a person was left in peace and, spreading his hands wide, he waited for the accord of his audience, the audience of course nodded once very seriously, but by then had already decided okay, this was fine, he would act as if he were paying attention for one more minute but then no more, he would go down from here to the ground floor, from there out onto the street, and out of here, because it was, all the same, ridiculous how a person couldn't get out of here because he had been attacked by a vision—because what else could have happened to him earlier than a vision, he didn't dare to move from here lest they grab him because of the ticket, well he hadn't done anything wrong, he hadn't taken anything, he hadn't even touched anything at all, the only problem was that he had no entrance ticket, so what, that's nothing, he would talk his way out of it somehow, later, but when he had already decided, and had launched himself off a mere hair's breath away from the wall, the old man started in again, at which he simply leaned back once more, for he thought it better if, for the time being, he was leaning against the wall, at least he could find a smoother spot for his back on the wall, and not that same bauble jutting out, yet still: he stayed there, and he could have heard that "I know you too, just came for that, I know, because everyone comes for that, everyone comes across that door, and I can see right away that they're disappointed, well of course I would be too, because the Rublev, the real one, that's something else, but that never, you understand, my dear sir, never will be moved from the walls of the Tretyakov Museum," and there it would stay, he continued to explain, it had turned up there from the State Institution of Restoration during the time of Comrade Stalin; the monks from Radonezh, from whom it had been taken to be sent to the State Institute of Restoration, received a copy in its place, so that the original could only be seen by someone who traveled specially to Moscow and looked at it there, the one here, however, inside, was not the one from Radonezh but a third variation, and from among the hundreds upon hundreds of copies prepared at that time, before Ivan the Terrible, the most beautiful of its kind, indeed a perfectly magnificent copy, he gestured toward the inner rooms, no one could even say that it's not, maybe Miss Iovleva or Yekaterina Zheleznyeva found it somewhere in the depositories, in a word it was beautiful and superb and everything, well, but the original, the Rublev, that was something else altogether, it was too difficult even to say where this very difference lay, because as even he could see, the figures, the contours, the composition, the measurements, the placement all corresponded near perfectly to the original Rublev, and, well, as a matter of fact, there was a divergence only in the table, because in the Rublev, there is a chalice on the table, and that's it, we don't even know what kind, because the paint peeled off, it didn't happen in the State Institute of Restoration, my brother-in-law's wife's younger daughter, Ninochka, worked there, it wasn't there but in an older time, still under the Czars, for as you know, these icons … the old man dug sadly into his beard—although it isn't clear that you do know, because, he pointed at him standing by the wall, he immediately saw, as he came through the door, that he was Russian and that he wasn't really an expert, but one of those art-loving types, the kind that speak very little as they view the exhibition, while the experts, they never stop blabbing on and on, that is how you can tell who they are, they haven't even come through the door yet and you can hear them blabbing away already, just like birds chirping back and forth, that suchlike and suchlike and Byzantine this and Theophanic Greek that, and Rublev this and Dionisy that, well, to put it briefly, it would be better if they kept quiet, and he pointed to himself, he during those forty years had come to know everything about these icons, there was no question anyone could put to him that he could not answer, because he had read everything, and so many things had stuck in his mind that even Miss Iovleva or Yekaterina Zheleznyeva herself sometimes asked him about a name, or a date, if they just couldn't happen to recall it right then, and he always answered too when he was asked a question, because he never forgot anything, because everything stayed in his head; he had grown up with these amazing icons at home, so that he could be trusted when he said these icons here inside, you understand, don't you, and the other ones too, all the ones back home, were very frequently repainted, restored, or simply painted over, yes—and that one too, the Troika—you understand already, and the one back home, the Rublev, it was painted over many times, they even say—the old man gestured for his audience to come close, who in turn, however, did not budge from the wall—that there is no point in restoring it to the original state with all of these modern tools, even then it isn't the original state, "because it is impossible by now to restore the original state and even sometimes you can hear"—the old man lowered his voice —"that this is particularly true for the Lord Our Father and the Holy Spirit, in a word, you know, I understand that in the Rublev the mouth of the angel on the left and the angel on the right originally curved down a bit more, thus they were sadder in the original, which of course I just happened to hear somewhere, I don't even know where, it could be that not even the half of it is true," what did it matter to him anyway, to a Russian who just happened to wander in here, it didn't matter here anyway, he could just delight in this copy, for it was beautiful, wasn't it? and as he held a slight pause here, and again just waited for a sign of consent, he leaned forward a little, toward him, again he had to nod once, but now somehow it was going a little more easily, because now he was convinced that the old man was not dealing with him in an unfriendly way, but rather gave the impression of someone who was trying to explain something, so that there was nothing in his voice to suggest that he was about to ask for the ticket, no, this was no longer about the ticket, but what then was it all about, the old man had clearly mistaken him for someone else, but if that were true, then what would happen if it emerged that he was not the person he had been mistaken for; or it wasn't even a question of mistaken identities but just that he was bored, very bored, and he had to sit down here, and his only hope was that he might latch onto someone coming from the last room, someone with whom he could while away the time; but what was he talking about, how the hell could someone just go on and on like that, and why did he even think that he was interested, because he wasn't interested at all, and even if he understood he still wouldn't be interested, and it was just for the sake of appearances, for self-protection, that he had stayed with him in this crazy building, where there were even angels; this was all he needed, well enough of this, he thought, and now he pushed himself away from the wall a little more decisively than before, but the old man right at that point raised his left arm and said to him, what, don't be in such a hurry, they'd been having such a nice conversation, he had to sit there from morning till evening, he wasn't saying that by way of complaining but it was just that, well, it was nice to talk a little with someone about these things, with someone who was interested, and it was just as if they were back at home in the Gallery; there too, if someone asked him a question, he always told them everything he knew, just as he was telling him now that all in all, in his opinion, the Troika was the most beautiful painting in the entire world, no one had ever succeeded in depicting Heaven—the imperceptible—with such staggering results, that is to say, like reality itself; never, declared the old man and he raised his index finger as well, at which the visitor of course began to retreat back toward the wall, never, no one, and that was exactly why every single copy is so important, and that is exactly why this one that he had seen at the entrance to the exhibit was so important, because the copy, as he obviously knew—the old man looked at him sternly—was not the same thing as here in the West; at home, if a copy was created from an icon, and then this copy was consecrated by the bishop, it was then accordingly acknowledged as genuine, and from that point on the very same sanctity would emanate from the copy as from the original, and it was like this with the Troika too, and in addition to that, a copy more beautiful than the one they had brought here would never be found anywhere, it had only come to light recently, and everyone had come to see the miracle, they even came from the highest echelons, all the restorer-colleagues were there, all of the historians, when Miss Iovleva or Miss Zheleznyeva—he didn't recall exactly who it was now—had found it and brought it up from storage, a small crowd stood there, he remembered it well to this very day, and everyone was amazed by this copy, because at first glance it really seemed to be the original, as everything in it tallied, if he could put it that way: the measurements tallied, the composition tallied, the proportions, the outlines, it was only on the table that something was different, but up to this very day no one has known, there is only speculation, what could have originally been painted on this copy, and chiefly as to why it was different than what was on the table in the

Rublev, they just stood there and they were all enchanted, and the guards were there too, and they wanted to exhibit it straight away, but then nothing at all came of that, because where should they put it? perhaps next to the original?! a nearly perfect copy?!—no, that was impossible, so then instead they didn't put it anywhere, yet when this traveling exhibit got started, there was no debate to speak of, they immediately selected it namely as one of the first items, because of course moving the original was out of the question, the original by Rublev, that one—the Director himself, Valentin Rodionov, stated—shall remain forever in its place, for where the Rublev Troika is hung becomes a shrine, even Director Rodionov said that; and he himself would say that it didn't really matter, where the Troika was, its sacred force was immediately felt, if someone looks at it they surely understand, and that is why no one dared to touch it; he—and again the old man pointed by way of explanation at himself—believed that this was the reason why no one had dared to move it since 1928, well who would take on the task of touching it without praying, without kissing it, it was trouble enough that it had been moved in the old days from the church at Radonezh because, well, it wasn't painted to be put in a museum, and for people just to stare at it like some ordinary picture . . . but no matter, one thing is certain, that at least no one was going to touch it anymore, in this way it would stay with them, in the Tretyakov, for even if the Tretyakov is not a church, the world—the old man lowered his voice and signaled with a movement of his hand, like a great lord, that he could go now if he wished, he had concluded all that he wished to say—the world should just look at this copy, and then try to figure out which one was real.

Many, many things demanded an explanation, as he nearly burst out of the building and rushed into the Carrer Provença, and onward from there, as if he were deaf and blind, and he had not the slightest idea of where to begin, as he had not the slightest idea of where he was at that moment, nor was he even interested; his brain was throbbing so hard that he could not bear, he simply could not bear to deal with anything else, only this throbbing in his brain; at first he thought it was throbbing because he was slamming his heel down too hard and that was making his brain tremble inside his head, but then he walked more softly and with that nothing improved, there was only this throbbing, in general he was thoroughly unhinged, the chaos inside him was total and he was dizzy, so dizzy that he had to keep stopping; certainly the passersby thought he was drunk or that he was going to throw up, but no, he was neither drunk nor was he going to throw up, he was just under assault from this dizziness and this throbbing, and by the fact that at the same time he began to see various things: he saw himself running through the streets, avoiding people; he saw faces as they arose before him for an instant then disappeared; he saw the old man from the museum or whatever it was that he had just left, and he saw at the same time that middle-aged couple too, as they separated while still behind him, passed around him, and then, moving in front of him, took each other by the arm again; he saw the staircase too, as it spiraled upward, and he also saw how in the middle of the big painting, and to the right, the colors were somewhat faded; then there was the staircase again, but now it was winding downward, and the gold leaf on the pictures gleamed, but what disturbed him the very most was that in between all of these simultaneous pictures flashing again and again were the three angels, as they bent their heads to one side, or more precisely, as the middle one and the one on the right bent their heads toward the one on the left, who bowed his head toward them, then all three of the angels looked at him, but just for a second, because almost immediately they disappeared, only the colors remained, the luminous blue and crimson of their cloaks—of course not just any old luminous blue or any old crimson, if these were even blues or crimsons at all, he wasn't even sure of that, and not even sure that it was even colors that he had seen, he wasn't certain of anything at all, because they just flared up and then flashed away, but in such a way that the other pictures were flaring up and flashing away at the same time, with such speed in his head, and it was probably that which was making him reel and making everything inside him throb, but the very worst was that he could not stop, which meant that he wasn't able to bring the entire thing to a halt, he wasn't able to say to himself, well enough of that, it's over now, stop, pull yourself together, and then he would stop and pull himself together, because it was precisely this he couldn't manage, the suspension of this speed out there, because it was inside him as well, he had to run—possibly in such a way that he would not bump into people too much, a lot of people were coming this way and it took a while for him to get out of the city center—and he came out toward the north, to the wide and heavily trafficked boulevard called Diagonal, and well, after that the situation was already better, in addition he already knew this area, so he kept to this northern direction, the one that he had to choose to reach his accommodations, for here already there were fewer and fewer people coming in the opposite direction, and that was exactly what he wanted, for fewer and fewer people to be coming along, so that at last the heavens could have mercy on him and free him from them as well, and then he could already bear to slow down a little, indeed, when he realized that no one was coming after him—of course he knew all along that no one had been coming after him—still it was somehow important now, it had become important that no one was, in any event; when this became unequivocal, and he was able to slow down his steps completely, when he was already proceeding at a walking pace along the narrow streets—he couldn't exactly say that on a day like today, Saturday, let there be no one outside, because there were people on the sidewalk or in the windows, or how could he not have seen here or there, where the little streets bulged wide, a children's soccer team now and then, but still, he no longer felt the presence of that monstrous strength that had driven him until now, so that now he could pose to himself the question of what exactly had happened, why was he running to and fro like a madman, and how had he, of all people, got mixed up in this story with the horrendous building, why hadn't he just left when he could have done so, why had he stayed, what did he even want from this exhibit, he had never before been to an exhibit in his life so why now, of all times, accordingly why and why and why; this had to be answered, he explained to himself, and he rapidly looked around, wondering if he'd been speaking aloud, but that was unlikely, as at least here the passersby did not stare at him, and so everything began to calm down, eventually even his brain slowly left off with the questioning, and with a few vulgar turns of phrase—that is to say fuck it, and really fuck it, and just fuck the whole fucking thing one more fucking time—he succeeded in gaining a psychological advantage in the face of another compulsion that drove him on, saying fine, if he was stopping too, or if he was even sitting down on an empty bench, then he should do so first and foremost to figure out what the hell had happened with him in the past hours, and why had he gone into that Perella, or whatever the hell it was called, and if he had gone inside why did he stay there, and why did he look at that picture, and why had there fallen upon him, with such force, what he had seen there, so that again just why and why and why, the only problem was that this advantage proved to be only momentarily effective, and he had stopped in vain, he cursed in vain, he sat on the empty bench in vain, namely this psychological advantage was all in vain, at the end it was not his more lucid self but instead the other that was triumphant, the one that wanted to find an explanation for why he had allowed himself to be swept into something of which he had not the slightest idea, and of which he never could anyway, I don't even know what that was hanging on the wall, I don't even know what building I was in, I—apart from restoration workshops—know the trowel, the mixing hod, the plane, because that didn't matter now, it didn't matter that there had been more than one restoration workshop in his life, just as it didn't even count that he had not become what he was all at once, this nothing who went in with the metro every morning, then out with the metro every evening, it did not immediately start with that foul-smelling, damp, dark room which he had rented during the past year, and where he lived alone, it did not immediately begin with this, but rather it ended with this, this was the end already, he thought now on the empty bench and this thought suddenly quieted down his brain inside, whoopee, the end is here, he said the words to himself, and these five words at last stopped the throbbing in his brain, certainly this is the end, old man, he repeated again, and he looked around the square, or well it wasn't even really a square, just a kind of forced widening of the street because one crummy house had been torn down among the other crummy houses, and there was just that much more extra space where he sat, and where a group of children were kicking a ball around, only now did he have a good look at them, one of whom moved fairly adroitly, he passed the ball well, it was evident at first that although he was the smallest among them, he was also the most intelligent, because not only did he skillfully dribble the ball, but it was plain that he understood what he was doing, while the others just kept running back and forth and shouted out obviously, I'm over here and the like, but that one, the little one, did not shout, one could tell that he took it seriously, indeed, now that he watched him more closely, his face remained surprisingly, even disconcertingly, serious at all times, as if something depended on whether he could stop the ball arching this way with his chest, or if he could make an accurate pass to the forward; he's serious, he decided, even too serious, he now only watched the grubby youth, always, unceasingly, unflinchingly serious, that is to say the youth did not for a single moment take part in the common joy as did the others when he kicked the ball, maybe for him it wasn't even joy but something else—and then at once his head was filled with a wracking pain, he quickly turned his glance away from the children, he didn't want to see them, and already he wasn't even there, he went on further in the narrow street, then again, just as the narrow street turned off to the left, he found himself suddenly facing . . . the three angels in the picture, the whole thing was before him in such detail as if it were real, which of course it was not, he stood there rooted to the ground and he looked at them like that, he looked at the miraculous faces, he looked at the angel sitting in the middle and the angel sitting on the left, and how their mantles were so dazzlingly blue, he looked at them for time immortal, then he stared into the gold, finally again at them, and he was disturbed to realize that they weren't even looking at him; they weren't looking at all at the person who was looking at them, or rather that, inside the museum or whatever it was, he had been seriously mistaken.

Everything went back to the definition of the Holy Trinity, practically the fate of all Eastern Christianity rested on this, indeed even Christianity itself rested upon the extraordinary concerns surrounding this fundamental question; as a rule, things don't usually occur in this way, because as a rule the fundamental questions only crystallize later, only later is it usually clear what is being debated, why certain principles are being put forward, why the quarrels, the schisms, then the heaps of massacred bodies; the questions occur generally speaking later; but this was not the case of the Christian religion of love, as here the discussions had been taking place since the fourth century, and finally it was because of this that the theological schism, made official back in 1054, occurred, although there actually had been an Eastern and Western Church since the creation of the Eastern Roman Empire, there was Rome and Constantinople; and this Eastern Church, to speak of only that now, this Constantinople, was none too reassured, neither at the time, nor later on, when an ultimate decision was reached as to the nature of the Almighty, the Christ, and the Holy Spirit, and what there even was in this realm that surpassed the human, because they had to make up their minds—on every occasion, once and for all—six times; the problem was that human beings—that is the Fathers of the Church, the patriarchs, metropolitans, bishops, priests of the synod, in a word the local and universal synods, and so on, the great Saint Athanasios, Saint Gregory of Nazianos, Saint Basil the Great, and Saint Gregory of Nyssa—had to make a decision in a question that clearly surpassed not only their extraordinary talents but their human capacities, because when the time came to say what was the relation between the Lord, the Christ, and the Holy Spirit, everything came into it: and there were the subtle and heretical distinctions of the most outrageous versions, heresies so subtle that it is not easy to comprehend the large quantity of blood, symbolic or real, that was periodically shed due to one or another miniscule detail of the so-called theological question, that was shed, therefore, because of the teaching of the Holy Trinity: for there were those who argued for the Lord alone, and there were those, too, who acknowledged the uniqueness and primacy of Christ alone, then there were those who argued for the precedence of the Lord and Christ together, but there were finally those who advised for the equal standing of all three, that is of the Lord, the Christ, and the Holy Spirit, and this school of thought was finally victorious, together with that peculiar formation which became the central tenet of Christian belief: the single essence of the Father but in three forms, so that there followed afterward, for those who can even understand it, the so-called filioque controversy, i.e., as to whether the Holy Spirit originated only from the Father, or from the Son, and this split the Christian faith into two once and for all, and there arose the Orthodox world of belief—this colossal mysterious Byzantine Empire—which remained for a thousand years even after the great collapse of the West, where there reigned a life subordinated simultaneously to the desire for pomp and sensual hunger, and additionally, with equal justification, a life subordinated to a theologically driven faith; and where the essential, earth-shattering attack on the entire Orthodox congregation following the Seventh Ecumenical Council no longer threatened this fundamental tenet of faith, which of course did not at the same time mean that the question was resolved, the question was not resolved; every decision concerning the Lord, as well as that of the relation between Him and the incarnation as Christ and, respectively, between Him and the Holy Spirit, remained in an unapproachable obscurity, or looking at it from the viewpoint of the later materialist heretics, on the terrain of a fairly indefensible logical failure, where only deference to authority and faith itself was of assistance, that is, as for the most profound saints of the Church, from St. John Chrysostom of the Golden Mouth to St. Sergius of Radonezh, the question of the nature of the Trinity never was problematic, it was and remained a problem only for the others, that is for the world, for all those who were not capable—since they were not capable of what the saints were—of seeing the embodiment of the Creator, of seeing the mystery of the Trinity, of not questioning but experiencing, experiencing for themselves and perceiving the extraordinary concentration of the created and the non-created world, the godly atelier and the supremacy—stunning, miraculous, inexpressible in words—of the strength of creation; allowing the decisions to be rendered upon them, through them, through their saintly beings, by the Church, that is the Holy Synod, as to what the tenet of faith was that could no longer be cast into doubt concerning bodily manifestation, concerning the mystery of the Trinity and its depiction, because it could be depicted, they concluded after some debate—a debate that did not forego destructive resolve—yes, they concluded that it could be depicted, yes, Christ the Son, the Embodiment of the Lord, it could be represented—as the order of the Ecumenical Council of One Hundred Articles conceived it—if Abraham had seen them beneath the oak-tree at Mamre, which indeed he had, then they could be represented, namely if Abraham saw Him in the depiction of the three angels, as was repeated by thousands and tens of thousands, from Athens to the Monastery of the Holy Trinity in Radonezh, then nothing could be said against the idea of the holy icon-painter depicting the Trinity, strictly on the basis of the prescription of the Council; and in the practical sense, on the basis of the descriptions of the monks of Podliniy, according to them, only Abraham, the most ancient of ancients, once, under Elonei Mamre, that is under the oak of Mamre, saw the three winged youths, sat them down at a table, and feasted them; Sarah's future was discussed, then after a similarly interesting dialogue between Abraham and the Lord during His celebrated appearance as the Three Angels on the topic of Sodom and Gomorrah, at the end of it, there was, briefly, a promise, that namely if He, the Lord, should find ten innocent people there, pure in soul, then He would show mercy to Sodom and Gomorrah, although inasmuch as later on he does destroy Sodom and Gomorrah, the conclusion can be reached that the Lord did not find even ten innocent people pure in soul in this Sodom and Gomorrah, but enough about that, let us return to the point where after this memorable dialogue, everyone went about their own business, the Lord in some form or another—contradictions arise in the relevant traditions as to what this form was—He went on toward Sodom and Gomorrah; Abraham could have reflected for a long time on what he saw and whom he saw, and what had been said to him under the oak, well then, after all this, from this renowned encounter of Our Father with Abraham, from this meeting's sacred Ordinance preserved namely in Moses 1:18, the precept of the Synod was established as such, after a good few hundred variations—in consequence of which, the divine grace descended upon Andrey Rublev, and his gentle hand and his humble soul, through the agency of his continuous prayer, and from the inspiring strength of the Unnamable Himself at the commission of Abbot Nikon of Radonezh, in memory of St. Sergius, it bore the title of "The Holy Trinity" and came into being, and was preserved, the extraordinary news of which, like a kind of storm of beauty, swept across the whole of Russia, so that Dionisy's imagination burst into flame a generation later when a copy of the Rublev perfection was commissioned on behalf of a church now unknown to us, and Dionisy set to work, he and no other, because, although it cannot be authenticated that the author of the copy in question could only have been Dionisy, at the same time, the thought that it could have been anyone else: say, one of his followers or someone from the artel of Dionisy, is inconceivable—it is inauthenticable and impossible—for this painting, which turned up later in the Tretyakov Gallery via a path equally unknown and which, thanks to the auspices of a traveling exhibition, arrived in Martigny, Cannes, and then Barcelona, some five hundred years later, was in its essence such a perfect copy of the perfect original, any painter less talented than Dionisy could not have been capable of it, either in that period or any other; after Rublev a magnificent artist such as Dionisy had simply not turned up for a long time, so that it was only he, and he alone, with nonetheless extraordinary help, namely that the condition of the fulfillment of the commission was nothing else than Dionisy receiving assurance that he could inspect the Rublev original without being disturbed, so that Dionisy must have had to spend a very long time in the Church of the Trinity—in the monastery of St. Sergius in Radonezh—for he would need a very long time to draw near to the spirit of this master-work, the spirit of Rublev, and to draw near to the presence of that which the icon of the Trinity on the iconostasis, located in the first space to the right of the Royal Gate, reveals, inasmuch as not only was it necessary to take within a hair's breadth the measure of the outline of the figures and all the items depicted in the icon, not only did he have to study the forms, the sketching, the placement, and understand the colors and the proportions, but he had to be able to pledge himself as well to the task, for he must have been aware, while in the midst of contemplating the icon, of the dangers inherent in the task: if word got out about someone, even about Dionisy himself—this celebrated icon-painter of the fifteenth century—that he was not worthy of the preparation of the copy of the Radonezh original, for surely Dionisy knew better than anyone else that if the soul did not feel what Rublev did in that time, then he himself would certainly end up in Hell, and the copy would come to nothing, because it would be just a lie, a deceit, a mystification, just an ineffectual and worthless piece of trash, which would then be placed in vain in the Sovereign Tier of the church's iconostasis, in vain would it be placed there and worshipped, it would not help anyone and would only lull them into the delirium that they were being led somewhere.

He went to get the linden himself, and as a matter of fact, he really would have liked to complete the entire commission on his own, but the others in the artel—among them his son Feodosiy—were convinced that the master did not wish to work alone, for surely they could, just as they had been doing for years, help him out with this or that, finally—already this was somewhat typical of the era as a whole, and many such matters were similarly concluded out of a love of comfort—it was permitted, and so they allowed him to select for himself the linden wood best suited to the original Rublev; but already they did not allow him to squander his sacred gift on completing the planing, the joining, and the gluing of the icon board, or the formation of the two sponki, that is the two crossbars crafted from beech wood, whose function it was to hold the board together, as well as the hollowing out of the space for the two sponki, the so-called "sponki vrezniye vstrechniye," they did not allow him to complete this work alone; there first came, accordingly, someone who sawed and planed and hollowed and fitted and glued and assembled the icon board and tautened the tightening bars, then someone came who completed the work pertaining to the sponki, then the polye was created to demarcate the border formed by the luzga—that is the border-area beveled inward—and the kovcheg—done by the one who was best at this—followed the direction of the luzga, already drawn; deepening the paintable surface, as it were framing it; because just as in the case of all other icons, the very first order of business was to ensure that the polye, the luzga, and the kovcheg were in good order, moreover in this particular case it was also mandatory for all three parts to correspond to a hair's breadth to the original, that is to say the polye had to be in the same place and of the same extent, the luzga had to be beveled in the same way and at the same angle, and at last the kovcheg had to be as deep and as straight as related by the descriptions of the original in Radonezh, so that after this the priming-master of the artel could take up his work and with his assistants prepare for the canvas that would be glued onto the surface to be painted; the levkas—that is the diluted glutinous liquid—mixed with chalk dust, was applied, in this case, in exactly eight layers, to the icon board, and when finally the last layer of levkas had dried, and it had become as smooth and clean as it possibly could, then there came the znamenshchik, the composition master, who was one of the most important personages in the artel, and especially here in the artel of such a famous painter, for he was the one who, for instance, could now, upon the surface of the completely dried levkas, sketch in, following the outlines of the Radonezh drawing originating from the Master's hand, with unerring assurance and fidelity, the three angels, infinitely gentle, with their enormous wings, gathered around the table; and behind them the outlines of the church, the tree, and the cliff, the table with the chalice and the platter filled up with veal; the entire artel stood behind his back with bated breath, as his instrument, the grafia, did not quiver even once in his hand; all of this, of course, from the assembly of the icon boards to the work of the znamenshchik proceeded self-evidently in such a way that it was not just the assistants and master of the artel who observed each other, but at each individual phase of the work the Master himself stood behind the backs of those who were working, and it remained so in the following phases up to the end, for this was not just any old work; the Master observed from behind to see if the paints, that is the lapis lazuli, the vermilion, and the rust and the malachite and the white, indeed, even the beaten egg-yolks corresponded exactly to that which had been chiseled into his memory as he stood immersed before the Radonezh original for all time; he stood there at the back, and he prayed, while first the lichnik and the dolichnik set to work, painting what was entrusted to them; the lichnik, in this case, exceptionally, just the arms and the legs instead of the face, the dolichnik, however the khitons and garments—and no matter, the Master governed every movement, practically guiding the hand of the lichnik and the dolichnik, so that it could be asserted with confidence that the Master himself had done everything from first to last, for it was evident that his assistants in the artel were obedient to his volition—namely, through the Master's prayers, the volition of the Highest—until the famous copy reached the phase where there was no longer any intermediary assistance, where the Master could not entrust the task to another, where he himself had to take the brush, dip it into the paint-stained dish, and paint the faces, the mouths, the noses, and the eyes and, although according to the accustomed order of things as the last great phase of the painting, at this point, the appropriate master would have followed next in painting the outlines, he did not, as the Master insisted that he himself would lay down the outlines of the asisti and the dvizhki, but at that point he prayed much more intensely, he recited the Jesus prayer, for perhaps he was thinking that in this too he should trust in tradition, and one must believe that Andrej, at all times, but especially while working, had recited this Jesus prayer to himself, he could hardly do otherwise as he worked, not only that, he didn't even stop praying, not taking his eyes off the icon for a second when he stepped aside for the assistants to put on the olifa, the transparent protective layer which, from this point on, had to protect all that had come into being so far, for it had come into being, said the people in the Master's artel happily, their eyes sparkling, the copy of the Rublev icon is completed, here before us again is the Holy Trinity, and whoever was able to come from the neighboring monastery, they looked at the icon, and they couldn't believe their eyes, because they were seeing the exact same thing, not a copy, and not an icon but the Holy Trinity in its own radiant beauty—the Master only stepped back from the workshop of the artel when the last layer of the olifa was being applied, and he stood before the completed icon, looking at it for a long time, then suddenly turned on his heel, and no one even saw him, in the time to follow, even cast the slightest of glances at the icon ever again; however, he had to have been there when the patron placed it in his own church, had to be there when the bishops consecrated it, had to stand there and listen as the bishops, after the opening prayer of the sanctification of the icon and the Sixty-Sixth Psalm, sang Our Lord, Our God, Who art praised and exalted in Thy Holy Trinity, hear our prayer, and send Thy blessing upon us, and may the icon be blessed and sanctified through the holy water, to venerate Thee, and bring salvation to Thy poor people—he heard this, he watched as the bishops consecrated the icon, he listened and he watched all of this, and he crossed himself and he said Amin, then immediately after that, Gospodiy pomiluy, and Gospodiy pomiluy, and Gospodiy, Gospodiy, Gospodiy pomiluy, but he was troubled, and he did not reply when later people went to him to express their recognition and wonderment, he was silent that day and he was silent for weeks on end, and every day he went to confession, finally completely withdrawing from life, and from that point on whoever, whether from curiosity or ignorance, dared to speak in his presence of how splendidly he had painted Rublev's Holy Trinity either risked having Dionisy gape at him in incomprehension, questioningly like someone who does not understand what is being talked about, or—and this was principally before his death, at the time when he painted the Blagoveshchenskaya in Moscow—the celebrated icon-painter of his age would suddenly turn pale, his face distorted, and with enraged eyes would scream inchoately at the top of his lungs at his understandably terror-stricken interlocutor—except if it was his son who was asking, for until the very last moment he always forgave him for everything.

Sundays were like a monster that settled upon a person and wouldn't let go, just chewing and digesting, biting, tearing, because Sunday did not want either to begin, nor to go on, nor to come to an end, it was always like that with him, he detested Sundays, much, but so much more than any other day of the week; all of the other days of the week contained something that slightly allayed the pressure, if only for a few minutes, of how intolerable it all was, but Sunday had never allowed this pressure to relent, that is how it was here, too; in vain had he come here to this country of Spain, in vain was this Barcelona different from that Budapest, in vain was everything here different, because in reality nothing was different, Sunday here settled upon his soul with exactly the same horrible force; it just didn't want to start, it didn't want to continue, it didn't want to end; he sat in the Centro de Atención Integral, in the homeless shelter of the city's social facility at Avenida Meridiana no. 197, which he had happened upon once by accident still at the very beginning when having temporarily despaired of finding any work here, he had set off on the so-called Diagonal and just kept on going and kept on going, he had no idea for how long, but at least for one hour, because he wanted to walk this temporary despair out of himself, and at one point he was just there in front of a building on the Avenida Meridiana, he saw that figures similar to himself were going inside, so, well, he went inside too; no one asked him any questions, he didn't even say anything, they pointed at a bed among many other beds, and since then he had spent the nights here, and now here he sat, on the edge of the bed, and it being Sunday, he had to spend the entire day here, because where could he go on a Sunday, especially after everything that had happened to him yesterday between the Passeig de Gràcia and the Carrer Provença; he could remain alone, remain on the bed, take the plate of food dished out at noontime, and be happy that it was already noon, only that he couldn't even bear to be happy about that, he was so nervous and chiefly not knowing why he was so nervous made him even more nervous, his legs kept moving; he jumped up, he could not bear to be still, he wasn't interested in the others, everyone was preoccupied with themselves, generally they were lying on their beds and asleep, or they made it look like they were sleeping, and he tried to think about the infernal stench that hung in the air so that he wouldn't have to think about how time was not passing; quite high up, on the wall facing him, a large clock had been affixed, and he would have been very happy to beat it down with something and stomp it apart into tiny pieces, down to the tiniest screw, but it was placed very high and he didn't want any commotion; but he could not bear it anymore, so, well, he tried to concentrate on the stink, and not pay attention to the time which he suddenly realized was not passing—his legs, however, unfortunately kept moving back and forth like a reel—it was still twenty minutes after twelve, my god, what was he going to do here, he could not go outside into the immediate neighborhood, someone had explained this to him at the beginning, gesticulating that if he went outside, all around there was La Mina, some kind of living hell where they would murder him, so don't go out there, La Mina, they repeated it several times over, si, he said in reply to this and did not go out into the immediate neighborhood, he solely used the dreadfully long street called Diagonal and that alone, this always took him into the city center, but he was too tired now, so tired that he couldn't even think that if he could head in there again, the day would pass more quickly, just the mere thought of the Diagonal made him feel ill, he had gone up and down the length of it so many times, it was so, so long that he too, like the others, remained on his bed; there was a TV, again stuck up somewhere high on the wall, but it didn't work, there was nothing else to do but to wait for time to pass on the clock-face, for a while he watched the hands of the clock, then he turned over on his left side and closed his eyes, and tried to sleep a little, but he couldn't, because when he closed his eyes the three enormous angels appeared, he did not want to see them, never again, although to his misfortune they kept coming back, either because—as just a moment ago—he'd closed his eyes, or because—as now—he opened them; so he got up from the bed, which was itself a particularly awful bed, sinking down in the middle, with some kind of hard wire mesh, or whatever it was below, pressing into his back or his side so that even at night he had to keep getting up again and again to try to do something about it, but in vain, because when he beat at the mattress it only relieved the situation momentarily, the whole thing immediately caved in again under the weight of his body, and there was that hard iron grating, or whatever it was; now, too, that he had gotten up and looked back at it, the whole thing had sunk in again in the middle; he looked back, and he went out to where you could smoke a cigarette, because it was forbidden inside, although he himself did not smoke but, he thought, at least there it's somewhere else than where he was before, only that even this didn't solve anything, because from here he saw the clock inside, in a strange way this clock could be seen from anywhere, there was no escape, it had to be seen, to be seen at all times and by everyone for whom this place was a temporary shelter, to see that time was passing, that it was truly passing, it was passing very slowly; one thing was sure, whoever turned up here was obligated to have be continually preoccupied with time, and especially right now, on Sunday, he thought bitterly, and he went back to his bed, and lay down again on the caved-in mattress and watched the old man lying next to him who was pulling something from underneath the mattress, he pulled out something from there wrapped in newspapers and he slowly unwrapped it, and when he took a long-bladed knife out of the wrapping, he looked up and noticed that someone was watching him, namely that he was being watched from the neighboring bed; then he held it up, and there was a kind of pride in him as he showed it to him, in any case he said cuchillo, and motioned with his hand that by this he meant the knife, then when he saw that the other one didn't even blink an eye, he showed it to him again, and he said by way of explanation, cuchillo jamonero, but nothing; he didn't understand, he let the old man pack the whole thing with an offended expression, but then suddenly he sat up on the bed, turned to the old man, and signaled with his head and hands to repeat the word, please, those two words, cuchillo, cuchillo jamonero—he had the old man repeat it again and again until he had it down, then he signaled to him that he would like it if the old man showed him the knife once again; the old man cheered up, took the package out again, and unwrapped it, and clearly kept saying it's beautiful, because somehow he had an expression like that on his face; he in the meantime took it into his hands, turned it over, and then gave it back, and tried to make the old man understand that he would now like to know where he had bought it, but the old man misunderstood the question and protested vehemently, quickly wrapped it up and shoved it under the mattress, signaling that no, it was not for sale, at which point he could do little else but try to say without words that he only wanted to know where he had got it from, the old man looked at him, trying to figure out what the hell this one wanted, for he didn't even know how to talk, when suddenly his face lit up and he asked ferreteria? of course he had no idea what this ferreteria was, but he replied si, at which point the old man dug out a scrap of paper and wrote something on it with pencil, and this is what was on the paper:

CALLE RAFAEL CASANOVAS 1

he looked at the clumsy letters, then with a movement of his head thanked him, and signaled that he would like to take the piece of paper, and the old man nodded in approval and wanted even to reach across to help him stuff the paper into the upper pocket of his shirt, but already for someone to touch him was too much for him, it was not possible to touch him, he had never been able to withstand that, during his entire life he had had a dread of being touched by anyone, even now no one could touch him, especially this old man with his putrid filthy hand; quickly he withdrew from him, just to make sure he wouldn't consider getting carried away like this, he turned his back to him and lay like that for a few minutes, until he was certain that his neighbor understood that he didn't want to talk to him anymore, nothing at all, as for him he had wrapped up, he had concluded the friend-making part, he lay motionless, closed his eyes again, and again the angels came to him above, then he opened his eyes, got up, went into the smoking room, stood around there for a while, then strolled into the toilets, sat there for a good long time; this was one place where he felt good, just like all the others there, because here it was possible to latch the door shut, a person could be alone, he could be alone now, no one saw him, he saw no one, but then it just bored him, because just sitting and sitting here above all the shit—because as it happened the toilet in the one free stall he had found was filled with shit—why didn't it go down, he even pulled the cord several times to no result, before he sat down and after a while he just got bored sick, and he went back into the large room, he lay down, he looked for a while at the dead eye of the TV up above, then at the second hand of the clock, then at the TV again, then at the clock again, so that the day finally passed in this way; he could not remain in control of his legs, his muscles were completely exhausted because his two legs kept moving—particularly the left one, it beat with tiny steps into the air if he lay down—or if he was walking on the floor or the sidewalk, or if he stood; he was dead tired by evening, and he thought at last he would sleep unbrokenly, but of course, just as before, even now nothing more was granted to him than a half-hour now and then, as the others snored, cleared their throats, and made rattling noises, continually causing him to awaken with a start, on top of that the angels too kept coming, then one evening a swarm of mosquitoes: if he pulled the blanket over his head to keep them away, he was too hot, then, well, he had to get up in the large half-lit hall and stumble out to the toilet to urinate, then stumble back again, and the whole thing started over again from the beginning, one half-hour of sleep, then the angels and the swarming mosquitoes and the snoring, in this way the hour finally came when he saw the first signs that dawn was breaking, so that by the time there was daylight he had already washed his face, largely tidied up his clothes and his shoes, and was outside of the building already, he did not wait for the morning tea, he was much too exhausted for that, and he couldn't take it anymore; he went along the street but not, this time, toward the Diagonal, but in the opposite direction, just like that, backward, so he could find someone who could give him directions, and at first he couldn't find anyone, the streets here were very empty, but then someone was coming from the opposite direction, he showed them the paper first, then to many other people, until he got to the Calle Rafael Casanovas, then it was still too early, everything was closed, he guessed fairly confidently which building it was that he was looking for, it bore the sign Servicio Estación; that's it, he thought, that could be it, and he began to pace up and down in front of it until a person came, pulled up the sliding gate on the entrance and opened up the shop, he was surly and rumpled, and he stared at him with distrust, indeed, when after a while he went into the shop after him, he looked at him with an expression that seemed to say it would be better if he just cleared out of here, but he didn't clear out, he stayed and went over to him, took out the fifty euros—actually, he had spent four last night on a sandwich and something to drink, he showed the money now, then creased it into his hand, and with this hand he leaned onto the counter, bearing down on it with all of his weight, finally leaning forward slightly, toward the shopkeeper, and in a soft voice said just this much: cuchillo, understand? cuchillo jamonero, and he added for the last time, lest there be no doubt as to what he wanted: a knife, old man, a very sharp knife is what I want.

34
THE LIFE AND WORK OF MASTER INOUE KAZUYUKI

I put down my crown, and in earthly form but not concealing my face, I descended among them, to seek out the Prince of Chu, the King of Mu, I had to leave the boundless plains of the Sky, the Radiant Empire of Light, I had to come from that world where form itself is resplendent; streaming forth it swells, and thus everything is filled by nothingness, I had to descend once more, and again, for I had to break away from the purity of the Heavens, and step into a moment; for nothing ever lasts longer, or even lasts as long as that, and thus so is my submerging below, not lasting longer than a single moment, if, yet, so much of everything can fit into one single moment; but the path did fit, as they put it, the path, as it is called in this coarse tongue, the sudden flash of light of that direction whence I have come thus far, the descent below, and the magnificence with which I made my descent as well, it all fit into that moment, because everything fit into it: the first steps in human form upon this earth, where my guide, my one mute escort led me, promptly and imperceptibly, so that I could take the path, and setting off upon it with human steps, I could then proceed among the troubling chaos of villages and cities, lands and oceans, valleys and peaks, the path fit into one single instant, the path, which led precisely over there to the theater corridor, for this time the meeting had been arranged in the Kanze Kaikan; the curtains—the agemaku—drifted apart before me, so that, in the form of a mae-shite, the hasigakari could open up for me there; I heard them from afar, I heard the drums of the hayashi musicians summoning me and that voice, comprehensible only in pain, of the noh kan, and then only this, the unscathed voices of the hayashi wolves, struck my ears; then I proceeded in my earthly form, in the noble radiance of the karaori kimono, through the familiar space of the Kanze, my feet hardly touching the smooth surface of the hinoki floorboards; as I moved toward the stage there was silence, there was unfathomable silence all around me, silence on the stage, for within me was merely the silence of the voices of the hayashi, and this directed me toward the palace, and I stepped in, and I interrupted the chant that rang out there, there too it became silent, already as I stepped in—although they could not know who had arrived—all became silent, unfathomably silent, maybe they were really looking at what could been seen by the eye, a noble lady, a being unknown, who suddenly is just there; the court of Chu, at my appearance, suddenly took a step backward, and with that, so to speak, the world too stepped back one pace from my path, so that it was not at all difficult for me to see where the throne was, the throne upon which the Prince of Chu, the King of Mu, was sitting, this upstanding ruler, creator of worldly peace in this scented and weighty earthly land, who, now in possession of a mirror—tawdry and broken but still a mirror of all that which is above him—truly has been worthy of the praise of the Heavens, a sign which I now must extend to him; but first there is the scent, at first only the indication of a scent, may the immortal fragrance of vegetation be the promise that I shall now disappear, but immediately be present in a true form, and already they can see the flowering apricot branches on my shoulders, they feel them, they have seen them until now, and they see my dance, while in reality I have disappeared, so that within that moment, I return as a nochi-shite, in my true form, for this is exactly what I promised, although they, immersed in the dance, see nothing but the illusion of the dance itself; however, I am there again, they see the phoenix crown upon my head, and the glittering lilac and scarlet silk of my attire: the simultaneous illumination of the ogushi kimono, the choken cloak at my side, and the sword attached at my waist, so that with every step I take, the whole becomes ever more and more visible, but all is woven through ethereally with gold, I see their startled amazement, only the Prince of Chu, the King of Mu remains immovable and disciplined, on his face is respect, distance, the precise consciousness of proportions; he watches me, he watches only me, he is the only one who truly sees me, who doesn't merely become giddy with the enchantment of the dance; I now extend to him, through my escort, the seeds of the plant of immortality, may this be an offering for the peace he has created, so there may be, in his hands, a sign to remind him of this peace, so it may remain; he looks at me, moved, he looks at my dance, but he sees me as well, as I relate to him with earthly movements that there is a Heaven, that high above the clouds there is a Light that then scatters into a thousand colors, that there is, if he casts his gaze up high and becomes deeply immersed in his soul, a boundless space in which there is nothing, but nothing at all, not even a tiny little movement like this one here, which now must slowly come to an end; slowly I must turn away from this staring, happy gaze, and I must set off on the hashigakari hinoki-wood stage boards, with my escort behind me, toward the agemaku, and by now I only hear the kakegoe-silence of the hayashi musicians, a body takes me, a body that is not my own, the colored curtains of the agemaku open up respectfully, and finally I can step away from the space of this stage and in front of an enormous mirror, remove myself from this body that has carried me, I may return, for return I must, I must put down my phoenix crown, I must free myself from this lilac and scarlet silken grace shot through with gold, and I must at once set off, go back to that place from whence I came, only my escort now appears before me, to show me the path, as they call it in this coarse tongue, yet again, and I slowly take my leave of the familiar world of the Kanze, the odors and the weight slowly vanish from around me, the sound of the drums and the cries of the hayashi musicians growing ever distant, yet still striking my heart now and then, but already I am ascending, I still see the troubling chaos of the villages and the cities, the lands and the seas, the valleys and the peaks, and the moment that enclosed so much into itself comes to an end, and as I ascend, everything ascends with me, a magnificence rises there, a magnificence—back to the purity of the Heavens, to the sphere inconceivable—which in its own form, resplendent, streaming forth, swelling, is nothing else than a return back to that place where nothing is, to the Radiant Empire of Light, the boundless plains of the Sky, for that is the place where I exist, although I am not, for this is where I may place my crown upon my head, and I can think to myself that Seiobo was there below.

They help him, but there are too many, too many assistants; to tell the truth even one would be too many, and still there's this crowd of people here; he would like to be alone here for a while, alone in the mirrored room, he would like to remove the zō-onna mask from his face by himself, he could certainly do so if he were alone, but no, this he cannot do, the theater assistants obligingly jump all around him, they have already untied the mask's cord at the back of his head, and they're even leading him out already, out of the mirrored room, the sound of clapping can still be heard from the audience in the Kanze, then it dies away; but even if it weren't dying away he wouldn't be able to hear it, because they have taken him into the dressing room and already they are pulling, unhooking, unbuttoning, unwinding off from him all that must come off, as if it were urgent, when it is not urgent, they are taking off the costume from him already, one of them is folding up the expensive kimono, the other is already folding up the hakama, it all goes completely smoothly like a well-oiled machine, everyone in a great rush as if it were important that he should not be the nochi-shite he was just now, but just as soon as possible Inoue sensei once again; yet he would like to be alone just for a little while, alone, but no, this is not possible, someone is running up to him and softly whispers in his ear that the sensei—that is to say he himself, has a total of fifteen minutes—then someone, Kaneko-san, is coming for him, who will take him to the car via the performers' entrance, then within minutes, he will be in the select presence of the venerable spectators, of the wealthy sponsors, at the reception organized by the Kanze, no, he knows that it has to be like this; he has done so on many hundreds of occasions already; still, every single time, just like now, one single feeling works within him: how unpleasant it is that he cannot be alone, it is especially difficult here in the Kanze Kaikan—although it is difficult in every Noh theater, for it is always like this, after the performance one has to rush so as not to be late in receiving the congratulatory bows in the eloquent banquet-rooms in the hotels or the restaurants; the nearby hotel, this time sensei Umewaka Rokura himself might be present, the theater assistant whispers, although it is not at all certain, as sensei Rokura as a matter of fact may well be heading to Tokyo on the Shinkansen, but maybe—the assistant tilts his head to the side with an endearing smile—and already they are giving him the shite's, that is to say his own, robe, so he can go into the shower; certainly, without the slightest doubt, he has to do this, the assistant is leaping in front of him with ultimate courtesy, but it's as if he were running behind him and pushing him forward so that he would go into the bathroom already, for on his arm already there hangs the pants and the shirt of the venerable shite, indeed, even his necktie, which then the attendant ties for him, but I could do up my own necktie, thinks the sensei tiredly, he doesn't even really admit it to himself, but now, at times like this, after the agemaku tumbles down behind him, and the performance has come to an end, the desire is always there within him simply to preserve this infinite joy and tranquility, to conceal the infinite fatigue that is within him as well, he would like to conceal it completely but his costume is already being removed, the cord of the mask is being untied from the back, the kimono and hakama are already off, there is only his sweating body, he feels that very much; another assistant however obligingly offers him a towel, and he is already wiping himself off, to free himself from much of the sweat, there is no time to think, there is no time to be immersed in thought, everyone unceasingly rushes around, as always the excitement is great, as if something had happened out there that he himself doesn't know about, he hopes that it is the performance itself that gives rise to such excitement behind the stage, in the rear spaces of the building, but no, he knows that isn't the cause, there are too many performances for that, too much superfluous repetition of meaningless insignificant things, as for example these successively repeating, superfluous, and meaningless receptions, where of course he has to be present to acknowledge the words of recognition and the bows, and maybe sensei Rokuro himself will really be there, in that school belonging to a branch of the Kanze Umewaka, the Kyōto-branch leadership of which has devolved onto himself in recent months—this hope always comes up—because that would make it worthwhile if the fifty-sixth sensei, Umewaka Rokura, the director of the school, would be there, the reception itself would at once be meaningful—of course as usual sensei Rokuro isn't there at these receptions, only his wife, in the best cases, is, although that too is rare—sensei Rokuro usually isn't there; it is to sensei Rokuro and none other, however, that the shite of today's performance, that is to say he, sensei Inoue, can give thanks, sensei Rokuro is unquestionably the leading authority of the Umewaka school, and for him, sensei Inoue—who never was and perhaps never will be a true professional Noh actor, as he started off with too many disadvantages, on the one hand he did not come from a Noh family, and on the other he began the Noh practice late in life, that is to say when he was already an adult—for him, it was only the sensitivity of sensei Rokuro, his recognition of sensei Inoue's particular abilities, in a word, that sharp eye that had discovered him, that is the reason why he is treated like a professional Noh actor and is given two or three shite-roles every year, just like the others, like anyone else among the membership of the Umewaka or the Kanze schools, in addition to which the distinction of the directorship of the Umewaka Kyōto branch has been entrusted to him, unambiguously indicating that sensei Rokuro favors him, and understands that for him the art of Noh is his entire life: where he, Inoue Kazuyuki, is just a medium who, so to speak, merely allows onto himself that which the Heavens shower down upon him—just let there be no reception, he shakes his head underneath the shower tap, although he doesn't have much time either for showering or head-shaking, for the assistant is standing there with the towels and with his clothes; in barely ten minutes from now, he will be there standing at the edge of the reception organized for the wealthy patrons, not daring to push deeper into the crowd, although he is forced inward, and he hears words of recognition coming from every direction, and with deep bows, everyone expresses how miraculous they consider what they just saw on the stage of the Kanze Kaikan; a glass is in his hand but still he doesn't drink from it, for a while now he has only drunk a special kind of water, which a Korean healer, whom he visits regularly, prescribes for him, for he only trusts in him and not in doctors; he has high blood pressure, ever since his life-threatening Dojoji performance last year it at times goes up to two hundred, and this could give rise to serious concerns, the doctors shake their heads, but the little Korean doesn't shake his head at all, he just nods once and prescribes the special water for two hundred thousand yen; he believes in it, and that is perhaps the most important thing, he feels the beneficial effect, he tells his experiences to the Korean who doesn't say anything in reply, he just bows and nods, and once again he prescribes the special water, gold is more expensive, Ribu-san, sensei Inoue's wife, jokingly notes to Amoru-san, his second wife, but of course it remains only between them; now, however, of course, there is a champagne glass in the sensei's hand, he steals a glance at the clock on the wall, he will stay for a bit longer, then after a long farewell during which he must take leave of every person there individually, he leaves the room, the taxi has already been there in front of the hotel for a while, and it has been waiting for him, we're going to the Mahorowa, the sensei says softly, which circumstance indicates that everything continues exactly the same as always, namely that we're going to the Mahorowa, and the sensei will continue his rehearsal, for him there is no difference between the rehearsal and the performance, there is only a difference between the practice of Noh and the non-practice of Noh—the latter, however is something that he hardly recognizes—his entire day from morning until late at night is filled with rehearsal, whether he is in Kyōto or Tokyo, as he divides his life between these two cities, for he has disciples in Kyōto and the surrounding areas as well, and he has disciples in Toyko and its surrounding areas, so accordingly two weeks in Kyōto, two weeks in Tokyo, that is how the sensei's life proceeds, in which of course are his own rehearsals are the most important, and these take place either in the Mahorowa or in the Shin-E Building, depending on what the sensei deems advisable, if he has to go to the Korean or wishes to return for a short while to his parents' home, then he goes to the Shin-E Building not far from Kyōto Station; if he wants to stay at home—and generally he does at the end of the day—then the Mahorowa; the Shin-E Building or the Mahorowa, the Mahorowa or the Shin-E Building, if he is in Kyōto, things proceed between these two places, but often enough, he creates the impression among the family members, and also his disciples, especially his most fervent admirers—Chiwako-san and Norumu-san, or Himuko-san or Raun—that he is simply improvising in the selection of his schedule; in any event, as soon as the expression "improvising" arises they drive it out of their minds, because—they affirm among themselves—that even if it seems that way, he never improvises, what happens is not improvisation, absolutely not in the everyday sense of the word, of that they are sure, since the sensei knows everything in advance, and knows it with dead certainty, and this is the general conviction, that's why only to them does it seem like improvisation, because while it is true that he has a prescribed schedule for every given month, the sensei is eternally open, like a book, which means that he is in direct contact with the Heavens, and for that reason he may suddenly be a bit unpredictable, since he follows the dictates of his soul in this direct connection, and thus he is constantly overturning all the things in the monthly-schedule notebooks he himself deems advisable to plan out for himself; the sensei himself does not, of course, sense this unpredictably, for he is entirely free, in this and every possible sense of the word he is free—rehearsal and teaching, teaching and rehearsal—in a word, only and exclusively the Noh; only rarely does he go anywhere different, for example, now and then, to the place before a performance where the play in question is being performed, so that he can worship there, or to the services of the Christian congregation at the corner of Oike Kawaramachi, but not for Jesus, as he puts it, but so he can take part in a shared collective joy, and of course only rarely, only sometimes, because as a rule there is only rehearsal, for hours on end, and there is only teaching, for hours on end, get some sleep, the family members say, he sleeps for only three or four hours a day, for he goes to bed only very late at night, never before two in the morning, and he is already up before the first birdsong, at such times he reads, he prays, then somehow the day begins, with rehearsal, with teaching; then again rehearsal, then teaching again, and finally rehearsal and rehearsal in the Mahorowa, generally, if he is staying in Kyōto, there the day's activities end, the Mahorowa is very close to his residence, which as a residence is, in contrast to those of the other Noh performers, a modest two-story little building near the Kamigamo temple in the middle of a hardly elegant district, the sensei does not wish for riches—the disciples and the family members note—except when he is traveling, they add, then of course he has to be accommodated in a hotel that is worthy of his status, or a place commensurate with his status must be chosen for him at a dinner, although not anywhere in particular, he looks for simplicity in everything, the simple and the transparent, as opposed to complexity, luxury, and superfluity; the taxi glides along; in the back seat sit the sensei and Amoru-san, and behind the taxi is the minibus with the disciples, and behind that are the family members in their cars, and thus they reach the Mahorowa this evening, and after a late dinner together and some more Seiobo-rehearsing, he withdraws, with only his close family, with Ribu-san and Amoru-san at his side, into the house that serves as his home; he prays for a long time at the house altar, then answers a question now and then put to him by Ribu-san, then they kneel down and they bow to each other, and that is how they take leave of one another, then he, the sensei, takes a bath, and goes up to his room, where at last he can be alone, he loves this best of all, to be alone before going to sleep, closeted in the bedroom, he turns on the electric light, it illuminates faintly, weakly, he takes up his book, sensei Takahashi's commentary on the Heart Sutra, which he reads regularly—and he begins somewhere, then he goes to the window, looks out onto the dark evening, prays for a long time, and at last lies back down, reads a few more pages yet, then closes the book, puts it in place on the small table next to the bed, and he is alone, enough now to be able to become tranquil, he is now capable of falling asleep, and then slowly he really does fall asleep into deep slumber.

His heart is very rich, explains Ribu-san in the Mahorowa: a rich heart, and a profoundly deep secret, that is the sensei . . . but it is difficult, she says, and she doesn't worry that the sensei himself hears this; it is very difficult to speak about him because he doesn't resemble me or us in any way at all, since he is entirely different in everything; I, she points at herself, I have been his wife for more than three decades, but often I don't know what anything means to him, he continually astounds me, because I am blind, whereas he sees, I am blind to what is coming but he already sees what things will be like, I have said many times it's impossible, or a miracle, and I've marveled at him because of that, but then I accepted that the sensei knows already in advance what is going to happen later, and also that this comes not from himself but from the world, from the true structure of the world, which he and only he sees and knows, but I could also express it like this: the sensei just feels things, and he is deaf, deaf, to those things that we are not deaf to, he is deaf to mundane explanations because he only feels, only grasps what his soul tells him, we are deaf to our souls, to him our mediocre imaginings and connections mean nothing at all, he sees them, he sees us, he knows what we believe, what we are thinking, and what we do, he knows the laws that are important to us, the laws that determine and circumscribe all of us here, yet these laws, in regard to the sensei, somehow ... just don't affect him at all, however absurd this may sound, still it is so: he also eats, showers, gets dressed, and goes and sits down and stands up and drives the car and checks his bank receipts and the money sent here from the Umewaka school, but with him nothing occurs as it does with us, in that moment, when he is eating, showering, getting dressed and so on, somehow at once ... everything is different, how can she even explain it; Ribu-san closes her eyes tight, and it could be a kind of illness with her because this happens every minute, she closes her eyes tightly shut and at such times her face contracts sharply, to make it clearly understood that well, it's difficult, she tilts her head to one side, because if she says that the sensei finishes everything, that he never leaves anything undone, that he is unpredictable, and that she never knows what he will do or say in the very next moment, then she hasn't said anything at all, and it is really as if that were so, that she has said nothing at all, because at this point the sensei interrupts her, until now he has been listening to Ribu-san in silence, with mute agreement and patience, with a kind of motionless gaiety in his eyes, but now in the Mahorowa he puts in a word and notes in his own particular way of speaking—that is to say that as he pronounces every single word, indeed, truly, every single word, he pulls his mouth back widely, like someone who smiles with each single word, so that after the word or the sentence has been uttered, the face at once settles back into those serious features that hold this face in that motionless perpetual serenity—every single day, he suddenly speaks, every day *I am prepared for death,* and then there is silence in the Mahorowa; the first time he met with death—he continues in tones even softer than usual—was when, in his childhood, a tall thin person came into the street where he lived, he came up to where he was playing, and greeted him and the other children; ohayou, he said, and he went on, on along the street, up to the end of the street, then he went out onto the Horikawa, and this happened every single day, the tall thin man, whether in the morning, the afternoon, at dawn, or at dusk, appeared again and again, and greeted him as he played in the middle of the street, and for him, the sensei says, this greeting became important, and he loved this person, and after a while he waited expectantly for him to appear already, and he was happy if he saw him at the end of the street; this person came, greeted him, and went on, and then one day he did not come anymore, and from that point on he never appeared again, and they quickly learned from the neighbors that he had been struck by a car out on the Horikawa, he had been taken to the hospital, where he continually asked for water, but the doctors did not give him water, but he just asked more and more for water, just water and water, he became dreadfully thirsty, but he did not get water from the doctors, they didn't give him any, and he died, well that is when, says sensei Inoue, I met with death for the first time, yet to understand what it meant, he still had to wait awhile, but then the time came, and he understood everything, and since then he has known that there is no tomorrow; I never think about that—he lowers his voice even more, and with every word that he utters he smiles, as is his custom, then his face closes up again—never, he says, because I only think about today, for me there is no tomorrow, for me there is no future, because every day is the last day, and every day is full and complete, and I could die on any given day, I am ready for it, and then the whole thing will come to an end, and by this he means that—he looks up at a guest sitting across from him on the other side of the room—that one whole will come to an end, and in the distance another shall begin, I am waiting for death, he says with an unvarying smile, I am waiting, he says, and death is always close to me, and I shall lose nothing if I die, because for me only the present means everything, this day, this hour, this moment—this moment in which I am dying.

That he was born, he says, he remembers exactly, he remembers that he was born, they lived on the first floor, and he sees himself, his body, down there far below, but he sees his soul as well—what did his soul look like?—well, it was white, and he couldn't cry, because the umbilical cord was wound around his neck; and with that everything began, his entire life, and he had to cry but couldn't, not figuratively, but because of the umbilical cord, he would have cried, but no sound came out of his throat, everyone watched him in fear, his father wasn't even there, he remembers everything clearly; the room where he came into the world, the windows, the tatamis, the washbasins, all of the room's objects, and where they were placed, and he remembers very well the feeling that he had been born, of where he had come from, and he understood immediately that he had now stepped into a different form, into a different existence, here somehow everything was harder: principally, breathing, and not only because of the umbilical cord around his neck, for someone immediately unwound it, the hardest thing of all was the breathing, that he had to take breaths or to put it more correctly, things weren't even more difficult, but generally, everything seemed to have weight, everything became apparent together with its weight, that was the new thing, and inconceivable, and so very heavy, everything slowed down, and this everything was still bloody and slippery, and everything was slipping and was in shadow, as if somewhere the light was shining, the shadow of which only extended to here; but even today, when he conjures this memory up, he doesn't know what was casting that shadow, he conjures it up with particular frequency, not even intending to, rather it just somehow floats into his consciousness, without any cause or precedent; that's how it must have been, that was his birth, his father was not there, he wasn't even there when they took him out of the room, he was not at home, during that time he was often away; the family was engaged in the respirator-mask trade, and the demand was great after the war, so his father didn't live with his family but no one knew where, or with whom; he appeared only once a month, when he brought home his dirty clothes for his mother to launder, your father is a bad man, his mother said to him, but he never, not for a single instant, felt that, in any event, his father, if he had money, really did not live at home, the business went well, so that a month went by before his father took him into his arms, he brought the dirty laundry, and he looked at his son, and it is there very clearly within him that his father somehow held him at a distance from himself and thus examined him, but he didn't sense that his father was bad: he was without any emotion at all, in the most objective manner possible, he determined that this is my father, while the father, in all likelihood, without any emotion at all and in the most objective manner, said, this is my son; this was his first meeting with his father, he recalls this as a very particular moment if he thinks about it, that first meeting, and in addition to its particularity, the most important thing was that it was the first, because later, afterward, for a good long time, he saw his father only very rarely, and his father hardly ever picked him up because he just showed up once a month, he took the money and brought the laundry, he waited until his mother gave him what he had brought one month ago—washed out and prepared—he hardly even sat down, or just for a little, and he always left immediately, hence it could be said that he grew up without a father, it could be said that his mother, abandoned, raised him, and the two of them lived together; he had no siblings, there was only him and his mother, altogether the two of them, his father showing up for only a few minutes once a month every month, so that he was alone very much of the time, indeed, in point of fact, he was always alone, all the time, this was his childhood and his youth, he says, and that is why later on he decided that if he reached manhood, he would have a huge family, and it turned out that way too, because here, he shows, is sensei Kimiko, and Sumiko-san, and Yumito-san, they are his daughters, and the littlest one, my son, is there, he says, Tomoaki, none of them are children anymore, and he has two grandchildren too: Maya-chan from Kimoko's family, and Aya-chan from Sumiko's family, he has a wife, Ribu-san, and next to her there is Amoru-san, but these are not the only people around him, but countless others as well, disciples in Kyōto, disciples in Tokyo, in Fujiyama and in Arayama, at least eighty people altogether, which of course doesn't change anything about his solitude, because everyone is a soul, everyone; the family members and students he is addressing nod respectfully, who—now the pause in the Seiobo rehearsal is longer than usual, they see that the sensei is beginning to speak at greater length this time, he is talking to the guest and, well, at that point, as if a sign had been given, they sit all around their father and their grandfather and their master, because sensei Kimoko is there and Sumiko-san and Yumito-san and Tomoaki-san, and Maya-chan and Aya-chan are there, and there too—always a little detached from the others—is the mysterious silent Amoru-san, too, and of course the sensei's most faithful disciples as well, Chiwako-san, Nozumu-san, and Himuko-san, and Ante-san and Haragu-san, and Gomu-Gomu and Raun, here in the Mahorowa, as the master calls his rehearsal space not far from the Kamigamo shrine, in the northwest corner of Kyōto, everyone is here, and they listen to their father and their grandfather and their master with the greatest of curiosity, although it is completely obvious that they have heard this quite a few times already and they know all of the master's stories, so they know too the ones in which he speaks of himself, but perhaps it is just that fact that impresses them so much, the master always tells them with the same, precisely the same words, he never mixes up his words, never mixes up the order of events in the stories, and he always begins by saying that I remember that I was born, we lived on the first floor, and I see myself, my body, down there far below, but I see my own soul as well—never a single alteration, and this is passed on: the family members and the students themselves try to follow the master's words exactly, when they begin to speak of him to someone with enthusiasm, in this way, the master's story is passed on, just like a fairy-tale, although with the difference that in this story not even one single word may ever be altered, not even a single expression, no one may add anything to it, and no one may take anything away, he was born on December 22, 1947, in Kyōto, he says, the family home is still there, and even today it is his property, the street however has no name, it is a completely narrow, tiny alley, and it was always like that, it lies not far from the Nanna-jo and the Horikawa-dori intersection, across from the enormous Nishi-Hongan-ji temple, you have to picture the alley running parallel with the Nanna-jo, just a few houses on it and among them, there in the middle, was ours, he says, where the lower story was always used for business purposes—for the respirator-mask trade—even today it is like that, we lived on the upper floor, my mother and I, because there were only two of us in the house, my father, while the business was still operating, turned up once a month, for a very brief time, to leave his dirty clothes and take his clean ones, my mama was always working, she hardly had any time to be with me, so that I was alone so much, so very much, so that my solitude was truly profound, as profound as solitude could be, he says, and roughly at that point, as if touched by a magic wand, the family members and the students begin, by mutual consent—as if from this point on the story doesn't really concern them—to return to their places, the places from where, listening to the beginning of the master's story just now, they had gathered around him, the children and the grandchildren move at least ten meters to his left; generally this is how the private rehearsals, when the master rehearses by himself, proceed, and completely apart from him, in the background, so that the master will not be disturbed, are the children, chiefly Kimoko, the eldest girl, who herself has already reached the level of master; accordingly then, farther away from the father and grandfather, the disciples seek out an even more suitable distance from him to the right, or sit facing him by the wall of the Mahorowa, for the place of the master is sacred, no one may sit close to him, only Amoru-san, but only so she can supervise, keep accounts of, arrange the master's affairs; Amoru-san, about whom someone not from here would hardly be able to say what it was she was doing, although she is always doing something during the rehearsals—he remembers a boy on a bicycle, he says; it was still before he himself began attending school, a boy fell down in the street with his bicycle, and he really had a bad fall, but everyone just laughed at him, just then there were a lot of us on the street, and everyone laughed at the boy, but not me, I wept, I felt so sorry for him, mainly because I felt how much his knee was hurting from the fall, my mother began saying enough already, stop crying, he's already gone, he dusted off his trousers, got onto his bicycle, and he's already cycled off toward the Horikawa, but he still just wept, he really felt sorry for him, so incredibly sorry for him, because the others had laughed at him; but this actually was not his own memory, he says, this was told to him by his mother much later, and so it remained like that, it became his own memory, and now he relates it as if he were recollecting something he remembered, which, however, he did, thanks to his mother, as, for example, when already in school, he says, we went to the swimming pool once, but there was one boy among us who did not dare to go in, he was afraid of water, he was afraid of the swimming pool, I understood what he was afraid of, though I myself was not afraid; yet everyone began to jeer at him, and I of course just burst out crying, I felt so sorry for him, they talked about it when I was older already, that as a small child it was always like that, I was always feeling sorry for somebody, and I was always weeping, and these have become memories that have accompanied me throughout my entire life, and so he continues unchecked, in his own particular way of speaking, repeating and repeating, there are numerous repetitions in the narration, but it's as if he were doing it just for the rhythm, because his memory—if it is a question of the Noh—is formidable; if he is telling a story, as he is now, he keeps returning to each point, each thread of the story, which he already related earlier, perhaps because he wishes to emphasize them, or because he wishes to preserve a content-rhythm of events untraceable by anyone else, it is impossible to know; in any event his memories from his nursery school years are innumerable, he says, namely that there was a nursery school nearby, facing the corner of the Nishi-Hongan-ji, yet opposite, in the inner corner of the Nishi-Hongan-ji, there inside, an enormous tower rose, and this proved to be a very particular building indeed, because no matter what time of day it was, whether morning or noon or evening, this tower, which in the time of the Meiji Dynasty had been called the shinseigomin, completely covered the nursery school in shadow, so that all of my nursery-school memories are connected with this completely dark nursery, because that enormous tower overshadowed us completely, there inside it was always dark, and I had to spend my entire nursery time there with the others, we played there in the dark, right up until when it was time to start school, and all the while, not one nanny or teacher turned up who even once mentioned or explained why it was always so dark inside, and that is why it stayed with me, that nursery school is some kind of dark place where children play in the dark, and where there is always an enormous tower rising somewhere nearby; but then came school and with that something different, as it happened the worst thing of all and completely suddenly, namely that from one day to the next our business went bankrupt, my father's business partner, with whom we ran the respirator-mask business, suddenly left, here was the problem now, thanks to him: he disappeared, vanished without a trace, we never saw him again, yet we stayed on there and it was really bad, because earlier we had had everything, we suffered no deprivation whatsoever, indeed, the master says, he believes that many considered his family to be well-off, they had a television set and a piano, and there were few people, few families that could permit themselves that, for after the Second World War nearly everyone lost everything, just their respiratory mask business flourished, until it went bankrupt, and from that point on they were plunged, completely unexpectedly, into the deepest poverty, they had nothing left, neither a television nor a piano, and the saddest thing of all, he says, was that my father who, while the business was successful, was never at home, moved back one day after we had gone bankrupt, and from then on until the day he died he lived at home; he sat in silence, I remember exactly where: downstairs where we used to run our business, facing the window, and even today in my memories he is still there, smoking a cigarette, and for years he didn't look away from the window, he never really took part in anything, he just sat there and smoked a cigarette, he left everything in the care of my mother; yet if I gave him some advice about anything, he immediately took it up—although at the time I was only nine years old, altogether nine, when he moved back into the house, and we were plunged into destitution—sometimes I gave him this or that piece of advice, and he honored these recommendations, that we had to address this or that problem, my mother also listened to me, but according to custom it was my father who had to say that this, that, or the other should be done, and he always agreed with my advice, my father wasn't interested in how old I was, he accepted my recommendations as did my mother, in fact, my relationship with my mother was the closest, no one was important to me, just my mother, she raised me, looked after me, took care of me, and I loved my mother very much, I spoke about everything with her, not only as a child, as a youth, but afterward as well, I felt her to be much closer to me than my father, or anyone else; she lived with her husband, that is to say with my father, in the old house until her death, near the Kyōto Station, there in the street that runs parallel with the Nanna-jo, in the parental house that is now close as well to the Shin-E Building, and after a while, when I moved back to Kyōto—because I was away for a while, I moved back here, to the Kamigamo: we were living quite far from each other, but nearly every day I came to visit her, and I talked about everything with her, it was like that up until her death, because she was the person closest to me, not even like a mother but like a friend, there was nothing that I couldn't discuss with her, I had no secrets before her, to keep a secret would have been totally senseless, I did, however, worry about her greatly, when my family sank into poverty, my father's business partner left, my father came home, and in general there was no money at all, the business had completely collapsed, but what could we do, we had to work, and then my mother did just what she could, namely there was a possibility of making Christmas-tree decorations, one yen for each piece; after the big collapse there was simply nothing to eat, we were in such a difficult situation, and we only got rice regularly from my mother's relatives in the countryside, there was that, rice and water, rice and water, every day, it was because of that that my mother had to work, my father was incapable of doing anything, most likely because he had collapsed as well, just like our business, we had to make these baubles for Christians, that was the only possibility, the value of the yen, however, was very low, and my mother had to make a lot of these baubles every single day, so I began to help her, I too was making these baubles for Christians to hang on their Christmas trees, the only problem was that I was still a child, and a child could not be treated as a regular employee, he says; so that he could only get half a yen for the same work, and that wasn't enough to live on, his mother's earnings and then what he earned, it wasn't enough; in addition it turned out to be a bigger problem that these baubles turned out to be very small, they had to be small, and after a while his mother's eyes couldn't take it anymore; how small they were—she strained her eyes, she fatally overworked them—she could work for a few hours but then her eyes were tired, she cried, and finally it was *painful* for his mother, she developed a kind of over-sensitivity of the optic nerve, in the evening she could hardly bear to look at anything; but it was all in vain, she could not stop working, so after a while, when in the evening those eyes were really hurting a lot, he said, a nun began visiting them, she took care of his mother, she cooked the rice, and this lasted until he, the master, was in the eleventh grade, during which time, he says, he was continually worried, he was very worried for his mother, he couldn't even pay attention in school, he only thought of his mother's eyes, and how they would hurt in the evenings, and he really wanted his mother to stop working, already he was in middle school but everything went on, and he was worried that his mother wouldn't stop, and that there would be a huge problem, he was so worried that he couldn't think of anything else, only about her, and he became more and more worried that she would be very ill, and wouldn't get up anymore; keep on studying, they told him, but he was incapable of that, he says, he wanted to stay home at any cost, to help his mother, and he did stay home, and he helped her too, he too began to produce these baubles for the Christmas trees, and he didn't go to university, even though his teacher advised him to do so, instead of university the Christmas baubles, really it couldn't be otherwise, he had to stay at home, because in any event he wouldn't have been able to concentrate on anything else from all the worry, and he was still in middle school when, at the beginning of the school year, there was the renowned mountain-climbing event, this was the occasion that he, along with every one of his classmates, awaited with great excitement, just that in his case the problem was that the other school children always, the week before the big mountain-climbing event, got a new pair of running shoes, yet so great was the destitution in their home that there was no money for new running shoes, so that his mother came up with the idea of polishing the old running shoes with some halfpenny chocolate, first she really cleaned them off and then smeared the chocolate on, and really they looked as if they could have been new, but he was distressed by this, and because he was not ashamed if, due to the family's poverty, he was the only one not to get new running shoes before the big mountain-climbing event, he took the shoes and scraped off the chocolate, and he never went mountain climbing with the others, this is just one example of how difficult it was, he says, but an example, too, of how difficult it was for him to be with others; it wasn't as if he didn't long to be among them, there was nothing he desired more than to play alongside them, it was just that some obstacle or another was always in the way, which meant that he always had to renounce their companionship, so when he was in middle school he became even more solitary than he had been in primary school: just his mother and he, the two of them in the street that ran parallel with the Nanna-jo, while his father sat the entire day in the old business premises, smoking cigarettes and looking out the window, although nothing ever happened out there, he was completely alone, and so the years passed and the compassion within him for those who could not make friends grew ever deeper, or for those who could not be with the people they wanted to be with, because he was always at home, or at school, or at school or at home, and because he was so worried for his mother and the entire family, and what would happen to them if he wasn't at home, during this time because of the worry he very often would not go out into the street to play, or go and join up with the others during school breaks, because there was only one thought in his mind, how to find an exit from this destitution so that his mother would not have to strain her eyes; he brooded over this incessantly, and of course in the meantime, he says, he did not have too much time to think about playing with the others; he could however have made friends, for example, with the boy who once complained that he felt very bad, and he was really afraid, because he couldn't go like this to his singing lessons in the mornings; I said to him, he says, that I would go in his place, and I even went, I went, and in the meantime I learned everything that he was supposed to learn, then later at the singing lessons I explained the situation with my classmate; I sang everything that he was supposed to have sung, and I was praised greatly, and the teacher said that they did not reproach my classmate for his absences, that it was alright, and of course the boy in question was very grateful for this, and they could have even been friends, but well he had to go home, at the beginning he just walked normally, then he began to move quickly, but finally he was already running, so afraid was he that while he was gone something had happened with his mother's eyes, and so it was not possible for him to be anyone's friend, for even if this boy had invited him on another afternoon to come along and play with him, in this dark period of his life he only thought immediately of what would happen at home if he weren't there, this was always his profound conviction, that no one would be there to help, as he was utterly certain, under this burden of continual suffering, that a larger catastrophe was looming; in the first place he thought of his mother, filled with concern for her, thinking that the catastrophe would be connected with her eyes, but it didn't happen like that, something completely different occurred, something completely extraordinary that turned everything upside down and changed their lives; no one thought that it could happen but it did; everyone, and in particular he himself, was convinced that the catastrophe was here, about to occur, and everything seemed so utterly hopeless that one day—such was the sorrow that overwhelmed him from his mother's and father's fate—he made a decision and went to them in the upper room, and his advice was that they should commit suicide, together, the entire family, because in my view, I said to them, he says, this is the only solution, this is what I can recommend, because we are so bereft of any future, there is no future whatsoever for us, all of our time is completely taken up solving the problems of everyday life, of what we are going to eat; well, of course I wasn't thinking of any future, I did not wish for any future, because there was no future at all, I went to the upstairs room, I knelt down before them, I bowed, and I said, let us all commit suicide together, but in the end we didn't do it, because an extraordinary turn of events came about, something completely unimaginable: one day in school a big white dog suddenly got into the hallway, I was in the seventh grade, when a stray, bedraggled, white dog came in, and it was in such a bad state that everyone just yelled and screamed at it, but no one dared or wanted to try to grab hold of it, it was evident, however, that the dog was getting close to the end already, its entire body was trembling, its fur was scraped off, and it was so skinny that its bones literally stuck out, of course it was chased out of the classroom somehow, and chased out of the entire building onto the street, it's just that the dog didn't leave but stayed there near the school and stayed right underneath our classroom window, it didn't move away from there for a whole week, it just trembled and cried and howled and whined, you could hear it very clearly, and in the end I couldn't hear anything else, I heard it even at home: so the dog did not budge from next to the tree, they tried to chase it away with a cane, but it was simply impossible to chase it away, so it stayed, no one bothered it anymore, only you could hear it crying, and I—as the week went by—looked at the dog, and I saw how it wanted to die, and then I said to myself, I have to take it home, somehow it will get along with us, and so, the master relates, that's exactly what he did, he took the dog home, he just said to it come, and at that one single word the dog came; but his mother said we can't do this, we can't have a dog here, whatever are we going to give him to eat, and this really did present a huge problem, as they had no meat that they could give to the dog, only rice, and moreover, dogs don't eat rice; his mother advised him to take it out to the monastery, it can't stay here, but, he says, he was not able to do that, he pleaded with his family, please let it stay here, he even made a doghouse secretly, he pleaded with his mother, but she said we don't have enough even for ourselves, to which he replied that he would give the dog his own portion, which of course sounded a bit peculiar, because dogs don't eat rice, but then he implored his mother so much that that night they gave the dog his nightly portion of rice, and the dog ate the rice, and then already his mother began to see things differently, and she allowed the dog to stay, fine, she said, we'll keep it, and really it turned out like that, he says, we took in the white dog, and two weeks later, altogether two weeks after the day that we had taken the dog in—people began knocking at the front door saying they wanted to buy an oxygen mask, suddenly they were getting orders, my father's business started up again, and even his business partner, the one who had caused the business to go bankrupt earlier, turned up again, and suggested that due to the change in demand they should go back into partnership again, and the telephone rang off the hook, and there were hundreds and thousands of orders, everything changed at once, the business flourished; at that time, the massive industrialization campaign was going on and due to the pollution, a huge demand for oxygen masks arose, and in addition, my father's business partner came up with a new kind of mask, a yellow one that filtered out the pollution more effectively, and it became so successful that even the state television, the NHK, did a program about it and advertised it, everything got better, the master lowers his voice, and everyone knew, my mother knew, I knew, and my father knew as well, that the change in our fate was because of the dog, it brought us luck, my father announced sitting on his chair in front of the window, and from that point on he prayed for it, for the white dog, and ever since he, my father, died, I pray for it, and when I shall die, my first-born child, sensei Kimiko will pray for it too.

It is difficult to express the joy of the practice in words, he then says, if there is a rehearsal—and for him there is always a rehearsal—then he breaks free from all indirectness and he is absolutely active, immersed, totally identified with what he is doing: with the next step to follow in the sequence, with the holding of the arm, the placement of the fan in front of the body, with the placement of the body in space, and then with the poetry and songs that began to resound in his voice, through his voice, which bursts out of the depths; in a word if he is rehearsing, as he has been just now with Seiobo, or if he is continuing the Seiobo rehearsal, as he shall do in a moment, then he feels in the deepest of depths that there is a soul; if he does the necessary dance-steps according to the prescribed order, then he doesn't think about whether or not the spirit is operating within him, because this spirit is perfectly ingrained in the order of steps he has just completed, he does not gape into the future thinking: after this, what step do I need to take, after this, what step comes next; it is a question of only one step that exactly fills the present moment, it is always this that he must concentrate on, says the sensei, on what I can do exactly in this moment, indeed, to put it more precisely, on what I am doing in this moment, this is altogether what concentration is for, not for anything else, not for the desire that this step here will be better, but that exactly in this moment, exactly this step in the dance is coming into being; that is all you have to know, and the rest is a matter of the soul; in a word, rehearsal is his life, so that for him there is absolutely no difference between rehearsal and performance, there is no particular mode of performance in the Noh, what happens in a performance is exactly the same as what happens in a rehearsal and vice versa, what happens in a rehearsal is exactly the same as what happens in a performance, there is no divergence, but as for him he is happier to view it all as a rehearsal, because this expresses the fact better that it is not about some kind of finality or completion, it better expresses the fact that the Noh has no goal, and this goal, in particular, is not performance, but that for him his entire life is a rehearsal, a successive awakening—or rather, he would just say, a waking up, since there is nothing to awaken to, namely that what remains is awoken to successively; this is a truly inexpressible catharsis for a Noh performer such as himself, for whom Noh is everything and the source of all things, the Noh only gives and he only receives, and he understands everything, because one then understands that things do not turn out for the better because a person has a certain level of apprehension of what will be correct in the future, but that things turn out for the better if a person has a correct apprehension of the present, namely, this is a kind of apprehension that is good not just for you but for everyone, that is to say it doesn't harm anyone, so thus it is good in general; no, says the sensei, smiling, he does not believe that those who speak so threateningly of an approaching catastrophe, some kind of a total collapse, a complete apocalypse, are in the right, for such people never take into account—and this is very characteristic—they never take into account the fact that there are higher potentialities; you have to know that your own experience in this is crucial for understanding how senseless it is to separate living beings, to divide up living things from each other and from yourself, for everything occurs in one single time and one single place, and the path to the comprehension of this leads through the correct understanding of the present, one's own experience is necessary, and then you will understand, and every person will understand that something cannot be separated from something else, there is no god in some faraway dominion, there is no earth far from him here below, and there is no transcendental realm somewhere else apart from where you are now, all that you call transcendental or earthly is one and the same, together with you in one single time and one single space, and the most important of all is that there is no room here for either hope or for miracles, since hope has no basis and there are no miracles, namely that everything happens as it must happen, miracles never changed anything in his life, he says, but he realized that it was a question of the endlessly simple operations of an endlessly complicated construction, so that anything can happen, anything can turn into reality, all told it is just the natural result of potentially billions of single outcomes, namely that—the sensei says this now in an entirely subdued voice, indicating that his words are being uttered only for the guest—namely that before we are born, the Heavens have innumerable plans for us, but after we are born there is just a single one; these recognitions, of course, do not always come easily; he, for example suffered greatly before he could encapsulate his experiences in a correct manner; and when the time was right, the personal teachings and written thoughts of Master Takahashi Shinji directed him, it was he, sensei Shinji, who was able to explain to him, when they met personally when he was a youth of nineteen, his story of losing God did not by any means lead him to suicide, that is to say, on one occasion, he related to him, that when he was praying, still at his home in Kyōto, on the upper floor of his old house, as he knelt with his hands folded in prayer, he suddenly caught a glimpse of himself in his own shaving mirror, and from that, all at once, he lost his faith; well as for that, sensei Takahashi explained to him, that is not the loss of God but on the contrary, it means that you have found God, whatever we call it, we might as well call it God, said sensei Takahashi Shinji, it's sweet all the same, that was the first thing that sensei Shinji said to him, and it had an enormous effect, similarly as when he sat next to his deathbed, there was a particular encounter when sensei Shinji, as a final admonition told him that at times the existence of the higher dimensions are veiled by those selfsame higher dimensions, that is what he heard from him, and it goes without saying that then, altogether in one single flash of illumination, like a blow, he understood all these things: he perceived, he felt, the other person, he saw what lay behind the other, he saw others' past lives, so that the day quickly came when he had to take notice that it was not just he who believed in something, but that people believed in him as well—of course through the agency of the art of Noh—and that meant that if people were turning to him, and he was able, exclusively, to lift them up through the Noh, that he should live with this word, with that same word through which the genius of Ze'ami lived, for Noh is the lifting up of the soul, which, if it doesn't occur through Noh, that means that the Noh is not occurring, but if it does occur, then anyone can comprehend that above us and below us, outside of ourselves and deep within ourselves, there is a universe, the one and only, which is not identical with the sky looming above us overhead, because that universe is not made of stars and planets and suns and galaxies, because that universe is not a picture, it cannot be seen, it doesn't even have a name, for it is so much more precious than anything that could have a name, and that is why it is such a joy to me that I can practice Seiobo; Seiobo is the emissary who arrives and says I am not the desire for peace, I am peace itself; Seiobo arrives and says do not be afraid, for the universe of peace is not the rainbow of yearning; the universe, the real universe—already exists.

In front of Amoru-san there is a low table, and for several minutes now Amoru-san has been counting out an enormous pile of money while the sensei speaks, first she separates the ten-thousand yen notes from the five-thousand yen notes, then the five-thousand yen notes from the one-thousand yen notes, then she arranges them nicely, stacking the notes up into neat piles, as if she were playing but she isn't, she counts how much is in each pile three times, then she begins to stuff the money into envelopes, she takes one note from each pile, adds one from the second, then from the third, then slips the total amount into an envelope lined up, and again she removes a ten-thousand yen note, adds a ten-thousand yen note, or two, or three—it varies, and then she adds a five-thousand or one-thousand banknote into the envelope with them, and then comes the next envelope already, she moves her lips as if silently, yet all the time she has to pronounce to herself how much and how much, and the banknotes on one part of the little table are diminishing, while at the same time the columns of envelopes on the other side of the small table keep getting taller, so that soon there isn't enough room for the envelopes, and Amoru-san places them next to herself, beside her sitting cushion; first she counts the envelopes, then when that is done she brings out a little notebook and begins to count again the amounts that she's placed in the envelopes, and she writes them down, very slowly, under the appropriate heading in the notebook, and that is how her work proceeds, while the sensei is speaking, and whereas the sensei is essentially grave and stern, Amoru-san essentially just smiles, from her long, thin, pimpled face an eternal serenity radiates, and she leans her head to one side at times, and holds it for a while, tilting her head now toward the left, now toward her right shoulder, but counting all the while, and arranging, and stuffing, and noting down, and at times she interrupts all of this so that she can fix her long, slightly greasy hair, so she can take out from her pink-dyed snakeskin handbag a little mirror with the name Vivienne Westwood on it, and a Dior lipstick, and she paints her mouth bright red, her wide thick mouth from which the smile never fades away, and never will.

He prays in such a way that first he enumerates the Great Cosmos, then comes the Great Spirit, then the Great Buddha, then the Spirit who watches over us in the Days, then the Protector in the Days, then—the Bodhisattvas! then the Self-Originated One, and then the Benevolence of the Higher Powers!—and following all of them he prays for the fortitude of his own heart and all this up until now, says sensei Inoue, are his own personal transformations of the prayers of Takahashi Shinji, so that somehow, according to his own sensibilities, as the prayer and the circumstances wish it to be, at the end he says: Guardian Angel within the Heart! I ask you, shed Light, O Creator, into my Heart! and then Grant Peace to my Body, O Great Spirit! and: Fill my Heart with Light! and Fill the Kanze Kaikan with Light! and Grant this Prayer to All Those who come to the performance of Seiobo! then I Call upon Those who cannot come! then I Call upon Everyone who once was here, in the Kanze Kaikan! and then he says: Raise up their souls here into the Light! and finally he asks the Great Spirit to Grant me the opportunity to be able to perform Seiobo tonight! and he asks, Grant me strength, and Grant that this strength may flow through me and from me to each individual person! and at the very end he says May the Kanze Kaikan be a torch now in Japan, in the World, in the entire Universe! and Reflect this strength in all Directions during the performance into the Universe! O God, cause this strength to permeate everything! and at the very very end he says: O God the Creator! May Your Strength be in the Performance, and when he says all of this, he concludes with the following words: I Give Over My Fate Entirely!

This is my prayer, says sensei Kazuyuki smiling, and then the stern face is once again impenetrable.

Sensei is everything, says Amoru-san, I'm not good at anything, I don't know anything, I hate everyone, I only know sensei and I only love sensei, because sensei is everything, and my father was a very hard man, he beat me every day, every single day, once I knocked over a porcelain vase, then he shoved my head into the iron stove, and he slammed the stove door against my head until I lost consciousness; in a word every single day was painful for me, every blessed day hurt, and I wanted to die, for a long time it wasn't possible, and then finally it was, and I was already an adult when I first saw sensei, and I knew immediately that I loved him, but nothing was possible, so that is why I jumped in front of a car, and I lay in a coma for seven weeks, the blow had struck my brain, I was between life and death, the doctors said there was nothing they could do, but sensei knew, he knew that I loved only him, so as soon as he found out, he came to the hospital and he called me back, I only know sensei and I only love sensei, don't ask me about anything, because I don't know anything, and I'm not good at anything, so, well, sensei is my goal, before him there was nothing and after him there will be nothing, and I hope that he, too, will love me forever.

They arrive at the stage door nearly two hours before the beginning of the performance, Amoru-san drove the car, she and the others already receive the more illustrious guests in the foyer of the theater, the tickets are distributed, now and then an older member of the audience is assisted to find a seat more easily there inside the theater; still there are nearly two hours, there is hardly anyone in the labyrinth in the back of the Kanza, but unfortunately for the sensei it feels already like a huge crowd, no one can ever truly be alone here, and that is precisely the reason—and everyone knows this, there are no secrets here—that is why sensei Inoue Kazuyuki arrives so early before the performance, because he wants to be alone, which is of course impossible, because it's as if the dressing room didn't even have a door, in vain does the shite have his own dressing room, the coming and going is continual, now this one, looking in, now that one, every single time he has to get up from his chair and greet the visitor, someone looking in at the door, asking if the sensei wouldn't happen to know when he will be paid, but the sensei just shakes his head, and now there could be a little quiet in the dressing room, when someone else slips in through the door, and after the ritualized greeting that person asks the sensei for advice, because the older brother of his female cousin has leukemia, what should he do; send her to me, says the sensei, but when, he is asked, well, if next week would be good, then, next week, I'm afraid, says the other, that next week might be too late already, well then, when can she come, asks the sensei: is tomorrow afternoon all right, asks the visitor, of course, replies the sensei, and he calls Amoru-san who will arrange the meeting, or if not her, then Chiwako-san, who is very accommodating, and she too can arrange perfectly for the older brother of the female cousin to come, and then she will escort the effusively grateful person out, but when he is about to close the door, two boys run into the dressing room with a large box, they have arrived just now directly from Tokyo on the Shinkansen, they have brought, they say, each interrupting the other, the phoenix crown; fine, nods the sensei, place the box on the table, he shall open it immediately and examine it, the boys, bowing, leave him to himself, but by now the sensei already knows that from this point on he will in no way be able to be alone, and that is why he chooses the same path as always, and not just here, in the Kanze Kaikan, but in Osaka or in the Tokyo Kanze Theater as well, it is an open secret, he accordingly leaves the dressing room, brushes away this or that other person trying to approach him, finally slipping out of their hands, and goes into the toilet of the Kanze, because he has even said openly at times to the people close to him, it is there and only there, in the toilet of the Kanze that he can find tranquility, in the toilet, the sole place where he can be alone for a while; still, before a performance, particularly now, before a performance of such special significance, he has an unconditional need for solitude, to just be by himself, alone, like in his childhood, alone, as in his entire life, disturbed by no one else at all, in peace and tranquility, because this is the place where no one else sees him, where no one else hears him, because only here and now can he finally shut the door—the door to the toilet—behind himself in the Kanze Kaikan, and then he kneels down, and he places his two hands before his face, leans forward a bit, closes his eyes, and begins to pray—he always has to recite in the same way—he begins to pray, from the Great Spirit all the way to I Give Over My Fate Entirely, he kneels on the cold stone floor of the toilet in the smell of disinfectant, he is alone, there is peace, tranquility and silence, and he expresses his gratitude to the Heavens for this peace, this tranquility and this silence in the toilet of the Kanze, then he presses the flush button, as if he had finished his business, and he silently sets off to the common dressing room, so that he may be dressed in the first layers of the garb of Seiobo, so that he may put on the wondrous mask of Seiobo, and so that then within him, in the mirrored room, standing before the as yet motionless agemaku, Seiobo may truly appear.

55

IL RITORNO IN PERUGIA

For the entire day they just sorted and packed and arranged things, they just hauled and hauled things from the atelier to the cart, and then that evening he sent the Florentines home, and sat the Umbrians down around the table; four mugs and one large pitcher of wine were placed in front of them, and he told them, when the last mixing pot had been safely placed in the chests strapped down onto the carriage, we're going home, and they all sat there with their mugs in their hands, he told them very meaningfully that well, Giannicola, well, Francesco, well, Aulista—in that way to all of them, looking at them fixedly and addressing them, so that he finally winked at Giovanni too—now it's time to go home, but not a single one of them believed what he was saying, everything was so complicated, because there was a great *on the one hand,* that nobody could believe the words of such a maestro who for his entire life had been wandering between Umbria and Tuscany and Rome, who continually, ever since that long-ago day, when as a small boy he had left Castel della Pieve, had constantly been on the road, like someone who is hounded by an all-consuming demon, but really, as if deep inside some dark corner at the back of even that hidden soul, a merciless demon lay in wait, in the very innermost part of that soul, for such demons do not exist here outside; all four of them, when this topic came up, nodded their heads in agreement, there is no way that a demon, here outside, could be capable of affecting someone with such strength, chasing him here and there continuously for thirty years, because this is how the situation looked, the maestro just went and went and went, the horses collapsing beneath him, and Rome came along, and Florence and Venice and Pavia and Sienna and Assisi, and who could even name them all, and of course always and again Florence and Perugia and Rome, and Perugia and Rome and Florence, and so whoever knew him just even a little would not have been able to believe it when he said, "well then, now," for the family was going to stay here in the house of Borgo Pinti—the beautiful Signora Vannucci and the countless children—and yet still this "well then, now," as if anyone could have entered into the spirit of the idea of them really finally going home, they knew very well there was no question of that, the only certain thing was that tomorrow, they were going back, tomorrow: back to Perugia, home to Umbria, and this was enough reason for joy in all of them, even for Giovanni, for at least now, for a while, it wouldn't be this insane city, but a little tranquility, he let out a sigh, although his true home, though he never spoke of it, was very far from Perugia; they took a swig from the mugs and you could see that everyone was thinking about that; since 1486—how many years, fifteen or how many, and now again, the beloved landscape of Umbria, the tastes and the smells of home—there was that much, so, well, Giannicola, Francesco, Aulista, and Giovanni . . . there was that much in the maestro's words, that much and no more, because in the depths of his words the idea of finally and forever was never enunciated, because for him, due to that consuming devil, this finally and this forever did not exist, it would never exist, so that, well, in vain was the cart already completely packed up, in vain did they tie up the last bundle with the cords with which they had fastened the canvas the previous evening for tomorrow's journey, in vain did the guard even stand there, to watch over it until dawn, for twenty soldi, until they set out; that they were finally returning home, that this really would be a true ritorno, as they, the Umbrian apprentices, after fifteen or how many years, may have still hoped, after the maestro had brought them here to the bottega in Florence, well, not a single one of them believed it, they just sat there, they nodded to each other, they avoided the gaze of the maestro, then after the maestro left they just sipped away at the wine, in the workshop in the Via San Gilio, a cheap piquette from last year, from the hills of Chianti to the south of here, and they said to themselves, fine, just let him talk, just let him say it, but let's forget about this ritorno, let's forget about this *finally* or that after fifteen or how many years, that there will again at last be the landscape of home; the only thing certain was that the workshop here in the Via San Gilio was being closed down, they had canceled the lease for the premises with Signor Vittorio di Lorenzo Ghiberti, and with that they were going back, and for how long would depend on the maestro's concealed, troubled soul, on this concealed soul, and on that consuming hellish whoreson within it, the creature that never left him in peace, and never would leave him in peace, but let's forget it, Giannicola noted, and he took a swig from the mug, and for awhile none of them even spoke, because all of them knew that all the same, there was here an even greater *on the other hand,* for if the whole thing was so, and if despite the temporary nature of this journey home, it was still the source of a kind of joy, if not that for which they truly yearned, there was no doubt at all among the apprentices that this so-called journey home had only been incited by the bitterness of failure, as it was occurring not at all from the maestro's free will, as—regardless of how much it was really final, and how much the four of them were really rejoicing or not at the return to Umbria—there was a great need, for some reason, for this move, to call things by their proper name; the maestro, who had become not so long ago one of the most celebrated painters in Italy, was compelled to take leave of his Florence, and the worst of it was that it wasn't because somebody was chasing him away, or because he had had a run-in with some authority, or because the commissions were lacking to such an extent—as they were provided after a fashion by the monasteries or the more pious families—but because for the maestro, one had to say, things, for some reason . . . just weren't going well these days, they hardly dared to speak of it among themselves, so frightened were they of this mere fact, but it was so, the maestro wanted to entrust them with more and more tasks, and he hardly even came into the workshop; when they got to the point in the preparation of a picture when they could tell him that he could come into the workshop, that everything was all ready for the painting of this or another panel, even then he didn't come, sometimes days went by until he finally stood there in the doorway in the Via San Gilio, so silently that they didn't even notice him when he came through the door, suddenly he was just there among them, asking why this, why that, fiddling with this or that mixing pot, addressing one of them, saying this or that was no good, or that it wouldn't be enough, or that it was too much, there was already much too much, let's say too much turpentine in the linseed oil; he hemmed and hawed, he muttered, and no one ever dared to mention to him the "obligations long due" to them, it was so obvious that he was in a bad mood, in a word he did everything, but he avoided the brush-rack, no, it's not that he went over to the brushes and picked out the right one and began to work on a certain canvas, no, instead he hemmed and hawed and just kept mumbling for a while, then he tossed out the remark that he would be right back, because right now he had some business to attend to; when, however, he appeared the next time, the entire thing started all over again, the panel lay there on the painting table all ready, and everything on it had already completely dried, to find a mistake in it would have been impossible, for they themselves were not just any old assistants, it was nothing for them to prepare the most perfect gesso or imprimatura, and already no one could have even found fault with the underdrawing, only he, because it had been done by his, the maestro's, own hand; he had already run out of ideas of how to avoid it anymore and he had to start painting, even then he tried avoiding it by saying that this or that—this cloak-hem, this eye-wrinkle, this contour of the lip in the underdrawing—is not how it should be, he could well say such things to them, because they knew very well that this was not the problem, so that on the basis of the maestro's "instructions" one of them, without saying a word, stepped up to the panel, or someone from among the Florentines, but in most cases it was Giovanni, as he had the quickest and the cleverest hand—and he visibly repaired something on the underdrawing, of course just in such a way so that he wouldn't ruin it, as what was there already was good, everyone knew this, including the maestro himself, as he himself had sketched out the underdrawing onto the clichés earlier, and they only had to copy it onto the prepared base in the appropriate way, and they always copied these wonderful drawings accurately and without error, in this the maestro was always amazing; that is, that they experienced the extraordinary talent of his old hand in these drawings on the fine paper, and there were really no mistakes, he outlined perfectly, with the finest of sensitivities he marked on the primed panel just what kind of wondrous Madonna, child, or saint would soon be appearing here, it was just that in recent times these figures were appearing ever less frequently, as he delayed everything; to no avail was the workshop full of the more serious disciples and assistants from both Florence and Umbria, it had nothing to do with them, but with this inexplicable impotency of the maestro, there was some spasm within him, or something, they guessed, because it decisively appeared that he *did not dare* to reach for the brush, sometimes the pigment, based on his own order, stood there, all ready, broken up and on the palette mixed in with the porphyry, just waiting for him to motion and then everybody would leave the workshop so that the maestro, as they put it, could "make the paints," that is conjure up, according to his own secret recipe, in his own inimitable fashion, this crimson or blue pigment, such a hue that according to the assistants, and all of Italy, did not and would not ever exist on the painting of any other painter; but he brushed it all aside, he retracted everything, he told them to do what they wanted with the broken pigments, accordingly that they should do something with them so that they would not be wasted, which of course was impossible, as within a few days, no matter how they tried, the strength of the pigments was lost, and because of that they were essentially ruined, they just didn't talk to him about it, and he already acted as if he hadn't noticed, he never used to be like this in the old days, things like this simply did not happen, that the expensive vermiglione, moreover the prohibitively expensive ultramarine, would simply be wasted, this would simply be impossible to even imagine in such a workshop as the maestro's, who was renowned for detesting so-called extravagance, whereas he himself these days was the cause of exactly such extravagance, just so that he wouldn't have to reach for the brush, this is how it went, and of course it could not go on this way for long, tomorrow they were setting off at dawn, somehow things here in Florence just weren't going well anymore; the four of them, sitting here around the table, the mugs in their hands, knew very well what it was, that the problem was not with Florence, that is, the problem was not such that tomorrow they were leaving this rich, lively, glittering, dangerous, or as Giovanni put it, this "insane" city and later on, in Perugia, in the quiet, sleepy, dusty, peaceful little town everything would proceed very nicely again—no, this journey of tomorrow, in its manner and fashion, was a retreat, or at the very least, the beginning of a retreat, from Florence, and what made them hang their heads the most around the table now was that it was a retreat from the profession, from the profession in which the maestro, it seemed, was ever more unsure, for in the past few years, but particularly in the past few months he truly looked like someone who was certain of the fact that he no longer knew what he had once known, and in vain did they get the news that in Perugia the maestro would immediately be honored by being appointed prior, this could not help the maestro, could have no effect on their wonderful maestro, because he did not dare to take the brush into his hands, only at the price of a dreadful inner torment, and so the result . . . was not at all what it used to be, and who could have seen this more clearly than they, his disciples and assistants of the past few years, from Girolamo to Marco, from Francesco to the Umbrians, but first and foremost the maestro's most faithful disciple, Giovanni di Pietro, who had served him for years and who after his first independent works, already began to take the name Lo Spagna, referring to his place of birth, and whom the others preferred to ask when they were debating the matter of the unpaid wages with the maestro, namely, in such discussions as these, they frequently wanted him to negotiate on their behalf, just as now they expected from him more than anyone else some kind of adjustment of the situation; they watched him, Giovanni, to see what he would say to this, but it was precisely he who was the most silent, a general wordlessness fell upon them in the closed-up workshop in the Via San Gilio, and it was as if he just wanted to signal that yes, to be sure, that is how it was: the master's luck had run out, and that is why they had to go back, that is why they could not prolong the lease on the workshop with Signor Vittorio di Lorenzo Ghiberti, and that is why they were signing another, that is to say, that they had already entered into an agreement from the first of January with the Hospital of the Brethren of Mercy on the Piazza del Sopramuro—in Perugia, so they were withdrawing from the world, because well this is what was happening, the maestro was withdrawing, and he would just withdraw more and more, Giovanni commented to the others, he would withdraw from the world, but don't be afraid, he added, because as for work, there will be plenty of that, in particular, he winked humorously at his companions, especially if it proceeds at the accustomed pace, at which of course laughter broke out for the first time that day, they poured out the final drops from the pitcher, and raising their mugs to their "bounteous" maestro, they clinked their mugs together with a great whoop, and gave no more thought to the matter, everyone went to lie down in their lair, for the next morning they had to rise very early; and the little birds had just woken in the break of the April dawn when they were already fixing the cords onto the cart, and finding a suitable place for themselves where they would be able to bear the vicissitudes of travel, and because, well, everyone knew exactly, as it had been their experience often enough, that in the strictest sense of the word the days to come would be jolting, namely, the cart would shake the very breath out of them on the old Via Cassia, upon which they would be traveling, for they always used that route between Florence and Perugia; of course they could have gone toward Siena as well, joining in with the crowded pilgrimage route, and they could have gone that way for a while toward Rome, then turning off to the left toward Perugia, but the maestro knew the roads in Tuscany and Umbria like the palm of his hand, and he had his own reasons for not taking the crowded Siena pilgrimage route, but instead the less-traveled Via Cassia Vetus to Arezzo, and in addition to his own experiences, there were the accounts of the postal coachmen from Rome, as well as those of the Siena foot messengers, just think for a moment with the mind of a bandit, they explained to him for a few soldi, where is there bigger and better plunder to be had, on a busy road or on a less busy road, well, my lord, you can see that you have to think with their minds if you want to be well informed in the question of travel, so that this time there could be no doubt whatsoever of which way to go, the cart will set off at dawn, the maestro said to them, when he put down in front of them the large pitcher of Chianti (but no more!) and the four mugs; he himself, however, as usual, would follow after them, on horseback and with a certain retinue, perhaps on the following day, or on the third day, or on the fourth day, which meant, that there was no way they were all going to return home all at once, they should not count on that; then he began to explain the route to the coachman, that as a matter of fact they should go along the Porta alla Croce, and with this he really began to issue instructions, as they had already taken their places beneath the tightly drawn canvas, and everything was ready for departure, the maestro never entrusted anything to chance and would make sure of every single step a hundred times while he thought it over, for there could never be enough circumspection, so he himself got up at dawn's very break and came over from the Borgo Pinti house, just to check up on everything and to see them off on their journey himself, in a word you should turn off at the Borgo de Croce here, he said—as if a coachman from Florence would not have known himself, as if they themselves had not made this journey there and back maybe twenty or how many times already in the past fifteen years—then, continued the maestro, go through the city wall at the Porta alla Croce, but be careful, he motioned toward the assistants, that there should be neither sword, nor dagger, nor knife anywhere, because of the sentry, well, Aulista, you understand, and then he gestured with a wide motion again to the coachman, straight along the road to Arezzo, straight as an arrow, and thus crossing S. Ellero and Castelfranco you should be able to reach Loro on the first day, there you should spend the night—he turned now to Giovanni, who had been entrusted with the travel expenses—but not in the Pieve, just to be made drunk by the wine of the friendly brethren of Gropina, in a word, Loro, Giovanni! and don't spend more than two golden florins, including dinner, and go on the next morning, passing through S. Giustino, past the Castiglio Fibocchi to the Buriano, there you should cross the Arno, the bridge toll should be twelve soldi, no more, Giovanni, and that evening in Arezzo you may not give them more than three, under no circumstances whatsoever, they will ask you for four florins and forty soldi, but you give them three—food, lodgings, fodder—well, Giovanni, you understand, and then early the next morning to Passignano, and then accordingly you should stay in Passignano that evening, there once again two florins will be enough for everything, and then by the evening of the fourth day you will already be in Perugia, coachman, drive carefully, it's not flour that you're transporting, and don't drive the horses too hard, feed them well and give them water, and as for you, he finally gestured toward the four assistants blinking sleepily, don't end up getting drunk somewhere, because you will regret it if I find out and I will find out, for surely you know that nothing can remain a secret from me on that route, in other words may God's blessing be upon you, the maestro bid farewell to them, and with that he dismissed the entire company with all of the expensive pigments and brushes and oils and turpentine and chests and frames and all of the wooden panels, half-prepared or just now begun, he turned on his heel and did not look back, he did not look back even once, but just went toward the Borgo Pinti, and then his entire bottega from Florence disappeared amidst the sleeping houses of the San Gilio; the two horses pulled at the first crack of the whip, the cart gave a great jolt, so that they nearly fell onto their backs, they turned out onto the San Gilio, then went all the way along the deserted Borgo la Croce, through the Porta alla Croce, already they had passed by the guard at the gate, and already they were outside in the open countryside; behind them was Florence, enchanting and beautiful and dangerous and insane, with its fiasco, and before them were the springtime Tuscan hills, gentle and covered in green, they were setting off on the road to Arezzo, in a word they set off, rattling greatly as they went along, tossed about here and there underneath the cart's canvas, they watched the city slowly disappearing behind them, they watched the land slowly becoming smoother ahead, and they thought, oh, what a journey, Perugia, oh, how far away it is!

No matter how much they were jolted, for a while it was not the terrible bumpiness of the road that made them suffer, but that contrary to expectations they only reached, before Pontassieve, the hills of Valdarno very slowly, which also meant that they did not hesitate even for a second when they glimpsed the first vineyard; they immediately instructed the coachman to head that way, and they were already turning down to the left off the main road, and so they left the Cassia Vetus as if they had never even been on it, they turned off, they stopped the cart in the shadow of a large olive grove, and leaving the coachman there to watch over the cart and get water for the horses to drink, they immediately climbed up the gently sloping hill, looking for the first cellar entrance; they knocked back the vintner's wine so impetuously, that it was as if they were not coming from Florence, but rather from some Arabian desert, already completely tortured by thirst, with leathery tongues and bone-dry throats; they simply dashed back the young wine from the tiny glasses, tastier with every sip, and for a good few minutes they didn't even ask the price, they just poured it down their throats, one after the other, they just panted and sipped and swallowed, and the vintner watched them, wondering what madhouse they had come from, and just where they had gotten so thirsty, and, well, what kind of master it was who, as he found out, locked away his own assistants, so that they could only drink just a little bit on occasion, ah, he doesn't let us do anything, they told him, lying nonsensically, just a tiny little drop of wine and he kicks you out of the workshop, once they had caught their breath, they went on saying things like that, and they went on to tell him just who they were, where they had come from, and where they were trying to get to, by God, Francesco fixed his gaze on the vintner, their master was so dreadfully strict that one little drop was too much, he never even permitted that much ever, just because he himself refrained from drinking any sort of liquor, like someone who had taken a vow, although none of them would have been able to say why they were babbling so much nonsense, namely things that were not true, namely, that the maestro really didn't like it if his assistants drank, moreover strictly regulating, as long as they were within view of him, just how much they could drink; accordingly they themselves didn't even understand why they were babbling such idiocies to this total stranger, maybe because the speed with which they were drinking compelled them to make up some kind of explanation, in any event they drank for about one half hour continuously, all the while just talking and talking, the words flowed out of them, just as the wine flowed down their throats, but by that point all four of them were so drunk, that the vintner just pointed at the entrance of the cellar, where a few sheepskins were spread out on the hard-packed earth, and already they were falling over in a row, and already they were snoring; the coachman was still waiting for them down there below in the shade of the olive grove, that is, he waited for as long as he could stand it, because as the sun began to rise and it became warmer and warmer, he had no desire to miss out on anything good, so, well, he tied up the two horses, and reassuring himself that there was not a single soul anywhere nearby—he could leave the carriage for a little while—he set off in the direction he had seen them going earlier, but by the time he, too, found the cool cellar, they were already snoring deeply and regularly so that he just pointed at them, indicating that the gentlemen would pay, and ordered a jug of wine for himself, and began to chat with the vintner, and time passed very pleasantly, but, however, it also really passed in actuality, the coachman kept looking with ever growing disquiet at the four figures sleeping on the sheepskins, because he remembered the unattended carriage and the unattended horses, as well as the warnings the maestro had issued at dawn, and what was going to happen if there would be a problem, and what would happen if he found out somehow—the thought arose within him—which was anyway altogether unlikely, but still, who knows, and he began to awaken the assistants, who awoke with great difficulty, but only so that they could order some more jugs from the vintner, well, the coachman couldn't really understand how they could be so bold, because this maestro, or whatever they call him, he explained to the vintner, seemed like a great lord, so, he convinced them to fill up a few flasks to take along on the road, for now the best thing would be, he said very uncertainly, crumpling up his cap, the best thing would be ... because, well, even these assistants were kind of gentlemen-like themselves, to go now, because the maestro had said that they had to be in Loro by the evening, of course we'll get there, they shrugged their shoulders, don't be afraid, just you have one last glass with us, and they drank one last glass, and then one more, and then one really last one, after which they made their way down the hill toward the grove, all four of them were black and blue by the time they got to the cart, because they either kept tripping over their own legs, or they fell on top of each other laughing, or they tripped over a stone or the stump of some old grapevine stuck in the ground, so that when they were finally able with great difficulty to climb up onto the cart, and settle down there again, and the coachman, just to make sure that they were all hanging on properly, as they had up till now, looked back and he saw that the entire illustrious company in the bed of the cart looked like they had been attacked, or had gotten a good thrashing by a band of marauders—well, how the gentlemen looked there behind him was the least of his concerns, he muttered to the horses, snapping the reins, and already he had turned back onto the main road and there on the Via Cassia they continued their journey where they had left off, just that, well, the coachman looked up and to be sure the sun was already very high, so high, that to be sure he could tell that there was no way that they would get to Loro in time, so that as they left Pontassieve, every time it came into his head, he cracked his whip for the horses to move along, the result being that the illustrious company in the bed of the cart were only jolted around all the more, and how could it have been otherwise; they were continually being startled awake from their drunken stupor, and they upbraided him not to drive those poor horses so hard, didn't he see that the sweat was pouring off of them, did he not remember that the maestro had said to drive carefully and not hound them, and mainly Giannicola raised his voice, he really shouldn't be shaking the breath out of the travelers like this and shouldn't be so worried, they'll get there when they get there, Loro was not the most important thing, the most important thing was that they be in Perugia by the fourth day, and to be sure that was true, the coachman said to the horses, as it really turned out to be, he decided that tomorrow he would speed up a bit, there were hardly any other travelers and as he recalled, from Loro onward, things would be a bit better for a while, but he did not remember well, or he was just deluding himself, because to be sure, after they arrived, late that evening, at Loro, installed themselves at the inn, unloaded the chests, washed themselves off, gave the horses water and provisions, and then started off again, that accursed Via Cassia, to be sure, was not even a tiny bit better, so that just as before they could only make progress at the price of painful tortures, the cart was jolting and rattling and getting stuck and coming to a dead halt so many times, and those four were constantly yelling at the coachman that they couldn't sleep because there was so much jolting and rattling and getting stuck and coming to a dead halt and what was true was true, it was jolting and rattling and getting stuck and coming to a dead halt, the coachman acknowledged to the horses, well, but Arezzo is still far away, namely Arezzo was his goal for that evening, as the day after tomorrow, in the evening they had to be in Perugia, this maestro, back there in Florence, when he bargained with him, seemed to be a very strict person, all he needed now was to know that they were late, under no circumstances whatsoever, said the coachman to the horses, and he cracked the whip over their haunches, upon which of course they again jumped, the four assistants at this began to yell again, and that is how they went, how the cart went along the Via Cassia; sometimes the coachman had to turn off the road if a horseman or another carriage was coming from the opposite direction, and sometimes just gently prodding on the two horses, the assistants were jolted awake, and began to yell at him again, at which point he once again slowed down the cart, then the road began to get a bit better, the assistants fell into a deep sleep, so that with Loro behind them they passed Terranuova, and even crossed the famous Ponte Buriano and reached the opposite bank of the fairly wide Arno, he didn't have to wake them up, because most likely due to the unusually small amount of travelers, nobody was standing there at the bridgehead, so there was no question of a toll, the assistants were completely still, they didn't even take the slightest notice of this crossing, indeed, the road after the bridge remained smoother, and so they proceeded onward in a more tranquil fashion, of course just for a while, because then afterward, once again, came all the bumps and potholes, the large stones half turned over on their sides, the treacherous ditches of the hollowed out wheel tracks; the assistants woke up irritated, and began to yell, but they had to slow down anyway, as the two horses couldn't really take it anymore, in consequence of which the coachman was forced to acknowledge that they were proceeding toward Arezzo too slowly, so that in the middle of that afternoon even the four assistants, who were coming back to their senses somewhat, realized that it would look better if they did not stop at every single turn to attend to their personal needs, or to rest the horses and let them drink at every single watering place, namely they too began to restrain themselves, and as for eating and drinking, they ate and drank on the road, and it was only in this way that they were able, on the second day—although it was already late in the evening—to reach Arezzo; they bargained for lodgings at the postal station, they unloaded the chests, they got water and fodder again, and they ordered something for themselves as well, they consumed a warm meal, but they were so tired, all five of them were so exhausted that they didn't even really know what they were eating, they just chewed and swallowed, then the five of them were already asleep, the four assistants inside, the coachman in the shed next to the horses, so that when on the morning of the third day they set off yet again they could not imagine how they would be able to withstand this all the way to Passignano, because that was the third goal in their journey, the northwestern tip of Lake Trasimeno, if the horses could bear all of this—the degree to which the journey was wearing the horses out was quite visible, as well as how much the coachman was worried about them, although of course he did not only have just these two horses, he explained as he kept turning his head back toward Aulista, who was just then watching him—but look at them, the coachman motioned with his head, look at the light in the eyes of these two, he would not be separated from them for any money in the world, no matter how much anyone might offer him, he would not just give them over to any human being whatsoever, he knew every single one of their movements, he could tell just from their gait if it was going to rain in the next half-hour, or which one's tooth was hurting just at that moment, he knew everything, just everything that you could know about them, of course he wouldn't deny it, part of it was that these two also knew him, the gentleman assistant won't believe me, said the coachman, but if he was in a bad mood, these two just hung their heads as if they understood exactly what the problem was, there were no two horses like them in all of Florence, yes, he nodded toward them, turning toward the horses now, and looking at the road, yes, they're getting on, you can't deny that, but well, as for him, wasn't he too?—he'd passed his forty-ninth, too, after Carnival, although he knew that he didn't look it, in a word the three of them here were just made for each other, the gentleman could see it for himself, that maestro there in the city had a good eye to pick him out from all the other drivers, because he had a sharp eye—the coachman turned again for a moment to Aulista—and he immediately knew that he could trust him and that he could trust these two horses, but at that point the coachman had to leave off because although the landscape had become more even, another very difficult section of the journey came, where the old Roman stones were nearly completely turned out of the surface of the road, he had to watch very closely if he did not want the cart's axle to snap in two, or some other huge problem to develop, he turned here, he turned there, and now not a living soul was coming from the other direction, or from behind—no nobleman, noted the coachman to the horses, or courier, delegation, or anyone, either from Arezzo or Trasimeno, as if everyone, he muttered to the horses, wanted to bypass this section of the road, but the horses said nothing in reply, they just suffered on with the whip cracking above their backs and the wheels always getting stuck, they tried to haul them out before the whip lashed yet more strongly, and nothing meant anything to any one of them in this continual torture, not to the horses, nor to the apprentices, nor to the coachman; and it was perhaps just some obscure mitigation that above them the sun shone, that the warm April breeze played up and down across the land, that the gently sloping hillsides of the Val di Chiana, and the general dominion of all things fresh and green in the entire springtime realm of Tuscany radiated such peace and tranquility, that nothing at all was lacking, in which already nothing else was necessary for someone to become conscious of this, a profound peacefulness, and a kind of unperturbedness that was not of this world: in this peacefulness and unperturbedness stood immersed the olive groves and the vineyards, the hills and the roads winding among the hills, even the undulating flocks of starlings—as again and again they furrowed through the rows of the grapevines amid the playful breezes—they were refined into an entrancing motionlessness, as if they had just stopped in midair in utter silence, or as if everything—the dense fragrance of the noble rot of the grapes, the silvery green of the olive groves and the vegetable gardens, the shimmerings and shadows of the gently sloping hills of the Val di Chiana—as if everything were just watching the silence, the silence created precisely by this attention—and all the while a weak little noise was a part of the silence too, bumping along in the little full-laden canvas-covered cart with its iron-girded wheels clattering on the stones, as slowly, with difficulty, past the villages of L'Olmo, Puliciano, Rigutino, toward Passignano, it proceeds.

They could not have said if they reached Passignano that evening, because if the first two days had rattled their bodies, the third, between Arezzo and Passignano, destroyed their souls, that is to say, first they became insensible, then later they revolted, namely, that with the cart continuously throwing them around here and there, at first they were despondent, then they announced things could not go on like this, this was not travel, but inhuman torture, and was strictly prohibited in letter and in spirit by the Republic of Florence: these two feelings alternated for hours on end, as all the while the road, without pause, tossed them about mercilessly, beat them, thrashed them, crushing their willpower completely, but then they rebelled again, and then again just resigned themselves to the whole thing, and gave themselves over to fate, because it was one and the same, for if rebellion was followed by acquiescence, then acquiescence was again followed by rebellion, so that at such times they stopped the coachman, but all they accomplished was that the cart stopped, which meant however that it did not move, namely that in a carriage that is not moving, there is no end of suffering, all four of them knew this, and the coachman kept repeating it too, so that then the whole thing just started again from the beginning, they piled back into the cart, got back into place moaning and groaning, hanging on, and let themselves be shaken, thrown, beaten again—until the next spell of acquiescence—but then after a while they couldn't stand it anymore, and once again mutiny reared its head; the next time, they did not clamber down, but in the strictest sense of the word they fell off the cart, every bone in their bodies ached so much already, they couldn't move a single limb, they lay in the fragrant grass like the dead, enumerating the wildest ideas, that they would proceed from now on by foot, that each one would sit upon the back of a bird, that altogether they would not go any further and stay here in the grass alongside the road, and they would all just die, but at this the coachman began to urge them on, really, stop this already, there's just a little way left, they would be there right away, look at the horses, they are also properly worn out and they're not lying down in the grass, so stop this already, really you're all like children, get up right away, climb back into the cart and take the rest of the trip like men, later on in Passignano you can have a rest, so that Passignano became a variation of Paradise in their minds, Passignano, Passignano, they repeated before every turn in the road so that when the turn in the road did not reveal Passignano, they were thoroughly embittered, and they began to curse the coachman, then the two horses, then this rotten road, then the Romans who had built it, and then all the travelers of the past millennium who with their wheels had carved such deep ditches into the road, then the rains, the winters, and the sunshine, in a word everything and everyone that had ruined the Via Cassia to such a degree; finally, just as much as they could, they cursed the maestro, so that when evening came, and darkness descended upon them, and they were ready to nail the coachman up onto a cross—where the hell was this damned Passignano already—but just at that moment when the horses were being driven very quietly, and back there in the bed of the cart they had begun to talk in undertones about how Giannicola would now stab the coachman with a dagger, the coachman said, well, there's Passignano already, but he said it so softly, that they really almost stabbed him by mistake, what's that, they yelled out from behind, Passignano, I'm telling you, gentlemen, it's Passignano, the coachman shouted out in a rage now too, because he had noticed the knife, and he gestured forward into the pitch-dark blackness, the knife was returned to its place, and they just stared fixedly ahead so they could finally see the end to this torture, to see that they had finally arrived just as the coachman had said, that they were in Passignano, and when the cart turned in they just motioned to the innkeeper, they motioned something, which could have meant anything, somehow they were led to their lodgings, there they collapsed, and immediately within the blink of an eye all four were asleep, so that when Aulista was startled awake after one hour, every molecule in his entire body was hurting so much, he was so exhausted, that he simply couldn't bear to sleep, and after he had first seen Saint Bernard and Saint Francis, the maestro immediately appeared somewhere above his pallet, and that made him come to his senses somewhat, and he looked at the maestro above his pallet, and he tried somehow to fall back asleep, but couldn't, then he was able to, but not even for a half hour, because his eyes sprung open again as if it were already dawn, it was, however, not dawn but still late evening and in addition he was starting to come back to normal consciousness, that is after the maestro, Saint Bernard, and Saint Francis had began to vanish, and the pallets had begun to regain their own true dimensions and form, there inside was one tiny little window, out of which Aulista watched the heavens playing into dark blue, he sensed a gentle breeze that occasionally blew across him toward the sleepers, and there suddenly came into his mind one of the panels under preparation, which, fastened to the back of the cart, was now being transported, that altarpiece, commissioned by the clerk of Perugia, Bernardino di ser Angelo Tezi, and which they had begun perhaps six years ago, and that inasmuch as it would be finished one day, would be placed in the church of Saint Augustine in Perugia in the Tezi family chapel named after Saint Nicolas of Tolentino, the commission of course had been arranged years ago, but they had gotten nearly nowhere with the picture, only the gesso and the imprimatura were ready, and they had finished the underdrawing a long time ago, that is the sketched-out composition of the painting was already recognizable, a predella below, above it in the middle of the picture a little ciborium, and as a matter of fact in the middle of the picture, above, was the Virgin Mother in the heavens as She was being held by three cherubinos, with little Jesus in her lap, and beside her to the left was San Nicola da Tolentino, to her right was Bernardino da Siena, and all those who were seeing this as a vision: down below, to the left of the ciborium, Saint Jerome was kneeling, and on the other side, Saint Sebastian, this picture now flashed through Aulista's mind, as did that afternoon, when in the still sufficient light the maestro painted the lower garments of the Virgin Mother with ultramarine, but then suddenly stopped painting, and flung out the comment that they should daub a deep blue spot with azurite onto the edge of the sleeve, which was still just sketched out but not painted, and they should finely inscribe there MCCCCC, namely that according to the desire of the family this picture would be placed in the chapel exactly at the turning point of the quattrocento and the cinquecento—which of course did not occur, Aulista now thought—and with that the maestro left the workshop, and since then hadn't even touched the picture, and here he was now lying awake from exhaustion, and instead of resting he was seeing the blue of the garments of the Virgin Mother, that glimmering, that wondrous, that inimitable blue, the likes of which he had never seen in any painting by any other Italian painter and this blue, now, as he lay almost completely awake in the sleeping quarters of the inn, made him think, and made all the maestro's colors come into his mind, as the green and blue and crimson blinded him, indeed, in the strict sense of the word, what blinded him was the dreadful strength of these colors, as each picture was finished, and they stood around the panel, or the fresco, so as to look at it, to view it as a completed masterpiece, with a fresh eye, so that the entire workshop could look at it together, just to see if as a whole the work truly was satisfactory, and it could be said that it was final, that it could now be delivered, really, Aulista now remembered, he was nearly blinded by this extraordinary ability of the maestro to work with colors, because this was the secret focal point of his work and his talent, he now added to himself, and he looked through that narrow little window slit at the evening heavens above Passignano—the astonishing *sharpness* of the colors, he thought, and with what overpowering strength, the green and the yellow and blue and crimson, placed next to each other, for example, on four draperies loosely thrown upon each other, the viewer was raised into the heavens, that is, Aulista noted to himself, the maestro ravished people with his colors, well, but the maestro can still create these colors even today, the thought wracked him, and sleep finally deserted him, for surely that unfinished picture back there, tied up there to the back shaft of the cart, that blue piece of fabric in it, as it spilled across the knee of the Virgin Mary, that was *the same* blue, that was *the same* color that was in the Santa Maddalena and Madonna della Consolazione and the altarpiece in Pavia and on the Madonna painted for the Pala dei Decemviri, and in the Lamentation over the Dead Christ for the Order of the Poor Clares and all the other innumerable depictions of the Christ and the Madonna and Jerome, but if that's where things stand, Aulista thought amid his snoring colleagues, if the problem is not with the proof of the greatest ornament of the maestro's talent, with his colors, then with what, that is the question, he said to himself, speaking aloud now, because although he wasn't conscious of it, he clasped his hands underneath his head, and fixed his gaze onto the ceiling, then in a single moment complete wakefulness was succeeded by the deepest sleep, although even the next morning he had not forgotten his nighttime thoughts, so when after a mutual attempt on the part of the coachman and the innkeeper to awanen them—lengthy yet in the end yielding results—and the assistants finally succeeded in shaking themselves into their pantaloons, and had consumed some warm panada and climbed back up onto the readied cart, like martyrs onto their stakes, starting off for Perugia, Aulista even brought up the topic; however, there wasn't really anyone to mention it to, for the others were still so badly off from the trials of yesterday and the day before, that they shouted him down just as much as they could, just as rudely as they could, only much later on, when after a while the road became somewhat better on the bank of the lake, and the last flask was brought out, which made them a bit more cheerful, they thought of Aulista and immediately began pestering him, what is it, Aulista, are you delirious, are you so worn out, that you can no longer bear the tortures, and you spend all night thinking about the maestro's colors?—you're looking kind of feeble, pretty boy, Francesco said to him sneering maliciously, and he took a swig from the flask, I don't even know how the maestro let you leave his side, and why you didn't travel on horseback with him, he should have made an exception for you, and so on, right up until the old injurious accusation, with which his colleagues had badgered him ever since he had shown up at the workshop, that namely he was the maestro's particular, very own favorite, and only because he was the one who posed as a model of Saint Sebastian for the maestro one time back then, and this crude banter, as so many times already, if they wanted to get out of some kind of difficult rut, led to their just not being able to stop, and the jeering just went on and on; the cart, however, shook and tumbled and swerved just like before, but their attention was absorbed by the subject of Aulista's relationship with the maestro, so that this time too he wasn't spared, they just kept on talking, the jibes, each one more malicious, more crude than the last, just kept on coming and there was nothing that could stop them, they were simply not capable of getting off this topic; he however was aching all over just as they were, he was just as eviscerated as they were by the sufferings of the last three days, so that he asked them, just asked them, and in the end weeping he asked them to leave him alone already, well but it was exactly this, the sight of a man bursting into tears that threw more oil onto the fire, and they attacked him, causing even deeper wounds, calling him a feeble woman, and the only help for Aulista, as always in such cases, was that he suddenly closed himself off, sunk into himself to such an extent as to become unapproachable, he spoke not a single word to them, he no longer took any notice of them, he wedged himself between two rolled-up carpets, and just waited for them to stop already, as eventually happened, because after a while there was no more pleasure in the thing, and Francesco, pointing at the Trasimeno, told the tale, related already at least a hundred times, about his adventure with some whore from Florence, who sometimes was called Pantassilea, and sometimes Pomona, and sometimes Antea, thus they went along the northern shore of the Trasimeno, and as they passed beyond it, everything began to be a little more easy, because they knew that now Perugia would follow, that there in the distance Perugia was waiting for them and the coachman said to the horses that surely it was very good, and if the gentleman assistants were finally in such a good mood, but that it would be good for them to conserve some energy for the last stretch as well, and he was really right, because in the falling twilight when they truly had reached the base of Perugia, perhaps the most difficult part of the journey followed, namely that they had to somehow get the cart up to the Porta Trasimeno on the notoriously steep route, accordingly they all had to get down, the coachman held and jerked the reins from the ground, while the others, putting their shoulders to the sides of the cart pushed the entire thing up, because this upward route toward the gate was not only very difficult for the two horses, who were nearly totally enervated, but even going on foot alone would have worked up a proper sweat in the travelers returning home; the coachman was worried about the horses, and the assistants were worried about the load on the cart, which until now had escaped damage; then their strength gave out, and it became increasingly obvious that they were hardly pushing the cart, the coachman yelled, because he was afraid, with good reason, that the exhausted company and the weakened animals would suddenly just give up, and then the entire thing would plummet back down, back down to the foot of the city, and then not only would the cart burst apart into matchsticks, not only the load, but his two beloved horses would be finished off as well, which he would not be able to bear; so he just yelled at the assistants to start pushing already, for God's sake, they were already almost halfway up, but it seemed nearly a hopeless task for these five and the two horses to get the cart up to the gate, so the coachman could do nothing else then to commandeer the company with some incredible luck up to the big turn in the road, where he then wedged stones behind the wheels of the cart, and ordered them to take a rest, the assistants, gasping for breath, collapsed onto their knees, the horses' legs trembled, no one spoke a single word, there they rested for perhaps a quarter of an hour, until the assistants looked at each other, and then at the coachman, then at the horses, and as if in some mute pantomime, they agreed all at once, fine, the last stretch would somehow have to be made in one go; the coachman positioned the four assistants next to the supporting stones, then he cracked the whip above the two horses just as much as he could, he tugged at the reins, and at the same time the assistants grabbed the stones from underneath the wheels, so that the wheels would turn more easily in the right direction; the horses just pulled the cart, the coachman yelled, the whip cracked, although the coachman was very careful to make sure that the strap didn't even touch the haunches of the two horses, and in that way they finally reached the gates of Perugia, and they finally stepped through the Porta Trasimeno, and when at last, gasping for breath they stood, beyond the gate, on the beautifully paved Via dei Priori, Francesco simply could not stop, he just kept saying, just saying, well, my friends, I wouldn't have believed it possible, I wouldn't have believed it at all.

Everything begins with the commission, with the patron, in this case Signor Bernardino di ser Angelo Tezi, the notary of Perugia who, representing the Tezi family, registers before the appropriate authorities all of the requirements relating to the commissioned picture, usually—as on this occasion as well—with the stipulation that the Virgin Mother and the two visionary saints be painted by the maestro himself, that the very best ultramarine and the very best vermiglione be used, and so on, including precisely designating the composition of the desired scene and the portrayal of the desired figures in the picture, and of course the price and the time are also registered, saying—that is writing—that for the preparation of the altarpiece the aforementioned maestro will be owed one hundred and fifty golden florins by the patron, in such and such installments, the maestro for his part consents to prepare this altarpiece in the propitious year of the turn of the century, and the delivery will be arranged by the patron, as the altarpiece is to be placed in the family chapel, Chiesa di Sant' Agostino, and with that the entire operation began, precisely, it began with the maestro going to his own carpenter—this happened already in Perugia—and he said to him, look, Stefano, I need it from poplar, but from the very highest quality poplar, you know what kind, the dolce, moreover, the dolcissimo, that's what I need, but cutting it so that no part of the edge of the trunk is inside it, saw it along the grain, in a word, it has to be six feet long and four and a half feet wide, yes, master Stefano replied in the carpentry workshop, so one piece, six feet wide and four and a half feet long; no, said the maestro, six feet long and four and a half feet wide, yes, the slightly thick-witted carpenter interrupted, nodding vigorously, accordingly six feet long and four and a half feet wide; yes, said the maestro, a poplar panel of those dimensions, I will be painting an altarpiece on it, in brief how much do you want, asked the maestro, so that the back will be smeared with minium to protect it from insects, and the painting side will be smoothly planed, but then go over it a little bit with the toothed plane, you understand, Stefano, that there should be completely fine little ridges running through it, so that the whole painting side will be able to absorb the size, go over the back though with the rough planer, because you know, Stefano, that then it will be easier to press in the cross-lathes, those, too, will be necessary, of course, of course, echoed the carpenter standing before the famous painter and bowing his head slightly, from oak wood however, oak, nodded master Stefano, you know, continued the maestro, it needs dovetailed grooves, or what do you call it, that's what we call it, approved Stefano, which you can then press the cross-lathes into, but you know, the maestro admonished him, the cross-lathes should always be placed crosswise to the grain, Stefano, yes, of course, maestro Vannucci, the carpenter nodded again, everything will be just as you wish, and when do you need it by, well, by when can you have it ready, that is the question, answered the maestro, if it were ready by next Saturday, would that be good, the carpenter asked, smiling, because he knew that nobody else could complete the order as quickly, because well, if it was for him, the greatly esteemed Pietro di Vannucci—so for how much, the maestro grew impatient, six by four and a half feet, asked the carpenter, and relying on his old habit, if the talk was about money, he continually rubbed the tips of his fingers together behind his back, as if he were rummaging around in a money pouch; from poplar, mused master Stefano, and the maestro nodded at every sentence, but he didn't say a word, and so, muttered the carpenter, with cross-lathes, Signor Vannucci appeared once again to grow impatient, and when he finally heard the price, he was completely crestfallen, and stared intently at master Stefano as if he had just cursed the Holy Mother Church, and he simply could not catch his breath—the maestro was a master of performance as well, and was capable of bargaining for a single soldo—or even one single caldera—for an entire hour, or even longer, as the situation required, so that on this occasion as well, a good half-hour went by, as they continued to bargain, and they enumerated the specifications again and again, and then the maestro stepped out of the carpenter's workshop, having quickly concluded the deal, and having got the price down to one quarter of the original stated amount, and next Saturday quickly came around, and the panel was there with all the agreed-upon measurements and requirements, so that work could begin, the maestro entrusted Francesco—not the Francesco Bachielli, who was still working in the maestro's workshop around the year 1495, but Francesco Bettini, who still counted as among the most inexperienced—with the initial preparatory operations, informing him to proceed with a large degree of circumspection, because from this point onward each individual phase of the work carried great significance, there were no tasks that were any less important or more important, he had to treat the tavola in such a way that if any phase of the work was completed badly, negligently, or in a heedless fashion, it would render the subsequent work meaningless, and the panel worthless, because the panel would be unusable, and the picture would be unpaintable, that is, even just the slightest negligence or lack of attention would be enough, and the commission would be gone, and that also would entail repercussions for Francesco, the withdrawal of wages, and other reprisals left unexpressed, so he should not disregard his, the maestro's, orders, he should begin by placing the panel in a perpendicular position, so that he could have access to both the front and the back surfaces, and wash them down, rubbing thoroughly everywhere, he should wash it down, but on the back side of the panel with only a damp sponge; with this, however, Francesco—the other Francesco—could help for a while, so that in a word as he thoroughly scrubbed the back surface with the damp rag, the other at the same time would be smearing boiling vinegar onto the painting side, but they had to be very careful to do it at once, truly at the same time, for the entire thing to occur simultaneously, otherwise the panel would begin to warp toward the back, and it would be like a barrel, and that would be the end, he hoped that Francesco understood, the maestro raised his index finger warningly, and with that work could begin, so that the two Francescos did everything exactly as had been prescribed, the back surface of the panel with a damp sponge, on the painting side with warm vinegar, to open up the pores of the wood, so that then the size would be absorbed more easily into the surface of the wood, and they really did all of this at the same time, so that there was no problem at all, they could continue with the following phase, but only the next morning; the two Francescos put the tavola aside for that day to let it dry, and the next morning, when, according to custom, they placed it horizontally onto the two trestles that were set up obliquely, they looked to see if they had the right kind of bristles, and what was most important, the surface smeared with vinegar had to be completely dry, and since it was, the unpleasant operation of sizing the panel could truly commence: because even expressing it as delicately as possible, it was unpleasant due to the unmistakable stench, for if here, in the maestro's workshop, the assistants weren't obligated to cook it up themselves from parchment, but rather got the size from the glove-makers', they still had to boil it, to warm it up on a so-called gentle fire, and keep it there while the work continued: and already from the mere fact that somebody brought it in from the courtyard and put it onto the fire, an infernal stink arose, there was always a great contest to see who could escape this particular task, but in this the maestro divided the work evenly among them, so that sometimes the Francescos, sometimes Aulista, sometimes Giovanni, sometimes Giannicola, sometimes the others—in the beginning the assistant who worked in the workshop in Perugia completed the task—in any event, this time the honor of applying the boiling size onto the tavola had been conferred upon the Francescos, that is to say in accordance with the instructions: employing a short hard brush of pig-bristles, and not dipping, but dabbing it into the size from above perpendicularly, so that just the tip of the brush would touch the size, then drawing it across the edge of the basin; they began to apply it to the surface of the panel, sprinkling it in circles, rubbing it in as much as they could, very thoroughly, not a single corner, detail, the tiniest little spot could not be left out, and when it was ready, when the first part had dried enough that a second nice fine layer could be applied to it, well, then it was ready, but before they got to that point they had to keep thinning the size so that it would not get too thick, and the maestro was always coming in, as he was always the one to check on things, to see if it was diluted enough, or if it was already too thick, he stuck two fingers into it, then holding them up slowly spread them apart, and if a nice film was formed, then everything was fine, and it wasn't at all bad for the maestro to continually supervise every movement, but for the fact of the stench, namely he, Francesco, and everything around him stank dreadfully; the assistants approached him plugging up their noses, and if they came toward him, they of course repeatedly bombarded him whose turn it was—this time Francesco—asking what it was that made him stink so much, and what would his sweetheart say if he were to embrace her right now in one of the back rooms of a nearby tavern on the Borgo la Croce, because it was like that to be sure, not only around the wooden panel, but wherever he worked in the workshop became suffused with an unbearable stench, and he himself as well, or perhaps he himself the most of all, and to be sure he could only get rid of this smell with great difficulty, it remained on his hands for days, he washed them, washed them in vain, it just wouldn't come off properly with water, in short at least a week would go by until he could somehow get rid of the stench; work went on however, and when the size was completely dry, which in this case was in two days, because just then the weather was very rainy, they began to work on the panel again, only that now this work was not for them—that is for the Francescos—but rather was entrusted to Giannicola, as the maestro said, look here, Giannicola, I know that you are already a great master in this, still it won't hurt for you to hear one more time what you have to do, so that well, first rub down what Francesco has made very finely with the pumice stone, only then can you put on the gesso; use the cauldron for this plaster, fill it with clean water from the brook, and warm it up, warm it up, and then you start to sprinkle the plaster into it nice and slow, and with your other hand all the while mixing it and mixing it, and put in enough water so that there will be enough for it not to start to harden, in a word put in enough for it to dissolve and stay liquid, and do it nicely, sprinkle a little more water onto it, cover it well, and when you see that already the plaster doesn't want any more water, then it's good, but make sure that it remains at boiling point until you begin to apply the first rough layer onto the tavola ... well, you understand, Giannicola, but in the meantime don't forget that you have to keep working on the back surface of the panel properly with a moistened rag, and when however it is dry, in other words, the first layer of gesso grosso, then you know what you have to do: take up the drawing knife, and apply the next layer, be very careful for it to be even, over the entire surface, and really even, but I will be here for that, the maestro reassured the assistant, who of course was not reassured, but became nervous, because to have to work with the maestro standing behind his back, after so many years, would be like having to listen patiently all over again about what he had already done a hundred times, and he had already listened a hundred times, but really, why was the maestro saying this again and again, neither Giannicola nor the other assistants could ever really understand, they suspected that it was because he was dreadfully anxious about the plaster, the size, the panel, and maybe even the water in the rag with which they rubbed the back surface of the panel continuously and perhaps his boundless miserliness was the reason that he never tired of repeating the same thing one hundred times, he so was lacking in trust in them just as he never trusted anyone at all almost like a sick man, whose illness consists of an unconditional lack of trust, and maybe that was the source of everything bad in him; because he was not lacking in that either, he was not exactly considered to be an easy master, indeed, he was thought of as notorious, but still better to have him there behind one's back, thought Giannicola, than to be without him—because that also meant that he was not coming into the workshop and that was always and unconditionally bad—in any event now here he was, and everyone was happy that the work on the Pala Tezi was proceeding and it really did look as if it would be ready in MCCCCC, and so Giannicola applied the two layers of gesso grosso, and then he began the gesso sottile, but here the plaster should only be lukewarm, Giannicola continued from here so he could show to the maestro standing behind him that he understood things, that he did not have to be taught—but one of the brand-new assistants should be instructed, you know, just be very careful, but very careful, that there are no bubbles; everything depends on how clever you are when you apply the gesso, the best is if we ask for a drop of spirits from the maestro—and the maestro was already holding out the flask—and from this, Giannicola continued, you pour out a glass and then you pour out this entire little glass into the bottom of the basin, yes, like that Giannicola praised the assistant, who completed the task quickly, the spirits, Giannicola explained to the assistant, get rid of the bubbles, but the main thing is that when you are mixing it you should almost not be mixing it, but rather let it sit for a day, for it to settle, and then you mix it again without hardly mixing it; you sprinkle the plaster until it sinks into it, then however when a little hill begins to form in the middle, you have to stop immediately and then mix it again one more time very carefully, and make sure that it remains lukewarm, the whole thing depends on this as well, you understand, Domenico, or whatever your name is, because the base of the panel must be smooth, perfectly smooth, and that depends on whether or not you end up making bubbles, so it all depends on you, take note, Domenico, Giannicola said threateningly; then, he added, you know the rest, you know that you have to apply it with your flat heavy brush, at first rub on the initial layer, but then you should smear on the next layer right after it, don't worry, I'll tell you later how many layers there should be, don't worry, I'll be here; I'm sure about that, thought this Domenico and you could see this is what he was thinking—because Giannicola, standing behind his back with the sarcastically smiling maestro, looked at him for a moment fairly strangely, but then he let it pass—and he continued by pointing out that when the entire surface was being brushed, he should make sure not to forget that we do not begin at the edge, and at this word Giannicola strongly raised his voice, but from the inside, and first we stroke inward and only after that outward, because otherwise a spot will remain there which you will be unable to get out, well you understand, Domenico, I don't have to explain so much to you, you've done it and you've seen it before since you've been here, and you've proven already that after you've finished we don't have to go over the whole thing with the hake brush, because if you do what I say, then your gesso will be as smooth as a copper mirror, and that's what we need here, said Giannicola, exactly, the maestro said, taking up the thread behind him, and looking directly at Giannicola, he said to him, yes, a perfectly smooth surface, but take note, that if by any chance I find even just one single bump, one single furrow, one single spot, then you'll get such a slap in the face, Giannicola that you will rue it for the rest of your life, you understand, at which point, to Domenico's greatest delight, Giannicola turned completely red from the chagrin of desperately wanting to somehow reply to the maestro, but not doing so, he just continued to listen to the maestro's words in silence, who however only now noted: don't be afraid, there won't be any problems, I'll be right here, and if I'm not, then call for me, always call for me if you are not certain of something, you may ask anything you want, just don't make any mistakes, this is not painting, this is the gesso, it cannot be repaired, you yourself know best, you've already been working for me long enough, the maestro said this in 1495, and although actually it not had been so long ago that Giannicola di Paolo came into the maestro's studio, he remained silent, and he would have been very pleased to take out all of his chagrin on Domenico, but instead set about to work, which, however for some unknown reason the maestro only permitted them to begin the following day, and Giannicola, instructing Domenico, prepared the gesso with him that same day, the gesso dried quickly, so that was it already possible to sand the whole thing down, and to draw a moist rag over it, very gently, but really just barely, as delicately as a breath, and the priming was completed, then came the application of the alum solution with the hake brush, as the maestro considered it to be extremely important for the base not to absorb the colors to such a degree, and there was the perfectly smooth, matte surface, and the underdrawing could begin—it's just that it did not begin, because from that point on the maestro stood the sized tavola up against the wall, and the Tezi family was forgotten, he simply took no notice of the picture, as if he had given up on it, he was not at all interested in the fact that it was there, as if it had ceased to exist for him; sometimes still they mentioned it to him, either Aulista or Giovanni, but he just pushed the whole thing aside with an incomprehensible gesture, and just continued with what he had been saying and doing at that moment, so that accordingly the prepared panel just sat there, and then—perhaps two years or maybe a year and half later—when everyone had forgotten about it already, the maestro came into the workshop one day, but this was already in Florence, where in the meantime it had been delivered with a large shipment, saying that now the time had come for the underdrawing, and at first of course they had no idea what he was talking about, because they had forgotten about it themselves, it was only when, in the bottega in Florence, the maestro pointed to the panel leaning up against the wall that they realized that he was talking about the picture for the Sant'Agostino, but at that time there were already two who could be entrusted with the commission from the maestro, that is, Giovanni and Aulista, who had already gained serious reputations outside of the workshop as well, but in the workshop ultimately, if the maestro wanted to be fair, then he had to divide the task up between the two of them, and contrary to their expectations, since he always made capricious and erratic decisions, this time he really was just, giving one part of the underdrawing to Aulista and the other to Giovanni, and so it happened that Aulista began, the maestro entrusted the drawing to his hand, and everyone who was in the workshop immediately gathered there, and watched in great wonder over Aulista's shoulder, because the drawing, as always, now too was wonderful, they were dazzled, especially the newly arrived apprentices—foremost among them Domenico—all would have liked to know immediately how the maestro prepared the drawing, so that as Aulista began, the maestro said to the apprentices, who were gathered in a circle, that in a good painting the drawing is of extraordinary importance, which always begins first by having to render the paper transparent, this can be acheived by using linseed oil diluted with turpentine, that is you must rub it onto the paper until it becomes translucent, transparent, and then after that you have to dry it, and then bring it out when it is time for the underdrawing, as is the case now, he motioned toward Aulista, the underdrawing, he repeated, which means that from among the previously prepared drawings you need to choose precisely the right one, just as I did at home one half-hour ago, and you place the transparent paper onto this drawing, and with a sharpened piece of charcoal, you trace it nicely, carefully, your drawing is now on the transparent paper, and then you lay some kind of carpet or a thicker piece of felt underneath it; then following the contours nicely you pierce through the paper, puncturing, densely with pinpricks, the maestro motioned to the assistants, along all of the contours of the drawing, and now all you have to do is smooth down your punctured drawing, because otherwise nothing will permeate through the tiny pinpricks; then you place it on the painting surface, and you put charcoal dust ground very fine into a fine rag so that the dust can pass through, you form the rag into a little ball, and tie it up with something, then with this tool, with the charcoal dust you transfer, through all of the tiny little pinpricks onto the panel—or onto the canvas, it depends on what you are painting—the original drawing, well then, so you understand, don't you; the master looked around at the assistants, then he watched for a while to make sure that everything was all right with the silently working Aulista, then stating that from this point on they should watch him, and then tomorrow they themselves could give it a try to see if they could do it; he left the workshop; the precise, faint underdrawing had been ready on the tavola for a long time, but the maestro had not come in to begin painting, they didn't dare to take the tavola down from the trestles, but they couldn't just leave it there, they had to keep walking around it, because well, they still needed to use the trestles, and when it had became obvious that for now the work had proceeded thus far and the maestro had lost interest in it again, instead of putting it back on the painting easel, Aulista traced the lines with a fine brush, and the panel was taken down, thus freeing up the trestles; then cautiously, the entire thing was sprayed with a mixture of milk and honey so that the drawing would not be damaged, and finally they put it back against the wall facing inward, so that life could go on in the bottega in Florence, and for a good long while even the maestro himself never mentioned the Tezi altarpiece, and didn't even ask Aulista, and chiefly did not look to see if the underdrawing was ready, or if it was, what the result was like; even then, and, when one day a half-year later—not in the morning but in the middle of the afternoon—he arrived, and there was still light in the workshop, he did not speak to anyone, but just put the long untouched panel back onto the easel, and instructed one of the Francescos to immediately take out one of the painting pots with some ultramarine prepared earlier for something else, and to break it up with the pumice stone; Francesco, of course, was greatly amazed when the master took up his cloak, wondering what the maestro could want with the ultramarine so late in the day, but he began to break up the exorbitantly expensive pigment without a word, all the while measuring out so cautiously, almost drop by drop, the egg yolk, already separated and mixed with linseed oil, and to prevent spoiling, disinfected with the juice of fresh fig buds, so that he even held his breath, and as in the case of ultramarine, the color is always best if the crystals of the pigment are left coarse, he, too, broke them up coarsely, and was ready with it relatively quickly, he poured it into a seashell, and was already giving it to the maestro, who took it without a word and began to paint with it the wondrous material of the lower garments of the Virgin Mary, their ethereal lightness, in that color at which Aulista had marveled already so many times when on occasion—if he was alone in the workshop—he turned the picture away from the wall so he could make sure that it had not been damaged by mold or something else; only Bastiano, Domenico, one of the Francescos, and he, Aulista, were in the workshop, the maestro painted, everyone went about their business silently, but so carefully as to not make a single sound, and as a matter of fact, the maestro was quickly finished with this blue, then he painted in, with a black that happened to be at hand, but originally prepared for something else, the folds and the waves, to the point of perceptibility, then he called for Aulista to come over, and for a while they looked at how the blue glimmered, then the maestro gestured for Aulista to come completely close to the picture, and pointing at the lowermost edge of the blue garment on the left side of the picture, he allowed him to paint there, onto that surface, a little more dark color, and to write there, with the finest brush—but you know, he grabbed Aulista's shoulder, just in such a way that it almost can't be seen, and with gold—MCCCCC, then he turned away from the easel, he took off his cloak, he handed his brushes to Bastiano so that he could wash them out with soap, and then he wasn't even there, he left the workshop and from that point on all that happened was that the next day, or the day after that, when he came over again from the Borgo Pinti, he took the picture down from the easel, placed it again next to the wall with the colors facing inward, and no longer bothered with it, as if he had forgotten that it was there, so that in Perugia a completely new story began, not the continuation of the old one, as the whole thing started with the arrival of the four assistants, who had somehow collected themselves after the fatal exhaustion on the Via dei Priori, then in a complete state of despair they directed the coachman to the door of the leased workshop on the Piazza del Sopramura, and there to their greatest alarm the maestro himself awaited them, like some kind of ghost, but it was not a ghost, it was he himself, as for some reason, he was not willing to say more than that, essentially he himself had started off toward home on horseback on the same morning as they, with some kind of paid accompaniment, when he had sent them off on their journey in the cart, only that he went by a different route, and of course reached Perugia much more quickly than their cart, in brief, the whole thing began with him seeing the state that the assistants were in, he let them have a proper rest, and when they were rested they should come to his house in the Via Deliziosa, and report that they were ready for work, and that is how it happened, the maestro left them and they immediately collapsed onto the floor of the new bottega, and already the four of them were asleep, the locals, Girolamo, Raffaello, Sinibaldo, and Bartolomeo, together with the coachman, brought in the contents of the cart—the coachman was not in such a bad state as the others, he was cut from somewhat harder wood, as he kept saying to the local assistants—so that after the cart-load had been brought in, they led the horses to the nearby postal station and handed them over to a stable boy, then they went back into the workshop, and the coachman got something to eat and drink, and finally they let him sleep as well, and they left silently so as to come back the next day, when the coachman was already awake, but the others were still snoring like horses, so getting some work out of them, because they lay strewn across the workshop, was not really possible, they left the coachman with his wages as sent by the maestro, and they waited, they waited for these four to finally wake up, but well they just weren't waking up, only on the following day; altogether they slept through an entire night, and an entire day, and an entire night again, however when they did wake up, all those who knew some of the others already were glad, for example, Bartolomeo knew nearly everyone from the workshop in Florence, but Aulista also knew Sinibaldo from somewhere, it was only Raffaello whom no one really knew, he was a fairly new assistant even for the Perugians, they had just heard of him of course from the maestro in Florence, he was wholly exempted from priming and the preparatory work in Perugia, because the maestro was teaching this Raffeallo exclusively how to paint, that is how to make the paints, how to take care of the brushes, and how to paint this or that—an arm, a head, a mouth, a Madonna, a Jerome, or a landscape—but frankly speaking, said the maestro, I really don't know what to teach this Raffaello, because he already knows how to draw very well, and he learns everything that he sees me do so quickly, that he could even already be entrusted with a picture, even though he is only, I don't know, how many years old, maybe sixteen, or seventeen, I have no idea, said the maestro and, well, that's all that they knew about him, and here in the workshop they did not find out much more, only that he came from Urbino, and that was all, and that he was good at drawing and painting, that was it, and so they didn't really take much notice of him, he somehow always worked apart, and the maestro always treated him differently, in a special way, not the way he treated them, which could have been a cause for anger, but it wasn't, because this assistant from Urbino charmed everyone with his amiability, maybe he was even too gentle for such a workshop as this, one thing was certain, he had no wish to push himself forward just because he was granted such exceptional treatment on the part of the maestro, he did not want to, nor did he stand in the forefront, in that forefront stood Bartolomeo, he was the center, the workshop was entrusted to him, so that everything somehow happened around him; Raffaello became friends with Aulista, who was also fairly quiet; the whole thing began with the arrival of the Florentines, who had a good sleep, gorged themselves, and became thoroughly drunk, then they went across to Via Deliziosa 17 to report that they were ready for work, and then the next day the maestro came over from the Ospedale della Misericordia to the newly leased bottega, and to everyone's great surprise, extorting them to continue with the work underway, took out at the very first the Pala Tezi picture, and put it on the easel, and that now this panel would be at the center of the activities of the workshop, and no one really understood why it was exactly this one, because work on it had begun and then had been left off so many times, maybe because since returning to Perugia the Tezi family was urging him to finish it; of course this was just a guess, no one but he knew anything about it, and the maestro actually never spoke of such things as patrons and commissions and honorariums and family and friends and suchlike, not even to Bartolomeo, or if he did so, then it was always with the order that the matter remain strictly between the two of them, in any event the tavola intended for Sant'Agostino turned up on the painting easel, and from that point on the fate of the panel changed, because no longer did it only happen that the maestro would paint another fold or figure onto the picture and then put it back against the wall, as he had done until now, but that from this point on the picture wasn't even taken down from the easel, the maestro was occupied with it continually, which of course did not mean that at times Aulista, or Giannicola, or even the young Raffaello would not work on it a bit, but really, the fact was that the maestro basically took the work into his own hands, and kept it there, maybe, really, one of the Francescos noted one evening, the esteemed notary and his family had reminded the maestro that the picture was supposed to have been ready one year ago, in 1500, the entire altar must surely be ready in the family chapel, only this picture was still missing, they reflected, but they didn't know for certain why this picture had suddenly become so urgent, one thing was certain, it was urgent, and the maestro was working, already this counted as something very new, he was working continuously, coming into the workshop every single day, and picking up where he had left off before, and the approaching event of his appointment as prior visibly did not seem to interest him, he just painted every day for at least two or three hours, and at his age—for surely he must have been at least fifty years old—this was not very common, old people, particularly in the case of the maestros who were renowned all across Italy, usually just visited their workshops once a week, and usually just taught a little, instructed the disciples, they themselves worked only very infrequently, and that was how their maestro had lived as well—in Florence, but not here in Perugia, here somehow, after the great fiasco, his fervor was renewed, or maybe he really needed the money from the Tezis, who knows, in any event he was painting, only this much was obvious: the lower garments of the Madonna were already done, with the upper part of the cloak in the gentle shading of the medium dark malachite green; the bodies were ready, the face of the Madonna, the entire figure of the little baby Jesus, the head and arms of the four saints, just as the landscape in the background was ready, in which everyone joyfully recognized a detail from Perugia with the Palazzo dei Priori, but he finished as well the ciborium and the garments of the saints, with the exception—and this was very striking, especially to Aulista, who had been watching the maestro with special attention since this feverish work had begun—with the exception of: the book in the hands of Santo Nicola da Tolentino of the Lily, the upper garments of broadcloth of the Madonna, the cloak covering the body of Saint Sebastian, and Jerome's renowned bishop's mitre on the ground, at the bottom of the picture, next to the saint and in front of the lion; no one knew why these parts were never painted, especially not Aulista, Raffaello was visibly uninterested as to why, or why these parts were to be painted at the end, before the completion of the entire picture, Aulista didn't know why, he just waited for the day, the hour, the minute for the time to come, and he did not wait in vain, because the day did come when every element of the Pala Tezi picture really was painted, already the yellow shone there, the blue glimmered, the green swelled, the brown appeared gently, and all across the border of the sky was a strong glaze of whitish blue, but it was already obvious that it was the painting of the red that the maestro had left for the very end, and Aulista simply could not wait for that day and that hour and that minute when he would say to him to begin breaking up the pigment, because he truly hoped that he would be the one to whom the maestro entrusted this task, and he was not disappointed—not that the maestro selected him himself, but Aulista positioned himself in such a way so that if there was even the tiniest chance of breaking up the vermiglione, it was he who had something to do right there, accordingly the maestro spoke to him one day, Aulista, please be so kind and break up the vermiglione, I ask you, and Aulista flew, already there he was with a tiny sack of fragments of vermiglione from the monastery of the Jesuit order in Florence—San Giusta alle Mura—directly from brother Bernado di Francesco, from whom the maestro ordered the pigments personally, regularly, and in great quantities, he was not willing to order from anywhere else, he only ordered this kind of pigment, even if it was a little more expensive than at the apothecary's, there was something in these paints, first and foremost in the vermiglione, due to which the maestro never used, under any circumstances, any other kind, only this and exclusively this, the breaking up of which Aulista was now preparing for, and really there was something special in it, which an experienced disciple such as Aulista, noticed immediately, this time as well, something extraordinary, this kind of vermiglione was different from every other kind, because as he broke it up now, he saw once again how the crystals in it glittered, and how something else was glittering too, just that Aulista did not know, and no one knew, only the brothers and the maestro; whatever it was, in any event, it was truly unique among pigments, not a single property of which the maestro's assistants and disciples in any workshops could ever discuss, because it was a secret, in addition to that, it was a secret, the meaning and essence of which the assistants and the disciples of the maestro's workshop did not know too much about; beyond the fact that through its mere use a most wondrous light could be made to appear, with this ultramarine that came from the brothers of Florence, with these malachites and azures and golds that they got from them, but especially with this vermiglione, something was happening here, when after the paints were prepared and according to custom everyone had to leave the workshop, accordingly it was some kind of thing about which they, the assistants and the disciples, could not know anything, and they did not dare ask what it was, because when following custom, after a few minutes they were allowed back in and they found the maestro already at work, who would have had the courage to disturb him in the midst of work with such questions, one thing however was sure, the maestro had a secret with these paints, in these paints there was some kind of secret, and Aulista knew that it was with these that the maestro dazzled all of the patrons who bought his pictures, but at the same time he dazzled the assistants as well, Aulista just broke up the vermiglione on the pumice stone, and he was not thinking now about what the secret could be, he was just thinking that for two or three hours he would be breaking up the vermiglione, then he would hand it in the seashell to the maestro, who then would send them out, and do something with the paints; then he sets to the upper garments of the Madonna, then the folds of the cloak on the tortured body of Saint Sebastian, and the mitre on the ground next to Jerome, and when he is ready, and they can all look at it, they are dazzled by the eternal light of this red, as it nearly shines out between the green and the yellow and the blue, then finally it becomes hopeless to them, as it does to his most trusted follower, Aulista, to answer the question as to what could have happened in Florence, in what accordingly did this fiasco consist of, why they had to return to Perugia, and why he felt that it was the end for his adored master, to answer the question of whether the maestro, Pietro di Vannucci, born in Castel della Pieve, and renowned as Il Perugino, had simply outlived his talent, or whether he had merely lost all interest in painting.

89

DISTANT MANDATE

Concealed in its essence,
by its appearance revealed

We don't even know what it was called, not a single contemporary document refers to it as the Alhambra, in part because there is no such document, or no such document has survived; in part because even if such a document did survive, this name is the most unlikely one, for its builders—if they were the ones we refer to today—would never have designated it by a name altogether not in accord with the building itself; as this name is not: if you derive an attribution from the expression based on the color of the materials used for the masonry, "qal'at al-hamra" or possibly "al-qubba al-hamra," it could signify "al hamra," accordingly "The Red," which might refer to the name of the builder, a version which, although more faintly, does hold together in some fashion or another; the palace, with its breathtakingly harmonious magnificence within, surpassing the architectural beauty of any earlier or later period, is itself, however, inconsistent with this hardly exalted vernacular clarification, so distant from the nature of the Arab spirit; if we were to rely upon those whom we have to thank for this structure for the attribution, then they would certainly have found a loftier designation for it; so already we're off to a bad start, it doesn't even have a name, because "Alhambra" is not its name, that is only what we call it, moreover in distorted Spanish, that is to say that "Alhambra" could refer to anything at all, it just stuck somehow, not to mention that in Islam it was just as frequent for a sacred or secular building not to have a name as to be given one, because what was the name of the Mosque of Córdoba? the Aljafería of Zaragoza? the Alcázar in Seville? the al-Kairaouine mosque in Fez? and on and on along the North African shore onward to Egypt, Palestine, and northwest India? there were no names; so there are examples, if we think upon it more deeply, hundreds of examples that there can be good reason not to give a name to an immortal artwork, it's just that this reason is indecipherable to us, just as indecipherable as the date of the construction of the Alhambra, because the records are fairly contradictory in this matter, as the whole thing depends on what the first one doesn't know, the second one misunderstands, and where therefore the third puts the emphasis, that is to say how far away this or that one strays from the unverifiable facts; certain individuals report that there are Roman and Visigoth ruins on the mountain that served as the location for the later Alhambra—either the part of it known as Sabīka, or the entire locale—others are of the opinion that until the building of the Alhambra, this mountain, rising above the swift-flowing waters of the narrow Darro, thus including the Alcazaba, a fortress dating from the eighth century on the top of it, never played any kind of significant role, and that maybe there was some sort of battle between the Arabs and an ethnic group known as the Muladi after the Arab conquest of Al-Andalus in the ninth and tenth centuries; but yet again in the view of others—in opposition to those who say that the Jews only lived in the district known as Garnatha, that is to say down below, in the area of today's Granada—there is only one fact worth mentioning, that in one of the centuries preceding the Alhambra, hence certainly by the eleventh century, starting from some point in time and ending at a later point in time, there existed, on the part of the mountain that was to become truly important later on, a Jewish settlement; after the fall of the Caliphate of Córdoba, an early Berber ethnic group, the Zirids, belonging to the Kutama tribe and thus to the Umayyads, who founded the city of Granada, located its center here and tried to "protect" the Jews; in any event there was a Jewish vizier by the name of Yusuf ibn Naghrallah, who built a so-called hisn, a fortified palace; we know, other scholars remark, that on the mountain beside the Darro there was, as far back as early Roman times but also after the Arab invasion of Iberia in 711, a strongly defended fortress, or at the very least from the eleventh century, an extremely well-built wall; and of course in opposition to this view there exist other opinions, according to which regarding this place—starting from Granada and the district known as Albaicín, from the nearly unverifiable fortress of Elvira nearby and the Jewish community of Sabīka, all the way to the Berber dynasties (the Almoravids and the Almohads), and the never-ending sheer butchery known as civil war—there's nothing, nothing at all, from which we might glean a bit of certainty, and so then we finally arrive at the first Arab sources such as they are, because up until this point—here and now is the time to say this—there is no kind of usable historical material at our disposal whatsoever, because the location we are discussing never had any usable historical records or they have not survived; hypothetically, because this place, during the first centuries of Iberian subjugation, did not play an important enough role for it to have something like its own history, that is to say its own place in historical events, because this place began to acquire an important role only with the emergence of the Nasrid Dynasty, the sudden appearance of which coincides with the genesis of the Alhambra in today's sense of the term, and it is better if we say at once its genesis, and avoid the question of who built the Alhambra, because this is already the third question after "what is its name" and "when was it built," that we cannot answer, as even this is not certain, it never was, maybe not even to those who were involved with it, someone began it, of that there is no doubt, but as for the true founder, to take a huge leap forward in time, the true initiator and first patron of the Alhambra is said to be Yusuf I; supposedly it was he who commissioned it, who paid for a new palace complex on the ridge of the mountain—roughly the middle section—following the various and obscure initiatives of the Nasrids; because there are many already who said that the first Nasrid was the one who built the Alhambra, he, the earlier ruler of Jaén, Ibn-al-Ahmed, his full name being Muhammad ibn Yusuf ibn Nasr, but better known under the name al-Ahmar, that is to say the prince known as "The Red," who moved his residence from Jaén to Granada, and proclaimed himself Muhammad I, he became, after the Umayyads, the Almoravids, and the Almohads, the first grandiose founder of this place, previously not so splendid; in addition to this, in the history of the western Arabs, he simultaneously became, with his own last dynasty, the luminous ruler of Islamic ambitions westward, because he began by reinforcing, to a degree never before seen, the walls of the Alcazaba; and, well, if we can believe a so-called contemporary account, the beginning of the story of the Alhambra began with him, Abdallah ibn al-Ahmar, namely, the ruler himself, at least according to the somewhat adventurous manuscript baptized as the Anómino de Granada y Copenhague: "In 1238, he went up to the place later known as Alhambra, inspected it, designated the foundation of a castle, then instructed someone to build it," the visit from which, supposedly, six palaces emerged, the royal residence in a northeastern orientation, with two round towers, as well as countless bath-houses, so somehow it got off to a start, it was begun like this and it became like this, and perhaps the romantic history of the Alhambra really did occur like that, but it's also possible that it didn't, as the description originates from a chronicle that—and here every self-respecting professional scholar, from Oleg Grabar and Juan Vernet and Leonor Martínez Martín up to Ernst J. Grube, raises his index finger—is completely unreliable; I for example, Ernst J. Grube writes in a letter to a close friend, have never once seen this account; so that they—all of these aforementioned scholars, including, as well, the amicable and as yet unpublished index-card notations of the scholarly team of four that authored the minor masterpiece The Language of Pattern—all agree quite clearly that the Alhambra was planned, commissioned, and built nearly one century later by Yusuf I, the Nasrid Sultan who ruled for eleven years after 1333, whose palace most likely bore within its embryo, or in its foundations—how shall we express it in this obscurity?—the concealed essence of the final Alhambra, although at this point one becomes completely uncertain, because it is necessary to add immediately that it was he, and after one of his own bodyguards ran a dagger through him, of course, his son, because this whole has to be imagined in such a way, that they, so to speak, built this work of uncertain depth together, Yusuf and his son Mohammed V, both of whom, as it were, passed the trowel from hand to hand—an expression wishing to allude to their inseparability—therefore we can conjecture that in all likelihood both knew very well what they were doing, because in the end, after them, there is nothing else, it could have only been them; for if it is certain that this origin is as unclear as the origin of any work of art can be, moreover if one would venture to state that nothing is more unclear than the origin of the Alhambra, the end, however, is as certain as death: after Mohammed V and his long reign, ending in 1391, there can be no doubts about the end; about one hundred years then follow, during which the Sultanate of Granada, among others, consume seven more Mohammeds and four more Yusufs, but this period of one hundred years is one single chaotic tragic drama where, in relation to the Alhambra—apart from the construction of the Torre de las Infantas—nothing essential even occurs, so that when the last Nasrid ruler, Mohammed XII, known just as often as Boabdil, "The Unfortunate," in 1492, upon the fall of his Granada and his Alhambra—seen from here, the conclusion of the great Reconquista—lamented, according to hearsay, that this was the end, no more, he must depart from all of this beauty, the Catholic Kings are marching into the Alhambra, kings who of course see the magnificent enchantment but do not understand it, but even more importantly, do not even wish to understand anything; yet they do not destroy it—how kind of them—which the non-Hispanophone historical accounts truly recognize as their one irrational, if beneficial act; in short the Alhambra's fate was sealed, and with the victory of the Reconquista it was occupied by foreigners, and in the centuries to come they built this and that in the surrounding area, for the most part insignificant structures, so that the essential thing, looking at it from the reference point of Alhambra, was that the Arabs definitely vanished from the scene, and thus the Alhambra ended up in the most haunting of conditions imaginable, for if there was anyone at all who understood it, it was the Arabs, yet they had vanished from here for good, which means, in our case, that there remained no one, from this point on, who could approach its meaning, this is absolutely true, because there is no one up to this very day who has been able understand the Alhambra, it stands there aimless and incomprehensible, and no one can comprehend even today why it is standing there, so there is no one who can help in this situation, it is not the interpretations that are lacking, but the interpretive code through which it can be deciphered, and it will remain like this from now on, because it is not even worthwhile to keep going on in this direction, but more worthwhile to turn back, to wander back a little to the probable creators, and in the most well-founded uncertainty to say that yes, after 1391—not including the interior of the Torre de las Infantas in the mid-fifteenth century—no one added anything anymore to the Alhambra, it came into being with Yusuf I and his son Mohammed V, and with them it also came to an end, in a word, it is more worthwhile to pronounce them indecisively as most likely to have commissioned the Alhambra; winding our way back, we cannot speak any less cautiously than this and perhaps what we have stated about Yusuf I and Mohammed V may be permitted, if one proceeds cautiously, a caution that at any single tiny point of this story is not in the least bit superfluous, particularly if we reach—as we are reaching right here and now—that point when it becomes clear that leaving aside the fact that we don't know what the name of the Alhambra was, or even if it had a name at all, and that this isn't even something without precedent, and so it is thus tolerable, that we cannot find a clear answer to when it was built and finally even to who built it; but now comes the point where the next thing we don't know must be revealed; namely that we don't know *what* the Alhambra is, that is to say we don't know why it was built, what was its function—if we don't view it as a residence, a private palace, or a fortification, because we don't view it as that, then, well, how should we regard it? generally we don't know, we have no idea at all, and this is difficult to explain, difficult, because now it seems as if everything is in order, one picks oneself up and travels to Granada, goes up the left bank of the Darro, then turns right and crosses above the Darro's bubbling froth, reaches the road that leads to the Alhambra, drags himself up in the heat—for let us say that it's summer and there is a dreadful, dry, scorching heat, and he has no parasol—and he buys the *expensive* entrance ticket, then a great surprise, more precisely an unpleasant surprise awaits him when at last, wandering with difficulty here and there up above, up here are all kinds of structures, from various gates to the chill, icy, unfinished, supposedly Renaissance palace of Charles V, but one feels that not one of them is *it*; then he finds it, because in the end, he finally realizes that it is there, at that little gate, where he has to go in, and then he finds out that he can't go inside, that he has to wait, because visitors are only allowed in at certain intervals, and he is a visitor, he has to follow the rules, to wait in the inhuman parching heat, there is no refreshment stand, so accordingly he withdraws to a more shaded corner, and if he is lucky, and let's assume that he is, then he has to wait for only twenty minutes, then he goes in and his jaw drops, because something like this, but like *this*, he says to himself, utterly stupefied, he has really, but really never even seen, this, the person says to himself, surpasses anyone's imagination, but in the meantime it doesn't even occur to him that something isn't right; he thinks it is a royal palace, well yes, he reads the brief explanatory sheet that comes with the ticket, or he hears the bellowing of the tour guides, that Yusuf I, was it not, and his son Mohammed V, they were the ones who created this wondrous masterwork, this unsurpassable wonder of the Muslim Moors, he hears this and he reads the same, and it never even occurs to him to question whether this is a palace, or a fortress, or perhaps a private residence, or all of these things together—why, what else could it be?—well, the sultan lived here, or didn't he? and here, living in his proximity, was the ocean of courtiers, and the women of the harem, courtly life, in a word, went on, there were huge feasts, splendid concerts, glittering receptions, the renowned baths, radiant celebrations and, well, of course, because this too is known, there were the thousands of ugly intrigues and machinations, secret associations and plots, and danger and murder, and chaos and blood and collapse, after which there always came the next sultan from the Nasrid dynasty, in a word everything went on just like it should in such a sultanate, one thinks to oneself, or perhaps doesn't even think, as the images already precede the thoughts, when that which a person is thinking about gives rise to just one question, yet a question that remains unspoken because, well, who would ask it, maybe the tourist guide with his hand-held megaphone?—no, really no, the suspicion does not even arise within him that he now in such a place, for the first time in his life—because in the world there is only one such place as this, the Alhambra, where innumerable signs indicate that everything here, called only by their Spanish names—from the Patio de los Arrayanes to the Sala de la Barca, the Patio de Comares to the Patio de los Leones, the Sala de las Dos Hermanas to the Mirador de la Daraxa—everything here does not constitute a palace but something else; innumerable signs indicate to the visitor taking part in the immortal beauty of the Alhambra, that no, this is neither a fortress nor a palace, not even a private residence, but again and again—something else, and well, here, then we start with the walls, about which we should first know that they were originally whitewashed with lime, so that from below, from today's Granada, or concretely the Darro or the Albacín quarter which once provided the Alhambra with water, the predecessor of the Alhambra was white, not red, and that is enough here about the name just one last time, but what is much more important is that these walls, for the most part towers connected to each other haphazardly—no matter what kind of well-intentioned expert sets to examining them—they were suitable for many purposes but it becomes ever more certain that they did not truly protect whoever was the ruler of the Alhambra, so then what were the walls for, what were they protecting: the Alhambra, fine, but from what, because in a military sense they were not really capable of defending anything; their significance, however, is as obvious as anything else in the Alhambra, or in relation to the Alhambra, so that then here, in the matter of the walls it is not really possible to arrive at any other decision than that the walls of the Alhambra—it is of course the outer walls of which we are speaking—did not provide any function of defense, but that their construction... perhaps... was intended as a kind of manifestation, namely to manifest that these walls were on the one hand like those of a fortress, accordingly high and wall-like, hence they could unconditionally protect something, something located behind them, yet on the other hand the people who commissioned these walls wanted to indicate that life within was unassailable, that it was not possible to enter here, not possible to breach these walls, and it was *not even allowed*, perhaps this sort of deliberation lay in the depths of the wishes of those who ordered it, who knows, no one has ever seen their specific plans, neither Yusuf I nor Mohammed V left any sort of trace behind as to what they were thinking when they built these walls here in this state, we can only guess, just as we also guessed as to why generally no written trace was left concerning the construction of the Alhambra, because nothing remained, and this still is not without precedent, for in the enormous territories of the Islamic empire, documents about this or that building are not too frequently available; it is however unprecedented that in the case of the Alhambra not even one single tiny piece of data has ever emerged about the construction itself, as if it would have been of particular importance to its commissioners that their work—how should one even express it, so as not to obscure things unnecessarily—would remain concealed, concealed in its essence, but by its appearance revealed, that is more or less the conclusion reached by one who lingers over these dilemmas, and this is just the beginning, really, because as one progresses in this Alhambra research, it will be ever more obvious that what earlier seemed self-evident here is anything but, that is to say that it can hardly be seen as an exception that in the case of a very old building, written sources do not survive, or that there are today very few experts to be found who can evoke, in spite of all their expertise, evidence, pertaining to how, for example, the days were spent in the Alhambra, or in any edifice, say, similar to the Alhambra; just that this complexity, this perfection appears to manifest itself as well in the concealment of any knowledge pertaining to the Alhambra at all; an attention extending to all things, that even of the tiniest, the most insignificant of facts, nothing at all should remain; this nonetheless causes one to ponder, because, well then, the question inevitably arises within one, if it isn't this way because *there were never any traces at all, it just appears that they were hidden,* Professor Grabar, coming from the Marçais school, and towering far above the other scholars of the Alhambra as he is the only one who notices that in this wondrous masterwork there is too much obscurity, briefly he, an instructor at both the University of Michigan and Harvard, the son of André Grabar, wrote an entirely serious monograph about how the story of the Alhambra is in fact nothing but the story of a great conspiracy, and the Alhambra itself, in his view, is a singular attempt at the art of disguise, and clearly the reason why he thinks so, being a knowledgeable expert, is that he cannot resign himself to there being no explanation; it is simply palpable, as one reads onward in Grabar's book, that this scholar of exceptional aptitude is hardly capable of conceiving that something could exist without a story, circumstance, cause, or goal; he can't even conceive that its formation, its origination would have no logical continuity, to put it more forcefully, this Professor Grabar neither considers it possible, nor is capable of accepting, that an effect can appear without having been elicited by any cause, hence that ripples would appear on the lake's tranquil surface without us having thrown a pebble into it, namely, in the case of the Alhambra that this, the Alhambra, could come into being without there being any real commission, and in addition, that the ones who commissioned it had no tangible intention and so on, but in the end Professor Grabar cannot, neither at Harvard nor at Michigan, cannot withstand that inasmuch as all of this is extant, that ultimately it all cannot *finally* be attributed to something logical, in this case then, perhaps in this unique case, we must confront the disquieting possibility that the Alhambra—already far beyond its really being neither fortress nor palace nor private residence—stands there with no explanation, it is wholly extant, the outer walls are extant, the entrance is extant, the spaces inside, ultimately traversable if with some difficulty, are extant, the presumed function of each single spatial element is extant, they point out, for example, that here is where the throne was, and here were the baths, and over there was the tower of the captive Infanta, things like that, they analyze the exceptional craftsmanship of the ornamentation, they look for correlations, and they find them in the universal regularity of Islamic architecture, and they do not grow perplexed when a less perceptive observer, in their view, does grow perplexed; they are not; we, however, are; for our gaze does not glide over self-evident things so easily, well, because we take one more step forward, and we note that no one is perplexed—only Professor Grabar with his own conspiracy-theory, but that is going in a different direction—accordingly then there is no one, although clearly this must have been obvious, or is obvious to every expert: no one is sincerely troubled by the Alhambra's outwardly very restrained, almost desolate, characterless, attention-deflecting walls, the negligible mortar of these walls built from negligible materials, in a word, the Alhambra places a great deal of emphasis on showing nothing outwardly of the nearly inhuman enchantment with which everything dazzles there within, like the starry sky of a summer's night above Granada; put differently, that the Alhambra from without betrays nothing of what is inside, and at the same time, from within, it does not betray what awaits a person outside, that is to say that the Alhambra betrays nothing about itself, and generally this or that quality is never shown in this or that direction, it never indicates here that over there this or that will follow; namely that the Alhambra is always the same, and is always at every point identical only with itself, by which statement one does not wish to express, on the other hand, that one knows what this means, but precisely that one does *not* know, he just stands there and acknowledges it, and he acknowledges it by saying oh my, how peculiar that Alhambra is from the outside, a completely different building than within, and utterly different inside than outside, and so it goes, truly one step at a time, when one enters through the little gate; so that his own Alhambra story may begin within a truly insignificant place in the greater whole, the entrance, let's call it that, but we don't think of it as such, as we know very well that this entrance is only the present entrance, at one time it was not located here, this is claimed decisively by a few, although already not so very decisively as to where exactly it was "in olden times," in short the entrance is concealed, says Professor Grabar from Boston or from Michigan, because who could imagine that the path into a palace of wonders would not pass through a gate of wonders, although, no, it isn't like that in the Alhambra, examining either the presumably earlier or current entrances, it is as if the entrance neither wants to invite anyone in nor to lead him anywhere, it simply allows one inside, an opening, a point where a person may obtain access to the interior spaces if he so wishes, an arbitrarily selected place which merely happened to come about in the course of time, and which offers nothing, is just open and is always open, hence it is possible to step across it; well, after, of course, it is another question of what to do after one has stepped across it, because let us take the simplest scenario, twenty minutes have gone by, the sweat trickles down in the horrendous scorching heat, he pays the *extortionately* high entrance fee, glances at the brief description that comes with the ticket, and sets off in one direction that would appear to be the right one—just that there is no such thing, the Alhambra does not recognize within itself the concept of a right direction, one is rapidly convinced of this when he realizes that fine, he headed off toward the Cuarto Dorado courtyard, and if he is moving inside a work of Islamic architecture for the first time, then certainly a few minutes will go by, perhaps even more, until he comes to, because the first encounter with a space determined by Islamic ornamentation—anywhere in the world, but particularly here in the courtyard of the Cuarto Dorado—completely overwhelms one: but let's say he regains his senses and establishes that most likely he has approached the inner wonders of the Alhambra from the wrong direction, *the courtyard of the Cuarto Dorado itself tells him this*, as if it was saying, indicating in every one of its single elements, that here is the courtyard of the Cuarto Dorado, and the path does not *lead* here, and from here it does not *lead* any further, the courtyard of the Cuarto Dorado offers only itself, and again just completely by accident he "deduces" from the building's construction that possibilities of coming into here and going out from there also exist, on the one hand inward, toward the Cuarto Dorado, on the other, away from here, finally from the Mexuar there are the two same directions and potentialities, but by then one is so stunned by the beauty, by this beauty that is so, but so unbelievably *beautiful*, that he thinks he is struck by vertigo, and consequently he just goes here or there, because he feels that the walls and the columns and the floors and the ceilings, the ornamentation carved with breathtaking refinement, have dazed him, the unendurable, immeasurable infinities of the tiles, the surfaces of the walls, the Moorish arches and the stalactite vaults, are collapsing onto him; that is why he proceeds in utter confusion, because only much later does he realize that no, his vertigo and his daze are not the reason why he does not find the right way in the interior of the Alhambra, and it is not because of that he continually feels that he is not stepping into one or the other room or courtyard from the desired direction, consequently, he realizes, his cloudlike enchantment is not the explanation, but that in the Alhambra there *is* no correct path, moreover, after a while he suddenly realizes that in the Alhambra there are no paths at all, the rooms and the courtyards were not formed in such a way as to link to each other, to flow into each other, to be contiguous at all with each other, namely that after some time, with a little good fortune and much spiritual exertion, one also comprehends that here every single room and every single courtyard exists for its own sake, the rooms and the courtyards have nothing to do with each other, which does not mean that they turn away from each other, or that they close themselves off from each other, that is not the case at all, every courtyard and room just represents itself, within its own self, and at the same time within its own self, represents the whole, the entirety of the Alhambra, and this Alhambra exists simultaneously in parts and simultaneously as one single whole, and every one of its parts is identical to the whole as well, just as the reverse is also true, namely the entire Alhambra represents, in every moment, the incommutable universe of every one of its parts, this runs through a person's mind with crazed speed even in the resplendent light here, yet he has hardly even entered the Alhambra, he is still only in the Cuarto Dorado, he has hardly seen anything and yet he has already seen everything, just perhaps it has not entered his awareness, he however only really now is starting with the Mexuar, then on from there, as if turning back from a dead end in a labyrinth, then the alarming visit to the Sala de la Barca with its maddening wooden ceiling—a visit to the Alhambra—where every visit is alarming, as the Alhambra offers everyone the understanding that it will never be understood, it offers the incomprehensible in the Sala de la Barca, and it offers the same in the long mirror of water of the Patio de los Arrayanes, in the marble-lace intangibility descending ethereally onto the slender columns in the Baths or finally, arriving at the fountain in the Courtyard of the Lions, the Patio de los Leones, one already suspects that he is not a visitor here but a sacrifice, a sacrifice to the Alhambra, but at the same time he is honored by the radiance of the Alhambra as well, a sacrifice because everything is forcing him to take part in a dream that he himself is not dreaming, and to be awake in another's dream is the most horrifying burden—but at the same time he is a favored being, as he can see something, for the sight of which there is only a distant mandate, or there isn't one at all, this cannot be known, he can see, in any event, the moment of creation of the world, of course all the while understanding nothing of it, how could he even understand anything of it, for if we know nothing about the story of the Alhambra, it does seem indisputable that its creators, let's call them Yusuf I and Mohammed V, didn't even know, it was only through their genial stonemasons that they experienced that knowledge, formed by the Greek, the Jewish, the Hindu, the Persian, the Chinese, the Christian, the Syrian, and Egyptian cultures, in enormous unity permeating the emirates and the caliphates, and creating the highly refined civilization of the Arabs; and it may be, as was already mentioned, that it was the two of them although it is also possible—and this was not mentioned earlier—that the construction of the Alhambra originates solely with Yusuf I, in any case it doesn't matter, what is certain is that if the creator of the Alhambra was solitary, he had something to rely upon, if however both of them took part equally, then they were also not alone many times over, because until that thought, the thought of the Alhambra, could reach Granada, it had to make its way through an enormous cultural space, spanning continents, countries, and epochs, where Mohammed Bin Musa al-Khwarizmi and Yaqub Ibn Ishaq al-Kindi and Abu Ali al-Hussain ibn Abdullah ibn Sina and Omar al-Khayyam and Abul Waleed Mohammed Ibn Rushd lived and created; Bayt al-Hikmah, the renowned academy of Baghdad under the reign of the flourishing caliphate of Abdallah al-Ma'mun Ibn Harun-ar-Rashid was needed; the nearby caliphate of Córdoba was needed as well, and the spirit of Al-Hakam II, that philosophical spirit, which transmitted to the contemplators of the imagined Alhambra, across inspirations that were so Greek, and yet not Greek, Jewish and yet not Jewish, Sufi and yet not Sufi, the splendid captivating argumentations and world-explanations of Abu Ishaq Ibrahim ibn Yahya Al-Zarqali, Abu Bakr Muhammad ibn Abd al-Malik ibn Mohammed ibn Tufail al-Qaisi al-Andalusi, Abu Mohammed Ali ibn Ahmad ibn Sa'id ibn Hazn, and Abu Bekr Muhammed ibn Yahya ibn Badshra, those learned men so sensitive to the mystical and universal veins of thought, although in the first place it is necessary to mention the exceptionally great figure of Arab culture, Abu Zayd' Abdu ar-Rahman bin Mohammed bin Khaldun, that is Ibn Khaldun should be mentioned, and named yet again, and even then it would still be impossible to make palpable how great his significance was in the genesis of the Alhambra, even if we pronounce his name again and yet again, namely that originally he was born in Tunisia, but, in an important period in his life, this genius who had returned as one of the followers of Mohammed V became, in al-Andalus, that is, in its center, Granada, the advisor to the sultan, and it is very likely, but not demonstrable, that he had a fateful influence upon Mohammed V, who perhaps continued to build, or was starting to build, the Alhambra on the basis of these inspirations; if it were not the case that it was Yusuf I alone, and not the two of them together, and if just Mohammed V himself were alone the creator of the Alhambra, then Ibn Khaldun as the lion of the Arab spirit truly sufficed, or could have sufficed to persuade the sultan to build such a universal masterpiece, such a monument to the contemplation of universal mysticism, as is the Alhambra, and not just to persuade him, but also to grant the most essential information and spiritual assistance necessary for the creation of such a structure, so that, well, it cannot be excluded—hypothetically, but not demonstrably, because nothing here indicates that the role of Ibn Khaldun in the creation of the Alhambra was much more than we think it was today, but by then one has already gone beyond the Sala de las Dos Hermanas, the Mirador de la Daraxa, and the Sala de los Abencerrajes and their wordless enchantment, and his attention begins to be concentrated on one single aspect of the Alhambra, that is to say he begins to examine the *surfaces* of the walls, the arches, the window-frames, the moldings, the columns and their capitals, the pavements, the wells and the cupolas, the *surfaces*: accordingly, the profound depth of the Alhambra, which starting from below, from the level of the flooring up to chest height, is written onto tiles of varying color, and from that point upward onto the plaster-work, or respectively the stucco, because yes, the entire Alhambra has been written into here, completely, in a faultless alphabet telling a faultless narrative; here, as if with inhuman detail and nearly terrifying solicitude, as if in one thousand, ten thousand, one hundred thousand forms something was being written, continuously, until the end, on the material of these tiles and stuccos; one does not think of the actual verses inscribed onto the Islamic buildings, which have aroused much attention on the part of researchers—whether they are quotations from the Quran in various rooms of the Alhambra, or the mediocre hymns originating from the work of a certain Ibn Zamraq, or other poetic excerpts of similar value taken from the work of an early poet known as Ibn al-Yayyab—no, it is not at all a question of these specific writings but of a language, arranged out of the so-called girih motif based upon the pentagon, but in any event, an inaccessible language rendered from a geometry sacredly conceived; which at first one experiences as pure decoration and considers as a form of ornamentation assembled from tiles or engraved or pressed into the stucco, and at the beginning it really is possible to be satisfied with the impression that this is decoration and ornament, because the dizzying symmetries, the suggestive colors—not only the plentiful but simply immeasurable glittering form-ideas—do not leave behind themselves any questions or uncertainty; yet few are those who have entered, proceeded through all of the rooms, towers, and courtyards of the Alhambra in whom the realization arose that these decorations aren't even decorations but the infinities of a language; few, but there are some, and they all wander between the rooms, the towers, and the courtyards, and they have absolutely no idea of where they are and why they are exactly there and not somewhere else, there are those for whom, after a while, their attention begins to turn to these enchanting surfaces, they stand still ever more frequently to examine the patterns, ever more frequently are they utterly absorbed by this or that crazed symmetry on the wall, it happens to them ever more frequently that underneath one cupola or another, for instance in the Torre de las Infantas, they simply become incapable of movement, there is a spasm in their necks, as their heads are fully tilted back to look, they look into the heights and they try to rationally comprehend how all of this is somehow possible, well, just who could those people have been—the thought flashes through those numbed heads—who were capable of such wondrous efforts, maybe angels? but there isn't even a Heaven, let alone angels! these heads are thinking, or maybe two of them are thinking this, in any event one is, and really we don't know about angels, yet we do know about stonemasons, so that it is nearly certain—inasmuch as one can speak of such coarse certainty in this divine or infernal complex—that there were stonemasons, and it's interesting—it flashes through the benumbed head atop the neck that is already demanding a massage, through the head of at least that one person, as he looks again and again into the heights of the cupola—how peculiar that we have no, but in the entire God-given world, absolutely no knowledge as to who they could have been, these stonemasons, these geniuses of carving, these genius tile-setters, these pattern-makers and arch-constructors and well-builders and water-engineers, how many hundreds of them could have been here, and from where? from Granada? from Fez? from Al-Karaouine? from the Heavens?—which don't exist?!—it is truly astonishing what unbelievable skill, experience, knowledge, and technical ability were alloyed here across the decades, and yet something else too, one thinks, as he returns to the close examination of the surfaces of the walls, these innumerable figures, these innumerable formations, these innumerable outlines ... as if there weren't even so many, as if there were merely a few figures, a few formations, and a few sinuous outlines on the walls' surfaces, just repeated, repeated a hundred and a thousand times, but how? here the question needs to be posed, in wonderment, but it is not possible to answer, that is to say as these figures, formations and lines repeat, occurring and recurring, it is so terribly complicated, like the entire Alhambra, they do nonetheless repeat, the person leans closer to this or that pattern in the wall, it really is so complicated, he steps back a bit to look at it from the requisite distance; but, now, is it simple or complicated, he asks himself, well, it is just that, exactly that which is difficult to decide, although it isn't even difficult, but actually it's *impossible* to decide, namely the question has occupied every serious geometrician, in particular from the beginning of the eighties of the last century, when in 1982, in an article in the journal Science entitled "Decagonal and Quasi-Crystalline Tilings in Medieval Islamic Architecture," written by a certain Peter J. Lu and his colleague Paul J. Steinhardt, the two researchers discovered that five hundred years ago Islamic architecture, inspired by the Arab geometricians, was already familiar (how could they not have been?) with that peculiar—because forbidden—instance in symmetry that the rest of humanity, apart from the medieval Arabs, discovered only in the twentieth century, sometime in the seventies, through the findings of the researcher Penrose, the essence of which is that there is a certain geometrical and thus mathematical pattern in five-fold rotational symmetry, which, however, in crystallography, is not possible; we can transform each point of a pattern, that is we can shift, reverse, reflect it countless times, as with a crystal, but not the pattern as a whole; to explain it differently, there exists in the *mathematical* crystal such a divergent, just a minutely divergent case, where, as opposed to a real crystal, it is not possible to transform any point at all into any other point, so as for attaining the given pattern, we do not attain it, we do not call such a figure a crystal, but, since the discovery by Roger Penrose, a quasi-crystal, well, these forbidden symmetries appear in Arab architecture, said this Lu from Harvard and this Steinhardt from Princeton, then others also confirmed that in this Islamic architectural art, the basic figure is what is known as the Persian girih, which is comprised altogether of five different geometric forms: a regular decagon where every angle is 144 degrees; a regular pentagon, where every angle is 108 degrees; an irregular hexagon with angles of either 72 or 144 degrees; then a rhombus where the angles are 72 and 108 degrees; and finally an irregular hexagon where the angles are 72 and 216 degrees; well, and with these five forms any sort of surface plane can be put together, that is it can be assembled faultlessly, without any sort of gap, this would accordingly be the girih, and it is this geometry as well as the mathematical knowledge that pertains to it that we discover, if we lean in closer—in imagination or reality—to the surfaces of the walls and arches and pavements and ceilings and columns and parapets of the Alhambra, and we see these peculiarly behaving formations pressed into the fresh plaster-work or engraved into solidified material, carved into the marble columns, arched vaulting, cupolas, laid out or drawn onto the floors, the ceilings, and the tile walls—to put it more precisely, as this is the case here—growing dizzy inside the labyrinth of the Alhambra; much more significantly, we discover these peculiar symmetries, we recognize them and immediately we are lost in them, because this quasi-symmetrical space is on every ornamented surface of the Alhambra, here every, but every single square millimeter is ornamented, it fixes our gaze in the face of the infinite; our gaze is not used to this coercion into the infinite, not used to looking into this infinity; and it is not just that this gaze looks into the infinite but it looks into two infinities simultaneously: not just a monumental, expansive infinite perceived by this gaze, as, for example, in the case of the already mentioned Torre de las Infantas, but also, there are its completely tiny elements, a miniature infinity as well, if, for example, one turns back toward the Sala de los Banos and in the proximity of one of the stairs leading this way next to a gallery, one tries to find underneath the left-hand capital, the bordering-elements of one of the patterns, where one narrow, parallel motif follows the path of a line leading upward until it loses itself entirely; again he just grows dizzy and doesn't understand how these lines, constructed from star-shaped points, can lead into infinity, the entire space allotted to them is so tiny, and it is this that leads to the thought that in the Alhambra, a truth never before manifested reveals itself, that is to say that something infinite can exist in a finite, demarcated space; well but this, how can this be? because it is as if here all these little infinities are independent of all the others and at the same time are connected, just the individual rooms were at the beginning, as was his first impression, this can be determined; but then it is better, if he stops and seeks out a spot where, given the circumstances, he can gain a moment of relative rest, his legs, his back, his neck are hurting, his head is buzzing, his eyelids, especially the right one, are twitching—really this is the moment for a bit of transitory peace, otherwise the time originally apportioned with the *scandalously* expensive ticket to one or another visitor for the viewing of the Alhambra has most likely run out, it is better if he lingers a little in the Alhambra in a place suitable for this; all the same it is not possible to sit; to touch any space here that could be used for such a purpose is clearly an insolent desecration, but stopping for a little bit and closing one's eyes, and trying to breathe with regularity, inasmuch as this is possible, to be tranquil, already even just the intention is healing, such a behemoth weighs upon one by now, and this behemoth is the Alhambra; at least inside him there is a need for a little silence, an inner slackening, so that the thoughts and the suppositions and reflexes and conclusions and the recognitions and images—the images!—would not vibrate so dreadfully beneath his trembling eyelids, and after a while it is already clear that this intention really was beneficial, but not enough; it is necessary to withdraw, gradually, from here, a few steps yet to those rooms that draw one back with particular strength, back one more time to the Mirados de la Daraxa, and with that, it is enough; yet one feels that a bad decision brought him here, for he will remain and not gradually withdraw: he looks at the rooms' stalactites swimming in gold, preparing to break off, but never breaking off, he grows blinded from the radiance of the vaulted fenestration as the light streams from without, he allows once again for this unearthly ornament of the patterns of the walls and the ceiling to descend upon him, and the thought is already there, too, in his head that ah, the essence of Islamic pattern is not to be found in what it seems at the beginning, not in the genial application of geometry, but rather in how it is used as an instrument: this glittering, delicately-lived pattern points to the unity of the nature of various experiences, the unity holding all as one in a net, because the geometrical composition used by that Arab spirit, across the Greek and Hindu and Chinese and Persian cultures, actualizes a concept, namely that in place of the evil chaos of a world falling apart, let us select a higher one in which everything holds together, a gigantic unity, it is that we may select, and the Alhambra represents this unity equally in its tiniest as well as its most monumental elements, yet the Alhambra does not make this comprehensible, even just this once, it does not demand comprehension but rather continuously demands that it be comprehended, but then one is already standing sadly in the magnificence of the Mirador de la Daraxa, and really will begin, slowly, to leave; he stands in not-knowing, a garden yet awaits him, the celestial Generalife, which is not far from here, the hill known as el Sol will admit him, enchanting the visitor with its heavenly panoramas—he stands in not-knowing, and despite all of this dazzledness there is something of disillusionment within him, it is as if a mild, unwished-for gentle breeze of recognition strikes him as he departs, it is as if he already suspects that the Alhambra does not offer the knowledge that we know nothing of the Alhambra, that it itself knows nothing of this not-knowing, because not-knowing does not even exist. Because not to know something is a complicated process, the story of which takes place beneath the shadow of the truth. For there is truth. There is the Alhambra. That is the truth.

144
SOMETHING IS BURNING OUTSIDE

Lacul Sfânta Ana is a dead lake formed inside a crater lying at an elevation of around 950 meters, and of a nearly astonishingly regular circular form. It is filled with rainwater: the only fish living in it is the bullhead catfish. The bears, if they come to drink, use different paths than the humans when they saunter down from the pine-clad forests. There is a section on the further side, less frequently visited, which consists of a flat, swampy marsh, known as the Mossland: today, a path of wooden planks meanders across the marsh. As for the water, rumor has it that it never freezes over; in the middle, it is always warm. The crater has been dead for millennia, as has the lake. For the most part, a great silence weighs upon the land.

It is ideal, as one of the organizers remarked to the first-day arrivals as he showed them around—ideal for reflection, as well as for refreshing strolls, which no one forgot, taking advantage of the proximity of the camp to the highest mountain, supposedly one thousand meters high; thus in both directions—up to the peak, down from the peak!—the foot traffic was fairly dense: dense, but in no way did that signify that even more feverish efforts weren't taking place simultaneously in the camp below; time, as was its wont, wore on, and ever more feverishly, so did too the creative ideas, originally conceived for this site, they took shape, and in imagination reached their final form; everyone by then had already settled into their allotted space, which they fixed up and organized themselves, most obtaining a private room in the main building, although there were also those who withdrew into a log hut or a disused shed; three moved up into the enormous attic of the main house that served as the camp's focal point, each one partitioning off separate spaces for themselves—and this, by the way, was the one great necessity for all: to be alone while working; everyone demanded tranquility, undisturbed and untroubled, and that was how they set to their work, and that was just how the days passed, largely in work, with a smaller share allotted to walks, a pleasant dip in the lake, the meals, and singing, fueled by fruit brandy, in the evenings around the glowing campfire.

The use of a general subject for this narrative proved deceptive, however, as the fact slowly but surely became manifest—it appeared to the keenest eyes on the first working day; for most, however, it was largely considered a settled matter by the third morning—that truly there was one among the number, one out of the twelve, who was absolutely unlike all the rest. His mere arrival itself had been excessively mysterious, or at least had proceeded very differently from that of the others, for he had not come by train and then by bus; for however unbelievable it seemed, the afternoon of the day of his arrival, perhaps around six o'clock or half-past six, he simply turned into the campground gates, like a person who had just arrived *on foot*; with nothing more than a curt nod when the organizers politely and with a particular deference inquired as to his name, and then began to question him more insistently as to how he had arrived, he replied only that someone had brought him to a bend in the road in a car; but as in the all-encompassing silence no one had heard the sound of any car at all that could have let him out at any "bend in the road," the thought that he had come in a car but not all the way, only up to a certain bend in the road, only to be put out there, sounded fairly incredible, so that no one really quite believed him, or more accurately, no one knew how to interpret his words, so that there remained, already on that very first day, the only possible, the only rational—if all the same, the most absurd—variation: that he had traveled entirely on foot; that he had got up in Bucharest and set off on the journey: instead of boarding a train and subsequently the bus that came here, he had simply made the long, long trip to Lacul Sfânta Ana on foot—and who knew for how many weeks now!—turning in through the campground gates at six or six-thirty in the evening, and when the question was put to him as to whether the organizing committee had the honor of greeting Ion Grigorescu, he dispensed his reply with one curt nod.

If the credibility of the tale depended upon his shoes, then no one could have any doubts at all: perhaps originally brown in color, they were light summer loafers of artificial leather, with a little ornament stitched in at the toe, and now completely disintegrating around his feet. Both of the soles had separated, the heels were trodden entirely flat, and by the right toe, something had diagonally ripped the leather open, rendering visible the sock underneath. But it didn't just depend upon his shoes, and so it remained a mystery until the very end: in any event, more than a few of the garments he was wearing stood out from the Western or Westernized dress of the others in that these items of apparel seemed to belong to an individual who had just stepped directly out of the late eighties of the Ceauşescu era, out of its deepest misery right into the present moment. The roomy trousers were made out of thick flannel-like material of nondescript hue, flapping limply at the ankles, yet even more painful was the cardigan, hopelessly swamp-green and loosely woven, worn over the plaid shirt and, despite the summer heat, buttoned right up to his chin.

He was thin, like a water bird, his shoulders stooped; bald-headed, in his frighteningly gaunt face two pure dark-brown eyes burned—two pure burning eyes, yet eyes not burning from an inner fire but merely reflecting back, like two still mirrors, that something is burning outside.

By the third day they all understood that for him the camp was not a camp, work was not work, summer was not summer, that for him there was neither swimming nor any of the pleasant restful joy of holiday-time, which tends to predominate at such gatherings. He asked for and received new footwear from the organizers (they found a pair of boots for him, hanging from a nail in the shed), which he wore the whole day long, going up and down the camp but never once leaving its confines, never ascending the peak, never descending the peak, never strolling around the lake, never even going for a walk on the wooden planks across the Mossland; he remained there inside, and when he happened to appear here or there, he walked around this way and that, looking to see what the others were doing, passing through all of the rooms in the main building, stopping to pause behind the backs of the painters, the printmakers, the sculptors, and deeply engrossed, observing how a given work was changing from day to day; he climbed up into the attic, went into the shed and the wooden hut, but never spoke to anyone, and never replied with even a single word to any of the questions, as if he were deaf and mute, or as if he didn't understand what was wanted of him; perfectly wordless, indifferent, insensate, like a specter; and when they, all eleven of them, began to watch him, as Grigorescu was watching them—they came to the realization, which they discussed among themselves that evening around the fire (where Grigorescu was never seen to follow his companions, as he always went to sleep early)—the realization that yes, perhaps his arrival was strange, his shoes were odd and so was his cardigan, his sunken face, his gauntness, his eyes, all of it was completely so—but the most peculiar thing of all, they established, was what they hadn't even noticed until now, yet it was the very strangest of all: that this illustrious creative figure, always active, was here, where everyone else was at work, yet idle, perfectly and totally idle.

He wasn't doing anything: they were astonished at their realization, but even more at the fact that they hadn't noticed it right at the beginning of the camp; already, if you cared to count, it was getting on to the sixth, the seventh, the eighth day; indeed some were preparing to put the finishing touches on their artworks already, and yet only now did the thing in its entirety appear to them.

What was he actually doing.

Nothing, nothing at all.

From that point on, they began to watch him involuntarily, and on one occasion, perhaps the tenth day, they realized that at daybreak and throughout the mornings, when most of the others were asleep, there was a relatively long stretch of time during which Grigorescu, although commonly known to be an early riser, did not appear anywhere; a period of time when Grigorescu went nowhere; he was not by the log hut, nor by the shed, neither inside nor out: he simply wasn't to be seen, as if he had become lost for a certain period of time.

Propelled by curiosity, on the evening of the twelfth day, a few of the participants decided to rise at dawn on the following day and try to investigate the matter. One of the painters, a Hungarian, took the responsibility of waking the others.

It was still dark when, having confirmed Grigorescu not to be in his room, they circled the main building, then went out through the main gate, came back again, went back to the wooden hut and the shed, only to find no trace of him anywhere. Puzzled, they looked at each other. From the lake, a gentle breeze arose, dawn was beginning to break, slowly they were able to make out each other; the silence was total.

And then they became aware of a sound, barely audible and impossible to identify from where they stood. It came from a distance, from the most outlying part of the camp, or more precisely, from the other side of that invisible border where the two outhouses stood, which itself marked the boundary of the camp. Because, from that point on, although it was not marked, the terrain ceased to be an open courtyard;

nature, from whose grasp it had been seized, still had yet to take the terrain back, yet no one expressed any interest in it: a kind of abandoned, uncivilized, and rather ghastly no-man's land, upon which the campsite's owners made no visible claim beyond its use as a dumping-ground for waste matter, from dilapidated refrigerators to everyday kitchen garbage, everything imaginable, so that with the passage of time tenacious, feral weed-growth, nearly impenetrable and almost head-high, covered the entire area; thorny, dark, and hostile vegetation, without use and indestructible.

From somewhere beyond, from a point in this undergrowth, they heard the sound filtering toward them.

They did not hesitate for long regarding the task that lay ahead: uttering not one word, they simply looked at each other, nodded silently, threw themselves into the thicket, breaking forward through it, toward something.

They had gone in very deep, a good distance from the buildings of the campsite, when they were able to identify the sound and establish that someone was digging.

They might have been near, for it was clearly audible to them by now, as the tool was pressed into the earth, the soil thrown up, hitting the horsetail grass with a thud, spreading out.

They had to turn to the right, and then make ten or fifteen steps forward, but they got there so quickly that, losing their balance, they almost went plunging downward: they were standing at the edge of an enormous pit, approximately three meters wide and five long, at the bottom of which they glimpsed Grigorescu as he worked, deliberately. The entire hole was so deep that his head was hardly visible, and in the course of his steady work, he had not at all heard their approach as they just stood at the edge of the giant pit, just looking at what was there below.

There below, in the middle of the pit, they saw a horse—life-sized, sculpted from earth—and first they only saw that, a horse made from earth; then that this life-size earth-hewn horse was holding its head up, sideways, baring its teeth and foaming at the mouth; it was galloping with horrific strength, racing, escaping somewhere; so that only at the very end did they take in that Grigorescu had eradicated the weeds from a large area and dug out this tremendous ditch, but in such a way that in the middle part he had stripped the earth away from the horse, running with its frothing ghastly fear; as if he had dug it out, freed it, made this life-sized animal visible as it ran in dreadful terror, running from something beneath the earth.

Aghast, they stood and watched Grigorescu, who continued to work completely unaware of their presence.

He has been digging for ten days, they thought to themselves by the side of the pit.

He has been digging at dawn and in the morning, all this time.

Below someone's feet, the earth slipped, and Grigorescu looked up. He stopped for a moment, bowed his head, and continued to work.

The artists felt ill at ease. Someone has to say something, they thought.

It's superb, Ion, said the French painter, in low tones.

Grigorescu stopped again, climbed up a ladder out of the pit, cleaned the spade of the earth clinging to it with a hoe lying ready for that purpose, wiped his sweaty forehead with a handkerchief, and then came toward them; with a slow, broad movement of his arm, he indicated the entire landscape.

There are still so many of them, he said in a faint voice.

He then lifted his spade, went down the ladder to the bottom of the pit, and continued to dig.

The rest of the artists stood there nodding for a bit, then finally headed back to the main building in silence.

Only the farewells remained now. The directors organized a large feast, and then it was the last evening; the next morning the camp gates were locked; there was a chartered bus, and some of those who had come from Bucharest or from Hungary by car also left the camp.

Grigorescu gave the boots back to the organizers, put on his own shoes again, and was with them for a while. Then a few kilometers on from the camp, at a bend in the road near a village, he suddenly asked the bus driver to stop, saying something to the effect that from here it would be better for him to go on alone. But no one understood clearly what he had said, as his voice was so inaudible.

The bus was swallowed up by the bend, Grigorescu turned to cross the road, and suddenly disappeared from the serpentine route downward. Only the land remained, the silent order of the mountains, the ground covered in fallen dead leaves in the enormous space, a boundless expanse—disguising, concealing, hiding, covering all that lies below the burning earth.

233
WHERE YOU'LL BE LOOKING

Anywhere, just not at the Venus de Milo—this was written on their faces, he could really say that, this was written so unambiguously on his colleagues' faces that he nearly found it amusing to sit among them during the weekly or monthly meetings for assignment of duties, to sit there among them, and in part to hold out without laughing, as no one wanted to be assigned there, in part because he, to the contrary, was just waiting for the departmental director to look up at him and to say again and again, so well, Monsieur Chaivagne, you shall stay in your accustomed place, you know, LXXIV, and then, XXXV, XXXVI, XXXVII, and XXXVIII on the first floor of the Sully in the hourly shift rotation, when of course the emphasis was on LXXIV, the Salle des 7 Cheminées, and at such times, when he heard that he was assigned there, not only was he filled with immeasurable satisfaction, but it was also gratifying how on each occasion he always sensed a kind of complicit recognition in the departmental director's voice, a gratifying praise, some granting of distinction beyond words, that as for LXXIV, XXXV, XXXVI, XXXVII, and XXXVIII, since he was trustworthy, Monsieur Chaivagne was the man—this had been trembling in the voice of the departmental director for seven years now, ever since he, Monsieur Bruno Cordeau, had been named Director—he was the man who could be trusted with the Salle des 7 Cheminées, the present location of the work, with all the crazed tourists; and he did all of this—for which Chaivagne was especially grateful—without in the least mocking that which every older museum guard knew, of course, and which everyone regarded as a question of individual temperament, namely that he, Chaivagne, had a special relationship to the Venus de Milo, and because of that, for him, as he expressed it himself on several occasions during his first few years, the daily routine of eight hours was not work, but a blessing, such a gift as can never be repaid, that he would do anything to win, if it hadn't fallen into his lap all by itself, having been hired at that time—thirty-two years ago—and found to be suitable for the task of tactfully yet decisively protecting it for the eight hours of the day, from ten in the morning until six in the evening, that had been determined as the museum's opening hours; he'd been found suitable for the task of safeguarding it from the careless, the crazy, the ill-bred, and the loutish, as these were for the most part the four categories which Chaivagne was obligated to identify among a certain percentage of the museum's visitors, a certain percentage, but not all of the museum's visitors, because in contrast to the majority of his colleagues, he did not clump the problematic figures together with the merely inquisitive, the latter namely never did the kinds of things which he himself, given similar circumstances, would never have done, because well, how could one not be jostled or pushed forward a little, if one has already drifted into the desired room and is then in the presence of the great work, he, Chaivagne, deemed this to be an even very tolerable weakness, and he never even intervened; in general, he did not really wish to call attention to his presence, in the end he was not a military sentry, but a museum guard; not a prison warden, but a guardian of the work, so that accordingly he tried to remain as invisible as these particular circumstances permitted, because there was, during the course of the day—in particular surges, completely at random, but on the basis of Chaivagne's three decades of experience, still arriving in certain predictable time-intervals—there was always a certain kind of "event," as they termed it among themselves in the professional jargon, when one had to intervene, not conspicuously, albeit decisively, not disturbing the general, although fairly clamorous, rapture, but with an unequivocality that brooked no dissent, and it was not a question here of someone touching the cordon surrounding the work, and you have to dash over there immediately—he motioned to the younger, chiefly female colleagues, eagle-eyed and ready to leap into action, who were more inclined to wait for that moment when they could finally pounce upon an unruly child or adult—no it wasn't about that, but when you sense that someone, perhaps a tourist who has forgotten himself, is about to step across this symbolic boundary by sheer accident, well then, in that case, the person in question must be unconditionally ushered out, not to speak of those instances when somebody not only creeps behind the cordon, but when you sense that they are headed toward the work, well, those are moments which one has to be able to feel, Chaivagne explained to the beginners and to the less experienced, the crazy, the obsessed, the nut-cases, the confused, the despoilers, in a word, those figures posing a real danger to the work must immediately—Chaivagne, who was not particularly stern, raised his index finger sternly to the younger colleagues, or to the women—those figures must immediately be removed not just from the room, but from the museum as well, there are ways of handling this; the security system is adequate, in the last few years in particular it has developed a great deal, but at the same time, in his opinion, the dangers must not be over-exaggerated, and for that reason, he considered with decided aversion those museums where the guards are authorized to stand, as it were, between the work and the visitor; here, of course, in the Louvre that did not pass muster at all, that was not admissible, and for that reason no one must ever forget that normality has its limits, and the Louvre operates within these limits, hence it should be thought of first and foremost as the most important museum in the world, which is open to everyone, and where it is the experience of a lifetime for every visitor to glimpse the inconceivable treasures of the Louvre face-to-face; the flood of tourists, the jostling and thronging crowds are just to be endured, it is part and parcel of the age we live in, such is the world, there are too many of us—Chaivagne expounded on his simple opinion of the world to his older colleagues—and in this world anyone can be a tourist; so that he did not consider himself to be one of those museum guards who hated tourists, it would be then as if he hated himself, no, this was not his standpoint, the fact that they come, they run around, they click their cameras, this must all be borne, well, my god, there are cameras, and there are circumstances that turn a person into a tourist, and in this situation a person is helpless, should he not then even look at the Venus de Milo?—isn't that so? this is a difficult question already; Chaivagne looked around at his colleagues at such times, well, should they close the Louvre?!—and then no mortal being whatsoever, no one would ever see, all that is here, only here—from the classical Greeks to Hellenistic statuary—yes, this was his opinion, Chaivagne nodded at his own words, his opinion had been formed over many years, and that is why those who knew him considered him to be as gentle as a lamb, so mild in the face of the tourists' wolf-like onslaught, that was already in and of itself perilous, well it was only Chaivagne who could neither be damaged by it nor induced to better judgment, for example, acknowledging that sometimes it was good to kick a Japanese tourist in the crowd there near the cordon, when no one was looking, but no, Chaivagne did not even react to such provocations, he just smiled—of course he always smiled just a little, his colleagues every morning recognized him from far away by that little indelible smile on his face, and not by how he parted his gray hair accurately in the middle with a damp comb, combing it closely across his skull, or his invariably ironed suit, but by this little smile, this was his token of defense, of which they only suspected—because Chaivagne did not reveal all—they suspected that it originated from the joy of being here again, which all the same seemed like pure absurdity to the colleagues, who just like all other Parisians hated coming into work, but the cause could not be anything else, they were obliged to state that this person was overjoyed if he was here, overjoyed if he could start work in the morning and take up his place, so he's an imbecile, one or two of the more talkative museum guards noted, and with that they closed the discussion concerning this matter on that very day, because it was boring as well, one could not really talk about Chaivagne—the older guards in general didn't even really talk about him—because Chaivagne was so much the same every day, every week, and thirty years ago he was exactly the same as today, yesterday, and he would be the same the day after tomorrow, Chaivagne did not change, they just brushed the matter aside, and there was something in it too; Chaivagne, too, just nodded, smiling if they taunted him ironically, saying you, Felix, you really don't change, as if, with that little smile of his he wanted to convey that he felt the same way: but the reason why was that what he was guarding, the Venus de Milo, wasn't changing either, just, well, they never talked about that, so that it could have gained ground and become a central theme if they ever discussed it, but, well, they discussed it only very infrequently, namely that Chaivagne and the Venus de Milo, those two, were living as if in some kind of symbiosis together, but here, at this point already, they were wrong, and they betrayed that they really knew nothing, but nothing at all about the essence of Chaivagne, because the situation was such, Chaivagne looked at them with that little smile of his, that there was the Venus de Milo, and beyond that there was nothing else at all, this was his, Chaivagne's opinion, how could anyone even think that there could be any kind of connection between them, but even if there was, it was just that kind of one-sided connection, that is, an amazement, the intoxicating feeling of knowing that he could be here for the whole eight hours of the day, if among the colleagues it was agreed that for him there would be no two-hour shift rotations, here inside, because he belonged to the inner world of the Venus de Milo, namely he was one of the chosen of the Venus de Milo's internal security, this was an uplifting feeling whenever it occurred to him—and it frequently occurred to him for more than thirty years—it continually flashed through his mind what a person as he could feel in an exceptional situation like this, and well, of course he didn't talk to anyone about it, and not a single colleague ever really tried to discuss the topic with him, as that was not how they saw it, for them it was simply work from which their arches were going to fall in, their backs would become hunched, in consequence of which after a while it became habitual for them to keep unconsciously massaging their necks, as that gets worn out the most, well and of course the foot, not just the sole of the foot, that too, but the entire heel of the foot, the ankle, and the calf, and the waist, the entire spinal column, and so on, it's difficult being a museum guard, and amid that difficulty, if there is even at the beginning some kind of sensitivity to one of the artworks, it usually is quickly dispersed by the fatigue that comes with the job, with the exception of Chaivagne; it was simply not possible to uncover in his case if he was particularly worn down by all that occurs to a person while standing—with the sole of the foot, the ankle, the spine, and the neck muscles—it wasn't possible to state that his body did not ache, just that he somehow did not preoccupy himself with this, did it hurt, well yes it hurt, of course it hurt, a person, if he is a museum guard, is on his feet for nearly eight hours at a stretch, the breaks are measured in minutes, and that could never be enough for complete rejuvenation, eight hours on your feet, yes, it's true, smiled Chaivagne, but at the same time it was eight hours in the inner world of the Venus de Milo; if someone asked, that is always what he answered, but nothing more, although as to why it was precisely this artwork that replenished his life to such a degree, and not the Mona Lisa, or Tutankhamen, and so on, he never spoke a word to anyone, because the answer was excessively simple, and no one would have been able to understand, because on the one side here was the Venus de Milo, on the other there was Chaivagne, who altogether could have said by way of explanation that it was because this was the greatest enchantment he had ever seen and ever could see, because among all the treasures of the Louvre, this ravished him the most, and that was all: it was due to the aura of the Venus de Milo; even if he had wanted to he could not produce more than that, the fact that this was the greatest of wonderments, at least to him, could hardly explain his peculiar life, which was in its entirety subordinated to the wonderment of the Venus de Milo, it would have sounded too simple, a blatant platitude, if he had tried to explain his extraordinary relationship with the Venus de Milo in this way, so he didn't even say anything, he preferred to be silent instead, and to go on smiling, seeking, as it were, forgiveness that he could not really know more about himself than that, for if he were to relate what had happened to him when he was a youth, at the time of his first glimpse, even that would not have led anywhere, as he could not have said more than that he saw it, and his feet were rooted to the ground, and the Venus de Milo mesmerized him; since then nothing had changed, with no explanation; they had simply come in from the provinces, from a little village next to Lille, where he lived with his father, and his father brought him to the Louvre, and then a couple of years later he moved to Paris, applied for the position and was hired, his life story really altogether consisted only of that, namely, this would not have caught the attention of his colleagues, perhaps they wouldn't even have believed that the whole thing was so simple, or that he would be so incapable of providing an explanation, so that, well, he remained silent; if from time to time someone tried to badger him about this strange devotion to the Venus de Milo, he just smiled but said nothing, preferring to stroll a little further on, and in the absence of an answer the secret remained as well, whereas he, Chaivagne, knew perfectly well that the secret was not within him, because inside of him—he acknowledged this at such times when at home—if he reflected upon it, there was absolutely nothing at all, he was completely empty; the Venus de Milo, however was completion itself, inasmuch as a museum guard could be permitted already, from time to time, to fling around big words like these, so that the secret was only in the Venus de Milo, but why is it exactly the Venus de Milo—Monsieur Brancoveanu, a particularly friendly and very sophisticated colleague once asked—with whom you stand in the most confidential of relations, why not the Medici Venice, or one of the countless Cnidian Aphrodites, and there is also the Aphrodite of Ludovici, or the Venus of Capua, or the Capitoline Aphrodite, or the Venus of Barberini, or the Belvedere Venus, or the Kaufmann head, in the world there are innumerable Aphrodites and Venuses, each more beautiful than the next, but for you—Monsieur Brancoveanu looked questioningly at him—for you, this Venus of scandalously ill-repute stands above all else, you cannot seriously think so; but yes, he nodded gently, he did think so, in the most serious manner possible, although it would be difficult to state that the Venus de Milo stands *above* all the aforementioned, in his opinion this was not a competition, here, not even one stands above the other, but yet and yet, what could he do, for him personally, this, the beauty of the Venus de Milo meant the most, he knew—he bent in closer to his colleague—it is difficult to justify such things, perhaps it is not even possible, at one time his heart was smitten, and that was all, no need to look for anything else here (at least he was not in the habit of doing so), moreover, he would even own that thinking was not his forte, because just as he embarked upon it, one thought immediately leaped out, while another was already pushing out the first one, but his head couldn't even remain with that for too long, along came another, then another again, and so on, the various thoughts, having absolutely nothing in common, practically hounded each other, and so, the smile that otherwise always played upon his face disappeared for a moment, no, it was not possible to think, he owned that much to Monsieur Brancoveanu, but then they never again spoke of such confidential matters, and Monsieur Brancoveanu had already been gone from here for a good ten years now, so that there was no one with whom he could then continue the discussion, otherwise, he had never before, never after, ended up in such a close relationship with anyone, which of course did not mean that he felt solitary among the colleagues—because *he* was still there, he noted to himself, if he examined this question now and then on a weekend, when in his boredom he had too much time to ponder things—the colleagues, for the most part, were amiable, if occasionally there was even a little so-called scurrility, but, well, this, in such a workplace, where one had to comply with such solemn demands, and where the work itself entailed a physical burden, was really no wonder, people have to let off steam somehow, he tried to resolve the question of these scurrilities within himself in this way, as when, for example, precisely he was the target; and he went home on the number one to Châtelet, and from there to the teeming Gare de l'Est, from there finally on the seven to Aubervilliers, and he just couldn't drive what had happened that day out of his head, he kept repeating to himself that he had to get away from the tension somehow, but somehow the matter could not be so easily resolved; he soaked his aching feet in a wash-basin filled with cold water for a while, then he just sat in his striped pajamas on the bed, looking at the countless reproductions of the Venus de Milo on the walls, nicely framed and all arranged proportionally in a nice row, so what is the problem if I find that which is beautiful to be beautiful, he posed the question, and he shook his head uncomprehendingly, and it still hurt, although ever more dully, that latest affront still hurt, because of course one or two of them had just pestered him about his attachment to the

Venus de Milo, but the steam, he thought, really has to be let out somehow—he sat on the bed, hunched over in his striped pajamas, his hands in his lap, and he just looked, looked around at the countless reproductions, and on such occasions as this he could not fall asleep for a long time.

Praxiteles, he is at the center of everything here, or if you wish, he said, everything goes back to him, and if one looks away, i.e., looks away from this fact, everything is a mistake, or will immediately become a mistake—that was usually how he began if anyone in the crowd turned to him, or if one or another guideless group happened to surround him to get some kind of orientation as to what was going on in this room, Praxiteles, he answered, and he didn't bother with what the question was—such questions, as what the statue was made of, or how old it was, why wasn't it in its place on the ground floor, and why was it so renowned all over the world, and did he not know its Christian name, and so on—he was not annoyed by such questions, he did, however, immediately brush them aside, or more precisely, he didn't even hear them, he didn't notice them, but if he could, he just said Praxiteles, and inasmuch as it appeared that the person or group in question was not turning away from him, but demonstrating interest as to what he was getting at with this Praxiteles, then he just came forward with the center and with everything here going back to him, namely in this case he tried to explain—at times more briefly, at times more elaborately—just as much as he could, that Praxiteles, this extraordinary genius from late classical Greek antiquity, that Praxiteles, this genial creator from four centuries before Christ, this inimitable artist of the decades after Pheidas, created, with his statue of Aphrodite intended for the island of Knidos, the ultimate form, the ultimate sense, and the ultimate realization of Aphrodite as an extraordinary archaic cult, and just as Knidos, the capital city of the Doric Hexapolis partially built upon the island, became the starting point of the Aphrodite cult, so too did the Cnidian Aprodite—its name derived from this place—become the starting point of all the Aphrodite statues that were to follow, this was how he understood it, he looked around at the members of the group, or looked smilingly at the person posing the question; everyone, therefore, should be acquainted with the name of Praxiteles, everyone who wanted to know even just a little bit about, well, what the Venus de Milo was anyway, and since the one, or the ones, who had addressed him, were generally of that sort, they decided that they would continue to listen to the chatter of the museum guard; at this point he always without exception paused for just two brief seconds, and if the interest proved to be genuine and more sustained, he then continued by saying that well, of course, when one spoke of the cult of Aphrodite, then one had to add immediately that in point of fact we have no certain knowledge of what that Aphrodite cult even was, as one was also compelled to disclose immediately that in reality, certainly, not a single work of Praxiteles, but not a single one, but really not a single statue at all remained, only Roman copies—and here Chaivagne raised his index finger—or at most, copies created in the Hellenistic Period, from Alexander the Great to the beginning of the golden age of the Roman Empire, furthermore, here is the essence of the matter—these are works of art that grew out of the legacy of Praxiteles, as yet preserved, and in a word we know nothing about the original, as in so many cases, all we can do is to try to trace things back to this lost past, or—and then Chaivagne once again raised his index finger—we don't look back at all, but we say here is the Venus de Milo, this statue originating most likely in the second century before Christ, which was discovered in pieces by a peasant named Yorgos Kentrotas in the nineteenth century, at least in two pieces and damaged, missing this or that; he found it on the Greek island of Melos, and although he supposedly also found an arm with an apple, or an apple by itself and also supposedly found a plinth with the name of the sculptor, unfortunately, from this point on, we cannot be convinced of what is true in the story, and we—speaking here as one of the personnel of the Louvre, Chaivagne winked with complicity at his audience—we cannot say any more than that, being bound in this case by self-evident loyalty; but enough about that, because in addition, if a person looks at this wondrous artwork, the whole story isn't even interesting, rather what is interesting is how the path led from Praxiteles' Cnidian Aphrodite to the Venus of Melos, or more correctly, how it leads backward, as one had to be aware as well that hypothetically, with the copies of Praxiteles' Cnidian Aphrodite, with the numerous Aphrodites generated through its established tradition, the goddess is depicted in a certain place, a certain state, and a certain moment, namely in such a manner—Chaivagne leaned, in a courteous, friendly way, closer to his listeners, or to the one who happened to be there—she covers her modesty with her right hand, and with her left she generally holds up her robes falling down in folds, or raises them from a jug, which maybe had been added earlier, which is in contrast, is it not, to this one here—Chaivagne motioned toward Venus placed upon the high podium in the middle of the room—due to her missing arms, we cannot know what she is doing, but in all probability it is *not the same thing*; although it can be imagined that with that right arm of hers she is reaching for the robe that is about to fall down, one cannot know, let us at least not speculate, there has been enough speculation, because you can just imagine what happened when we Frenchmen—in the persons of a certain Olivier Voutier and a certain Jules Sébastien-César Dumont d'Urville—when we Frenchmen got hold of the Venus de Milo on Melos, and had it brought back via adventurous means and various individuals to the repulsive Louis XVII in Paris as a kind of gift, which is ridiculous, isn't it, an artwork of Praxiteles as a gift; there were those who said this, and those who said that, the most varied kinds of reveries flared up, moreover, of course, there were those who created maquettes, Monsieur Ravaisson, for example, who pictured her with Ares, then came Adolf Furtwängler, who had her with her right arm, as I myself described a moment ago, reaching for her robe, and with her left arm leaning against a column, I won't innumerate them all, because it is already obvious that in the sense in which we usually know something about an artwork, when it comes to this artwork, as a matter of fact, we know nothing that is essential, even the identity of the sculptor is doubtful, as the inscription on the damaged plinth, which later mysteriously disappeared—if it even really belonged to the statue at all—permits us to believe that the artist was Alexandros, but it also permits us to believe that it could have been anyone whose name ended in "... andros" who came from Antioch, but you know, Chaivagne said in a more reticent manner to his auditor—if there was one at that moment, and of course, remaining, wished to hear more—you know, said Chaivagne, if I look at this magnificent goddess, namely if I—believe you me, nearly every blessed day, it's been a long time now, already a very long time—if I look at her, then the least painful part for me is not knowing the name of the sculptor, who perhaps came from Antioch, and who maybe really was the son of Menides, as the plinth immortalized him, who knows; because then the least troubling for me is that I don't know what the right arm was doing at one point, and what the left was doing, because I feel that instead what is important here is the connective thread that leads the Venus de Milo back to its own original, back to the one-time Aphrodite created by Praxiteles on Knidos, that is what is important to me; if I look at her—and here Chaivagne, sensing that he could no longer deprive his audience of their time, lowered his voice, as it were signaling that here he intended to conclude, and took one step backward—you know, if I look at her, he said softly, all that there is within me—and maybe this is truly a form of pain—is that this Aphrodite is so enchantingly, so ravishingly, so unspeakably beautiful.

He had said enchanting, he had said ravishing, he had said unspeakable, but he was silent, however, about how in the course of the past years he increasingly felt the beauty of the Venus de Milo to be a rebellion, he was silent about this in the Louvre; only at home—reaching it by the one, then the four, and transferring at the Gare de l'Est, and then the seven to Aubervilliers, returning home at the end of one day or another, and quickly filling the wash-basin with cold water, and quickly pulling off his shoes and socks, and arranging the basin by the armchair and slowly lowering his feet into it, and there and thus sitting quietly—what he had related to a group of older American ladies or a young Japanese man that day in the chaotic crowd came into his mind, and he was ashamed, ashamed of himself for not telling the entire truth, because the entire truth was that the secret of the beauty of the Venus de Milo was its rebellious strength, if the secret of her beauty could be named at all, this was largely the attribution that he had arrived at in connection with the Venus de Milo in the past years, for it was futile to say to him, as Monsieur Brancoveanu did that time, that the entire valuation of the Venus de Milo was greatly exaggerated, it was the French who made her world-famous when they propagated the notion that it was the work of Praxiteles, and in general, Monsieur Brancoveanu noted, curling his lips, how could such an artwork as this—trite, falsified, enervated, gnawed down, grossly overpraised, over-aggrandized, and hence in this way made utterly commonplace—be deserving of the all-encompassing attention as he paid to her; he—namely, Brancoveanu—could not understand this in such an informed person as Monsieur Chaivagne, but the latter just smiled, and shook his head, and said that one must be detached from the circumstances, we cannot allow ourselves to be pressured to believe that just because humanity has for some reason or another placed a work of art upon the highest pedestal, it is already well on its way to becoming commonplace, Monsieur Brancoveanu should believe him, he stated; he looked at the statue almost uninterruptedly: it was possible to be detached from the crowd, to be detached from the statue's unpleasant—as far as they, the French, were concerned—early history, it was possible to disregard every manipulated, mercantile, hence false, devotion weighing upon it, and possible just to look at the statue itself, and the Aphrodite within it, the god within the Aphrodite, and then one saw what an unsurpassable masterpiece the Venus de Milo was; but you really don't think—his colleague, much more passionate than he, then raised his voice, that when you look at the Venus de Milo itself, that you are also seeing all the Aphrodites created earlier by Antiquity and then Late Antiquity and then all the other Hellenistic artists, you surely don't think that?!—but of course, Chaivagne smiled at him, how could he not think that, well, that was the point exactly, in the Venus de Milo there was the Cnidian Aphrodite and there was the Belvedere Aphrodite and there was the Kaufmann head, everything was there, Chaivagne gave a broad movement with his arm, everything that happened from Praxiteles, from the presumed fourth-century original onward up until Alexandros or Hagesandros—then he gestured toward Venus, still in her old spot, that is to say on the ground-level Galerie de la Melpomène, and he said: but at the same time the sculptor of the Venus de Milo imbued his own Venus with such a kind of strength, as he nearly let the robes fall down upon her, a strength that does not originate from this Venus' earthly sensuality, not from her alluring nakedness, not from her cunning eroticism, but from a higher place, from whence this Venus truly comes, and at that point—even today he remembered it well—he did not continue his train of thought, in part because he was not prepared to do so, in part because he was frightened by what he was thinking, for already at that time, at the time of Monsieur Brancoveanu, he was already aware that the existence of the Venus de Milo, that is to say, her being there in the Louvre, and how she stood there in proud sanctity—across from her were the crowds, lining up, jostling, surging with their cameras and their complete ignorance and vulgarity—in that place in this Louvre, exactly where she, the Venus de Milo, stood, a kind of distressing scandal erupted, it was just that Chaivagne didn't dare express it, even to himself for a while, or even to formulate the thought that namely the Venus de Milo in the Louvre was . . . unbearable, even to admit to himself, for a long time he even dismissed that word from his mind, trying to quickly think about something else, to think, for example, that he was a museum guard and nothing else, and it was not for him to be concerned about these matters, only with those things that pertained to being a museum guard, but well what could he do, he *had* become such a museum guard, and so, well, the thought just took shape more and more, as he looked, he looked at the statue, as when for example it was moved, due to reconstruction, one story higher, and turned up here temporarily in the Salle des 7 Cheminées, and they set the statue upon a high—and especially to Chaivagne's taste, not particularly appropriate—podium, and then the scandal somehow just became all the more obvious, because the statue still rose above the people, but it was not very suitable here, because she, the Venus de Milo, in Chaivagne's opinion, did not belong here, more precisely, she did not belong here nor anywhere upon the earth, everything that she, the Venus de Milo meant, whatever it might be, originated from a heavenly realm that *no longer existed,* which had been pulverized by time, a moldering, annihilated universe that had disappeared for all eternity from this higher realm, because the higher realm had itself disappeared from the human world, and yet she remained here, this Venus from this higher realm remained here, left abandoned, and this, as he explained to himself of an evening—while soaking his aching feet, he sat down in the armchair and tuned into the news on France 1—he understood this abandonment to mean that she had lost her significance, and that all the same here she stood because that Yorgos dug her up, and that d'Urville had her brought here and that Ravaisson put her together and exhibited her, yet she *had no meaning*, the world had changed over the past two thousand years; that part of humanity, thanks to which it had not been in vain for the Venus de Milo to stand anywhere and to signify that there was a higher realm, had vanished; because this realm had dissipated, vanished without a trace, it was not possible to understand what the one or two remaining fragments or pieces dug up could even mean today, Chaivagne sighed—and he moved his toes in the cold water—there was nothing higher and nothing lower, there was just one world here in the middle, where we live, where the number one and the four and the seven run, and where the Louvre stands, and inside it is Venus, as she looks at an inexpressible, mysterious, distant point, she just stands there, they put her here or they put here there, and she just stands there, holding up her head proudly in that mysterious direction, and her beauty emanates, it emanates into nothingness, and no one understands, and no one feels what a grievous sight this is, a god that has lost its world, so enormous, immeasurably enormous—and yet she has nothing at all.

And yet she had nothing at all, not even any meaning—this was a very sad thought; Chaivagne even tried continually to drive it out of his head, he didn't want to think about it, he tried to convince himself, well, why was it not enough that every morning he could get up and immediately stand there again in her presence?—of course it was enough; at such times, he relaxed, and sleep really did chase these thoughts out of his head, and once again the next morning he appeared at his workplace with the same little smile on his face, and he took up his designated position in the room entrusted to him, tactfully withdrawing into one of the inner corners—from where he could keep an eye on the visitors, but could simultaneously also see the rising figure of Venus—another year went by like that, and again it was autumn, and it frequently rained in the city, although he took virtually no notice of this, because he did not move from his place, and the Venus de Milo did not move either, the reconstruction was still going on down there, and no one could even predict when the statue would turn up in its old spot, and neither he changed, nor did the Venus change—nor did that long crack in the Parian marble, which extended from the back of the statue along the back contour of the right thigh, and which of course was kept under strict observation by the restorers, but no, nothing happened—and well, really, nothing happened even with him, nothing, the days came and went, the crowds flooded in every morning, and flooded out every evening, he stood in the inner right-hand corner, observing the eyes and face of Venus high above, but never where the eyes and the face were looking, he observed the crowd as they trampled on each other, then once again he raised his gaze to the statue, and he just stared on and on from one autumn to another autumn, he diligently soaked his feet, he went in with the seven, the four, then the one, then he went home with the one, the four, and the seven, he meticulously parted his hair in the middle of his head in the morning with a damp comb, he stood and stood with his hands always clasped behind his back in the inner right-hand corner, he always smiled a little, so that he was always being approached, now by a group without a tour guide, now by a solitary visitor, and he always started by saying—and never saying anything else but—Praxiteles, always just Praxiteles.

377
PRIVATE PASSION

Music is the sorrow of one
who has lost his Heavenly home.

Ibn al-Faradh

The end has come and there is nothing, he said, and even if there is something, it is only the squalid fulfillment of that process, hidden at first, which has made chance, ever more blatant, and then finally insolent vulgarity—shaming even the most horrifying premonitions—completely victorious; because there was an age when something reached its own culmination, the height of its own boundless possibilities, for it is not the case—no, not at all—that each age is granted its own articulatory world, a world incomparable with the others, and that the art of every single epoch, for each given genre, carries the inner hypothesis of its own internal structure to perfection; no, decisively no; still, it is true, well; I, he added, am speaking of something else, that is to say that there lies before us, after the hazy bestial zero, a long continuum arising from all the noises and rhythms having to do with music, which then reaches—as it did indeed reach a perfection no longer perfectible—the roof of a seemingly infinite celestial vault, a particular border of Heaven close to the godly spheres, so that something—in this case music—comes into being, is born, unfolds, but then it's all over, no more, what must come has come; the realm dies away, and yet lives on in this divine form, and for all eternity its echo remains, for we may evoke it, as we do evoke it to this very day and shall evoke it for as long as we can, even if as an ever more faint reflection of the original, a tired and ever more uncertain echo, a misunderstanding ever more despairing from year to year, from decade to decade, in a disintegrating memory that no longer has a world, no longer shatters people's hearts; no longer elevates them to that place of such achingly sweet perfection, because this is what happened, he said, and he straightened his suspenders, such a music came into being that shattered people's hearts, if I listen to it, I still feel, at some given point, after an unexpected beat, I feel, if not that my heart is being shattered, that at least it is falling apart, as I collapse from this sweet pain, because this music gives me everything in such a way that it also annihilates me, because how could anyone think that they could get away without paying the price for all of this, well, how could we even imagine that it is even possible to traverse that distance where this music exists and not be annihilated one hundred, one thousand times—if I listen to them, I am in a thousand tiny pieces, because you can't just roam around in the company of the geniuses of inexplicable musical fulfillment and at the same time, say, be able to fill out a personal income tax form or prepare the technical blueprint for a building while this music is sinking to the depths of your heart, well, it doesn't work, either this person filling out tax forms or completing technical blueprints is annihilated, or will never understand where he has arrived, if this music strikes him from above, it definitely comes from above, of that there is no doubt, and I—he pointed to himself, on the podium, with both hands—I am speaking solely and exclusively about music, not about anything else; the discussion here cannot be generalized, it is not possible to extend my train of thought to include all of the arts, and blabber about those kinds of absolute generalizations; what is being referred to, what one wants to say, must be stated precisely, and I too say it now, that I am merely reflecting on music, and that I consider my statements valid only with regard to that, so that I cannot begin by stating, ladies and gentlemen, this evening, within the framework of this widely promoted lecture that you shall hear, through an analysis of music's essence, about the essence of so-called art itself, when my subject, the subject of this widely promoted lecture, is only music; that is while delivering this lecture, it's as if I were standing here with a smoking bomb in my hands and I were telling you that it was going to explode in a minute; now, try to imagine that I began by saying, ladies and gentlemen, and so forth, with this bomb in my hands, you would all rush headlong out the door, would you not?—which would not be a bad idea, well, perhaps at one point I shall turn into a real bomb; anyway, for now just imagine a smoking bomb in my hands, as I try this evening to share my thoughts with you about that moment in time when the pinnacle of music, within the world history of music, came to be, so that you will hear such things from me tonight that you never heard from others, nor shall you ever, because I myself represent—truly, like an anarchist holding a bomb—my own thesis, and, as it happens, it is precisely because of this thesis that I am, even from our own degenerate society, excluded, exiled, expelled; so that I am an object of scorn, indeed, put more crudely, I am jeered at; it is possible that there are those among you who are thinking but, well, you are an architect who shall give a lecture about his private passion, about music, and how can an architect be excluded from society when he is at the exact center of society, in that case, perhaps, someone among you is thinking, that he, an architect, is as deep as anyone can possibly be in the whole thing, only that in my case that person is mistaken; I am an architect who has never seen a single plan constructed, I don't know how many buildings I have planned already in my life, I am now sixty-four, so you can imagine how much I have planned and planned and planned, how many maquettes and drawings and who knows what else rose up beneath my hands, it's just that not one of them was ever built, this is the situation, you see here today a lecturer who is also an architect, but who has not built a single thing, who is himself a total architect-fiasco, who moreover does not even deal with architecture in his free time, and is not even peddling architecture here from village to village, thanks to the Kíler district library's program, "Village Cultural Days," and who will not even speak of architecture, but of something perhaps unexpected from an architect: of music, of one of its highly particular embodiments, because that of which I am going to speak is truly unique, a sacred fact, because I shall, with this finger—and he raised his index finger—draw your attention to a certain age of musical history, an extraordinary, a peerless, an unrepeatable moment of what we call music, or, put more simply, you will hear about the essence of music of the very highest order, a music whose time had come, so that from the very beginning of the seventeenth century until the middle of the eighteenth century it came, let this suffice for a starting point, in place of a more precise designation, as you cannot really expect dates from me, generally I do not believe in dates, things flow into each other and grow out from each other, the whole thing proceeds somehow like tentacles, so that there are no definite eras or other such askininities, the world is much too complicated for that, because just think about it, where does an accident begin and where does it end, so there you are, there is no point in looking for dates or demarcations of eras, let us leave that whole thing to the experts, to those who are either feeble-minded or pig-headed know-it-alls—those who, thanks to their position, instead of simply saying what happened, what largely came to pass between these two time-designations—could trumpet throughout the world how music, the story of music truly has a pinnacle from which it doesn't go on, or rather it does, but this is only and exclusively the so-called *sad descent*, because afterward, nothing else occurs but the slow degradation of the form, so it is perhaps more correct to express it by saying that the whole thing isn't even sad, but pitiful, a mockery, a long, drawn-out vulgar ceremony, but no, those who take part in this perpetually clamoring, false, base propaganda, hammering into us that music is, like art in general, a science, and altogether, that culture and civilization only advance in such a way that the whole thing, starting from some confusingly designated cause, goes onward and moreover surpasses itself again and again, that is it develops, and according to *their* conceptions, attains ever higher and higher levels; look upon them as people who, in a word, are there to mislead you with their prestige, and who not only keep silent, but try explicitly to ter-min-ate, to an-nih-il-late the fact that the history of music has its pinnacle, after which the entire history of music, summa summarum, begins to decline, in the end it simply rushes into vulgarities masked as a crisis, and drowns in a kind of sordid sticky flood, but enough about that, let us speak instead of how I ended up in all of this; perhaps it might be interesting if we were to pause for a moment at a little anecdote, for surely I, too, am aware—even though I'm not a professional lecturer, apart from these appearances organized by the district library through which, strictly between ourselves, I merely try to supplement my meager income—I am well aware that from time to time a little relief is called for, a small personal touch, as they say: a well-placed comic sentence, a little material drawn from experience, and in this case, I will offer just a brief account of an afternoon in the office where I go now and then as an early-retired pensioner, that is to say about that afternoon when, with maybe thirty similar architects, I was plying the trade completely senselessly, bent over a meaningless architectural blueprint for who knows how many times now, and the colleague sitting next to me, fiddling with the little pocket radio set out on the desk finally settled on one particular station, and left the dial there, and this, this random movement with which the finger of my co-worker stopped the dial right at that point, was fateful, I am not exaggerating, it had a fateful effect upon me, because there began to resound forth, of course in terrible quality and not for the first time in my life, but audible to me for the first time in my life, a *faultless, eloquent* melody, produced on the strings, together with a second faultless, eloquent melody, and then with another, and this, this melody-architecture having become wondrously complex, created with the leading part high above, such a heart-wrenching harmony, causing within me such joy, in that large, soulless, bleak architect-hangar, under the fluorescent lights, that I was simply breathless; well, I will stop here, although I recall with exactitude every single moment of that afternoon, and of course as well, what music was wavering, crackling, whining right next to me: an Oratorio of Caldara, one of the arias for Santa Francesca Romana, it was the Si Piangete Pupille Dolente, and so I have now incidentally betrayed that I entered the Baroque through a small side-gate, if I may express it in this way; he said and then again adjusted his suspenders with his right hand, and managing it only with difficulty, because his trousers, in spite of the suspenders, continually wanted to slip down beneath his gut, rolled into thick protuberances, in the meantime with his other hand he reached for the glass of water set on the table behind him, where otherwise he had also thrown his coat when he arrived, during which the eight people—six old women and two old men, who comprised, here in the village library, the courageous audience of this completely incomprehensible lecture, entitled "A Century and a Half of Heaven," were given yet another opportunity to scrutinize the older gentleman who had arrived from the capital city, and to determine that naturally he had many peculiar features: the short, fat, yielding build, the few strands of hair brushed to the right side of his balding pate, the soft flabby double chin tipping over onto his chest, or his voice, which sounded as if someone were trying to scrape out stew-scraps from a saucepan with a wire brush, and the old-fashioned eyeglasses with black plastic frames that might have turned up on him only by mistake, because they were so large as to conceal that entire upper section of his face like scuba goggles, but it was really his gut that captured the attention of the locals, because this gut with its three colossal folds unequivocally sent a message to everyone that this was a person with many problems, it was no wonder that he was continually adjusting the elastic straps on his trousers, like someone who didn't even trust in them himself, or like someone whose confidence in the straps built up gradually and cautiously, but had been lost time and time again, one nearly felt that one wanted to help him, because everyone sensed how these trousers were continuously, ceaselessly sliding downward across those three thick folds of fat, down toward the thighs, it is doubtful that any kind of trousers can be of any use at all with a gut like that, and that this gut could be of any use whatsoever to any kind of trousers, so that in a word the listening public, comprised of eight persons, was without exception preoccupied with these trousers, these suspenders, and this gut, for they understood not one solitary word of what the gut's owner was talking about, and, moreover, the person in question spoke without pause, never lowering his voice once and never raising it, never subduing it and never strengthening it, and there was no pause and stop and rest and forbearance, he just spoke and spoke and spoke, he put the glass of water back on the podium borrowed from the school next door, and he said: well now, let's get to the point, and let us take one of the masterpieces of Johann Sebastian Bach, the Quia Respexit Humilitatem from the Magnificat, in which the greatest musical genius of all times, in an aria for alto, created a kind of compound from pain and humility, from sorrow and supplication, clearly due to heavenly exhortation, which in and of itself could serve as enough of an example here, it would be enough just to speak of these small individual compositions for us to arrive at an instantaneous understanding of the essence of the Baroque, of that entire era, for that is our subject today, the Baroque, and this is what I have spoken of so far as well, and this is what I shall continue to speak of, for I maintain, and I can prove, that it was through the Baroque that music reached that divine sublimity I mentioned earlier, from where there was no going any further; and yet as it was only possible to sustain for a brief time—that is, it was not possible to sustain it—for that star within us that could have sustained it has inevitably died out, that star is extinct, its geniuses vanished into death, those who came after transcended them, transcended the so-called Baroque musical world, because this is the phrase the experts use, they "transcended" them, which is already itself a scandalous expression, and perfectly betrays just who we are dealing with here, what kind of characters employ such turns of phrase, because what does that mean, transcend them—transcend Monteverdi perhaps?! transcend Purcell?! transcend Bach?!—still, to transcend them, we should have transcended them by not listening to them—but that accursed 18th century, those accursed last decades, poisoned everything and destroyed everything, and made everyone unsure if they should listen to the words of the soul—or the mind, as they put it, the mind—the lecturer now shouted, and there was no one in the room who did not sense that a great wrath was trembling in his voice, even if, still, they had not the foggiest notion as to the meaning behind this wrath—and the mind, he shouted again, and to transcend—he raised his voice more and more, so much so that the more timid members of the audience began to steal cautious glances toward the exit, for, all of this—to speak in this vein—is not just baseness but iniquity, for they, the experts, knew full well whom they could honor in this Monteverdi, this Purcell, and this Bach, they knew exactly, and yet they still spoke of how time had passed them by, they announced this in unison, as if time could pass beyond something for which the medium is eternity—Sublime God in Heaven—the lecturer raised both of his hands toward the ceiling, freshly whitewashed not too long ago, he raised his hands and vehemently began to shake them, so then, after Monteverdi, after Purcell, after Bach, there comes someone who would be a greater genius in music?—or what?!—so who came after them?!—I ask you, the lecturer asked, now with lowered hands, and the public really began to feel uncomfortable, because it seemed, since he was looking at them, that they were the ones causing this problem, they were the ones he was angry at, saying: perhaps you're thinking of Mozart?! about this child prodigy?! who was capable of everything as well as its opposite, are you thinking of this genius of *pleasantness*?!—the *charm* of this undoubtedly amazing showman?!—this truly dazzling *entertainment artist*?!—at which point one or two members of the audience tried to indicate an uncertain "no" with their heads, who they?!—never would they think of any such thing, never would it even have occurred to them, they could cautiously indicate this with their heads, the lecturer was already seized by zeal and went on saying no, it was not his obligation, and particularly not here, within the context of a lecture such as this—to pronounce his opinions and analyze those who came after this Monteverdi, this Purcell, this Bach in the Classical era, it was generally speaking not his task to slander them—although he could slander the Classical era, or launch into an attack, although he could attack the Romantics and so on; his task here instead, he opined, was to praise that which can be praised, and the music of the Baroque unconditionally fell into this category; precisely, only *it* belonged in this category; because only this was praiseworthy, to which it was now important for him to add, he said, that he, first and foremost, wished to share his perceptions concerning the *vocal* music of the Baroque; he did not, in every one of his lectures, speak only of that, but today yes, perhaps because at the center of the anecdote he had selected in this lecture, there was a vocal piece, the aria that Caldara wrote for a certain mezzo-soprano, perhaps this was the point where he might betray that although he did not always speak about the vocal music of the Baroque, when he did speak of it, as today, he did so with the greatest pleasure, because there was something in the human voice that he loved more than anything else, if a melody sounded upon this, the human voice; and if he had to choose between this one or that one, if he heard a melody on a certain instrument, he would instead in an instant choose the human voice, there was something in it, the human voice, in the cultivated human voice, the expression of which for him was such a powerful enchantment, irreplaceable by any kind of amazing instrument, whether the harpsichord, violin, viola, oboe, horn, church organ, or even all of them put together; nothing, but nothing could attain the same level as the cultivated human voice, and if they were pausing here, then he would have to make the personal remark that within this genre, it was the cultivated female voice that made the greatest impression on him, a dramatic soprano, a dark alto, always had, so to speak, a power within, difficult to explain; in any event this was the situation, so that heaven for him was when that organ, that harpsichord, those violins, violas, oboes, horns, and so on sounded forth at once together, raising above themselves that certain cultivated female alto voice, well, when they were all together like this he was filled with unspeakable happiness, at such times he felt something like the Old Believers of the Orthodox Church when they kiss the icon of the Virgin Mary and the Infant, or like a Japanese Zen monk in the kyūdō jo as he releases the arrow from his bow toward the target, really and truly, he was not exaggerating, not thinking figuratively: never did he feel the direct closeness of the presence of God from any other sort of art form, he had never gotten it, never found it in any other kind of music, not in the music that came before nor in the music that came after, only, only from the Baroque; picture to yourselves now the fantastically variegated musical world in Europe of that time: the essence of music resounded in a hundred ways, and from our perspective, it resounded simultaneously, because the essence of music is the Baroque; and now he enumerated who and when, pronouncing the names one after the other: Reincken, Porpora, Fux, then Charpentier, Paisiello, Böhm and

Schütz, then Buxtehude, Conti, and the greatest ones, Vivaldi, then Handel, then Purcell, then Gesualdo, then Johann Sebastian Bach?!—but just imagine alongside them, the endless rank and file of musical lackeys, truly in the hundreds, perhaps in the thousands, who lived and sustained the Baroque with their works, from the English court to the villas of the Italian princes, from the chateaux of France to the castles of Hungary, because this was the case, the music of the Baroque filled those approximately one hundred and fifty years granted to it, you can hear one continuously resounding work of musical art—wondrous intonations, wondrous harmonies, wondrous compositions and melodies—if I think back on it, he said, if I picture myself back in the time of the Baroque, and I hear the first few bars of the Matthäus-Passion as the orchestra becomes audible, I am choked with tears, and I can understand, I truly understand how even one composer of a later era, who, at a performance of the Matthäus-Passion, could not bear to hold back his tears and lived for days in painful ecstasy, yes, I can understand, for I, too, have lived through that each time, if for example I hear an undisturbed performance of The Indian Queen, or the great Messiah; undisturbed, I say, said the lecturer, and the wording here is no coincidence, because I suffer dreadfully, unspeakably, if one of those Karl Richter-types, one of those coarse dilettantes sticks his ugly snout into the Baroque, because these people destroy everything that is the Baroque, because they understand so little that they debase all that is the Baroque, it is horrible when they wreck the artwork that serves as their prey, but what is even more horrible is *how* they wreck it, here words fail me, because they play Bach as if they were playing Beethoven, which in the end is the real scandal, characters like this should be cast out from the orchestral world of Baroque performance, or they should simply be locked up in prison, that would be the most fitting, because then on principle they wouldn't be able to get at any sort of music, let alone to scourge the Baroque with their filthy hands and insensate souls; the performance, in a word, must be undisturbed, there is no doubt that the spirit of the Baroque is present only in the case of an undisturbed performance; then it appears, then it resounds, and then it subdues one, breaks one's heart to bits, knocks one to the ground, and what this means is that a mistake may not be made in the choice of conductor, so that—if we take into consideration the circumstances of today—then the coarse Harnoncourt NO, and Christie YES, the airy Bartoli NO, but Kirkby YES; then the enfeebled Magdalena Kožená NO, but Dawn Upshaw YES, the so-called Barock Kammerorchester of Zugdorf NO, but Les Arts Florissants YES; in a word, with a faultless selection we can attain a level where the Baroque begins to resound, insomuch as today the Baroque can even make itself heard, because even this is not so self-evident, for just think about it, if you listen to the Scherza Infida from Handel's Ariodante, with David Daniels, under the direction of Sir Roger Norrington recorded at EMI's Abbey Road studio, or not even that, let's drop it, it isn't obvious enough—because it is actually too much so—but let us assume instead if you were to go to a performance of Ariodante, where the Baroque makes its appearance, without its own world—as there is no more world of the Baroque, because in the chaos and disintegration of that dreadful eighteenth century, as has already been mentioned, it went to rack and ruin—there one sits in the audience and before one is, let's say, the Ariodante with Lorraine Hunt, in the Stadthalle in Freiburg, but in vain is Lorraine Hunt the right one, in vain is the Barockorchester of Freiburg the right one, neither Handel nor the Ariodante is there, only the memory of them, for the Baroque isn't there, the entire world has already become anti-Baroque, the theater is anti-Baroque, the curtains are anti-Baroque, the stage, the theater-boxes, the audience, Freiburg itself is anti-Baroque with its innumerable reeking beers and with all those innumerable reeking tourists, and all of Europe is anti-Baroque, there is not a single nook in all of Europe where this anti-Baroqueness is not palpable, only, the annihilation of something that doesn't even exist anymore just goes on and on, for the so-called Baroque musical performances keep on coming, one after the other, and they do not call forth but instead demolish the essence of the Baroque written down in the scores, scarcely has it begun when the whole thing is already ruined, so that a person truly needs an enormous ability to read into things, unbelievable imagination, inhuman endurance, unparalleled patience, and I almost forgot, said the lecturer, that beyond all of this he needs an incredible amount of luck, in order to catch an occasion now and then where with all these gifts the Baroque might touch him once in a while; yet this concentration, this patience, this persistence is worth it, if at such a performance of Baroque music—as for example with Lorraine Hunt in the Stadthalle in Freiburg—a person may glimpse within himself at least the shadow, for nothing more is possible, of the essence of the Baroque; then that person will be taking part in such an experience, in such an encounter so as to grant one true strength, if I may say—the lecturer appeared to reflect for a moment—true strength to live, because then afterward life without the Baroque shall not be as torturous, after one or two encounters with the shadow of the essence of the Baroque, brought about through enormous luck—thanks to the inhuman strivings of Lorraine Hunt and the Freiburg Barockorchester—one staggers out of the theater, pinches his nose shut against the sticky reek of beer and tourists, he can be certain that the godly sphere at least existed, he may rest assured—with profound and sincere thanks to Lorraine Hunt and the Freiburg Barockorchester—that the Baroque did exist at least at one time as a living reality, written down for us and performed, but at the same time, it is a reality so frail that it proves too easy to perform, and we perform it at the first possible opportunity, as soon as we possibly can, and perpetually, we have played the whole thing as if the stakes were those in a poker game, and we can regard it as our greatest fortune if—this time too, with gratitude and thanks to Lorraine Hunt and the Freiburg Barockorchester!—we can stagger out of a concert hall and wander through the reek of beer and tourists with, however, the shadow of the Baroque in our hearts, about which I simply cannot repeat enough times that in it, in the Baroque, music made by humans attained its pinnacle, and if at the beginning I promised that I was not just going to keep lecturing to the air, not just keep gabbing on and on, but actually confirm that this is true, then now the time has come for me to do so, for you have heard enough now of the details, I've touched upon this and touched upon that, but the real confirmation awaits, for which of course you should not wait, said the guest, once again tugging at the suspender-clip on the left side to see if it was still holding, as just now he had felt that side to be a little uncertain, you should not wait, he repeated, for some kind of complicated heaven-and-earth-shattering demonstration of musical elements, I shall, if you permit me, pass over that and instead attempt to make my thoughts more concise, which then shall contain this confirmation, namely, it shall call your attention to what occurs in the very first moments of the sounding forth of a given work; I ask you then very kindly, please, to close your eyes, to allow yourselves to enter the spirit as, let us say, you hear the first measures of the Matthäus-Passion, the first thirty-two measure, when the two orchestras—as you know, there are two orchestras, two choirs, two sides, entering into a dark, swirling, tragedy, pain, finality—the first thirty-two measures, I ask you, the lecturer asked his public, raising both of his hands as if placing a benediction upon them, he held his head high, closed his eyes, and he waited, but in vain, because when he checked to see if they were doing what he had asked of them, just squinting between his eyelids so they wouldn't notice, he looked at them and saw that in the meantime his listeners, comprised of eight persons, had become utterly exhausted, no longer even preoccupied with his suspenders, nothing interested them any longer and because of that they had refused his request, at least that is what he thought, that they had refused it, they simply were not paying attention, as for a long time now they had become incapable of any such thing, that is to say to act like people who were watching what was accumulating here, so that they failed to close their eyes, and because of that, they only did so when the guest speaker, halting his flow of speech for a moment, cast such a wild look at them that it immediately occurred to them what he wanted them to do, and everyone quickly closed their eyes; there sat the eight members of the audience and they had absolutely no idea as to why, but they waited with closed eyes to see what was coming next; after a long silence—because the lecturer also needed a bit of time to find his way back to his train of thought—he spoke anew and everyone was relieved, for the speaker picked up exactly where he had left off just a moment ago, asking: do you hear? do you hear this dark strength? this terrifying beauty? this threatening spiral, as the separate melodies whirling above each other strike across the entire orchestra like the tumultuous waves of the sea?! yes—he raised his voice—like the inconceivable, the fathomless, the mysterious sea with its waves striking upward, the whole is here, the beginning, it is evident immediately, a perfect, intricate, dazzling harmony, an intensity of musical resonance never reached until then and never again afterward, whoever hears it does not need any sort of proof whatsoever that this is music of the highest order, because the music itself is the proof, whoever hears it will hear the harmony of the voices as never before brought together in such richness, will hear in this harmony the enigmatic free beauty of the leading part, and so the heart speaks—the speaker struck his heart with his right hand—the so-called proof; the heart speaks it, for this is something never felt anywhere else, not before the Matthäus-Passion nor after the Matthäus-Passion, and you should understand this to mean, of course, not before the Baroque, nor after the Baroque, but if you wish, he said, and he raised his voice a little again, it can also be expressed like this: that in no other instance can we speak of such a virtuosic knowledge of the art of musical composition, of the virtuosity of this rainbow-spectrum-like versatility, of such an extraordinary virtuosic unity of musical language, of such clear melodic contours, of such an unparalleled art of counterpoint as the fulfillment of musical conciseness learned from Vivaldi, of the web woven in such an unrivaled fashion of the inner parts, and generally speaking of such refinement of the harmonies, not deduced from any predecessor, as in the case of Bach; just as we can never even speak of a finished work by him, only of a kind of continuously swelling music, to be amended, enriched, edited, built, ameliorated over and over again, a music that only indicates the way to perfection but is not identical with it, so that when it is a question of Bach—and so it shall be until the end of this lecture, he said—for if the essence of music is the Baroque, then the essence of the Baroque is Bach, in him there is embodied in one all that is present, in dispersed fashion, in Vivaldi, Zelenka, Rameau, Schütz, Handel, Purcell, but also present partially in Campara, Cimarosa, Albinoni, Porpora, Böhm, Reincken, but altogether and as a whole, only and exclusively present in the singular genius of the Baroque, and thus of music, and in its entirety, Johann Sebastian Bach—it is inconceivable how all that Johann Sebastian Bach represents could have come about, inexplicable, if we hear these first measures from the Matthäus-Passion, as the chorus resounds with its broad tempestuous strength, sweeping all away as it rises, as it becomes ever more intricate, ever more richly woven, namely as the miracle—this Johann Sebastian Bach right before our eyes, in every single work and so in this case the Matthäus-Passion—resounds as well, is born and again is born, because we hear, we must believe, and that is what is so unbelievable, but we hear it, yes? we hear the heavenly weight of these voices falling in infinite density, falling below from there above, like snow, and there we are there in this landscape and we are amazed, and we have no words, and our hearts ache from the wondrous beauty of it all, for the Baroque is the artwork of pain, for deep down in the Baroque there is deep pain, more precisely, in every single chord of every single musical work created by the Baroque, every single aria, every single recitativo, every chorale and madrigal, every fugue and canon and motet and in every single voice of the violins, the violas, the bassoons and the cellos, the oboes and the horns, this pain is there, and it is there too if on the surface a kind of triumph, serenity, sublimity, joy, or praise is being offered, each individual voice speaks of pain, of that pain that separates him, Johann Sebastian Bach, from perfection, from God, from the divine, and that separates us from him; namely, the Baroque is the art form of death, the art form that tells us that we must die; and how must we die: it must be in that very moment when the Baroque resounds in music, because we should have ended there, at the pinnacle, and not have allowed everything to happen just as it might, and then to lie, to blurt out these morbid lies and learn how to enthuse over such music as this Mozart or that Beethoven or over whatever it was all those ever more modest talents, those ever more commonplace figures, were able to conjure up out of their hats, to give our enthusiastic acclaim to the composition of The Magic Flute, or to that dreadful Fifth or Ninth, or to be amazed that the horrific Faust can be heard, that tawdry Fantastique, not even to mention the most repulsive of all, this imperial criminal named Wagner and his zealous supporters, let's not even mention it, because if I even just think about it—the lecturer shook his head, giving expression to his disbelief—it is not shame that overcomes me, not the consciousness of degradation, but rather a dark desire for murder, because this sick megalomaniac of unprecedented incompetence impoverished music exactly in that land where the Baroque and the great figure of the Baroque, Bach, was active; a dark desire, if I think about it, he repeated, and he looked at his audience, and it was obvious that for quite a while now he had not been engaged with them, and hadn't looked at them because, it seemed, he was appalled by this public: the public, that is to say, that just sat slumped in the room, completely drained, not daring to escape, their hopes that at one point there might be a normal end to this lecture long since extinguished, and moreover these eight people—six old ladies and two old men—had reached such a state of sheer exhaustion and renunciation, like those who have given up, who no longer even propound, no longer even conjecture any kind of possible ending, they just awaited what must come, because after that would come hope as well—and this was inscribed upon their faces—the hope that the moment would arrive when everyone in the village Cultural Center would receive the signal that their guest, this guest from the capital city, was finished with his lecture about music; and when a good ten minutes later, which, to put it mildly, was as if two hours had gone by, that moment ensued, no one budged, because no one could believe it, for hope, being useless, awakens only slowly, yet what could have given them cause for hope is already here, if only in the last ten minutes they had paid closer attention: for the lecturer is, just now, threatening to return to an analysis of the individual works, namely, now it would be the time to evoke, choosing rapidly but a little haphazardly from the most sublime of the sublime: the aria for alto, beginning "Bereite dich, Zion," from the Christmas Oratorio; the aria for soprano from the Magnificat, "Quia respexit humilitatem," BWV 243; as well as, from the much-mentioned Matthäus-Passion, the aria, similarly for alto, "Erbarme dich, mein Gott," but then he purses his lips, he could do it but he isn't going to, so accordingly he renounces the evocation of the "Bereite dich, Zion" and the "Quia respexit humilitatem" as well as the "Erbarme dich, mein Gott" and, seeing and perceiving that he has gone a little over the time, and exhorting his audience to listen only to the music of the Baroque, he now bids them farewell with the most fitting words for this time and place, that is he now cites the very greatest masterpiece of the cathedral of pain closest to his heart, saying thus:

O selige Gebeine,
Seht, wie ich euch mit Buß und Reu beweine,
Daß euch mein Fall in solche Not gebracht!
Mein Jesu, gute Nacht!

he cites it; the guest inclined his head a little, as it were, in farewell: he cites it and leaves its spirit here; he then reached for his coat thrown on to the chair, picked it up, and as slowly as he began to button it, he reached the door of the room, and to the greatest shock of the still incredulous, long-faced gathering, he looked back with tears in his eyes, then he waved once, adjusted his enormous glasses, went out, closing the door behind himself, and finally they could still hear from outside as he walked away, how he still yet shouts back to them a few times, saying mein Jesu, gute Nacht! Mein Jesu, gute Nacht!

610

JUST A DRY STRIP IN THE BLUE

He stands in line: there are still five people in front of him, but that's not what is making him nervous; he will catch his train, it isn't because of that, and actually, to say that he is nervous does not even accurately describe his frame of mind, because instead he cuts the figure of someone who has lost his mind: his eyes are burning, they shine dementedly yet are completely still, like those of a wild animal ready to pounce in the last moment before the attack, it is much better if no one looks into them, and no one does look into them, and whoever by some misfortune does happen to catch the gaze of the celebrated painter—those standing in front of him don't dare turn around even once, and those behind him try to turn their heads in the other direction—this gaze cannot be endured, as it is completely apparent that Monsieur Kienzl is beside himself, it is evident that just a little harmless nothing will be enough and Monsieur Kienzl will immediately explode, will attack anyone at all, really like an animal infinitely roused, like a feral beast surrounded, one clearly facing a stronger power, when any resistance is as hopeless as could be, that is why he is the way he is, and that is what everyone observes in him, on this early morning of November 17, 1909, everyone in line to get a ticket for the number one express.

•

He has no idea why they are looking at him so much, he would be only too happy to knock them all down, to smash all those curious figures into many pieces with one single blow of his fist, how could they even imagine they could do this, that they could assault him like this, with this aggressive moronic gaping again and again, just what are they thinking, he clenches his teeth now, for how long will he be able to withstand such a brutal intrusion into his mourning, because no one can claim that they don't know, since yesterday the entire city has spoken only of that—from the last bakery to the first salon, from Eaux-Vives to the Rue de Grand—the news traveled everywhere, and now this insolence, he presses his fist into his palm, in the face of his mourning, a completely unforgivable, intolerable, treacherous intrusion, and this damned line is moving so slowly, why the hell is that ticket clerk taking so long with those dammed tickets, and there are still five people in front of him, let the sky rot over their heads, how long will he have to stand around here, the train is leaving soon, and in general he's not even sure if he should go, really, wouldn't it be better to turn away from this accursed line and go home instead, and leave the whole thing as it is?!—because then at least he wouldn't have to see these shifty faces, because then at least he wouldn't have to be incessantly afraid that in the end some idiot, thinking things over, would feel obliged to approach him, and then turning to him would express his condolences, well, no, not that, Kienzl says to himself, if someone here among these people even dares to try that, then he will not hesitate for a moment, but grab him and without a word strike him dead, anyone who gives even the slightest hint of anything like that, with one blow, he won't hesitate even for a second to do it—really.

Hector brought the news in September, but then there was already nothing to be done: there was nothing that could be done in the entire God-given world, because there is no cure for this; everyone dies:

his father died, his mother died, all his siblings and relations died, and now Augustine had died as well and now he had no one from the past, only Hector from Augustine, because Augustine was dead, and with that the past was dead, she too lay recumbent, since yesterday; everyone lay recumbent, everyone lies down one day, and nothing remains of them, just a dry strip in the blue; the person who remains does not want to acquiesce to this, cannot even do so, it's all arranged so that that the person who remains cannot bear it, he knows, he is aware, that, well, Augustine is dead, his old lover, who knew everything, who knew who he was at one time, and who at the end bestowed to him dear Hector, and this Augustine, his one-time Augustine is already being eaten up by worms, she is no more, and already is just a horizontal strip in the blue, and so too were they all here, in essence, all those here with him—he cast a glance around—all dead, here stands a pile of the dead in the blue, Kienzl thinks to himself, but what is even worse is that these five people keep standing in front of him and there behind the ticket window is that decrepit turd who is incapable of issuing a single ticket, this much is already obvious, there will be no tickets here, the train is leaving and they will remain here, this pile of the dead, here in the Geneva Station, finally perishing in a matter that seemed simple, on November 17, 1909, when already in the very first minutes they had entered a hopeless situation by wishing to buy a ticket for the train from Geneva to Lausanne.

The landscape painter is confronted not with the landscape, but with the blank canvas, namely that it is not the landscape he has to paint, but the picture, and he has stated this already many times, he begins to chew his moustache in rage, but well, he stated it already many times before, completely in vain, however; people think he paints so many landscapes because this is a *rewarding subject* for the canvas, they think that what they see is beautiful, but they are just blind, and they don't see that it isn't beautiful, but that it is—everything, but he repeats this over and over in vain, and chiefly he paints in vain, no one who looks at one of his pictures sees that he is not simply a painter but much more than that: a landscape painter, the kind who cannot do otherwise than paint landscapes: meaning this is so if there is some kind of landscape on the canvas, but also—and to the same degree—if there is a figure, so, well, what can be painted by the landscape painter is always, in this sense, a landscape, and nothing else, exclusively a landscape, even if there is a figure, he could never repeat this often enough, and he could never paint enough, but now he doesn't say anything, he just paints, because why say anything, no one understands anyway, better to be quiet and paint, without expecting the wealthy clients to follow him, as they had never done so before—only in Paris and Vienna maybe, yes maybe there; here however, no, and this is not even surprising, if a person looks around—this world never ever changes—in Geneva and Bern and Solothurn and Zurich, this entire spiritual torpidity proved once and for all that it was incapable of comprehending anything at all, because they never bothered to think about anything at all, and never could, not here; he could paint well, among these figures, ever more awe-inspiring canvases toward the final, the great, the cosmic end, here, however, it was completely hopeless; before, until now, they didn't understand and they didn't buy the paintings, now they still don't understand and they buy the paintings, so that, well, only that has changed, now he is not poor but rich; unchangingly, and in full measure, he was, however—alone, exactly when he might have believed that this barren misapprehension might have come to an end, because no, there would be no end, they would never understand even what it means to paint a landscape, to stand before a scene, and then it doesn't matter if the scenery is that of Grammont or Augustine on the deathbed, to stand there, to look at this life withdrawing for all eternity into death in the human and natural landscape, and to depict what is before him when he looks up from the blank canvas: that is everything—who should he explain this to?! maybe to these people in the station, who are only capable of trampling upon his mourning?! to affront him yet again?! for if there is anyone at all, well, he really cannot rely upon them to show some respect, now in this mourning he must be silent, he must be silent and continue to paint all that Augustine was and what Augustine will be, and what remains of Augustine.

She lay recumbent and he pulled the sheet off her, so he could see the whole of what Augustine had become, when his heart, shattered by the pain, nearly stopped in his chest; he pulled off the sheet, because he is used to doing this in other cases as well: when he sits outside on the slope of the Grammont, or at Chexbres in the heights of Saint-Prex, and his brain, his soul utterly tautened, he pulls the sheet down from the landscape, and he sets to looking above the blank canvas, then to take up evenly, from left to right, with a thick brush or ever more frequently with the painting knife itself, the blue, the violet, the green, and the yellow, namely, when he begins to work on a canvas, or to make it even more plain; for years now he has been painting a single picture where only the canvas is exchanged, but the picture is almost always the same, where the colors too, and the parallel planes, and the proportions of sky and water and earth, too, in the picture are, in their essence, the same—he pulled the sheet off, and he saw what remained, what there was, and this lasted for a long while, as he watched with his tautened brain; until he can smooth the sheet back into place; and he feels not only his heart but his mind is shattering from the loss, because he must think, and his mind very nearly shattered in the thinking, during the entire previous evening, which he spent next to the dead woman, and it will shatter again, he determines with his clattering brain here before the ticket desk, for as much as he knows that he is really within the proximity of what he sees, he still does not however see it in its final form in that picture—its essence constructed according to already inviolable principles—he knows that he still has to modify something, maybe the yellow has to be a little more dirty, maybe the blue a little harsher, something somehow has to be modified from what it has been until now, with Lake Geneva he's headed in the right direction, but to know exactly where to now, what is to be the next step, for that he needs that brain in his head, and he would need the ticket already, which he can't manage to get to as he is still standing here in front of the ticket counter and there are still four people in front of him.

Valentine, too, is going to die, the thought lacerates through him suddenly as he stands in line, Valentine will also lay recumbent, the dreaded thought slashes through him, and he will not be able to bear that either, then so it shall be, Valentine as well, that inconceivably beautiful, immeasurably alluring, maddeningly sensual, exquisite woman, his current lover, to whom he is rushing with this loss and with his mind tautened in pain; she too will end up like everyone and everything, recumbent in the blue strip, falling into bed, becoming gaunt, her skin drying up, her face falling in, her chest caving in, and that marvelous flesh will come off her down to the bones, just as it did with Augustine, just as with his mother and his father and his siblings and his relatives in his beloved Bern, exactly the same, exactly the same as every dead person here and there and everywhere, but first, the news will come, if it indeed happens like that, and finds one in the midst of this atrocious life, and he will start to go to her again and again, maybe with the number one express every afternoon, just as he did with Augustine since September, to always be there, so as to be there beside her bed, day in and day out, just so that she would not have to die alone; if the time comes maybe everything will be exactly the same as with Augustine—he just stands in line, there are still four people in front of him, and he tries to brush off the thought, but it doesn't work—Augustine and Valentine—it throbs in his brain, and he sees them already, the two of them dead, one atop the other, stretched out at length, like the strips of color on his canvases, like the beginning and end of existence in the Cosmic Whole, two bodies emaciated to skeletons with sunken-in eyes, tapering noses, lying stretched out above each other as the water lies above the ground, the mighty sky lies above the water, swimming in the blue of death.

Maybe everything truly does happen exactly in the same way—Kienzl finally steps forward one place in line—because every story repeats itself, life unto life, and at the end of course: death unto death, he thinks with a clouded countenance, well he is not the painter of death, he says, but of life, and now he even speaks the words aloud, nearly comprehensibly for those who are standing in close proximity to him, he doesn't know, nor is he even interested, if they hear what he is mumbling, the painter of life, he repeats it several times, of life, which he loves unspeakably, he loved it in Augustine and he loves it in Valentine, that is why he has painted even its tiniest vibration for these long years now, that is why it is so important, finally a matter of life and death, to place the most decisive emphasis on this vibration, in Augustine and in Lake Geneva, to give it emphasis, if he sees it in the local death, this is his task and so he does it, because it is right, he cannot do otherwise, he must be the painter of oneness, thus, well, he must give himself over to death, but nothing can compel him not to find a place for that mere wisp of a fact, the presence of life, its eternal rebirth, in the green and gold—not to put it up there where it flashes, he will search for a place for it, and he will put it up there, thinks Kienzl, and now in his horrifically tautened brain, a picture appears from the Geneva material, painted not long ago, in which the gray-blue of the water extends toward a strong, earthy yellow strip below, in layers of color that follow and distance themselves from each other, giving depth and majesty to the scene; then there is the opposite shore of the lake, depicted with a thin green, a pale violet, and a more poisonous green: all of this is below, enclosed in the lower third of the canvas, so that then he can paint the sky into the gigantic space, into the two-thirds of the canvas extending above it, above the horizon of the far shore, some kind of weak, paler than pale sunlight, declining in gold with its swirling fog, then high above, just the pure blue of the pure sky, repeating clusters of white clouds following upon each other, accordingly, then, roughly twelve layers placed above each other: and with these roughly twelve layers placed above each other, with these crude twelve deathly parallels, is flung down there, as coarsely as possible: This is your Cosmos, this is Complete, the Whole, in roughly twelve colors: EVERYTHING, from Kienzl—and now—he stands shifting from one leg to the other in the line—it is yours.

There are three people in front of him, and now he simply doesn't believe his eyes, such slowness as this cannot exist, the old man, the railway official selling tickets behind the window, he sees clearly from here, is slowing down the process in every possibly conceivable manner, after the destination has been stated, he repeatedly asks in confirmation, Morges, really? Nyon, yes? well that is wonderful, I wish you the very best, that truly promises to be a pleasant trip, so then you will want a ticket to Céligny, is that right? If I may ask, in which class of carriage does the gentleman wish to travel? First-class, that is simply marvelous, a demonstration of truly excellent taste, and I can assure you that it shall be exceptionally comfortable, so then, Morges? Nyon? Céligny? Lausanne? in a word it goes like that all the way up the line, in the most roundabout fashion possible, again and again bringing things to a complete halt through some discreet question, or through gushing inanities, in addition to which, Kienzl now realizes, his face reddening in rage, the people standing in front of him even visibly enjoy and appreciate it, what a sweet old man, someone notes, ticket in hand, as they turn away from the counter, passing by Kienzl—this blithering oaf, he shakes his head in disbelief, yes, Morges, he mutters loudly to himself, yes, Nyon, yes, yes, Céligny, and Lausanne, don't you hear, my good man, what they are saying?—Morges, Nyon, Céligny, yes, give them the tickets already, that should be your worry, to hell with it, and he flings all of this into the discreet silence, no one reacts, everyone tries to look as if they haven't heard anything, and as if they wouldn't even understand why Monsieur Kienzl is so impatient, for there is surely much time left before the train departs, and certainly not even three minutes have passed since he got into line, they don't understand, but they don't even really dare to contemplate the matter lest something be visible on their faces, because Monsieur Kienzl seems invariably and inexpressibly dangerous, the glances are turned away, the eyes cast down, then a tiny cough or two, then not even that, just the silence, and the patient waiting, and some kind of general agreement and forgiveness—which just infuriates him, Kienzl, all the more—for everyone knows what happened yesterday, that Mademoiselle Augustine Dupin, Mr. Kienzl's former model from the slums, died, and they know what this poor lady could have suffered, and what Monsieur Kienzl himself must be suffering, and how magnanimously he behaved with that poor pariah, he, the celebrated painter of the city, who in the space of a couple of years had become a millionaire, providing her with the very best, sitting every day—and for hours!—by the dying woman's bed, thus giving proof of his strong, faithful nature, for he certainly did not abandon her in any way, she who in his one-time destitution was not only his model, but in the most intimate sense of the word, his companion, moreover the mother of their little boy, in a word the city knew everything, but everything about the events of yesterday and the events proceeding yesterday, and of course here among the people waiting for a ticket, the situation was no different, they, however, also recognized and knew well that it would be better not to confront his vehement nature, namely that he was increasingly giving evidence of being incapable of mastering his pain, and one inappropriate word would be enough and he might just hurl himself at one of them, and finally, out of the present-day gentleman—the wealthy and dignified artist—the former ill-mannered, scruffy vagabond of Bern, just as familiar to everyone there, will burst out.

Augustine and Valentine, it echoes in his head, and he cannot he get that picture of Lake Geneva out of his mind, the one that arose earlier, the painting as yet untitled but completed the other day: the obsessively pursued sequence, he cannot drive away those twelve obsessive parallels out of his mind, and in a sudden terror of the contiguities he says to himself that later . . . later, instead of the yellow, a metallic matte blue-green should be burning below, then to spatter a GHASTLY quantity of ochre and brown and crimson, and onto the sky as well, so that it will be ablaze in the ochre and in the dead crimson-brown, only above will there remain some kind of grayish ominous blue; then the mountain ridge on the opposite bank should burn intensely in a dark deathly, final blue, because in the end this picture must be aglow, must be ablaze, must burn, and then suddenly in a flash he sees himself as the train takes him to Vevey: somewhere between Nyon and Rolle he suddenly perceives there below, from the window of the well-heated carriage, a ragged figure struggling against the strong wind, his own self in 1880, walking with all of the paintings he has completed mounted on his back and under his arm, to Morges, so that he can sell them, and then there is a beaten scruffy dog in the storm; the wind is blowing against him, still mainly coming from the lake, and it strikes down upon them again and again; and it is still very far away to Morges on foot, it is 1880 and he is hungry, and the train from 1909 runs alongside them, the dog runs after the clattering wheels, and barks, the train disappears from view like an unreachable dream, one in which he will take his place in just a moment in one of the second-class compartments, and exclusively on the right-hand side next to the window, because he wants to see the lake, nothing else but the lake, for really, as never before, he wants nothing else than to see this lake, as this lake replenishes its own enormous space, with the rather tenuous shore here below, and the rather tenuous shore, there, on the other side, and above, the whole, the enormous sky—if he could only manage to drive that rotten mangy dog out of his mind, he mutters to himself, but speaking so loudly this time that everyone standing around him understands his words clearly, although they don't know what to think about Monsieur Kienzl, who now wants to get rid of some dog that won't budge from his heels, he kicks it aside in vain, it just won't leave him alone, it just keeps on coming, says Kienzl irritatedly, just dragging itself along beside him, as if there would be any sense at all in this entire devotion.

He's cold, they say, repulsive and unfeeling, he's heard it hundreds and hundreds of times, that he is harsh and merciless and brutal and unsympathetic and decadent, by that, however, they only betray—he takes one step forward—that they are afraid of him, because it is terrifying, really, when they have to be confronted with the fact that he is here, he who amidst eternal death and in the greatest of need, had to break out in a truly harsh, merciless, unsympathetic, and decadent world, with that truly unassailable desire in him, so that at last someone could state something about the truth, but what kind of a statement is that—he is cold and repulsive and unfeeling! and his mind is filled with rage yet again, and now he is the one who would be called repulsive and unfeeling! exactly him, who could be called the fanatic of reality, if anything at all; but not cold and unfeeling, no, not that; in his anger he begins to pull at his beard impatiently, in front of the ticket desk window, no one will ever get there, will ever get to the point of being able to understand, only Valentine understands, no one—just Valentine, and Valentine alone—understands what he is searching for so obsessively, and no one can say that he is unfeeling, because that was exactly what was so unbearable in his dreadful life, that he wasn't brutal, but everything was—from Geneva through Bern and all the way to Zürich—it was he who surmounted everything with the greatest of sensitivity, because he alone had a heart, and with this heart he looked at the landscape, and he looks at it now too, and it is with this heart that he sees now that everything is woven into one: the earth with the water, the water with the sky, and into the earth and the water and the sky, into this indescribable Cosmos is woven our fragile existence as well, but merely for just one moment that cannot be traced, then, already, it is no more, it disappears for all eternity, irrevocably, like Augustine and all that Augustine was as of yesterday, nothing else remains, only and exclusively the landscape; in his case, then the locomotive's whistle sounds from the direction of the tracks, and with that, this line, where there is only a woman with a hat in front of him, suddenly speeds up; he speaks once again out loud to himself, in his case, Lake Geneva remains, the recumbent monumental strips in the dead blue space, the Great Expanse, those two words begin to rattle around in his head, just like, in a moment, the wheels beneath the carriage pulling out of Geneva Station: the monumental, the inconceivable, the Great Expanse that includes all within itself, the ultimate painting of which is, of course, right here in front of him, and he will paint it, he finally reaches the ticket window—he will go that far, he flings out, with his two insanely burning eyes, to the visibly frightened elderly railway official, that he wants a second-class ticket to Vevey; he knows already what title he will give to the painting of the lake completed not too long ago, he knows already, once he comes back from Valentine, his first order of business will be to go into the atelier, take the picture down from the easel, and note down on a piece of paper, and finally to attach to the back of the painting those few words, which he cannot express more precisely than to say that he, Oswald Kienzl is on a journey, a journey in the right direction, just a few words, namely "Fomenrhytmus der Landschaft," hence the most appropriate possible expression for the painting, for it not just to have a title, but in his own succinct way to let the world know, inasmuch as it may be curious, to let the world know who he was, what kind of figure he was, upon whose gravestone would one day be written the words: Oswald Kienzl, the Swissman.

987

THE REBUILDING OF THE ISE SHRINE

He didn't say I am Kohori Kunio, he didn't even return their bow, nor did he accept the handshake offered by one of them, he didn't say anything at all for quite a while, he just listened, namely he listened with barely concealed reluctance till the end of their account as to why they were here at the Jingū Shicho, who they were, and what they wanted; then he informed them that as for the name they had mentioned, Ms. Bernard, although he knew who she was, from here and from Harvard too, in terms of their request, he could neither say yes nor no, as the matter did not fall under his jurisdiction; he for a long time now—and here he repeated the words very meaningfully, stressing *for a very long time*—had not worked in the Department of Public Relations; then, with an unfriendly grimace, he gave them to understand that he did not in the slightest wish to discuss his present position with the two uninvited guests, moreover he did not wish to discuss anything with them at all, nor did he wish to have any dealings with them whatsoever, he did not in the least wish to get mixed up in a conversation with the two foreigners, he already even regretted having to come down from the Jingū office here to the public area of the Naikū, in a word he deliberately behaved in an unfriendly manner in order to humiliate them, and a little threateningly as well, as if he wanted to let them know that it would be better if they gave up their plan; if they went ahead with their request, they would meet with refusal everywhere, even if they handed in an official application, the grudging recommendation with which he wished to close this conversation that was debasing for him, they would receive exclusively one and only one kind of response from the Department of Public Relations at the Jingū Shicho: a refusal in the most decisive terms, and they should not even count on anything else, the Jingū Shicho and the two of them simply did not go together, they should leave off even trying, they should leave the Naikū and in particular they should quit trying to cast their presence, so inappropriate here, in a newer and newer light, so really, he turned the corners of his mouth down and looked off somewhere into the heights above the forests of Naikū, how could they possibly imagine that they could just show up here, accost him, cause him the trouble of coming down from his office and ask his permission, in the area of the parking lot in front of the Shicho building, to take part in the 71st rebuilding of the Ise Shrine, in the ceremony known as Misoma-Hajime-sai, and all the other things as well, how could it turn up in the head of a European novice architect and a Japanese Noh-textile designer, as they called themselves, that they could even step into the most sacred spot in the entire country, he could see very well, his contemptuous gaze suggested as he looked around with increasing irritation, just what sort they were: the kind of people who neither in their attire nor their bearing nor their way of speaking nor their manner were suitable, neither were they acceptable in their social status, and, in particular, the manner in which they had conveyed their request scandalized him, so that while they tried with ever more servile bearing and ever more humble words to reverse the direction of their incidental audience, already now completely hopeless, Kohori Kunio simply left the two supplicants there; they stood for quite a while, completely scalded, without even the strength to move, this reception had taken them so much by surprise because while they had suspected—

chiefly, the Japanese friend had—how complicated it would be to obtain a general mandate from the Jingū Shicho, while they suspected that there would be serious obstacles, they—at least the guest from Europe—did not suspect that their first attempt would end in such a fiasco, not to mention that the so-called conversation that took place with Kohori-san excluded even the possibility that he would ever again communicate with them, either personally or in writing, so that they left the otherwise public area of Naikū with their heads bowed and with the speed of people fleeing, and they didn't even feel like looking for the most important spot for them in Naikū, in this sacred forest, they just wandered around *there outside,* along the streets of Ise, they hung their heads and for differing reasons did not utter a single word to each other, in this way an hour passed until they were able to make their way back to the main entrance, so that this time they would go along the shaded dirt path leading between the majestic trees, at least as far as the center of the main shrine, to have a look at the honden—to put it more precisely, what interested them the most—the so-called kodenchi, the fenced-in empty space in *direct* proximity to the honden, which twenty years ago served as the location of the old honden, but since the demolition and complete removal of the honden twenty years ago, it was now, following the stipulations, strewn and made completely level, just like the other subsidiary shrines in this sacred forest, with roughly cut pieces of white limestone; they wanted all the same to see the place that—as the Japanese formulated it to his Western friend—was the honden's reflected image but without the honden, because it is really like this in Ise, in the two sanctuaries of this small city, that is in the forests of Naikū and Gekū, there lies, in direct proximity to each significant complex of buildings, pressing up, as it were, against the existing group of buildings, an empty space of the exact same size as in the existing group of buildings, the empty lots stand there next to the building complexes, covered with white stones cut into fist-sized pieces, and they literally shine in the pure moonlight for twenty years: a group of buildings, an empty space, an empty space, a group of buildings, this is how everything has proceeded here in Ise since the edict of Temmu, because according to legend he was the one, the Emperor Temmu in the seventh century, who first commanded in six hundred and something that every twenty years the entire structure of shrines in both Naikū and Gekū, that is both the inner shrine to Amaterasu Ōmikami, as well as the outer shrine to Toyooke Ohokami—would be rebuilt again and again, namely that on the neighboring tracts of land, left empty and corresponding with complete accuracy to the basic plan of the buildings now standing, the individual buildings would be constructed again and the old ones would be demolished, although Temmu's edict states that not just the copy of all these buildings has to be rebuilt again, but that the *same* buildings must be rebuilt once again, and everything—every beam, piece of masonry, dowel, corbel, overlay—really, with a hair's breadth accuracy, must be rebuilt in the same way and at the same time and in the same place, so that it may be renewed, so that it may be maintained in the freshness of birth, and if we are speaking of Naikū—and we are speaking of that because of the two visitors—it is so that Amaterasu Ōmikami, the sun-deity, would not leave us and would remain among us, and then—delighting in the radiating strength of the freshness—she does not leave us, and remains among us, as long as this renewal truly sustains the two great shrines in time: sustains the hondens of Naikū and Gekū, i.e., the shōden within the hondens, which serves as a residence for the deities; the three treasures, and the fencing encircling them as well, are all as if they had just come into being today, in the true vividness of creation, in the realm of a truly eternal present, because in this way all of the hinoki-wood is always fresh, because in this way the gilded beams are always fresh, the roofs and the steps are fresh, all of the joinings and planings are fresh, one can always feel that the carpenter has left off his work just a moment ago, that he has just lifted his chisel from the plank of wood, and so that every single piece of hinoki always has the sweet fragrance of hinoki; the Ise shrine, accordingly, has been shining forth in freshness ever since the year of six hundred and something, just as the main shrine of Naikū shines as well over there, where the two of them are now looking, but they turn their gaze away already, to here, onto the kodenchi, onto this emptiness, onto this unbuilt-ness, onto this pure possibility with its white stones, where altogether this emptiness is broken only by a little hut, serving as the basis for future work and protecting the sacred column, the shin no mihashira, in the middle of the back part of the area; they are looking at this space, which burns, so to speak, in anticipation, this space that will be the location of the 71st Shikinen Sengū, that of the 71st rebuilding, that is to say immediately, as it is now March, and the 71st Shikinen Sengū begins in May, that is, there are eight years left before the change that occurs every twenty years will take place in 2013, the Jingū Shicho gets eight years from Emperor Temmu until the twenty years are up, and for the new, that is for the current assembled buildings of the Ise Shrine, to be regenerated; this is what they wrote to each other, this is what they analyzed in their letters between Japan and Europe, when the idea first emerged of what a wonderful thing it would be for an architecture student and a local resident interested in Japanese culture to follow, in its entirety, how a Shikinen Sengū such as this proceeds in its countless ceremonies, moreover not just to follow it but to understand something of it, the Western friend wrote innocently, yes, the Japanese responded with a certain disquiet, perhaps suspecting something of that complicated process about which no one could have any knowledge in advance, so closed to the entire world was this process, no one could know anything about it, only the Emperor and the relative of the Emperor who represented the imperial family, as it happened the Emperor's older sister—then, of course, the dai-gūji, the high priest, himself closely tied to the imperial family, the priests of Ise, and finally the miya-daikus, the actual instruments in the hand of continual divine creation, or more simply put the temple carpenters, and only in this case, the case of Ise, it is necessary immediately to add that we are speaking of the carpenters of the Ise shrine, because they were trained by the Jingū Shicho itself, it named them, it engaged them, it employed them, it took care of them and buried them, and they could not undertake any other line of work, only this; they could not enter into any other kind of employment, only this; the work, in the strictest sense, lasted until the end of their lives, for they were not just any sort of carpenter but ritual carpenters who worked, in the operation of the rebuilding of the shrine, with particular tools, particular materials, particular methods, in a word with a particular consciousness, completely secluded from the public, in secret as it were, just as all of the participants of the Ise Shikinen Sengū worked in secret, from the carpenters all the way to the high priests, a secrecy which in the very first place could be explained by the seemingly greatest likelihood that the purity of the process—one of the most important objectives of Shintō—could be maintained from the beginning until its completion and that, well, then it was exactly this, this openness, this so-called modern Japan, and not least of all the thorough secularization of the system of patronage, that caused or compelled, from year to year, the confidential inner circle of the Shikinen Sengū to relinquish something from this great secrecy, with the Emperor's family at the forefront, Kuniaki Kuni by name, the current high priest of the shrine, the older brother of Princess Kōjun, the son of Prince Asaakira Kuni, who felt that the Ise Shrine should be opened up to the world, and this meant that already the previous Shikinen Sengū, at the time of the seventieth rebuilding, had admitted journalists and television reporters to certain ceremonies; moreover, under the patronage of the Jingū Shicho itself, a documentary film was made about the Shikinen Sengū process, which although revealing hardly anything about it, still gave a kind of superficial account, at the very least drawing attention, moreover the general public's attention, to the fact that there is something called the Shikinen Sengū; yet the high priest considered—and the previously mentioned confidential inner circle of the Shikinen Sengū agreed with him—that it would still be better if the Jingū Shicho would keep a firm hold on what was divulged and what wasn't, nevertheless it did happen here that a film was made in such a way that it seemed to be revealing something while still concealing the essence of things in the usual way; in a word, from the viewpoint of the initiators of greater openness, it proved to be the height of success; in the history of knowledge of the Shikinen Sengū, however, it proved to be an absolute hodgepodge, indeed directly misleading, everyone in Japan knew this, yet hardly anyone said anything about it, nor did anyone connected to the Emperor's family; people treated the affairs of the Emperor's family with the deepest possible sympathy, tact, attentiveness, and patience, and with gratitude for everything with which the Kunaicho—that is, the Imperial Household Agency, in its representation of the imperial family—honored Japan in bringing it to public notice, so that evidently the previously inconceivable could take place, that non-Japanese, but so-called scholarly researchers with strong ties to Japan and to Shintō—as for example, the recently deceased Felicia Gressitt Bock, or Ms. Rosemarie Bernard, the anthropologist from Harvard University—received permission from the Jingū Shicho to observe certain ceremonies at the 70th Shikinen Sengū, moreover recognizing, for example, the clarity of the attentive research of the latter scholar, as well as her proven sensitivity in the treatment of the matter, further permissions were granted to her, in fact she was employed as a consultant at the Jingū Shicho Public Relations Division for one year, so that, apart from the work she was given, she might further deepen her research relating to the Shikinen Sengū, which afterward was confirmed by the invitation to Harvard, at the initiative of Professor Bernard, of one of the most highly regarded personages of the Jingū administration, Kohori-san, who had not worked as director of the Department of Public Relations for a very long time now, and his participation in a symposium there, well it was precisely upon this that the western friend's plan depended, that they should try, relying upon Rosemarie Bernard's indirect support, to acquire permission to attend the ceremony, to follow the course of the rebuilding, in which he was even successful in winning the cautious ... hmm ... support of his Japanese friend, and this plan, it seemed just now, had proven a disaster, as they looked at Western friend Kohori Kunio's back as he walked away after their introductory conversation, then disappeared into the main entrance of the Jingū Shicho building, a disaster that made both of them equally bitter, for they sensed that there could be no doubt whatsoever as to the clarity of his message, they hadn't even begun to introduce themselves, the appraisal of whether they were qualified for the Jingū Shicho's attention could not even begin before it was immediately thrown back in their faces: they were not qualified, the world of this affair, so far beyond them, just beat them down, this world was so unapproachable and so opaque, and would manifestly remain so, they were embittered and were beaten down, if each for different reasons, and with different consequences as well, for while one of them, the European half—wounded to the bone in this matter that would contain great surprises even later on—was repeating over and over again to himself, on the train headed back, how in the world is this possible, and why, for god's sake, what sort of mistake had they made, and what a rude, arrogant, offensive character this Kohori is, they had really crashed hard against how sacred it was ... while what kept running through the head of the other, the Japanese side of this purportedly friendly relationship, was that they deserved it, he had felt it from the beginning, no good was going to come of this, what had happened was completely natural, they should in fact have counted on it, at least he, Kawamoto, should have counted on it, knowing well that you could not, just like that, as they had done—as his friend, with his European mentality, considered to be perfectly natural—you could not just send for a high-ranking official from the Jingū Shicho, Japan is Japan, and the Jingū Shicho is particularly so, and he, especially he, should not have pledged support to his Western friend, should not have accepted the general first-person plural and allowed himself to be swept up in the enthusiasm of the other when the great plan was beginning—first in their letters and then in person following the arrival of his friend—to take shape, but he should have dissuaded him in the most decisive manner possible from his insane idea, and should have explained somehow that this is not possible, this is completely out of the question; he should have stated clearly that to approach a person of such high status demands extraordinary discretion, it is simply not possible for us to go to him just like that, for us to have him called down by the porter just like that, no, Kawamoto-san shook his head, how could he even have mixed himself up in this insanity, why hadn't he warned his friend that proposals such as this are doomed to failure, later on in eight years they could go at the end of the Shikinen Sengū to the consecration of the shrine—that is possible, that is open to the public, well of course this is what he should have soberly recommended, Kawamoto was now thinking, his friend would have understood sooner or later and he wouldn't have got himself swept up into such a horrible mess, because what were they going to say later at home if they found out that they had gone to Ise, the Japanese side worried as they rushed homeward on the JR long-distance route, although this, the worry over this question, at least proved to be unnecessary, as later at home, in the Noh-textile workshop, luckily no one asked them anything, they were not plied with questions like: so how did it go, what happened; because those at home, the members of the Kawamoto family—the mother, the eldest son, and the two younger sisters—did not in any event really occupy themselves with the daily affairs of the other son in the family, rather unlucky, weak-willed, heaping one failure on another and thus still living at home, for they saw on their faces as they returned home that it had not gone well, that it had come to nothing, that it had been a fiasco, so why start asking questions of such a compendium of misfortune as Akio, so no one breathed a word about it, they didn't even speak, they just ate their dinner in silence, and went to sleep, and although the next day it appeared that this unfortunate initiative with Kohori-san had made their position impossible, they still wrote, that is to say, the Western friend dictated, Kawamoto-san translated, refining every phrase to the uppermost limit, into Japanese, and thus, because the other insisted upon it, though he, Kawamoto, said to himself that now the disgrace would be fully complete, that day they sent the application to the Jingū Shicho by post, then they just sat at home in Kyōto, that is in the Noh-textile workshop of Kawamoto Akio's family, they listened to the sound, clacking as it had for centuries, of the looms, and they sat there very dejectedly, and didn't do anything; the guest was now no longer interested in the Kinkaku-ji, nor the Ginkaku-ji, nor the Katsura Rikyu, nor the Sanjūsangen-dō, not at all; still, he explained responding to the question of the head of the family, who risked mentioning at times that it might be worthwhile for them to get out a bit, still, the architect friend decisively shook his head, what could they look for anywhere in this undoubtedly wonderful city—anything but to stand there as the tenth thousandth visitor immersed in solitary reflection in the Ryōan-ji garden, or to trudge along the corridors of the Nijō Castle, their eyes obligatorily dazzled in each room by the golden Kano paintings—when their plan, for which their Western friend had traveled here as a guest, their plan built up over the months, had suddenly and unjustly collapsed so terribly, but so terribly?... when one day a letter arrived from the Jingū Shicho informing them that they were granted permission to observe the Misoma-Hajime-sai ceremony, they should be there at such a time in such a place, and they could participate in the ceremony along with the journalists, all other information, it said in the letter, could be obtained from Miwa-san, who could be reached at such a number, from Miwa-san assigned by the Jingū Shicho Public Relations Division, and then they called him and already they agreed on the time and place and how to get there, in a word, they made the so-called arrangements, then they took out the relevant map and looked for Agemaku, and the forest of Akasawa, where the meeting place would be, where the minibus would come to pick them up to take them to the place, for there, Miwa-san emphasized, when the conversation turned to the details, no other kind of vehicle was permitted to enter, it was the private property of the Jingū, where the only kind of transportation possible was, solely and exclusively, those vehicles provided by the Jingū Shicho, it was not possible just to go charging around in one's own car, this is a dense forest, Miwa-san explained, a very dense, impenetrable forest, where there are no paths, and apart from this, Akasawa belonged to the Jingū Shicho, and the trees there, several hundred years old, represent an enormous treasure, so that in a word, no, your own car exclusively and solely as far as Agemaku, and there, across a little nameless bridge on the left, then to the right up a foresters' path to a special parking lot built solely and exclusively for the purposes of this ceremony—and there was the end, there they should entrust themselves to him, to Miwa-san, because he, Miwa-san, would be there, and he would guide them, and they would see, he said with more authority, that he would take care of everything, they should just get to the parking lot in the Akasawa forest, and the rest was up to him, with that they said goodbye, they put down the receiver, and again took up the map, but Kawamoto-san, though in one respect relieved that perhaps through somehow achieving some success at something, his position in the family would be a little less onerous, in another respect, beyond the Kohori affair, he felt in contrast to his friend, that it was not a time of rejoicing, but rather of fear, because he was decidedly frightened, as someone who knows just exactly what awaits him, that namely from this point on a series of horrifying situations would be coming one right after the other with his Western friend, completely uninformed as to the accustomed rules of conduct here, and whose faux pas would somehow be for him to smooth over, oh no, thought Kawamoto Akio, but then he didn't even bring up the topic, he didn't even mention a few rules pertaining to how one can ... well ... be more fortunate in conducting oneself according to the accustomed stipulations in Japan, but instead in his great confusion he began to speak, amid the clatter of the looms, that his guest would certainly like the region they were going to, because this, and he pointed to a splotch around Agemaku, is Kiso itself, this is the Kiso region where the postal route of olden times ran from Edo to Kyōto, between the Shōgun and the imperial court, and some of the smaller cities belonging to this route can be found to this day, ah, the postal stations of the Kiso Valley, oh that is a really beautiful place, the Western friend said to Kawamoto-san, then he quickly added: at least I think so—but the Western friend did not give any sign that he was particularly animated by the news, or that they could just conceive of the whole thing as some kind of tourist excursion, he just nodded, saying wonderful, wonderful, but from then on he was simply buried in books and notes, he only came down to the family at mealtimes and spent the rest of the day upstairs, in the room above the clattering looms, leafing through books and notes about the essence of Shintō and deities of Shintō, the ceremonies of Shintō and the hierarchies of Shintō, the history of Shintō and its origin myths, these were the themes of his research, not suspecting that there would not be any need later for this knowledge but, well, how could he have known this—from where, from what: instead, there was the fashioning of the wood and the measurement of the beams, the system of corbels and the jointing, the miya-daiku tools and the life of the hinoki cypresses and the means of crafting them, these accordingly were the subjects he should have been researching although before the Misana Hajime-sai he still could not have suspected anything, when he still wished that he could know, if only he could ferret out what was the dai-gūji, and what was the saishu: and the dai-gūji, is that the same thing as the saishu, or where are the Emperor's Three Treasures, the Yata no Kagami, the Kusanagi no Tsurugi, and the Yasakami no Magatama, are they all in Ise today, for that is the chief shrine, the most sacred of all the shrines, and well, in every shrine there have to be the three treasures: the mirror, the sword, and the jewel, for these are kept in the shōden, no?—he pondered over such things, but he was already sitting in the car, Kawamoto was driving—the steering wheel on the right would have been hard for him—he sat next to the silent and as far as he was concerned incomprehensibly sad-looking Kawamoto; the three treasures, the Sanshu-no Shiki, ran through his head, it was midnight, they were just turning out from Kyōto into the thick traffic of the Meishin Expressway, the road was completely packed, the lanes seemed narrow, but in spite of this, the speed limit was one hundred kilometers per hour, so that they proceeded as a single mass among the innumerable buses and trucks and cars, the guest did not even dare to look anywhere, he just asked his friend a question now and then about Shintō, what is this like and what is that like, but Kawamoto was already cautious, and every answer began with the words that he didn't know, and only if his friend forced the given topic further would he say something concerning his own knowledge with many reservations, but if he could, he instead tried to divert the other's attention, bringing up concrete questions as, for example, when would they reach the meeting place, it was now past midnight so it would be three in the morning, which means that they would have altogether three hours to sleep, at dawn, at six a.m., Kawamoto-san reminded his friend, they had to be there by the tent, waiting for Miwa-san, so that he could register them; and if new questions popped up, he tried to dodge them with such matters, and he did this for a while until he got tired, and from then on he either gave terse answers or no answers at all, as if he had not heard the latest question, he pressed down on the accelerator in the dark night; in front of them, behind them, to the right and the left everyone was doing the same, as if all were pressing on the same pedal, one hundred kilometers an hour, that is how they headed toward Nagoya in the tight disciplined traffic on the Meishin Expressway, so that a good hour later they arrived at the turnoff point above Nagoya from the Tōmei Expressway and went onto Road No. 19 toward Kiso-Fukushima, but there only Kawamoto was determining which way to go, because his friend had suddenly fallen asleep, so he was obligated to keep holding up the map himself to get his bearings in the empty district, but he located, after Agemaku, the little nameless bridge on the route given by the Jingū Shicho without error, then to the right and up the forest path, so that when the guest opened his eyes—he started awake, as he had begun to feel strange, but what was strange was that the car had stopped—we've arrived, said his host, and he pointed through the windshield, they had stopped in a specially constructed parking lot, recently nailed together and surrounded with beams; all around was the forest, plunging gloomily into the sky, no one was in the parking lot, but Kawamoto-san was very certain that they had arrived at the right place, although he was only fully reassured when, after a few hours of sleep, he was awakened by his travel alarm clock, which he had brought with him; and which truly and accurately woke them up at 5:45, dawn was breaking outside and the parking lot was full, among the few trucks there were mostly cars lined up close beside each other, from Tokyo and Ōsaka, Nagasaki and Aomori, Niigata and Matsue, journalists, reporters, television and radio crews, they were already preparing in silence, even it if wasn't clear for what, probably they had timed their arrival here for around five or half-past in the morning, and they did arrive, and they were preparing, that much was clear, but what wasn't clear was if they knew at all what was to follow, light was breaking around them in their kind of preliminary milling around, for a long time nothing happened, then further on down, below the parking lot, on the edge of a forest path, young people with sleepy eyes suddenly hoisted up a tent, then later on they put up one more next to it, but they didn't carry or set up anything else, didn't pile up anything inside, and each tent only had a roof, neither had any sides to it, altogether one table appeared from somewhere, well, that they put down, not inside either of the tents but in front of one of them, another young man appeared wearing a suit: judging from the seriousness of his expression, he was sent here for more serious tasks, he was Miwa-san, it turned out, when they went over to him and asked where they could find Miwa-san, I am Miwa Kitamura, came the reply, then he looked them up and down and asked—although it appeared he knew the answer, how could he not have known?—so, you are the architect from Europe and his friend from Kyōto, yes? and his gaze revealed neither good nor ill will, yes, that is us, Kawamoto-san replied respectfully, he handed a small gift and bowed, fine, then stand here over by the side and wait, you will be picked up by a minibus, and that is what happened, they waited for a long time and patiently too, in front of the empty tents in the middle of the forest with their name-tags that Miwa-san had given them hanging on their chests, when at last one hour later the buses appeared, the reporters quickly got into line and made a dash for the seats, the two friends were continually pushed farther and farther to the back of the line that was quickly forming and surging forward to the seats, but finally they too got a place in the last bus, and the vehicle was already taking this last group, driving with great caution across the bumpy terrain on a road that appeared to be brand new, because the road was new, just as the parking lot was, it was so new that it seemed to have been constructed during the brief hour while they had to wait in front of the tents, and one couldn't know that it hadn't been so, in any event there could be no doubt that they were decisively heading for the Misoma-Hajime-sai among the forest's trees, where they slowly proceeded forward, now lurching here and there, then at one point the minibus just stopped, and between them they really, but really had no idea whatsoever where they might possibly be, do you know where we are, asked the European, I have no idea, answered his companion, somewhere in the depths of the forest of the Kiso Valley, among the pines and the hinoki cypresses belonging to the Jingū Shicho; Kawamoto, smiling, only said that much, because only that much was certain, and there was a little bridge that they had to go across, to be led between the trees on a winding path strewn with wood shavings, the buses accordingly had stopped, the gathering had set off on foot, and at last, after one turn, they suddenly saw in the distance a huge wooden structure, the whole thing reaching into the sky from among the trees as if they were dreaming it, because the whole, viewed from here, decidedly created the impression of a huge stage, not only from a distance but also from close up, that is, an absurdity built out of fresh-planed beams, just what the hell was such a huge impossibility as this doing in the mysterious depths of the Kiso Valley, they looked uncomprehendingly at each other, yet it was not a dream, even if it remained an impossibility, in the mysterious depths of the enchantingly beautiful Kiso Valley that extended between the prefectures of Nagano and Gifu, a huge stage looked down upon them, they were not prepared for this, somehow they had imagined that there would be two trees in the forest surrounded by priests, visitors in the background, something like that—and instead there was this huge stage, raised several meters above the ground and sloping downward, and this surprise overcame them in their first astonishment as they drew near, because they saw, at the front of the stage, the two extraordinarily tall, broad-trunked live hinoki cypress trees, down to which the stage, as it were, sloped, extended, and they saw on the two wide tree trunks the cords signifying selection—these were the shimenawas and then the shides—the small pieces of snow-white paper cut into zigzags, and folded, below them, a protective covering from some kind of rice-based material, also fastened to the trees with cord, and one or two lathes: quite high above the level of a person's head, this might have been a sign, that below these lathes the sacred work would later proceed, in a word they noticed all this, and they saw it, and there could be no doubt that these were the two trees that today—in the Misoma-Hajime-sai—would be cut down, and in doing so would, as it were, inform the kami that the Shikinen Sengū had begun; still it was the stage that drew their gazes again and again, they looked to the left, they looked to the right, but they just could not familiarize themselves with it, although it also seemed obvious that in front and below, the two sides of the U-shaped stage surrounded the two chosen hinokis, so the whole thing, accordingly, was for these two trees, this stage, accordingly—enclosing a sharp angle with the rising forest floor—from the last rows to the first, from the back part of the stage timbered into the heights down to the two ceremonial tree trunks: this was a part of what was going to take place here, was closely connected with the ceremony to follow, and so on, the only problem was that they—at least the two of them—could not at all sense the import of this, because they could not come to terms with it, from whatever direction they looked at it, this stage did not belong here, in addition, what those who had made the foot-paths and those who had built this enormous stage had done escaped neither of their attention, because they had crushed, cut, and hacked down everything that had turned up in their path, they had chosen the trees, they had built the stage, they had formed the paths that led to it, but not with the proper degree of circumspection, neatly keeping things in order, but crudely, with a near-barbarous negligence, which was a little distressing, because the ceremony among other reasons was being enacted, as they had read in the written publicity materials given to them by Miwa-san, in order to beg for the trees' forgiveness, and to reassure them that if in one sense they were going to lose their lives, in another sense life, namely a new and noble life, would be granted to them; in the midst of so much devotion and veneration and consideration, it was, however, incomprehensible that this devotion and veneration and consideration was all the same so lacking, namely that they had laid waste to, and hurled aside, all that was not needed, on both sides of the path lay scattered about in confusion, twigs, wood-splinters, shreds of bark, wood shavings, and rotting tree trunks, which could have been cleared at least from here, from the two sides of the path, thought the two guests, who now really began to feel uncertain when they experienced the same conditions arriving directly underneath the stage, and they wished to perform as well, after the others, the temizu, that is, when they rinsed their mouths and washed their hands, and here, too, even in the vicinity of the water-trough, which had been constructed rather hastily, in truly slapdash fashion, and into which the sacred water, arriving from an undisclosed location, trickled out from a rubber hose, they experienced the same disorder as on the path leading here, which really made them uncertain as to why this was not important in such a sacred Shintō ritual, but not much time remained to them to reflect upon this, because they were already above, on the back part of the stage rising into the heights, namely, despite his better judgment, Kawamoto-san too climbed up after his companion, who with not a single word, had just ran up the stairs all at once, and already he stood there by the balustrade on the stage, as if he had personally been invited; apart from him and Kawamoto-san, coming after him in the great confusion, only the organizers wearing armbands were climbing up and down, and the organizers looked at them too in the great confusion, wondering, well what are these two doing here, from where however these two could see quite well what this giant stage that didn't belong here was good for, that is to say they could see that there was room for them, that there was room for the numerous privileged guests, for whom two hundred chairs or so had already been prepared, of course who knew exactly how many there were, in any event, a vast number of chairs arranged nicely in rows on the planks, inclining downward toward the two selected hinoki trees, that divided in two the populous camp of the privileged guests; they were already milling around, one group facing one tree, the second group facing the other, this was essentially the principle behind the arrangement, but then it already became apparent to the bustling organizers that they were not privileged guests, they could no longer, accordingly, remain here, this European and this Japanese could not remain among the occupiers of the chairs, namely they had no business whatsoever up here on the stage, and would have none, and in a split second they were cast out, and thus—to Kawamoto's greatest relief—they were compelled, as were the other nonprivileged guests, to climb back to the ravaged ground, going around the stage, up to a clearing, where they were ordered to go, and where in a tight group Miwa-san's people were already gathering, that is the already familiar faces of the frantic columns of television reporters, photographers, and journalists, and that meant that they could be placed together obliquely facing the stage, more precisely, facing the ever-increasing number of guests gathering there, obliquely facing the hypothesized presence of the priests, and thus obliquely facing the two sacrificial trees as well, because what else could you call them other than sacrificial, just like those other trees, eighteen in number, upon which the Akasawa forest rangers had honed their skills, as this special operation was presented only every twenty years, and for that reason required the white-garbed workers, who over time lost some of the freshness of their craft, to train again in the last few days—at least eighteen was the number given by one of the workers, who seemed to be some kind of mid-level supervisor, entrusted with the oversight of the iron cable that tautened each of the two trees from three directions, holding them in place, and who, in addition to this supervisory role, naturally had just enough time to readily answer the questions of the curious journalists, as well as those of the two friends among them, eighteen enormous hinoki trees had been felled, the cable supervisor repeated, all the same they had to practice here, he said, mistakes could not be made, and certainly all of them were fairly nervous as to whether the cutting would really succeed without error, as of course every participant knew full well that there could be no question whatsoever of any mistake, here everything had to be done perfectly, as he expressed it, which meant, as he related, that the trunks of the two trees ultimately had to cross each other at precisely five meters from the upper part of the trunk, as it were, the two trees had to lie upon each other after being felled, the one had to fall down onto the other, he explained, but this contact, this intersecting, had to take place at a precisely given height, otherwise the ceremony does not come about, and the Misoma-Hajime-sai must be repeated, so it is no wonder, sighed the cable supervisor, if—eighteen trees here, eighteen trees there—the two teams of woodcutters, specially trained, but over a period of twenty years understandably out of practice, were still fairly nervous, and that could be seen on his person, he himself was really nervous enough, sweat trickled down his brow, and he gazed flustered here and there, so that finally the journalists began reassuring him, don't be afraid, everything will be fine, if you have practiced so much, there will be no problems, and this individual looked at them with such gratitude that they felt inclined to console him even more, but there was no time for this as something seemed to be occurring in the direction of the seats on the stage, the reporters therefore scanned the seats of the stage more and more, the two of them as well began to observe the mysteriously uniform mass of the exclusive highly ranked guests gathered on the stage, where about two hundred men in identical dark-blue, somewhat rustic-looking suits were sitting, it seemed that this attire could have been mandatory as everyone was wearing it, suits and shoes from the 1970s, they looked at these suits and shoes, then they looked at the faces, and they tried to discover a more well-known celebrity—a factory owner, a banker, a noted politician—but from here it wasn't really possible to make out the necessary details of a face *like that* on the ceremonial stage in the Akasawa forest during the Misoma-Hajime-sai, then they observed that on the incoming side, young Shintō priests were carrying freshly carpentered boxes to the stairs leading up to the stage, then after them, on the path in a line, appeared the mute and stern-gazed group of the priests who would lead the ceremony, but they too were clearly agitated about something, because now and then one or the other stumbled on the precarious surface of the shaving-strewn path, in their high heavy black-lacquered priest's footwear, and so in general it could be said that everyone seemed serious and flustered, if not stricken by stage fright, even the male gathering of the exclusive guests was like that, as if the entire Misoma-Hajime-sai itself were suggesting that no one could be certain of how the proceedings would go, there were rules, and these rules had to be followed faithfully, without error, as if there were general doubt concerning this; something of this was perceptible in the atmosphere from here in front, from the clearing, where they sat among the journalists on the ground; then a shorter line appeared, a new group of priestly persons, who clearly now could only be the very highest leadership, although no one here knew who was the guji, the negi, the kujo, or who the joo was, or the mei, the sei, and who the choki was, or if everyone here even had received a mandate to take part, which was unlikely, there was total uncertainty among the journalists, they kept asking each other, although whoever was asked just laughingly shook his head, in a word no one knew anything, and somehow one had the feeling that the same bewilderment was felt among the chairs below them on the stage as well, when at last at the head of a little troop of priests the chief personage appeared, everyone recognized her features and her bearing, namely the elderly sister of the Emperor had appeared, the saishu of the Ise Shrine; she moved slowly along the path, completed the purification ceremony by the water trough, then with perceptible strain due to her age, she dragged herself up the stairs, and withdrew to the middle of the first row on the stage, taking her place there, which was so to speak the sign that the Misoma-Hajime-sai could begin, the highest-ranking priests were already kneeling, holding out their shakus in front of themselves in front of the hinoki on the left, then crossing over, in front of the hinoki on the right, so that the first part of the Misoma-Hajime-sai ceremony would be completed in both places, of which however it was impossible to understand, or hear anything, although there was silence at the ceremony, namely that here there was no music—the high screeching of the hichiriki and behind it the sounds of the ryūteki, and the shō, protracted and weeping, present at nearly every Shintō ceremony, could not be heard—the forest was enveloped in complete silence, the priest leading the ceremony, Kuniaki Kuni, mutely performed the ritual with his entourage behind him, and only at times was the rustle of robes audible, as the priest turned, stood up, then kneeled down, bowing again to the ground, because from that place, from where they were observing, this is largely what they saw, and this much was largely comprehensible from the ceremony: the priest kneeling in front of the tree, bowing down, getting up, bowing again with the shaku in his hands, behind him the entourage motionlessly kneeling, then they too at times bowed down and got up, and sat straight-backed and motionless again, this is mainly what happened in front of one tree, and mainly in front of the other as well, they had crossed from one to the other, after which the priest leading the ceremony took out from the wooden chests, carried up to the stage, and placed on the little tables slowly, and somewhat hesitantly, the food offerings: the shinsen, rice and saké, fish and vegetables, fruit and sweets, salt and water, they were placed as offerings on the little tables, and then this was repeated in front of the other tree as well, and then it was already possible to see, readying themselves at the bottom of the staircase, the white-garbed woodcutters, who at the given sign proceeded onto the stage, and splitting up into two groups placed themselves around the two trees, but first just the group on the left began their work, while the other group stood motionlessly and waited for their turn to come, and the two of them, the Western guest and the Japanese host, both felt that with this the entire Misoma-Hajime-sai was saved, because up until the point when the woodcutters appeared, it was simply impossible to take this entire Misoma-Hajime-sai seriously, no matter how sacrilegious the thought seemed to them, they were of the opinion, and they even discussed this between themselves in subdued voices, that it was the complete absence of sacredness, or a crushing of the sacredness of the departed taking place on the stage, because the whole thing was so untrue, and there was no credibility to anything, not one movement, not a single gesture of the chief priest, the dai-gūji, or of the kneeling priests behind him, betrayed anything but a tense indecisiveness for everything to go well, for there not to be any mistakes; sheer exertion, this was all that could be seen in every movement and ritual gesture, but not the rite itself, and this atmosphere characterized the spectators as well, the privileged invitees, those supporters who had clearly arrived with generous financial pledges: a tense indecisiveness, thus the movements and the gestures were not the movements and gestures of faith and devotion but those of fear; a fear that somehow it would become visible that here nothing was true, not true, not sincere, not open, and not natural: well, what was missing was exactly that which was the very essence of Shintō, this is what they thought, and this is what they both discussed, concealing themselves among the journalists, when the work began, and with which everything was suddenly saved, because from this point on, the entire gathering watched the operation for close to two hours with bated breath, they watched, and they could not believe their eyes, because what these simple woodcutters, the specially trained workers of the Akasawa forest preserve, were doing, was true and pure, and credible and natural; an art was revealed in their movements, for that matter, in their movements was a very ancient art, and it occurred in such a way that they did not merely fall to the trees with their axes, but employed a particular method, in which of the group of nine, altogether three workers used their axes at once, they always worked in this group of three, surrounding the tree as they stood on the stage, and they did not just begin to chop away in a circle, say from one side, but all three of them together began to chop three holes with their axes, all told, three holes on three evenly spaced balance points of the circumference of the tree, and they did not broaden these cuts, but deepened them, so that accordingly, they cut into the tree from three directions, the location of which was determined by the leader of the group, and particularly in such a way that the tree stood in the direction of the desired pitch, the leader leaned his back against the trunk of the tree, he measured with his arms a distance on this trunk, and with that a point; then another and then another, then he showed these three points, where the holes had to be, to the others, and they already raised their axes, and when the group of three workers grew tired from the axe blows, they stood aside, and three rested workers stood in their place and continued the work so that the three groups alternated with each other, and the three holes grew deeper; and as the two of them watched in the great silence, in which the only sound was the melody of the echoing axe blows, as they watched them from the circle of journalists both began to feel—and they spoke of this again and again—that these workers were undertaking the work they learned to do with hairsbreadth precision, but they did not know, they had not the slightest idea, why what they were doing was exactly the way it was, and mainly they did not know that with every movement as they raised the axe, as it fell backward and then struck down, as they accordingly deepened the three holes until they met and became adjacent with each other at one point in the trunk's inner part, namely that they were repeating—and with hairsbreadth precision—the momentum, the direction, the strength of the movements of their ancestors, in a word, the order, just as those ancestors had only just repeated the movements of their own predecessors, so that now, the Western friend whispered over to his companion, that is to say every movement of each worker, and every component of every movement—its momentum, its arc, its striking down—is one thousand and three hundred years old, they are artists, Kawamoto-san nodded enthusiastically, too, and only his glittering eyes betrayed that he too understood what the other was thinking, and he too, just like the other, was inspired by the thought; they watched as the cuts in the trees were deepened with the dull rhythm of the axe blows, they saw as they all then met at an inner point, the leader of the group of the woodcutter-artists, motioning, the others stepping back, a few shouts were heard, and it was as if this leader had uttered a short prayer, finally he himself struck the tree a few times at one spot on the trunk, but the two visitors could not see, as from here the figure of the chief priest was in front of that of the woodcutter-artist, at which point the tree gave a cracking groan, then it slowly began to lean downward, and then it was already down below on the ground, its peak turned a little toward the other tree; then someone began to relate, Kawamoto interpreting as well, that the true point of this ancient way of cutting down the tree was that in this way the position of the felled tree could be determined precisely, could be directed with a precision measured in centimeters; Kawamoto translated the words of an older journalist to his friend, but he was just watching the entire thing dumbstruck, mainly, when around the other tree, where the woodcutters had proceeded, the same thing happened, and the tree fell exactly where it had to, that is five meters below the peak of the other one on the ground, so there lay the chosen hinoki trees, and then

Kuniaki Kuni stepped closer to one of them, and then before the trunk of the other felled tree, and, if it was possible, the silence only grew deeper than it had been before; Kuniaki Kuni raised the broad piece of paper with handwriting upon it to the height of his head, and there was even deeper silence, and no one moved, the sister of the Emperor—the saishu of the Ise shrine—bowed her head, and at this point so did all of the privileged invited guests, and as they bowed their heads so did the journalists in the clearing facing the stage, Kawamoto was only able to whisper to his friend: "norito" in exhortation, and he followed the others, and the Western friend did the same, but he did not know of course what had happened and what was happening, of course he didn't know why, he stood with his head bowed, and he didn't know, just as he would never know what he might have heard if he had understood, but well how could he have understood, for what was audible from the mouth of the priest was, apart from him, not understood by many even among the Japanese, because these words, spoken for the first time at least one thousand five hundred years ago and since then with no variations whatsoever were takaamahara ni kami tsumari masu, kamurogi kamuromi no mikoto wo mochite, sumemioya kamu izanagi no mikoto, tsukushi no himuka no tachihana no odo no, ahagi hara ni misogi harai tamau toki ni, narimaseru haraidono ookami tachi, moromoro no magagoto tsumi kegare wo, harai tamae kiyome tamae to mousu koto no yoshi wo, tamatsu kami kunitsu kami yaoyorozu no kamitachi tomomi, ameno huchikoma no mimi furitatete kikoshimese to, kashikomi kashikomi mo maosu, and so on, they listened, hardly able to hear anything at all, as if the dai-gūji were reciting nearly mutely, then he folded up the piece of paper, stepped back, prayed before the one felled tree, then knelt, prostrated, then everyone raised their heads, the priests repeated the norito in front of the other felled hinoki as well, then the priests departed from the stage in order, and they could still be seen as they proceeded in front of the water trough, finally they vanished at the first bend in the path, but then the Emperor's relation stood up and she herself left the stage with her entourage, followed by the invitees, and this was the sign, because not only did the others remain there, but everyone pressed forward toward the stage to try to get as close as possible to the woodcutters, who now came forward to shake the hands extended to them, and they were happy, all of them were smiling, and they were touched, and the joy did not want to leave them, they gave everyone some of the wood shavings from the sacred trees, the two friends also went over to them, shook hands with one of the woodcutters, and received a handful of wood shavings pressed into their palms, and it was just then that they noticed, only then did they perceive what an astonishingly powerful fragrance was everywhere, the particular fragrance of the two felled hinoki trees practically burst onto the section of the forest like a cloud, it drew them in, what an extraordinarily sweet wondrous fragrance, rhapsodized the Western friend, it is, nodded Kawamoto-san, because he was happy that his friend was not just experiencing disappointment again, and they would not return home beaten down, although that really happened too; they drove back to Kiso-Fukushima in a decidedly liberated mood, the enthusiasm of the Western friend—at least for a while—somewhat rubbing off on Kawamoto-san, although he was mostly grateful to fate that no larger misfortunes had taken place, they had not gotten mixed up in any sort of unpleasantness, which however could still be counted upon, as it was only afternoon; they were for the most part discussing the norito, gliding along in the traffic on the Meishin Expressway, the norito, the Shintō prayer uttered by the faithful in complete silence, the recitation upon which the benevolence and receptiveness of the Kami addressed in the prayer is wholly dependent—if, that is, it is uttered faultlessly in every instance where it is recited—that was all he, Kawamoto, knew, he said, apologizing while still in the car, because the norito is the most sacred of prayers of the Japanese, he explained further, when he saw on his friend's face that he would like to know more, or, as he expressed it, to know as much as could possibly be known, and although Kawamoto-san enlarged upon it for a while inasmuch as he could recall from his school assignments: the norito is connected with the belief that the uttered word has power, but only the word uttered correctly, faultlessly, beautifully has the power to bring good; every time the opposite occurs, the word will instead signify something bad for the community, that is all that Kawamoto-san said: then in a strange confusion, a dispirited mood suddenly weighing down upon him, he became silent, and he did not wish to speak of this or of anything else, time imperceptibly slipped by, and they were already in Kyōto, there was much traffic, but still they made their way, Kawamoto however could see that due to their early arrival his friend really didn't feel like going home, and so he proposed showing him some of the more unknown inner districts of the city, but then they sat down instead in a ryokan, and they had a fine meal, finally they sat on the terrace of one of the bars on the Kamo River, they watched the river, the couples strolling across the bridges, and Kawamoto Akio listened in ever-growing agony, as his friend had already been speaking for a while about how he would like to continue his research, how he wished to return one more time to Ise, because he would like to talk with the carpenters from Naikū, he would like, namely, to know more, to know everything about how the team of carpenters prepares for each Shikinen Sengū, how do the felled hinoki cypresses arrive there, how does the operation proceed, how do they prepare the hinoki, and how are the dazzlingly simple, pure buildings of the shrine constructed, namely, he explained, he felt that perhaps here, on this path, he must take one more step, because it was obvious that the ceremonies of the Shintō faith were completely uninteresting and had ended up in a woeful state, still though, it could be that the Shintō was still in there somewhere, concealed within the invisible world of the everyday, because surely if this Shintō was still to be found in an ancient movement, as they had experienced today, an ancient movement which had been preserved for centuries, there could be other surprises here too, oh no, thought Kawamoto-san, surprises, most likely there will be some, he nodded on the terrace of the bar on the bank of the Kamo River, and deep in thought he gazed at the people strolling from Shijō, flowing into the Gion, all the while convinced that no, this was enough already, they had been able to see the Misoma-Hajime-sai, they had received permission for that, but the Jingū Shicho would not give them any kind of permission for anything else, yet still to speak with the miya-daikus, yet still, to find out about the toryō, the miya-daikus, and through them the entire construction-leadership of the Shikinen Sengū, my god, how could he explain, brooded Kawamoto, that all of this is not possible already, it was not possible to put the Jingū Shicho in an awkward position with yet another request, even the first one already had gone beyond the limit of the desired norms here, but the Jingū Shicho had been magnanimous, it had given them permission to observe the Misoma-Hajime-sai; anything beyond this, however, beyond expressing their gratitude in a letter to the Jingū Shicho office, to which—Kawamoto tried to get his friend to understand what the correct procedure would be here, they could even add a gift, for example—well, anything else beyond this was unimaginable, but his companion, as if it were just a topic of debate, immediately rejected the thought that he, at this point—as he expressed it—should give up, come on already, don't be afraid, you can smear all the discourteous things on me later, he said and laughed, but Kawamoto did not really feel like laughing at this, as his guest was already saying that tomorrow they would try to contact Miwa-san by telephone, and they would get to the carpenter's workshop at Naikū, the location of which, thanks to the previously well-studied map of the shrine, they were familiar with, we'll get in, the guest looked at Kawamoto encouragingly: but not only was it impossible to encourage him, from his constrained smile, and how he suddenly changed the topic to something else, it became clear that even the plan of this latest "action," as his friend put it, oppressed him, and in general he was beginning to be worn down by his Western friend's—of course, from his friend's perspective, entirely natural—audacity, he knew he would never be able to explain to him that *this* was not possible here, and not only regarding the Jingū Shicho, but . . . regarding himself as well, one could not conduct oneself this way toward a host, this was very unpleasant, to have such a friend to whom it clearly never once occurred, because looking at the thing from his world view, it would hardly occur to him to consider just how difficult this whole matter was for him, Kawamoto—that he was obliged on the one side to try to satisfy the requirements of his guest and in this case, those of the Jingū Shicho; on one side there was the guest, whose needs had to be met, on the other side the prescribed obligatory forms that could not be transgressed, this was impossible to fulfill, and then so what now? Kawamoto brooded on the terrace next to the Kamo River, what should he do: he brooded needlessly, however, he fretted senselessly, and it was in vain that he showed something of this brooding and this fretting, however discourteous it was, the guest noticed nothing, he couldn't have noticed anything, and thus there was nothing else Kawamoto could do but to dial Miwa-san's number in Ise, he did so early the next morning at his friend's tenacious entreaty, then he dialed it again one hour later, because he got the reply that the person he was looking for was not in, he dialed, then an hour and he dialed again, and yet another and yet another, his friend sat next to him with ever-increasing resolve, and ever-growing impatience, so that, well, it was actually a relief when he finally got through to Miwa-san, because at least he was freed from this resolve and this impatience, although it was true that with Miwa-san, however, another form of torture commenced, one in which he had to explain to him that no, what the Jingū Shicho had shown them of its good intentions and magnanimousness had not been enough for them, they would like to become acquainted with the workshops of Naikū as well, they would like to see how the trees were prepared, how they sawed and planed the wood, and then on the basis of what plans did they build the shrine buildings, Miwa-san of course, showed surprise, and his voice suddenly echoed back from a distance, he would see what he could do, and they should once again submit a request, he recommended, in perceptibly strained tones, and the Jingū Shicho would decide if permission would be granted, and with that the conversation came to an end, and Kawamoto-san felt that his arm was about to fall off, it had grown so heavy while he was on the telephone, as he had suffered the entire process of continually bowing and scraping whereas his friend, when he informed him of what Miwa-san had said, became almost feverishly excited, and said, just wait, you'll see, we'll get into the Naikū carpenters' workshop, and Kawamoto-san in the end did not even understand what was going on with this ever more complicated affair, because his guest turned out to be right, and already the second week after the submission of the application that immediately followed the telephone conversation, Miwa-san telephoned *him*, with the information that they should be at such a time at the main entrance to the Naikū, a certain Iida-san would accompany them to the carpenters' workshop, they could meet with two miya-daikus, moreover, the possibility of a conversation with the toryō was extended to them, they could take photographs, but could not use recording devices during the conversations, and he apologized for that in his own name and that of the Jingū Shicho, but this was the decision, he wished them a very pleasant time in Naikū, Miwa-san said goodbye, and he had already put down the receiver and they were already on the train to Ise; no, Kawamoto Akio clearly did not understand this, he was, however, even more anxious as to what would happen now, it was two o'clock in the afternoon, there they stood at the main entrance to the Naikū, the sun was scorching, it could have been at least forty degrees celsius, and at exactly two o'clock a short, fat young person, Iida Sato, really came for them, and while the sweat was pouring down off of him in his black suit in the scorching sun, he took them to a gated entrance in the northern part of the grounds of the Naikū, this was the entrance to the Naikū carpentry workshops, but—as Iida-san expressed it a little theatrically—this was also the symbolic entrance to the Shikinen Sengū, and every such banality in relation to the Shikinen Sengū just began to pour out of him: by the time they reached the office of the workshop area, Iida-san recited nearly word for word every single sentence that was in the promotional brochure, which the Jingū Shicho had printed to popularize the Shikinen Sengū, and they grew so used to Iida-san being the kind of person who always speaks without interruption that they didn't even pay attention to him, they just nodded politely, yet he—enthusiastically and with the serious look of an expert— just kept talking and talking, while they, in the meantime, noticed that on the left side of the road leading to the office building, numerous hinoki tree trunks were floating in a kind of canal-like body of water widening out into a lake, but of course, Iida-san didn't know the reason for this, they would get an answer once inside, and they sat around a table in one of the rooms of the office building, where two miya-daikus were waiting for them, a middle-aged one, and a fresh-faced youth, it seemed that the older one was the teacher of the younger one, in any event somehow they belonged together, this was evident, although at the same time there was no sign of the master-apprentice relation between them, the fresh-faced youth sat just as decisively and proudly in his chair and answered the questions as did his older companion, both of them in the Jingū's white work-overalls, and they gazed at them with a fairly suspicious yet at the same time somewhat curious look in their eyes, and in the beginning they didn't really seem to understand what this strange pair wanted from them, this gaijin and this fidgety Japanese from Kyōto, so they didn't even really respond to the questions put to them, instead they just warded the questions off, as if they were avoiding them, and they tried to give the most inane answers possible, particularly the older miya-daiku, he, as if he were laughing at them, was more and more aloof, and observed the two visitors with a somewhat derisive smile, he observed them, and uttered his replies from an ever-increasing distance, while incessantly looking up at the clock on the wall, so that, well, the fresh-faced youth was the one to say something occasionally, for example that the hinoki cypresses float in that canal to where the water naturally flows from the sacred river of the Jingū, from the Izusu River, because they *dry out* there for two years, that happens first, the younger carpenter continued, they bring the hinoki trunks, trimmed and stripped of their bark and branches, and these, he added, are delivered continuously every single day, already from the beginning of the Misoma-Hajime-sai, they are immediately placed in the canal, and they really float there, they are soaked for two years, but as to the visitors' question as to how is it possible to dry wood in water, he did not betray anything, because the older one took up the thread of conversation, he announced that every single piece for the Shikinen Sengū was prepared here in this workshop, for Naikū and for Gekū, and with that he fell silent, he crossed his arms over his chest, glanced up at the clock, then looked at Iida-san, and it appeared in any event that he wished to demonstrate to the employee of the Shicho just how much he did not have time for idle chatter here, he was haughty, he was uncooperative, and he was increasingly deflecting the questions as soon as the Western friend began to formulate them, because of course he was posing the questions, Kawamoto-san, as always, only assumed the role of interpreter, he was trying with every possible means, with his body and his posture, to make his friend realize: this conversation must immediately come to an end, and then it was not drawn out for too much longer, after a while, his friend also grew weary of asking in vain, he was not getting any real answers to anything, so that at last he got up from the table, at which point all the others jumped up as well, the two carpenters accepted the gifts that had been brought but didn't even look at them, and already they were gone, so if it was going to go like this then they had come here for nothing, the Western friend noted in subdued tones, but Iida-san heard, and in order to pacify them, he informed them that the person they were about to meet was someone, as he put it, whom worldly beings hardly ever saw, because he was the sacred person of the Shikinen Sengū, they didn't even refer to him as the director of construction here, in his case they used the old expression, and they called him toryō, everyone addressed him like that, and he enjoyed truly great esteem, even if of course, like for everyone else here, the Jingū Shicho was the lord above him, although as for that, the current toryō was the kind of person who did not really acknowledge anyone as being above himself, only his kamis of the Heavens and Earth, and in the very first place, Amaterasu Ōmikami, the sun goddess, Iida-san explained, Amaterasu Ōmikami, the resident of the shrine in Naikū, whose grandson, he continued proficiently, Ninigi no Mikoto, descended to the Earth in order to render judgment upon the squabbling people, and to deter them from further squabbling, he struck down his trident in South Kyūshū, where he had landed, into the peak of a mountain called Takachiho, so that people would remember him, and ever since then the trident is still there, he explained and he did not continue to speak about the first Emperor, though it appeared he would have been happy to do so, the visitors however did not ask, and since it seemed he was waiting for that, he leaned back in his chair slightly offended, pursed his lips, and sank into a brief transitional silence, and that is how the time passed in the office of the Naikū carpentry workshop; Iida-san scratched his head, he went out, he came back in, he looked at the clock, right away, he kept saying to the guests, and sat down only to get up and go out again, and while these long minutes of waiting were hard for Iida-san to endure, particularly without talking, he returned again and again to describing the character of the toryō, whom, the two friends had the impression—it was not difficult to figure this out—Iida-san did not know in the least, only from hearsay, and he was relaying this to them, practically elevating this illustrious personage to the status of a demi-god, thus they were informed that this meeting was an entirely extraordinary gift—and he greatly stressed the word purezento, that is, gift—of the Jingū Shicho Public Relations Department, extraordinary, because in the first place, he babbled on, the toryō had work to do, the work had begun, and he, bearing full responsibility for all operations in his one single person, had to be everywhere at once, every work-process was concentrated in his hands, without him not a single planing-machine could be switched on, not one single cut could be chiseled by anyone, but one must realize—Iida-san lowered his voice, and here, even in this somewhat air-conditioned room, he dabbed his sweaty forehead again with a white handkerchief, after which he folded it up meticulously—one must realize that his task, of the first order, or how should he say it, said Iida-san, his immediate task is to separate the tree trunks that are worked on according to a precise order, because the mikoshi was constructed from one kind of material—this was obvious, wasn't it—of the wondrous hinoki family, and the buildings from yet other materials, and a different material was used for constructing the walls than the columns—that too was understandable, wasn't it?—but not only that, Iida-san gasped for air—the thoughts were rushing out one after the other from his head with such speed, and he wanted to share them with the guests with the exact same speed, so that he could hardly catch his breath—not only that, he raised his voice, and here he had to state again that the toryō's very first task was that of drawing, apart from him no one else could draw, that was the most sacred and exclusive knowledge of a toryō, and he, the current one was particularly, extraordinarily gifted at knowing what to sketch onto the lower and upper parts of the evenly sawed-off tree trunk, how the saw should then proceed as it cut columns or planks from the hinoki-trunks, how finely the mechanical or the handheld planes should run along them, because his drawing decides how a column shall emerge from the tree trunk, moreover, it also decides what individual columns will serve which part of the building, and then in what function they will serve the higher interests of the shrine; Iida-san was so swept up that he nearly expressed himself in poetry, and who knows where this rapturous ardor for the toryō would have stopped if the person in question had not stepped in himself, true, not a demi-god, but an elderly man with snow-white hair, with a thin, tall build and enormous dark-brown eyes, himself wearing the attire of the others, that is white overalls: a dear, friendly old man, with a smiling look in his eyes, whose clothes still had sawdust on them, which he began to brush off himself; when after his entry, the customary presentation of gifts, mutual introductions, and the exchange of visiting cards—he said, laughing, he did not have any such thing on hand while working—Iida-san offered him a place to sit down, and signaling what an honor he felt it to be here and to be able to meet such prestigious interested parties sent by the Jingū Shicho, the toryō sat down cautiously so as not to begrime the chair too much, and then in time forgetting all about that, he immediately relaxed, sitting with his elbows leaning on the table, namely that he had learnt from Iida-san that these two were not visitors that had been sent by the Jingū Shicho but that they had been *permitted*, and they merely wanted him to tell them about the Shikinen Sengū, about the preparations, the trees, the work process—his eyes glittered gaily as he then began to speak, the words arose from him quickly, as one who lives in the impassioned shadow of great things, and who has stepped out of it just for a short time in order to speak of these things; but then would have to go back, go back to his passion, this aspect of him characterized the entire conversation: that he was burning now in a kind of truly great affair, and could not think of anything else, ever since he had been designated; only about this, the 71st Shikinen Sengū; and in the first place, he did everything possible to steer the conversation away from his own person, which they asked about first, because all the same, what could he say, he was a simple carpenter, a miya-daiku and that he remained so, he explained to the guests, only that the Jingū Shicho had honored him by naming him toryō, and as the toryō, he had now become a carpenter who bore a great, very great responsibility to the Jingū Shicho, to the Naikū and to the Gekū, but, most of all to Amaterasu Ōmikami; I am a simple person, stated this simple person, and he laughed at them and answered everything they asked very seriously, and gave them answers that cut straight to the heart of the matter, and if he felt that perhaps they were having a problem understanding something, or if he felt the topic immediately at hand to be of special importance, he repeated his sentences, even several times over, and at such times his brow darkened, now looking deeply into the eyes of the first, and now the second guest, and only when he was convinced that they understood what he was saying did he laugh again and wait for the next question, and the next, but after a while he digressed in order to speak of what he considered to be important, although they hadn't asked him about it, because they had begun with why the Shikinen Sengū takes place every twenty years, to which he replied that well, because the Jingū has to be rejuvenated, and according to the elders the time for that comes exactly every twenty years, for the Jingū goes forward in time with man, and the gods too do not age, thus in the eternally youthful Jingū, there is a place for the eternally youthful gods, this is what he could say altogether as to the reason, he smiled at them, and well, how does someone become a toryō: it doesn't matter what you say, it doesn't matter how beautifully you speak, the only thing that matters is how you work, and of course age and practical experience play a role, not just professional, but human practical experience as well, and so it goes on from there—he gestured with his hand to show

how it went on from there—but the essential thing, he raised his index finger, and looked at them very seriously with his enormous dark brown eyes, the essential thing is what is in your heart, the god looks and sees, and knows everything exactly, the god, he glanced at them with an impish look, and the Jingū Shicho too: after the latter remark those present, with the chuckling leadership of Iida-san, replied with complicit understanding laughter, and as for how someone becomes a good miya-daiku, that too, said the toryō, is very easy to understand, because here, in their native Japan, but especially here in the Jingū, the custom is such that the master does not teach, but that the disciple observes the master, and that is how he was with his master as well, he observed how his master, his oyakata, went about his work, he intensely scrutinized every movement, he watched what he was doing and how he was doing it and he imitated him, we call this, he explained, the "me de manabu" way, if someone is teaching, then it will certainly never be possible to learn anything from that person, this is what it's like, he nodded in affirmation and his audience nodded, too, as from this point, all three had been transformed into keen auditors, the personality, the directness, the friendly nature of the toryō, his frankness and openness, had quickly swept them off their feet, even Iida-san, who at the beginning, striving to ensure that the authority of the Jingū Shicho would not remain latent for a single moment in this situation, he himself, his countenance serious, impeded the toryō with questions, dabbing away in the strain of his great task at his fat head, from his skull to his neck; but then even he forgot all this and, like the other two, really listened to the toryō's words enthusiastically, as when, for example, he began to speak of that process of drawing, namely that it is here that everything begins and is determined, that is the essence of the entire activity of the toryō, namely that only he knows how to draw, and he only came to know this after having studied the drawing plans in the Shicho during half of a lifetime, of these, that is to say the drawing plans, there were altogether three kinds, the really old ones, the old ones, and the newer ones—for example the "kirikumu zushi," to follow this and draw it onto the wood is a frequent solution, a person, he demonstrated something with wide gestures in the air, looks at the old drawing plans and he stores them away in his head, that's what he did as well, as for books themselves, of which there were an innumerable quantity in the Shicho—he made a droll, wry face—well, books never help, because books are *someone else's experience*, they unfortunately can never help the toryō, only his own experiences can be of help to him, he must always try everything out for himself, of course, before he actually becomes a toryō, because then he cannot try anything out any more, just think about it, a toryō cannot make a mistake, if a drawing is not executed correctly on the tree trunk there will be huge problems, because then you might as well just toss out the entire tree, but you can't just throw out a hinoki like that, they had seen already, at the Misoma-Hajime-sai, what a tree goes through by the time it gets here, you can't be tossing them out just like that, every single hinoki is a soul, and this soul must be dealt with very carefully, firmly, very carefully, and because of that a toryō cannot make a mistake, more precisely he may never make a mistake, he gazed again into their eyes, then after a brief pause spoke about how in the first place everything has to be there in his head and in his heart, then he has to measure very precisely, look at the drawing plans continuously, and only after that carry out his sumi-zuke, that is the drawing on the tree trunk; ink, every toryō uses a special ink, of course he did as well, and still even with all that, it is not certain that all will be well, because it can happen that the daiku may not cut according to the drawing, meaning that, he explained, he may not cut with hairsbreadth accuracy along the line, then the problem is just as huge, and this can happen in principle, but in reality it never happens, because a daiku never makes mistakes, everyone here, every one of his colleagues had been through the most outstanding training, all of them, nearly all of them could be a toryō, at the very least all of the older ones could, unconditionally, everyone here understood every single phase of work to that degree, but there is no stampede, he laughed, lest they might think that in front of the door, where the selection of the toryō is taking place, there would be some kind of major fisticuffs, to be a toryō is a great, a very great responsibility, one is not only a toryō by day, but by night as well, when he is asleep, even then, he has no family, no amusements, no rest, no illnesses, no holidays, entirely up until the point that the Shikinen Sengū is fully completed, he said; then again he returned to the explanation of the drawing, so that they would understand his words without fail, accordingly the drawing, I look at the drawing, I look at it continuously, and I only draw on the basis of that, but I don't draw without a drawing plan right away, because then I can make a mistake, and if I make a mistake, it will not be possible to fix, to look at the drawing plan, measure accurately, and to draw accurately, it is only possible like that, and that was exactly what he did, and what he had not mentioned as of yet, he raised his index finger again, was the eye, because the eye has a huge role to play when using a tool, to see if everything is going well, and if the result is good, this must be examined with the eye, it wasn't like in Europe where some kind of tool was used for that; but the eye, and then—he lent forward above the table toward the guests—the tools, the toryō always makes his own tools, for example, he inspects the tree and he makes the tools *for that tree*, yes, he makes his own tools as well, every single one by himself, even if he is working on something at home, he still always does this, then for the Shikinen Sengū it will be particularly so, because it is only worthwhile working with such tools that are really meant for the given raw wood, it is clear when the raw wood is there, you just have to look, and a person sees what kind of tree it is, and then how he can make the tools for it, but machine tools are used as well, he says, because they don't look at whether the tool is new or old, but instead which is the most perfect to work with, he will show them later—he gestured to somewhere behind his back—how it all works; of course, mechanical tools, these are only used in the arabori phase, that is with the raw wood, not for the fine work; then it is time for the hand tools, and well there are no changes, no changes whatsoever, they do everything exactly the same as they did for the 70th Shikinen Sengū, and that was just like the 69th, say the older toryōs and so forth, going back to the very old times, and as to whether the new shrine is similar to the old one or is the same? he repeated the question, well, this seems like a difficult question, but it isn't difficult, because the answer is simple, that is, the new building is the same as the old one, and as to why this is so, it is because the deity who resides there, Amaterasu Ōmikami, is the same, it is as simple as that, and that is how you must think of it, because even though the whole thing is rebuilt again, and the Three Treasures re-created for every Shikinen Sengū, nothing ever changes, everything remains the same, you know—the toryō leaned again toward them above the table, with a gay expression—if I go over to one shrine or another to pray, already I can sense from the scent of the hinoki that everything is the same, and it is that way with me in life as well, the toryō nodded, his audience nodding in agreement, I think about it, and I feel that everything is the same, well that is what it is like, that is how I think, and that is how my master also thought, and the toryō before him as well, but now, the Western friend interrupted him, let's talk about the last day, what happens then; well, that too is very simple, the toryō spread his hands apart, because it goes like this, when all the materials are ready and beautiful, and the drying of the wood is as it should be, then the entire shrine is built, everything, but everything is built, assembled together, to see if it fits, if it is accurate, if it is correct, but all of this of course takes place within the workshop, and continuously, in the workshop, yes, because only human work can take place there; outside at the kodenchi, on the great day of the Shikinen Sengū, when they assemble the whole thing, there the work of the deities takes place, after that everything stands empty for one month, then it is tidied up for the last time and decorated, this however is the work of the priests, as is the final ceremony as well, before the sengyo, when they bring the deity from the old shrine, and then the people come, countless people come from all over Japan, and everyone prays, well it's like that, but if you'd like, said the toryō, I can enumerate again the whole thing from the beginning, that it all starts outside in the sacred forest of the Jingū Shicho, but you saw that in Akasawa: there we select the trees, that is the seizai, then comes the first drawing, the rough sketch, that is the sumi-kaki, this is followed by the drying process, which is followed by the kannabai, that is the mechanical planing, then there is another sumi-kaki, then they take, he explained patiently, the entire thing, all of the trees into the workshop, that is the individual tree trunks are divided up among the various storerooms—there are eight such storerooms here on the grounds of the workshop, four of them for Naikū, four of them for Gekū—so, there in the individual storerooms the toryō, that is to say myself, he pointed to himself, draws the sumi-zuke on the tree trunk, so I could say, he says, that I sumi-zukize them, then there is the drying, and then the daikus try to put together the individual shrines in the workshop, and they keep them all there, built, then comes the next, and they build that one, they keep that one, and then comes the next one, and so on, but then the Jingū Shicho issues a deadline, so they take them all apart, and they take them out to the grounds of Naikū and Gekū, and there they are constructed for the last time, things proceed in such a beautiful orderly manner during the Shikinen Sengū, the toryō lowered his voice, then he looked up at the wall clock, exactly one hour had gone by, and he said, one cannot work without a good heart, it was godly work that he was doing, therefore the chief mandate for him was that he must not be preoccupied with anything else, only with work, must not think of anything else, only work, he accordingly had to think correctly, he had to work correctly, when the guests yet asked him if the toryō's knowledge was concealed within his soul, he reflected a little upon this last question, then—like one who had forgotten what he had been asked—he said, *a good tree, that is the essential thing,* and with that he got up from the table, he bowed to the guests, indicating that the conversation had come to an end, and he offered to take them to the individual storerooms, which is what then occurred, Iida-san proceeding in front, having suddenly realized toward the end that he should have been representing the Jingū Shicho here in a more forceful manner, that is he became aware of having been somewhat pushed into the background, as events proceeded there inside the office, whereas he, as the representative of the Jingū Shicho, could not permit this, due to his rank and hierarchy, because of that Iida-san was now keeping abreast of the toryō with his rapid gait, with his own little roly-poly figure, his short rounded legs could hardly keep up, but he endeavored to do so with his round figure in the scorching heat, and he did keep up, and he withstood it, and they went forward like that, they in front and the two guests behind them, the toryō accordingly turning back to them now and then to explain what they were seeing, he went with them to all the eight storerooms, then he showed them, too, how finely the planing machine, to which the raw wood was entrusted, could cut, and he prepared a sheet of hinoki two meters wide, he ran the machine along it, and a fine strip of wood, hairsbreadth thin, was produced, curling before their eyes without breaking off anywhere, he looked at his guests with proud contentment, because they were of course gaping in amazement, and they touched the wood as if they could not believe this was possible, and they ran their fingers and ran them again along the planed piece of wood, they praised how much, but how astonishingly, how unbelievably smooth the surface was, then after this little demonstration concluded everyone received a piece from the hairsbreadth-thin strip of wood as a gift, at last only the farewells remained, the two guests bowed, the toryō bowed, then, lifting it up, he thanked them again and again for the purezento, which he had been carrying wedged under his arm during the entire walk, finally he bowed deeply to Iida-san as well, Iida-san just nodded at the toryō, and was already headed off to the door, with his own characteristic movements already waddling toward the exit like one who is in a great hurry, then when the guests caught up—it was exactly two o'clock—to their surprise he recommended that maybe they should eat something, he, as he remarked, had not been able to have lunch today for obvious reasons, and as they saw that their consent would be very gratifying to him, and that a negative response would leave him deeply embittered, they said yes, and went to a nearby restaurant recommended by Iida-san, and they ordered everything that Iida-san, as a local specialist, advised them to, and with that, when the last course had disappeared from the table, Iida-san, as if he been struck by a magic wand, was completely altered, changing from a stern, serious, and haughty bureaucrat into a dear, friendly, and good-natured young man, he began talking about his work, about how many, how very many important visitors had already been entrusted to him to show them the shrines, there had even been here—with him!—an actor from Scotland, he stated in meaningful tones, and he nearly hung onto his guests' reaction, to see what they would say to that, and when they praised his outstanding achievements, and prophesied a great future for him, he at last was appeased, and suddenly he began to talk about his family, and here too the words were flying off his tongue so quickly; and then he thought better of it and ordered two more local specialties, Kawamoto-san could hardly keep up with translating his words: he had an older sister, and a younger sister, he enumerated that the older sister was married already, and the couple lived in Kawasaki, the younger sister was still at home where he lived too, not too far away for that matter, Iida-san gestured to somewhere behind his back with the chopsticks, someone had to stay at home, his parents were old and sick, there had to be a man in the house, you understand, don't you, he asked, well, of course, the guests nodded, the family could not leave the sick parents all alone, he also thought so, said Iida-san approvingly, and then the two guests paid, and stepped out of the restaurant onto the street, he was already behaving in such a way as if they had become good friends and he said good-bye to them, sweet boy, said the Western friend, and watched smiling as Iida-san's roly-poly figure on those two rounded legs of his, teetering this way and that, grew distant, heading toward the Jingū Shicho along the street shimmering in the heat, but his companion didn't say anything to this, but instead began to speak about how ashamed he was that he could only show such a Jingū Shicho to his guest; of course, the meeting with the toryō, he hoped, had given him joy, but he, Kawamoto-san, asked to be forgiven for the events in the Jingū, which his friend of course had no idea of what to do with, he simply didn't know what to do with this abrupt change of mood in his host, because he, who had not been paying any attention to him at all, had been so utterly captivated by the toryō's entire being, that for hours now his host practically had not even existed, he was just an interpreter who was there, and who functioned invisibly and self-evidently, but who had no existence of his own, but now he suddenly stepped out of this non-existence, and not even just in any old way, namely it was as if something were bursting out of him, he spoke without pause, like someone who had been preparing this for a long time, maybe for days already, and it was already fairly strange that Kawamoto was speaking uninterruptedly, until now, that is, he had not uttered more than two or three sentences at a time, but rather listened to the other, now, however, he was dissecting the separate turns of fortune that had occurred to them with the Jingū Shicho, and was doing so even when, having reached the station, they bought their tickets to Kyōto and sat down on the platform, and not only that, but he even started up with Kohori-san as well, and asked to be excused for him, and for how they had to sleep in the car in Akasawa, he was very ashamed that things turned out like that, and he was ashamed that the ceremony in Akasawa had proceeded as it did, he was certain, he continued in the dreadful heat of the station, that his friend had been hoping for something else, and he surely must be disappointed now, and he, Kawamoto, regretted this so much that he simply did not know how to make it right, but the other just looked, and said nothing, and stared at him as he could not understand anything of what was going on, maybe the best thing, his friend continued, would be if they returned to Kyōto, and if he would permit him, as a way of saying farewell, as there were only two days left now, to go somewhere, to take him to a place that would perhaps meet with his liking, it wasn't much of a sight, just a little nothing, but perhaps the other would be glad for this, and this other just gaped at him, and now he was confused because he still could not understand what had happened with his friend, what this whole thing was all about, so that of course he agreed, and he thanked him for the offer, and all the way on the train he analyzed, to change the subject, the great beauty of the Shintō shrine, what a dazzlingly pure construction this was, how much elegance lay in its simplicities, in the lack of ornament and the infinite solicitude with which the materials were treated, although it was already evident that nothing could alter Kawamoto's mood, he just sat next to the window, and kept glancing out, as if speech would be very difficult for him right now, his friend sensed that the more he began to praise something, the gloomier his host became, he was completely bewildered, so that in his confusion he left off the conversation and thus the last kilometers back to Kyōto were spent in silence, and even afterward they didn't really know what to say to each other, as having reached the station they got onto bus number 208 headed homeward, which then became positively unpleasant, the confusion within them grew deeper and deeper, they lurched to and fro in the bus, which in addition was packed with a group of noisy American tourists, and they said not one word to each other, Kawamoto's complexion even changed, namely he was pale, as white as a sheet, his friend ascertained in fright; we get off here, Kawamoto said, and the guest found himself in the station of the famous Silver Temple: but they did not go toward the Temple, but suddenly turned off to the left on one of the roads leading up to it, and at another equally hidden point started heading somewhere on a somewhat neglected trail upward, up to the Daimonji mountain, as it immediately became apparent, and the whole thing was strange, Kawamoto said not one word the whole time, and his friend didn't want to start asking any questions, this must be the little surprise, so this is what he was talking about in Ise, he thought now, climbing after him, after the despondent, peculiar host, who was going on ahead of him, showing him, as it were, the way, and at times showing him where to step, because the path was becoming ever more steep and ever more rugged, and in the twilight he could hardly even see where to step, but Kawamoto was climbing upward with such determination, and due to this determination, he did not ask him even occasionally for help, to pull him up now and then on one of the tougher spots, he only sensed Kawamoto's back above, in front of him, and his attention was entirely focused on the path so was not to slip, not to fall, not to roll backward, smashing every bone in his body, because this already was no pleasant evening stroll, but real mountain climbing, one had to clutch here at this, grab there at that, a branch sticking out here, a larger rock edge there, and climb and climb upward, and all the while twilight was descending with great swiftness, as if a net were being cast down upon them, maybe Kawamoto is hurrying so we can get there while you can still see something, he thought, but he didn't understand anything, he was wrong even about that, Kawamoto was not at all rushing because he wished to reach the top of the mountain before the onset of darkness, there must be some monastery or a Shintō pilgrimage place, thought his companion, but it was not some monastery or a Shintō pilgrimage place that Kawamoto wanted to show him, but instead *all of Kyōto*; the Western friend perceived this when at last they reached the peak of Daimonji mountain, and Kawamoto-san stood aside, and he could look down from the heights, and there down below—completely encompassing the horizon—was in actuality the entire city, darkness had by this point almost completely fallen, the lights were burning down below in the distance already, and they didn't say anything; he, because the sight had left him at a complete loss for words, and Kawamoto because he was afraid that he was showing this in vain, that his friend—who had helped him form a connection between his solitary life and the world, due to which he owed him eternal gratitude—didn't understand, and it wasn't possible to explain: here, on the peak of the Daimonji, this was not the world of words; this gigantic evening picture of the city encircled by mountains said, without a single word, everything that he wanted to tell his friend before bidding farewell: an evening picture, as the glimmer of twilight was disappearing into nothingness, and darkness finally descended, down below there was an enormous city, with the tiny lights of its stars setting out an enormous surface for itself, and up here above were the two of them, Kawamoto Akio and his friend, who although he was pleased that his friend wasn't talking and was only staring downward below with dazzled eyes here from the heights, he was also aware that it was in vain, this friend saw nothing, the Western eye only saw the firefly-like sparkling of the evening city, but nothing of what he wanted to tell him, of what this hopeless, solitary, trembling land was signaling to one from down there below, certainly this place merely signified to him the wondrous gardens, the wondrous monasteries, and the wondrous mountains all around, so that Kawamoto had already turned around, and set off on the path leading downward, when this friend, his eyes filled with wonder, crowning an already irreparable misunderstanding, and, as it were, to offer thanks for this enchanting gift, spoke to him, and certain of an affirmative reply, asked the following question: Akio-san, you really love Kyōto, don't you; which in a single instant caused a complete breakdown in Kawamoto, and he could only say in a hoarse voice, as he headed downward in the thick darkness of the path, just this much, going back, that no, not in the least, I loathe this city.

1597

ZE'AMI IS LEAVING

Everyone says that he wasn't at all sad, that the cruel exile hadn't weakened him, on the contrary, that he understood the Sadogashima judgment to be a kind of completion, a sort of merciful judgment, the higher divine contradiction of "willing evil but creating good," and this is the opinion of Miss Matisoff and Erika de Poorter, Kunio Komparu and Akira Oomote, Dr. Benl and Professor Amano—no point in enumerating them—for it is Stanford and Leiden, Tokyo and Tokyo, Hamburg and Osaka, that most decisively claim, and in unison, that he was born Yuusaki Saburo Motokiyo, bearing the name of Fujiwaka in his youth, then Shio Zempoo as a monk, widely known as Ze'ami Motokiyo—that is to say, the condemned, who departed in 1434 for his exile in an almost happy state, and there, on Sado Island, the traditional destination of exile for the most highly ranked offenders, he felt that Fate had directly elevated him to Paradise: this is what they all write, this is what they imply, they spread this lie as if they—the Japanese and non-Japanese alike—had all previously agreed upon it: that the ignominy, monstrous and unparalleled, of even dispatching one of the greatest artistic figures in the history of the world, this tiny, frail, and otherwise already broken old man, seventy-two years of age, onto a perilous journey and then, to crown it all, to our even greater ignominy, if not to the direct cretinization of our ignorant present age, by having us believe that he felt just fine, he made the trip and on the distant island spent a period of time left unspecified, in accordance with custom, which therefore might as well have been for all eternity, in a harmonious, balanced state of mind; we have no sources to indicate the contrary, they all spread their hands wide in unison, we may rely, they proclaim, only and exclusively upon the enchantingly beautiful Kintoosho, referring to his short masterpiece written in 1436, and thus beyond doubt entrusted to paper during the period of the Sado exile; surely this farewell-pearl of his aesthetic oeuvre, this exquisite ornamental gemstone, this ravishing cadenza, cannot be read otherwise, cannot be interpreted as anything else but the ceremonial swansong of a soul sunk into silence, of a being who has overcome inconstant fate, capable of contemplating worldly existence only alongside heavenly existence; but this is all a deliberate intrigue and a lie, a mystification and a conspiracy, because he certainly was sad, infinitely, inconsolably sad; they injured him, more precisely they injured that artist in whom there was already hardly any strength to endure a verdict that was thoroughly unjust, both to him and to the instigators of this command; he was already very tired, he was weak, and life had worn him out; and in the impotent court and the residence of the crazed Shogun, everyone knew that even just the mere tone of a superficial, an insensitive, an unfeeling remark was enough for Ze'ami to feel eternally wounded; well then, after such a verdict as this, after all that had come before—his career, with its luminous beginnings, decisively shaken in 1408 by the death of Shogun Yoshimitsu, well, and still after that, his career approaching consummation, interrupted by the death in 1428 of Shogun Yoshimochi, and yet still after that, the final blow, crushing the genius so defenseless—indeed, he was already susceptible to even the slightest blows of fate—the loss of his utterly adored son, his heir, and the embodiment of the future of the Yuuzaki Association, and therefore of the Noh itself, Juro Motomasa, whom he, Ze'ami, held to be a greater talent than both himself and his own father; still, how could anyone, Japanese or non-Japanese alike, believe that after all this, that this thoroughly megalomaniacal, ignoble, idiotic, and arrogant decision, to send such an elderly person to certain death, would make that person, the subject of that decision, happy, and that in his eyes Sado would be truly identical with that described in the Kintoosho, identical with the center of the Wasp and the Diamond Mandalas, with the Cosmic Unity, the Endless Course of Regeneration of Gods and Humans—no, that is not Sado, just as no location in the Kintoosho is identical with even one location of the story of his exile; what a shameless deception, what a depraved falsification; for in reality—and not in the Kintoosho—it was a sad, wounded, broken old man that had to depart from Kyōto in 1434, subsequently reaching Wakasa prefecture by boat and from there the place of his exile; it is altogether as if we were expected to believe that when Ze'ami received the order to go into exile from Muromachi Dendoo, the residence of the shogun, he was filled with the greatest happiness, oh, at last I can get to Sado, oh, his heart was flooded with warmth, at long last here is the possibility for me to attain in this world, as a reward for my entire life, that which is not worldly, the Realm of the Wasp and the Diamond Mandalas—should we imagine it like this?! really?!—no! a thousand times no! in reality the entire thing happened completely differently, for there was every reason for him to sense that ill fortune, personified by Shogun Yoshinori, did not merely wish to drive him away, but wanted, like a sledgehammer, to crush him to bits, to destroy him, annihilate him, to clear this disobeyer of his wishes from his path; Ze'ami knew very well that if he left Kyōto, fulfilling the order of exile, a command that nonetheless he had to fulfill, that he would never see Kyōto again in his lifetime, so then in what other atmosphere could this have taken place than one of farewell for all eternity; everyone in the house wept, the servants of the retinue from the very youngest to the most hardened elders all wept; he gently reassured them that everything would be fine, but he knew full well that from this point, nothing would be fine, he bowed before all the members of his family, he bowed to his beloved wife, but all the while he was bidding farewell to the house as well: the objects, the rays of light, the delicate scent of incense; and the hour came and they set off through the streets of Kyōto, and then he bid farewell to the streets of Kyōto, farewell to the Gosha, to the Arashiyama bridge, then farewell to the Kamo River as well, it was the fourth day of the fifth month, the sixth year of Eikyo when they left the city in silence, at the time, with the retinue, specified in the command, and they arrived only the next day at the port of Obama in Wakasa prefecture, there stood the boat; Ze'ami tried to evoke his memories of the place because he was certain he had been here before, but he could not recall what had brought him to this place or when it might have been and in whose company his visit might have occurred, he hardly remembered anything anymore, maybe he wasn't sure that he had even been here before, perhaps it only seemed that way to him, the burden of more than seventy years weighing down upon his memories, and these memories functioned in a particular way, namely that everything swirled around, completely helter-skelter, in his shattered heart and mind, the memory-pictures came, flowed, surged, continually floating one after the other, and drawn from everything that he had encountered in reality, some old image drifted into his mind; there were no important, no essential memories, because now each and every memory was important, essential; although one single face returned again and again, one face kept continually floating into these transient memories: the dear face of his beloved son, whom he had lost, and whom he knew—until the day he departed from this earth and with the most merciless suddenness left him behind—to be his worthy successor; he saw Motomasa-san now as well, until the picture grew pale, and the mountains surrounding the shore, and the gentle clouds above the waves, evoked in his mind the renowned Chinese work "Eight Views of Xiao and Xiang", then he thought about this picture and a poem was beginning to formulate itself inside him, there was more than enough time for that, as having embarked onto the boat they were obliged to wait, and for a long time, in the dead calm and utter stillness; no wind blew the entire night, only in the morning and then in the wrong direction, not from the direction for which they had to wait, but then that wind came too, the wind blowing in the right direction; they raised the anchor, they sailed off, above the waves; and he looked back and he saw that they were moving farther and farther away, away from the land that he had loved so much, already he was very far from the city that he must now leave once and for all, he really must bid it farewell now, and although he had been hoping until the very last minute that perhaps it would not, after all, come to pass, now that the certitude was irrefutable, he could not master his emotions and there was not even anyone in his vicinity who would have understood why his tears were flowing down, when the sailing craft—although following the coastline all the way—put off so far from shore that one could only know, and not see, that it remained back there, somewhere in the fog: they left him alone on deck and he stood there leaning against the rails, and for a good long while could not even bear to sit back down in the chair that they had fastened there for the old man; for his soul was bidding farewell to everything that had been his life, which was now ending, because what could come now, he asked himself, but he only saw waves as the boat cleaved through them, the waves, that was the answer to his question as to what could come, because—well, what could come; waves, waves, one after the other, thousands and thousands, millions and millions of waves, already he had known that it was going to happen—this thing and in this way; once when he was very young, sometime between childhood and youth, he had fallen passionately in love with Shogun Yoshimitsu, from whom afterward—completely independent of their feelings for each other, and purely thanks to the Shogun's exceptional aesthetic sensitivity—he and his troupe—and with that the entire Sarugaki no Noh as they called it back then—were awarded the most elevated patronage; even then he already knew, already in the midst of this infinitely pure love known as wakashudo; and often he stood by the window in the Shogun's bedroom, which had a view onto the exquisite garden; he stood there; at that moment, dawn had not yet begun to break, it was still dark but something had already begun to relent in this darkness, promising that later on the darkness would slowly, utterly slowly, be sifted through, like a delicate breath, with light; even then it occurred to him many times that one day this would come to an end, and that fate would not be kind to him, and truly fate was not kind to him, executing its judgments upon him without mercy, one after the other, so that now the final one was brought forth and was dispatching him on the decrepit vessel; neither in front of him, nor behind him, nor anywhere at all was there anything in sight, just water and endless water, how far is it to Sadogashima, he asked the captain, who replied after what seemed to him like a remarkably prolonged silence that oh, venerable sir, it is yet a very long, long journey; this is what he replied into the wind that had risen to a storm, or rather he yelled it out from the helm, yelled it out through two smaller gusts of wind, it is still a long, long journey; and so it was, too, they proceeded along, following the coastline, just water and water everywhere: sometimes rain poured down onto them, and there was no sign of summer, and it was possible to sense the mountain Shirayama faintly in the distance, and Hakusan with the mountain-shrine and its snowy peak, then out alongside, the pilgrimage harbors of Noto and Suzu and the Seven Islands, and maybe the sun set once, and the sun set two times, and perhaps still at times the gentle sparks of fireflies could be seen above the water near the shore, or perhaps it was just the last embers of the sinking sun, who knows, thought Ze'ami, and he could hardly even decide anymore whether he was seeing reality or just the mechanisms of his imagination, in any event, later on he distinctly recalled the fishermen's boats: those were not the work of his not overly keen imagination, they definitely encountered fishermen's boats, and the days came, and the nights came, and at times it seemed to him as if the boat wasn't moving at all, but just swaying, and there next to him swayed the renowned pilgrimage temple on Tateyama, and then, one day, the peak of Mount Tonami, and they were just swaying there in the wind, while the prefectures of Echizen, Etchū, and Echigo slipped away; there was moonlight and there were smaller storms too, the days and the nights alternated with each other; he watched this, but the flashing pictures, between Shirayama and Echigo, were not pictures to stimulate his thoughts, because those, his thoughts, kept returning again and again to Kyōto, taking up the streets one after the other, the Suzaku Ōji running straight between Rashomon and Suzakumon, then Gosho above, and farther to the north, the Shogun's palace; he went in one direction, as if he had entered into a dream, he turned at one corner then strolled on some more, and he saw in sequence the most important figures of his life, and finally he stood unexpectedly in front of his own house: and he would have opened the door already, pulled the door at the entrance gate, when a wave rocked the ship and he had to clutch onto its side, as the wave otherwise would have swept him overboard, the sailors cried out, they reefed the sail, the boat returned to its former position, and from the captain's face one could see that nothing had happened, they cleaved on through the waves, and just water and water everywhere, and memories and memories, no matter where he looked, and the sadness, the pain in his heart now almost without object, and water and water, and waves and waves, he was tired, lonely, and very old, and then suddenly he was startled by something; he cried out to the captain where are we, to which the captain replied there it is already, it's over there, and he pointed in some direction, grimacing but with a respectful expression, there is Sado island, my lord, that is certainly Sadogashima, venerable sir.

Oota was the name of the gulf where such vessels, carrying the exiled, traditionally moored; namely that here they had to lower the anchor, at the gulf of Oota, where, in accordance with the command, they had to disembark onto Sado Island, and disembark here they did; day was already turning to night, and after the exhaustion of the trip, lasting at least a full week, though this full week seemed much longer to him, more like a week of eternity extending into some kind of timelessness; they did not remain on deck, of course, but embarked onto the shore, following the stipulation only to travel by day, and spent the first evening, in view of the narrow range of possibilities, in a small fisherman's hut; no sleep came to him that night, the journey had worn him down, his every limb was aching, in addition underneath his head was a piece of stone but even this did not capture his attention as they lay down in the kitchen to rest, but rather he thought of his children, his wife, and his beloved son-in-law Komparu Zenchiku, to whom he had entrusted those he loved; later on there drifted in among his thoughts a few lines from a poem by Ariwara Motokata, from the Kokinshu, about how autumn was approaching, and whether the mountain, with its shape like a rain-hat, would protect the maple trees from the ravages of the weather, or something to that effect; it was strange that exactly this mountain, Kasatori, shaped like a rain-hat, Kasatori of Yamashiro came into his mind from that poem, this Kasatori emerging from utter nothingness; he could not connect it to anything; as to why, he could not explain it in any terms, as to what caused precisely this verse to emerge in his memories in the depths of night—Kasatori, he tasted the word in his mouth, and he called forth in his mind the form of the mountain, recalled the wondrous colors of the maples of the land plunged into autumn, Kasatori, Kasatori, then suddenly the entire thing fell away from his brain; he looked at the unknown, cold, simple objects in the hut's gloomy dark; he adjusted the position of his head on the stone, turning now to the left and now to the right, but it wasn't good anywhere on the stone, which was his head-rest for this night, and although dawn broke with difficulty, with great difficulty, in the end he couldn't even have said that he was too exhausted as he awaited this dawn, at his age one usually spent one's time just like that, in a great waiting, even in Kyōto it was almost always like this, long hours in the silence after a brief sleep, a Kyōto dawn—Kyōto, a sacred, immortal, eternally radiant Buddha, it was all so far away already, as if it had been obliterated from reality once and for all, to exist from now on only within himself, oh Kyōto, he sighed, stepping outside through the door of the hut, sniffing the biting sea air, Kyōto, how horrendously far away you are already—but then he was helped onto one of the horses stationed here, as instructed by the Shinpo, and the procession began to head upward along a mountain path, his imagination was already taking him back to an autumnal dawn of long, long ago, not only did he see the unparalleled strength of its crimson, but he even sensed in the depth of the maple trees that unmistakable scent that made him so giddy at such times, for example, an autumn in Ariwara, on the mountain-side celebrated in song; they struggled upward along the path, he searched for the maple trees, but here they were not to be seen anywhere, the journey was wearing the horses down, the tiny path was serpentine and it was steep; the guide who had been entrusted to lead him on horseback slipped at times in his hemp-woven sandals—the worn-down waraji—on the stony ground, and at such times the reins grabbed him, rather than him grabbing the reins, it went on for a long time like this, and why deny it, he could hardly bear it, he couldn't even name the year when he had last been seated atop a horse, and now on this dangerous ground; their one bit of luck was that it wasn't raining, he determined, and in vain did he try to discover a beautiful glade in the forest along the path, or catch the song of a nightingale or a bulbul, continually he was forced to concentrate on not falling off the horse, on not sliding down from the saddle during a perilous washed-out stretch, he had no strength left for anything else, so that when they finally reached the Kasakari Pass and he addressed the peasant leading his horse saying, is this not Kasatori?—No, the peasant shook his head, but then there is something here in common with that word; the convicted man pressed him further, with the Kasatori in Yamashiro, no there isn't, the peasant replied in confusion, this is Kasakari, so nothing, the rider pondered, and was he completely certain of this? he asked, but did not even wait for a reply, almost simultaneously with his question he conveyed that the journey had worn him out a bit, and he requested a stop to rest, just a brief rest, which did him well, too, and they spent just one half-hour underneath the thick foliage of a wild mulberry tree, yet his strength returned, he spoke saying they could now go on, he was helped again onto the horse, the procession started again, and they quickly reached the Hasedera Temple, which as he knew from the peasant, belonged to the Shingon sect, but to whom else would it belong; he would have smiled to himself if this name hadn't evoked in him the memory from home of the Hasadera in Nara, which, however, was so painful that he said nothing to the peasant, only nodded, it's well that it belongs to the Shingon sect, and although magnificent flowers suddenly came into view by the side of the temple—from where he was it seemed for a moment that they could have been well-tended azaleas—he didn't call out to stop the horse, because he didn't want to, he didn't want a memory from Nara to torment him anymore, because right then he would have been tormented further by his daughter's dear face and his son-in-law's dear face and the picture of Fugan-ji, their family temple, the memory of an important prayer uttered there would have tormented him; well, better to be tormented by the journey, then, let us go on, he motioned, but the peasant, misunderstanding him or believing an account would bring joy to the venerable gentleman from Kyōto, spoke to him as they went along, and so the peasant was continually pointing backward toward Hasadera, where there, before the main altar, was a statue of the Eleven-Headed Kannon, but the gentleman from Kyōto didn't say anything, so the peasant did not even begin to enumerate in detail what this famous Kannon in the Hasadera even was; he just trudged upward along the pass, grasping the horse's reins, and he didn't even dare to speak until they reached Shinpo, when night was already falling, and thus the district regent, insisting fully on the strictest of formalities, had already designated for the exiled man a place in a nearby temple, the Manpukuji, which could not convey to Ze'ami anything of itself on that day, as Ze'ami was so exhausted that they had him lie down on the spot prepared for him, he had already closed his eyes, lying on his back as always, he adjusted the blanket and immediately fell into a deep sleep, and slept for nearly four hours straight, so that the temple displayed itself to him, not then, but only the next day, only then did the convicted man from Kyōto see what kind of a place he had ended up in, he pushed back his blanket, pulled on his robe, and went out into the temple garden, which later on, until he changed his residence, was to give him so much joy, particularly one pine tree which he discovered at the edge of a high cliff, and which grew out and clung to this cliff as if it were holding tight to it, and this sight was often heart-wrenching for him, and at such times, so not to be overcome again by profound emotion, in the face of which he proved, during this period, to be so weak, he listened to the mountain winds as they caressed the foliage in the trees, or in the shadow of a tree he watched water trickling down the tiny veins of a moss-patch, he watched and he listened, he asked nothing of anyone, and no one asked anything of him, the silence within him became immutable and this silence around him became irrevocable too; he looked at the water in the little rivulets in the moss, he listened to the murmuring of the mountain winds up above, and from every quarter he was inundated with memories, no matter where he looked, an ancient recollection, dim and distant, fell upon the image or the sound, and he began to pass the days in such a way that he no longer could sense that one morning had come and then the next, because the first morning was exactly the same as the one that followed it, so that he began to feel that not only were they coming one after the other, but that all told, there was just one single day—one single morning and one single evening—he stepped out of time and returned to it only occasionally, and even then just temporarily, and on these occasions it was as if he were seeing the Manpuku-ji from a great height, or the Golden Hall in the middle of the garden, with the Yakushi Buddha inside it on the main altar, all from a great height, from the height of a slowly circling hawk; well at such times it occasionally happened that he came back for a little while and, sitting underneath a beautiful cypress tree in the moss garden, he said aloud to himself: so, this is my grave, that of the blameless, this is my grave, here, this temporary residence in the Manpuku-ji, then he sank back into that particular inner silence, and this was not looked upon favorably in the office of the Regent of Shinpo, he should be doing something, he was advised one time when he, the District Regent, came himself to pay a visit, whereupon Ze'ami, in order to stave off any further exhortations of this kind, asked for a piece of hinoki cypress wood and tools, and he set about to carve a so-called o-beshimi rain-making mask, which was not in use in the Noh, as might have been expected, but in the bugaku, the renowned worship-dance: he worked out the forehead and the eyebrows in a completely detailed fashion, and the eyes and the ridge of the nose delicately and movingly, but then he didn't have enough attention for the rest: the ridge of the nose, the ear, the mouth, and the chin, remained in a crude state, as if in the course of things he had lost interest, or as if his thoughts had continuously wandered off somewhere between the ridge and the lower edge of the nose, and moreover he worked slowly, in contradiction to his nature, which was quick; he created this mask with many slow movements, and now he chose the appropriate, the precisely necessary chisel with great meticulousness, even with too much care, then he dug into the soft material with the chisel, so cautiously, so dilatorily, that anyone who knew him could well believe that he was working upon a truly extraordinary task, but here, of course, no one knew him, there was no question of any sort of extraordinary task, as among the higher-ranking officials no one was even that interested in what he was doing, just as long as he was doing something, the important thing was his person, and that he not be idle, and hence not die before his time, which for the higher-ranking officials and even the Regent himself would have meant only unpleasant questions and answers difficult to formulate, risks and obligations, so that, well, not even a flea was curious about this mask, they simply became aware of the news with acquiescence in the Shinpo Regent's office and in its environs, that the tiny exiled old man was not just sitting around in the garden and idling away the entire day, as they expressed it, but was working on something, he is carving a mask, they repeated to each other, which then quickly spread among the general population of Sado, because the news was spread, not so much among the higher-ranking officials, but rather the lower-ranking ones, so that altogether 208 years after the death of the great emperor, and 154 years after the death of the founder of the faith, if we do not take the poet-minister into account, the residents of the island noted among themselves that the next famous exile from Kyōto is already here—but he wanted to move his residence to Shoho-ji, he nonetheless informed the Regent, in the future, he felt, the Shoho-ji temple would be a better place for him, assuming this would not represent any kind of bother for His Excellency the Regent, the old man said one day in his faint voice; the Shoho-ji, the Regent started back in astonishment, and he really could not conceal how shaken he was by the request from the condemned man from Kyōto, it wasn't as if it would have made any kind of difference whether he was living in the Manpuku-ji or the Shoho-ji, that itself caused no problem whatsoever, but rather that—the Regent stammered in nervousness among his retinue—well, why is the Shoho-ji better, and why isn't the Manpuku-ji good, and the people in the retinue looked at each other and they were perplexed, because they said, it didn't mean anything if it were now the first or the second, but why the first and why the second, that was the question, and this question had to have an answer, they nodded enthusiastically, but then Ze'ami received permission and he changed residence, and no one ever asked him again why the first and why not the second, it was so inconsequential, it's just that the question was not inconsequential and somehow—no one remembers how it happened—the problem sorted itself out, the Regent issued a command that the man exiled by Shogun Yoshinori should be transferred from Manpuku-ji to Shoho-ji, inasmuch as, the Regent wrote in the necessary documentation, inasmuch as this would not cause a burden to the venerable gentleman, and so in this way the Shoho-ji forthwith became the residence of Ze'ami, he took with himself the mask he was working on, and at times he still worked on it, but he never got beyond the ridge of the nose, he found an enormous boulder and attributed some kind of enormous significance to it, because from that point on, every day if it wasn't raining, he went out to his cliff—there was no way of telling what he was doing there, the people covered all the possibilities: he was reciting poetry, singing, mumbling prayers, but in reality no one ever really knew, because no one ever dared to approach him, he could never make himself understood if some infrequent conversation might come about from time to time, he couldn't even get them to stop calling him Your Honor,

Venerable Sir, in vain did he tell them he was just an ordinary monk named Shio Zempoo, the Your Honors and Venerable Sirs remained, but it was also true that they really didn't dare approach him, not because he was frightening, he wasn't frightening in the least, rather he was just a small, emaciated, frail, gentle creation, his hands trembling, ready to be blown away by the first large gust of wind; the only problem was that he was so different, they simply didn't know how to approach him, his world and theirs were so far away from each other, like the stars in the heavens from a clump of earth in the ground, his movements seemed so peculiar here, he raised his trembling hand in such a different way, and the way he held his fingers was different too, his eyes as he slowly looked at someone were as if he were looking through this someone, as if he were seeing their great-great-grandfather through them, and they found it odd that his face, despite his advanced age, was like a young boy's, and moreover that of a very beautiful boy; the smooth, white skin, the high smooth forehead, the narrow tapering nose, the finely chiseled chin, they were confused if they had to look at him, because he was beautiful, very beautiful, and no one had any explanation for this, here in Sado, where everyone, including the Regent himself, was cut as if from the same cloth, everyone's face with the same dark-brown skin, and this skin pockmarked from the eternally blowing winds, and the women from higher-ranking families hardly dressed any better than the women from lower-ranking families, boats rarely arrived, and it was even rarer for something to arrive on these boats that these women could have used to smarten themselves up: the exile was truly, in a word, the envoy of a distant realm, and sometimes he alarmed the local gentry and their subordinates by speaking fluently in verse, if he felt so inclined, and he mixed up his words, it was impossible to tell if he was speaking of a dream from yesterday or a memory from twenty years ago; one thing was certain, he never spoke of what was here on Sado, or he always changed the topic, talking about things that had happened twenty or thirty years ago, or he gave an evasive reply, saying when they asked if everything was to his liking that, yes, it was to his liking, they were in fact heaping too much on him, he didn't need so much food, during the day he ate just once, in the morning, and very little, a little cooked vegetables, fish, beans, that kind of thing, he was satisfied with everything, he never once complained about his circumstances, he nodded at everything in approval, he praised the people who brought him things and who served him, he seemed tranquil and peaceful, or impassive, it was only when he was near his boulder that he cried, sometimes they saw it, the group of children among the servants gave an account of it, they dared to come near him and they spied on him, and the most simple and most high-ranking residents of the island did not even say anything upon hearing this news, this at least they could understand, he's thinking of home, they said to each other and they nodded, as those who are fully able to comprehend, they understood the matter very well, and no explanation at all was necessary as to who this man was and what he was feeling; nevertheless it was precisely the case that they understood nothing, absolutely nothing of the matter, in this entire god-given world, because of course how would they have been able to understand, how could they have even suspected that precisely on this occasion, not only did they not understand—this was in the end to be expected here on Sado, in this godforsaken place—no—but not a single person in the entire world existed who could have truly understood him, neither in Kyōto nor in Kamakura, neither in the Emperor's Palace nor in the Muromachi Dendoo, nobody, nothing, never and not even in the slightest possible degree, not even the infinitely cultivated advisor to the Shogun, Nijo Yoshimoto, and not even Ashikaga Yoshimitsu himself, that Ze'ami was not one of many, not just a sarugaku performer whose star had risen and then set, no, altogether no, he had created the Noh, he had called into being and determined a new form of existence:

he had not created a theater because the Noh is not theater, but a higher if not the very highest form of existence, when an individual, by dint of a cultivated sensibility, unique intuition, and genial introspection, the competence of a profound engagement with a tradition of the highest order, creates revolutionary forms, never before experienced, and in doing so elevates all human existence, elevates the whole, to a very high level; and now this situation, this death sentence: because human existence holds its own needs at a very low level, they have always been held at a very low level and will be held at a very low level for all eternity, for the human being simply has no need for anything save a full stomach and a full coin-box, he wants to be an animal, and there is no strength that could convince him otherwise or recommend anything else, and so cunning is the human being that he instinctively senses when something or someone wants to dislodge him from that place where the stomach and the coin-box are the only things that matter; don't need it, he replies to the higher challenges, you can take your advice and shove it up your filthy ass, if he has to put it crudely, and at such times he does put it crudely, whether he is a nobleman or a commoner, it's all one and the same, let them strut and mince about, give themselves airs at any time and for any reason, but he still won't get up from the dinner-table and no one will be able to pry him away from the wonders of the coin-box, if the stomach and the coin-box are full then he has no need for anything else, leave him alone already, moreover he wouldn't understand, even if he had good intentions, he still would never be able to understand that which is great, that which surpasses him to such a degree that he hasn't the slightest hope of comprehension, and so, not even reverence, so that Ze'ami had to go, thought Ze'ami sitting on the boulder, and anyone could have executed him, he reflected, rolling a little pebble here and there with his foot; then one day he asked a servant for permission to go for walks on the island, special permission is not required, came the answer, in conformity with the Regent's order that he could go wherever he wished on the island, so he set off immediately, because the weather was good, and he sought out Kuroki Gosho Ato, the location of the exiled great Emperor; he bowed his head before the memory of his predecessor, he placed flowers by the first column, on the right-hand side of the entrance to the remains of the building; then another day the sun was shining nicely again, not too warmly, but the light was filtering down just so, the birds were particularly lively, he went on horseback with his escort to the Hachiman shrine, where Kyogoku Tamekane, the great poet and minister, had lived during his exile, and although he venerated him and held Tamekane's work to be truly great, at the same time he had grown very curious upon hearing the legend that circulated among the residents of the island, according to which the hototogisu, the cuckoo that could be heard everywhere, was here, and only here, silent, he did not wish to hear the legend again, although in his retinue there were many who, upon reaching this location, immediately wanted to relate it again, so that he allowed some of them to do so, but it was not the story that he wanted to hear, but *how* did the hototogisu not sing in this place; and actually it was so, he stood before the shrine, he prayed, then he stepped aside to listen to *how* the hototogisu did not sing, and it was so, the hototogisus remained silent all around the shrine, not one sound could be heard from any cuckoo, and as for seeing a cuckoo, he saw just one, which, however, he watched for a very long while, and the people accompanying him could not understand what he was up to with that bird for such a long time, the bird on its branch didn't move, nor did Ze'ami, as the procession to the horses came to a dead halt, he looked, he looked indeed for a long time, then finally the bird flew into the thick of the trees, the venerable sir somehow—with assistance—agonizingly got himself into the saddle, and they returned home quickly, and that night he slept for not one single moment, he tried to force himself but it didn't work at all, no sleep came to him, he stared into the darkness, he listened to the night sounds, the rustling trees, and the gliding sound as a flock of bats returned or set off into the night, you cry out, Tamekane's poem came to his mind, and I hear you, I hear you yearning for the capital city, oh hototogisu of the mountains, fly away from here, and he spoke these lines aloud perhaps two times, then he himself didn't even know if he was quoting anything, or if these were his own words, he added something yet about the falling flowers, the first song of the cuckoo, the moonlight with its promise of autumn, then the word came into his mind again, hototogisu, and he played with the primary meanings concealed within this word, for examining it from another viewpoint, hototogisu literally means the bird of time, he tasted the word in this sense, nearly twisting it around—the cuckoo is signified by a compound, which is the bird of time—to see from which side it would be suitable to give form to his soul's deepest sorrows; at last he found the way, and the melody began to formulate itself within him—he was just thinking about it, not calling it by name—and the verse somehow formulated itself like this: just sing, sing to me, so not only you will mourn; I too shall mourn, old old man, abandoned and alone, far from the world, I mourn my home, my life, lost, lost forever.

No one even knew, neither the Regent nor the servants closest at hand, that Ze'ami was writing; it would not however have been too difficult to ascertain, as he asked for paper, just for taking some notes, he enunciated several times and with strong emphasis, when he called the Regent's attention—simultaneously sending him the half-finished mask as a gift—to the fact that what he was receiving only occasionally was merely an inferior imitation of real paper; please try, the exile beseeched him, to find something of better quality somewhere on the island, and if this is not possible, then—and this was his only request—have some brought from the mainland, but the Regent considered that Ze'ami was just a pampered court darling and was whining about a trifle, he can be happy, his voice thundered out in his office, that he gets anything at all, but frankly speaking he didn't even know what kind of paper Ze'ami was insisting upon, as in his entire life he had never seen such a thing, in a word he could not have the faintest idea of what kind of paper the temporary inhabitant of Shoho-ji had in mind, and what quality it was to which he kept referring, he could not even begin to comprehend that it very nearly caused Ze'ami physical pain to see, in the package sent to him when the messenger arrived from Shinpo, these coarse materials, pressed from the fibers of who knows what plant, horrible, crude, malodorous, on the other hand there was nothing he could do about it, his request had clearly not met with comprehension in Shinpo, so that, well, he began his work with the quality of materials at his disposal, although he himself would never have referred to what he was doing as work, because it had not been mere self-depreciation, when at the time of the submission of his request, he had designated the activity for which paper was required as note-taking: the thought formed within him very slowly that he could possibly in time put the fragments of quotations and fragments of his own versifications into some kind of order, which then at times ended up on this sort of, as he was to call it later, rustic paper—so, well, he started one morning by attempting to put into sequence everything he had composed so far, but the whole thing ended up being too contrived, he did not wish to write a drama, never again to write another Noh piece, nevertheless the thought of framing these broken fragments into some kind of coherency eventually would have led him to something that he didn't want, this wasn't his intention—why?—he shook his head, and he pursed his lips in disapproval as he sat in the cell of Shoho-ji arranged for him, in the light coming through the tiny window; puzzled, impassive he looked at the paper, at the lines written there, and he really had no idea of what the hell he should do with them, and he even pushed them to one side for a while, and just sat in the garden when the weather permitted, murmuring prayers, trying to find his bearings among his memories, or his attention was drawn for long minutes to a lizard warming itself in the sun at the base of a tree, then another morning he decided to put everything he had written so far into chronological order, but it was just then that the problem came up that he could not recall when one part or another had arisen, yet the idea seemed like a good one, to put these things here into chronological order, among the circumstances of his captivity, wedged in between the mute bird of time and the shriveled continuity of one single day; Obama came to mind, the name of the port in Wakasa, the journey made by sea came to his mind, the gulf at Oota, the fisherman's hut, then the journey to Shinpo—and then, somehow just like that, the brush in his hand began to move as if by its own accord, and he began truly to narrate the story of his exile, in chronological order as it had occurred; he did not wish to think of it and could not ever have even thought of it as something for a future drama, as something for the ceremonies at Kasuga or Kofuku-ji; no, not at all, what for, he shook his head again, it would make no sense at all to embark upon such an undertaking, I no longer wish to embark upon any kind of undertaking, it's just enough that I'm still alive, he said aloud to himself, it is just enough of a burden, so that he did nothing else but begin to describe how it had all happened—from Wakasa to Shinpo—but of course he also used everything that he had already committed to paper, the ink was suitable, he had brought the brushes with him from home, there was enough time, in that one single long day it seemed endless, and it didn't even concern him that the whole thing was turning out to be a little discontinuous, fragments of verse followed upon one another as they came to mind, with prose descriptions, verse fragments of which he frequently had no idea at all if he or someone else was the author, sometimes he hadn't the slightest idea about the one who wrote these lines, it seemed so, so unimportant; at a certain point, he felt the lines to be just right, and he played, as he had done so many times before, with the different layers of the meanings of the words, so that they would harmonize, and diverse places or persons or events would come into a sudden unexpected connection with each other, that is to say, he did what he had done throughout his entire life when he wrote a play, moreover when in his most enigmatic works, even his summaries of everything necessary for the Kanze School to be aware of, he could not free himself from this, from the play of this Chinese compositional mode, the growth of meanings, the concordance of meanings, the exchange of meanings, in a word the search for the joy of the meaning-rhythms, so that it didn't concern him when, on a later morning in that one long, so long, motionless day, he saw already that his work, the likes of which he had never before committed to paper, was changing, was transforming from the loosely woven story of his exile to the chant of his religious feelings; above the next chapter he wrote the words Ten Shrines and then Northern Mountains above the next, and he looked out of his tiny window, he saw from his cell a little sun-warmed patch of garden, and he thought of the infinite distance extending from Sadogashima to Kyōto, and that would always exist between them for all time, and as his heart was filled with bitter sorrow, he painted these words onto the paper: beloved gods, beloved island, beloved ruler, beloved country.

At the end of the Kintoosho he wrote that it had been created in the second month, in the eighth year of Eikyo, and he signed it as Novice Zempoo. His death was just as silent as the years of his exile. They found him one morning on the ground, he'd been on his way from the window to his sleeping-pallet, and by that point he was so tiny that even the smallest pyre, as if for a child, sufficed for his cremation in the funeral ceremony. And he was so light that one person alone carried the corpse and placed it on the wooden logs.

The cell was empty; they found the Kintoosho manuscript on the ground, and they were heading out the door when they noticed that there seemed to be something on the table. But it was just a little slip of paper, and on it was written: Ze'ami is leaving. They crumpled it up and threw it away.

2584
SCREAMING BENEATH THE EARTH

We ask nothing of the dragons, and the dragons ask nothing of us.

Zi Chan

They scream in the darkness, their mouths gaping open, their protruding eyes covered by cataracts, and they scream, but this screaming, this darkness, their mouths and their eyes cannot be spoken of now, only circumambulated with words, like a beggar with his palm extended, for this darkness and this screaming, these mouths and these eyes cannot be compared to anything, for they have nothing in common with anything that can be put into words, so that not only is it impossible to describe or convey, in the language of humans, their concealed dwelling-places, this place where the lord of all is this darkness and this screaming; it is only possible to proceed above it, or more cogently, to wander there above, that is possible, while having not the faintest idea of where the thing is that one wants to discuss—somewhere down there below, that is all that we can say, so that perhaps it would be wisest just to take the whole thing and forget it, take it and not force the issue anymore; but we don't forget because it is impossible to forget, and we force it, for this screaming does not cease of its own accord, no matter what we do, if we have heard it once, for example—between

Dawenkou and Panlongchen, after Longshan and Anyang and Erlitou—this happened: seeing the statues glued together from the shards, the green bronze slabs with the drawings, it is enough to see these artifacts, just one time, for that inhuman voice to be lodged forever in the brain, so that one then begins to wander: the knowledge that they are there is insufferable, insupportable, just as is that desire to see their dreadful beauty at least once, in short, that is, generally speaking, how we set off, we push off on our journey through the regions of the one-time Shang Dynasty from a point selected entirely at random, it doesn't matter from where or at what time, one choice is as good as another, for we don't even know where they are, either confidently or obscurely, yes, we say, sometime between 1600 and 1100 years before Christ is where we have to set off on our journey, walking somewhere along the Huang He riverbank to the East, proceeding with the river's current toward the delta and the sea, and never getting too far away from the riverbank, where the renowned capital cities were, that is where you have to go; roughly from 1600 to 1100 BC, the place of the dissipated memory of the cities of the Shang emperors, Bo and Ao, Chaoge and Dayi Shang, Xiang and Geng, imperial cities now vanished for at least 2800 years, where we say *China* but think of something else—if we do not wish to delude ourselves and mislead others, as they, the Chinese, have done themselves for several thousand years now—because it is only since the Qin Dynasty that it has been called China: as if China, Zhongguo, the Middle Kingdom, or in other words the World, were one unified whole, as if it were *one* Country, which actually it never was, for in truth there were many kingdoms and many peoples, many nations and many princes, many tribes and many languages, many traditions and many borders, many beliefs and many dreams, that was Zhongguo, the World, with so many worlds inside of it, that to enumerate them, trace them, recognize them, or understand them is impossible with one single brain—that is, if one is not the Son of Heaven—and even today it is impossible, one can only spin fabrications, blather and jabber nonsense, as anyone will do, setting off on the lower banks of the Huang He roughly between 1600 and 1100 BC, along the so-called "bends" of the Huang He, saying to himself, here I am in the Shang Empire, here I am going East, this is Chaoge here, or perhaps Dayi Shang, here below my feet, and the only truth in that statement is that they really are there somewhere below the earth, despite all of the accidental discoveries of the Dawenkous and Anyangs and Erlitous, uninvestigated and invisible, they are hidden deep below the earth in the darkness, and with their mouths opened wide they scream, the graves they were meant to serve collapsed onto them long ago; and collapsing in layers, buried them completely, so that they became walled into the earth, among the stolons, the ciliates, the rotifers, the tardigrades, the mites, the worms, the snails, the isopods, the innumerable species of larvae, as well as the mineral deposits and the deadly underground gullies—walled in, condemned to this final immobility, even if they hadn't always been that way, they are now motionless in their screaming, as their gaping mouths are already crammed with earth, and before their cataract-clouded bulging eyes there is not even one centimeter of space, not even a quarter-centimeter, not even a fragment of that quarter, into which these cataract-clouded bulging eyes could stare, for the earth is so thick and so heavy, from all directions there is only that, everywhere earth and earth, and all around them is that impenetrable, impervious, weighty darkness that lasts truly for all time to come, surrounding every living being, for we too shall walk here, every one of us, when the time comes, we who wander here among the unfathomable vastness of the Chinese millennia, we think to ourselves, so this was their Empire, here is the Shang Dynasty, and we wander along the enormous, hypotheticized splotches of their one-time capital cities, picturing to ourselves what is below the earth, where all that was Shang is sunken below; we cannot imagine anything, just as it is not possible to capture anything with words, it is impossible to bring them out of the depths through imagination, for those depths below us are unapproachable, as are the depths of time and its howling; they cannot be reached through any kind of imagination, the route is blocked already at the starting point, for so dense is that earth below the Shang Dynasty—roughly from 1600 to 1100 BC, beyond the bends of the Huang He, by the lowest river-reaches as it flows toward the delta and the sea—that imagination is blocked and cannot get to that place where they stand, in pieces, leaning to one side, corroded by the acids, almost unrecognizable, for only those who might have seen something during the perilous tomb desecrations known as the "excavations" at Dawenkou, Panlongchen, Longshan, Anyang, and Erlitou know how terrifying they were when still in one piece, how they were fear itself, and how those who made them did not realize with what terrifying strength they had expressed what was granted to them beyond eternity, below the earth, what it is like if everything in this dense earth is crushed together in the complete and final darkness; they, the artisans of the Shang Dynasty, perhaps then only wanted, when they formed the giant gaping mouths, the bulging clouded eyes, for these statues and bronze objects to be placed at the entranceways or within the inner chambers to preserve the tombs of their dead, to protect them by frightening away the malignant forces, to hold the Earth-Demon at bay, for the people of the Shang Dynasty possibly thought that the graves must remain inviolable; they could have thought that there should be a connection between the dead and the empire of death, but they could not have considered how time goes on even further than its own promised eternity—they could not have considered how time would also extend dreadfully from their own age into the vastness of eternities, one after the other, where even the possibility of remembering who is lying here with their *hun* souls is extinguished; they could not have considered that almost nothing would remain of the graves, the dead, the *hun* soul, of themselves, their empire, or even the memory of their empire; in the ravages of time from nothing, almost nothing remains, everything that once was, disappears; the

Shangs disappear, and the graves disappear with them, here by the lower reaches of the Huang He, along the bends toward the delta and the sea, and nothing else remains, only the screaming and the darkness under the heavy impressure of the earth, for the screaming, that does remain; they stand there below in their ruined graves, stand in tiny pieces leaning to one side, eaten away by the acids, wedged into the earth, but in their wide-gaping mouths the scream does not cease, it somehow remains there, broken into pieces, and yet through the millennia, that scream of horror, the single meaning of which nonetheless extends up until today, telling us that the universe below the earth, the locus of death, below the World is a colossal overfilled space, that that place where we all shall end most certainly does exist; that the World, life, and people will all come to an end, and it is there they will end, below, this time here below, below the dreams of the Shang, in the grave-statuary broken to pieces and the screaming of the bronze-cast animals, for there are animals below the earth, perhaps in immeasurable quantity, pigs and dogs, buffalos and dragons, goats and cows and tigers and elephants and chimeras and snakes and dragons, and they are all screaming, and not only are there cataracts in their bulging eyes, but they are all blind, they stand leaning to one side in pieces and corroded from the acids around the collapsed graves, and blindly they scream in the darkness, they scream that this was awaiting them, this awaited the Shangs, but that up there above, the same fate awaits us, it awaits us who now reflect upon the Shang, the horror, which is not just the residue of some cheap fear: for there is a domain, that of death, the dreadful weight of the earth pressing in from all sides which has entombed them, and which in time shall devour us as well, to close it in upon itself, to bury, to consume even our memories, beyond all that is eternal.